Totally Bound Publishing books by J.M. Powers:

Medieval Quest
Jewel of Ramstone

I0615155

Medieval Quest

JEWEL OF RAMSTONE

J.M. POWERS

Jewel of Ramstone
ISBN # 978-1-78651-938-2
©Copyright J.M. Powers 2016
Cover Art by Posh Gosh ©Copyright March 2016
Interior text design by Claire Siemaszkiewicz
Totally Bound Publishing

This is a work of fiction. All characters, places and events are from the author's imagination and should not be confused with fact. Any resemblance to persons, living or dead, events or places is purely coincidental.

All rights reserved. No part of this publication may be reproduced in any material form, whether by printing, photocopying, scanning or otherwise without the written permission of the publisher, Totally Bound Publishing.

Applications should be addressed in the first instance, in writing, to Totally Bound Publishing. Unauthorised or restricted acts in relation to this publication may result in civil proceedings and/or criminal prosecution.

The author and illustrator have asserted their respective rights under the Copyright Designs and Patents Acts 1988 (as amended) to be identified as the author of this book and illustrator of the artwork.

Published in 2016 by Totally Bound Publishing, Newland House, The Point, Weaver Road, Lincoln, LN6 3QN, United Kingdom.

No part of this book may be reproduced, scanned, or distributed in any printed or electronic form without permission. Please do not participate in or encourage piracy of copyrighted materials in violation of the authors' rights. Purchase only authorised copies.

Totally Bound Publishing is an imprint of Totally Entwined Group Limited.

If you purchased this book without a cover you should be aware that this book is stolen property. It was reported as "unsold and destroyed" to the publisher and neither the author nor the publisher has received any payment for this "stripped book".

JEWEL OF RAMSTONE

Dedication

To Cheryl, the clever sister who inspired this story.

Chapter One

A Breath in the Forest

She winced at the sunlight and rolled to her side, a blanket tangled between her legs. Still thick with sleep, she noted a dagger lying atop a cracked leather pack, vaguely wondering why she'd left it out in the open. The moment she stretched, a cry escaped her throat. Every part of her hurt. Slowly pushing aside the blanket, she sat up, her gaze darting from the dagger to the smoldering ashes of a fire, then to where she lay atop a bed of leaves. Her breath quickened. Was this a dream? A breeze whispered through the clearing, whisking the sudden sweat on her brow. "H-hail thee?" The only answer, a squirrel chattering from a distance as if telling her to stop interfering in its peaceful existence. Her breath caught. A cold sweat crept over her body. Try as she might, she could not fathom why she woke in the midst of a forest. Or recall her name.

The crack of a branch wreaked havoc with her heartbeat. She dove for the dagger, nearly rolling into the hot coals. "Who" — she cleared her throat — "who goes there?"

The unmistakable nicker of a horse just beyond the tree-lined clearing spun her attention forward. Sweat trickled down her face, stinging one side, but she ignored the pain, too frightened to look away. "Make th-thyself known!"

A black stallion, resplendent with rippling muscles, broke into the clearing. Upon the saddle, a man raised his eyebrow and shook his head. "Put that away. I am not a foe." He dismounted, still locking eyes with her.

She tried to decide what startled her most. Was it the man's immense bulk or the fact that he didn't seem surprised to see her? Dizzy with pain, she shook her head, refusing to lower her weapon.

"Come now." Wisps of ebony hair brushed his broad shoulders and fell into his blue eyes as he dismounted. With a slight shake of his head, he cleared it from his brow and turned his sun-bronzed face her way. "I ordered you to put that away." A shadow of a beard lined his angular jaw and dipped into the cleft on his chin, somewhat softening his surly expression. Each muscle pulsated with strength when he placed his hands on his narrow hips, as if waiting for her to cower.

She gripped the dagger tighter, hoping he did not detect her tremble.

As if to show certainty of how little a threat she posed, he calmly untied two rabbits from his saddle. "Hungry? We shall discuss everything as we sup, starting with why you are still pointing that at me." He sighed. "Now sheath it."

Her palms sweated so much she feared dropping the dagger. Thoughts shot like arrows, one splitting the next. Not a foe? She inhaled sharply when he smiled at her, though it failed to reach his eyes. Gods! He was

trying to trick her. Mayhap he was her captor and…
Wait. Hadn't she wakened at liberty to move about?
Why could she not recall anything? What had he done
to her?

"All is well, lad."

Lad? She nearly looked behind her, but then realized
he didn't know she was a maiden.

He approached and she jabbed the dagger in the air.
Her whole body seemed to vibrate from the inside out.
She countered his steps with a backward one, relieved
when he stopped. The moment she chanced a glance
over her shoulder to assure nay other was about, she
spied him slipping the quiver of arrows from his
shoulder and she cried out.

"Easy." With a quick nod, he held the arrows to the
side.

She kept her stance as he hung the quiver and bow on
the saddle, and tried to calm herself. Mayhap he
believed she shook from the morning chill, and not fear.
She hoped as much, for she detested the fact he
witnessed her trembling at all.

"I understand your wariness, but I have done naught
to harm you. You have but a moment to obey.
Relinquish the weapon on your own, or I shall take it."
His eyes narrowed. "Now."

His steady advance vibrated through her boots. The
hairs on her arms stood. "Stand fast or I shall—" Her
voice cracked as she swung.

In one swift motion, he avoided the blade and
wrenched the weapon from her. He snatched both of
her wrists with his free hand and jerked her arms above
her head. Pain shifted through her body as her feet left
the ground. The man was immense. Damn the bastard,
handling her so roughly.

"Ungrateful fool!" he shouted in her face.

"Unhand me!" She kicked him in the shin, then smashed her forehead into his nose, nearly rendering herself unconscious. He let her drop. She fell hard, bursting into tears.

"You deserve a thrashing for your idiocy." He wiped his bloodied nose, then flung the dagger into a nearby tree. The thud of the blade's impact shattered what was left of her resolve.

"Cease your blubbering. God alone kept me from jabbing that dagger into your blasted chest. Get up!"

She stared at him.

His fury seemed to dissipate as quickly as it came. "Come now." He bent as if to assist her in standing. She scrambled away on her bottom, then bolted to her feet. Dizziness collided with pain, nearly sending her back to the ground.

He grabbed her arm. She jerked away. He swiped his hand across his face and wiped the blood on his breeches. "I did not intend to frighten you, lad, however—"

"I am not a lad, you oaf." Though she should not have dwelt on anything but her safety, something within her rankled about a man so undeniably masculine mistaking her for a lad. A flicker of confusion teased his face, but it was gone so quickly she wondered if she imagined it. He raised a single eyebrow, mirth filling his eyes. Odd it may be, but the motion infiltrated her fear, dousing it a bit. Nonetheless, she dared not trust him.

"Your attire." He gestured toward her, but spoke not another word.

What of it? She glanced at her tunic and breeches, and stifled a gasp. Blood-spattered. Tattered. And masculine.

He bowed, his shoulder-length hair momentarily curtaining his face. "*Milady*, might I offer a plea of forgiveness for my oversight?"

Something gave her the notion he was jesting. When she spied his crooked grin as he rose, she was convinced. She dearly wished to deliver another swift kick, this time higher than his shin.

"Daren't attempt it," he said, his smile still intact.

Damnation, the man had read her thoughts! "I attempt naught, brute."

He was silent for a moment. "I am Sir Galeron of Ramstone. Far from the brute you identify me as."

Was he waiting for her to respond? She crossed her arms.

"Your name as well?" When she failed to heed his request, he extended a scarred hand. "I assure you, your trust is safe with me."

Pulse throbbing in her throat, she raked her bottom lip across her teeth. A part of her wished to take his hand and draw comfort from his touch.

"Ah, no name then." He shrugged.

Alas, if he sensed the truth in that statement. She shook her head and a lock of red hair escaped from the confines of her hood. When she brushed it from her cheek, her breath escaped in a small whimper.

"Aye, I can tend to that. While you were unconscious, I—"

She took several steps back. Hell's teeth! What had he done to her?

He shook his head. "Have I not proven I mean nay harm?"

His tenderness seemed genuine, and quite unsettling. She leaned back when he reached for her face. "Daren't touch me."

"As you wish." He snatched the rabbits, strode a few paces and sat on a log.

She slowly traced a welt on her forehead then feathered across a gash on her check. He drew a dagger from his belt. Fear seized her breath until he began skinning the rabbit.

"Why am I here?"

He slowly met her gaze, his hand poised. "As I said, I found you unconscious."

"You did not say that! I feared I was your..." She bit her lip.

After a pregnant pause, he said, "My what?" He raised a single eyebrow. "My attacker?"

She clenched her fists. "Your captive."

He stared at her a moment. "I know not why I would choose that." He let out a laugh.

Did he fail to see her alarm? Mayhap 'twas fortunate he did not. She changed the focus of the conversation and eyed the fresh kill, her mouth watering at the promise of food. His smirk betrayed his awareness of how she was all but drooling.

"Pray tell, is there something worthy to smile about?" Mayhap the fact that she looked like a lad. She delivered the most evil squint she could muster, holding it until he resumed preparing the kill. Hunger aside, she eyed the horse, calculating an escape.

"Daren't attempt it."

She swung to face him. His eyes remained downcast. Was he a sorcerer? Had he clouded her memory and could now read her thoughts? She twisted the bottom of her tunic so hard it stung her fingers. 'Twould explain why she remembered naught. She glanced at the dagger still embedded in the tree.

"Daren't attempt that either." Her hackles poised, and she was unsure whether to flee or stay — unsure of anything at all. "You are pale. Sit before you fall to the ground again."

"You tossed me to the ground. I did not fall."

"True." He pulled the skin from the rabbit and started gutting the next one. "I tend to react aggressively when someone attacks me."

Sardonic arse. I held every right to attack. She looked away, but her gaze drew back to Galeron, as if her eyes had a mind of their own. *However, he has been naught but kind since then.* A rustle above distracted her. On a branch directly above sat a crow. Instinctively, she reached for her arrows, only to find them gone. "Where are my quiver and bow?"

He snorted, but his mirth vanished when their eyes met. "Ah. I see you are quite serious."

She jerked her head toward the bow and quiver he had hung on the saddle earlier. "Are those mine?"

"I trust you should wait before touching another weapon."

She sorely wished for her dagger back and dared a glance to where her blade remained plunged into the bark of a great oak. Would she have the strength to remove it should she reach it before Galeron? She glanced back in his direction, then flinched at his nearness. When had he approached?

"Perchance 'twould do well to lie down until your confusion passes."

"Stand fast!" She backed away, her bit of trust dashed. "*Perchance* divulging the whereabouts of my weapons would ease my confusion. Or mayhap 'tis due to the fact you drugged me? Or cast a spell."

"I — what?" He took another step toward her.

"I said stand fast!"

He stopped midstride and it seemed everything else halted as well. The stillness of the moment teetered, as if weighing who would speak first.

"What is this place?" Her question echoed in the dense forest and she realized she was still shouting and lowered her voice. "Why am I here?"

"'Tis but a clearing in the woodlands." After a moment he added, "Do you not recognize it?"

She shifted from one foot to the other, unsure of which way to run — or why the need to flee reared its head. Sweet angels in heaven, the woodsy scent of the man made her want to draw *nearer*. His manner, gaze and that damn raised eyebrow made her wish to confide in him. "I must take leave." Before she made an utter fool of herself. Why with all that was wrong, did she wish to stay? "Now."

"Ah, I see." He cleared his throat, motioning toward his tethered stallion. "There is enough cover just beyond those trees."

She had not the need to relieve herself until he suggested it, and now cursed him for the reminder. Heat infused her cheeks. "'Tis not what I—" With a huff, she stomped deep into the trees.

Tears bubbled up and she finally allowed herself a solid cry while relacing her breeches. She crept to the stallion to untie the reins. She prayed the Lord would forgive the sin of theft and understand the need to escape. Galeron's broad hand covered hers and she inhaled a scream.

"Daren't attempt such a fool thing. You shall be thrown off without my presence in the saddle." He stated the words without emotion but his anger was evident by the vein throbbing at his temple.

"I needed…" Shamed, she pulled her hand from his grasp.

"Very well." He blew a sigh. "You can ride with me. Where do you wish to go?"

Alas, if she only knew. "I shall go alone, though your offer is kind." She strode to the makeshift bed and rolled the blanket to hide her growing confusion. She would be safer with this—she glanced up at him—brutally handsome knight. Ah, if she could but trust him. The way he eyed her was disarming. Mayhap 'twas herself she must be wary of. She blinked hard. *Fight the spell he has certainly cast.*

"You have yet to give your name," he said. "I should have one perchance someone enquires about a maiden in lad's clothing, with nay sense in her lovely head."

Whether 'twas in jest or not, it raised her ire just the same. Though he did call her lovely. Truly hating herself for such vanity, she dismissed the thought immediately. With newfound resolve, she secured the blanket with her leather belt and slung it over her shoulder. Though the strap barely grazed her neck, she winced, wondering how many bruises she had.

He sat on a log and crossed his arms. "You have nay mode of transportation."

Pompous, milk-livered...muscular, comely—argh! "I shall traverse by foot." She sensed, more than witnessed, his gaze follow her path to the dagger. Every part of her ached while she worked it out of the tree, but she did not intend to leave without it.

He rose to his feet when she freed it. "Wait. The dagger—"

"Fret not. I shall tuck it safely away." A slight grin tickled her lips as she picked up the sheath, slipped in the dagger and secured it in her boot. Aye, 'twas wise for him to be wary. She'd nearly sliced his gullet with it. She notched her chin a bit higher and turned away. "Fare thee well, Sir Galeron."

She set off without a destination in mind. Though foolish, anywhere else was preferable to here. With him. It did little good to add the undeniable feelings invading her body and mind. Could he sense it? 'Twas best she be on her way before he did. Something was wrong with her. Terribly wrong. How long would his spell last? Her identity should be uppermost in her mind, not confusing thoughts about this man.

Galeron stepped into her path just before she entered the trees. Her musings shattered.

"I cannot permit your departure."

She attempted to sidle past but Galeron took a side step, once again blocking her path. "Allow me to pass!"

"Be at peace. I merely wish to ensure your safety." He put out his hand. "I also need my dagger."

Only one thought came to mind. Without a weapon, she was defenseless. "*Your* dagger?"

"Of course. A maiden would not possess one."

She bristled at his comment, yet slapped the blade into his palm. His hand closed over the sheath. He stood so close she could feel his warmth. She wanted to melt into it and forget her worries — or add to them. Her reaction to him was disquieting. Gaze fastened to the weapon, she took a step back, the underbrush slapping against her boots. Did she dare continue on? She released a sigh, wondering what had happened to her weapons, finding it odd she recalled ever having them when she could remember naught else.

"Can you loan me a weapon?" she blurted, surprised at the calmness in her voice.

"A breech-clad maiden who carries a weapon. Quite extraordinary." He grinned.

She glared at him, biting the inside of her cheek to still the curses wishing to spill from her lips.

"I jest. Douse that ire." With a grin, he cradled her elbow, leading her back. She took a few steps, savoring his touch. *Savor?* Had her sensibilities taken leave with her memory? She pulled free and trudged the opposite way, shoving branches from her path.

"You cannot venture out alone," he called.

"I can do as I wish."

"'Tis not safe, fair one," he said quietly. The tenderness in his voice brought her to a standstill. She clenched her eyes and tensed at the crunch of his footsteps on the forest floor.

"Return with me," he said, just behind her. "I shall keep you safe."

Galeron's deep voice stilled her insides and she almost sighed. Slowly turning, her nose nearly brushed his broad chest, but he did not step back. Surprisingly, neither did she. She looked up, and whispered, "Safe from what?"

He cleared his throat and stepped aside. "Dare I remind you of wild animals and unsavory travelers?"

"If that is an attempt to make me feel safe, 'tis a lame one."

He made a sound between a growl and a chuckle. "At the least, stay and eat."

She drew her teeth over her bottom lip and considered his offer. Hunger gnawed at her indecision, but dared she stay? Why was she so untrusting? If he had wished to harm her, he would have done much worse when she had attacked him.

He raked his fingers through his hair. "I give my word. I shall take you to your home after we have eaten."

She threw up her hands. "I know not where my home is." Sudden hope struck her. "Do you?"

"Mayhap."

She grew concerned when he simply questioned with a crook of his brow. She could become accustomed to that endearing quirk. She met his gaze, waiting... hoping.

"What village are you from?"

She shrugged, hiding her disappointment. "What is the nearest one?"

He rubbed his chin. "The mystery surrounding you is intriguing indeed, fair one."

Intrigue was her only answer. She was nay further in the quest of her identity. *Stand strong.* She squared her shoulders, a chill coursing through her, but hell's teeth, she mustn't show fear at the voice in her head. Thank God she was able to retain her composure. Galeron seemed to sense her need for silence, and allowed her time. Her trust began to solidify in that moment.

As they made their way to the bed of leaves she had woken on, she stole a sidelong glance, wondering what he was thinking. She untied the knot, dropped the blanket to the ground, and sat, half relieved when he didn't join her. He leaned against a nearby tree instead.

"Ask me anything. Mayhap I can help." His deep voice broke the silence.

How was he to help? "Pray tell, how did we come to share the forest?"

"I shall explain." He bent and picked up a twig, then proceeded to peel off the bark. With each curl he tossed aside, she grew more frustrated.

'Twas better to allow mistrust. *Stand strong.* She gasped. Unexpected, the thought rang with such clarity it seemed someone else had spoken. "Perchance you should be honest. Did you drug me? Spell me?"

He tossed aside the twig. Though his eyes remained on her face, her whole body reacted to his scrutiny. "'Twould do you well to hold your tongue."

"I am beginning to dislike you," she said, knowing full well the opposite was true. She truly wished her insides would cease...prickling? And her head. Damn, it ached so. Tingles and pain aside, she tried to focus. "Do you intend to explain or not?"

"I seek a means to tell you gently."

With a slight shrug, she said, "No need for gentleness. You already tossed me about." She grinned despite the truth in her statement.

He sighed. "It appears you are lost."

"God's eyes, knight!" She shook her head. "You must be a great sorcerer to possess such insight."

"Your tongue shall be your undoing. Best you still it."

Twice he attempted to stifle her. She clenched her teeth. "Still it?"

Galeron's jaw twitched and she wondered if he were quelling a smile. "I found you here in the woodlands. I did not hold you captive, drug you or harm you." He blinked slowly. "Hold to that."

She nodded. "Forgive—"

"Nay need. I understand. You now stand a day's ride from Ramstone. Have you heard of it?"

He pushed off the tree and came to sit beside her, his thigh nearly touching her own. Nearly. It took a moment for her answer. "Nay, I do not recall Ramstone." The fact that she did not recall much of anything choked off the rest of her response.

"Odd," he said, more to himself than her.

A sigh escaped and she realized how badly her masquerade of bravery was faltering. Out of the corner of her eye, she saw his hand come toward her. Surprised at the urge to lean into his touch, she remained still and allowed him to brush back the wisps of hair from her brow. His hand lowered in a fist, yet his voice was laced with tenderness.

"It pains me that I cannot give you answers." His gaze strayed from her face, lowering to her neck.

She slapped the neckline of her tunic with both hands and glared at him. "Focus elsewhere." *He sees me as a woman after all.* She dashed away the thought. Almost.

"I intend nay disrespect. The bruising on your neck concerns me." Gently brushing her hand aside, he peered closer. "Fingerprints."

It took all she had not to cry out. Who had harmed her?

"When we discovered you, there was nay sign of anyone else."

She glanced around. "We?"

"I sent my men home."

She blinked. Then blinked again. "Your men?"

"My brother, a healer, assured me your wounds were not serious, so I decided to wait—"

She put up her hand. "Why not leave me under the care of your healer? Or leave me in the nearest village?"

He swallowed hard. "It matters not! Are you always so…so…inquisitive?"

Ah, this man was not used to being questioned. She tried to ease his surly mood. "A shame your men were sent on their way. No one laid witness when I kicked you and bashed your comely face before you so unceremoniously dropped a maiden to the ground."

He blew a long breath. "You insist on repeating that. Had you dressed appropriately, I would not have thought you a lad." His chuckle made her grin. "Although you certainly fight like a maiden."

She swiped her hand through the air. "Carry on."

"Carry on," he muttered. "I fear you shall interrupt again." He looked up through the trees, ignoring her huff. "We still had several days before reaching our destination when we found you. With that in mind, I postponed the journey and sent my men back to Ramstone."

"I see." She studied the frayed edge of her tunic. "How long have I been here?"

"I watched over you a single night. How long you were here remains a mystery. I was only gone a short time for I needed to boil meat into a broth to sustain you. Had I known you were a maiden, I never would have left you alone."

Her head snapped up. "Yet you would a lad? I am not defenseless simply because I am a female."

Galeron's eyes hardened. "Aye, 'tis so. I returned to find you brandishing a dagger. I left it in case you awoke in fright, not to use against me."

She ran her hands through the leaves and shrugged a silent apology, too stubborn to utter it out loud.

"Fair one?"

Damnation, she hated when he addressed her with those words, and yet it awoke something in her, for he said it with tenderness. She glared at his smiling face. "Why are you calling me that?" To her chagrin, what she'd meant as snide came out as quite curious.

He splayed his hands in question, "Would you prefer I call you lad?" Two furrows appeared on his brow at her silent glare. "Because you have yet to give your name."

Disarmed, she swallowed her spiteful attitude. "If I only could." She locked away her tears, her dismay, and did her best to keep her voice steady. "I had hoped you would…say it by now. Sir Galeron, I…I recall naught before I saw you standing before me."

Galeron seemed to battle with her revelation as his expression flitted from stunned to confused. Then his gaze bore into her with such tenderness it nearly undid her. "Nay memory?" he finally whispered.

She shook her head. He guided her head to his shoulder. Barely a moment passed before he released her, rose to his feet and strode away. Unsure of why he had left so abruptly, she frowned when he looked back.

"I regret I cannot ease your uncertainty." He stooped to gather twigs. "However, I am able to ease your hunger. After breaking our fast, we shall take leave."

She dabbed her impending tears as soon as his back was turned.

"We should arrive at Ramstone by nightfall."

"I am to stay at your home? What shall your wife think?"

"There is nay wife." He grabbed a branch and added it to his arms. "But there is plentiful family about."

She held the tree for support then stood, waiting for the dizziness to subside before she followed. When he turned, she picked up a branch, embarrassed at how silly she looked traipsing on his heels. While she gathered an armload of kindling, she stole glances at him, each time wondering how it would feel to remain in his arms. She piled the branches then watched him arrange them.

"Oh, are you preparing a fire?" Hark, she was a fool.

"Nay, I am building an abode." And he solidified the fact.

"I want my own chamber then." Several paces away, she sat. Sunlight peeked through the forest canopy. She closed her eyes and raised her face to the warmth. Like a constant itch, she sensed his gaze. She slowly peered through her lashes. Aye, he was staring — no — studying her face. Her gash. Her ugly face. She sighed and looked to the sky instead.

"God's eyes," he muttered.

She turned to him. *Very well, if he finds a need to gawk, I shall give him a full view of my battered face.* "Sir Galeron, what worries you so? Has my plight delayed your duties?"

"Nay." He jammed the skinned carcasses on a sharpened branch.

"You cursed. Was it in frustration of not reaching your destination?" Oh, how she wished to smirk at his rudeness, but she kept her poise.

"I was not delayed from anything that could not wait." Keeping his eyes shielded, he placed the meat across the spit before offering a weak smile. "I pray forgiveness for my curse reaching your ears."

She wrapped her arms around her legs and rested her unscathed cheek on her knees. "Curses are naught. I am simply thankful you helped me, Sir Galeron." Apparently he was too kind to mention her affliction. She hated the pity.

Seemingly distracted, he arranged kindling then retrieved a piece of hammered steel and flint from a pouch on his belt.

"I pray you can forgive my initial rudeness." When he didn't respond, she added, "Ah, I gather forgiveness shall come with time."

Galeron struck the steel with a bit of flint. "I never held ill will. I understood the reason you lashed out." He blew on the kindling until it caught. "You are forgiven for bashing your head into mine as well."

"Ha!" She rose and strode to the fire. Her gaze flitted over his body. He looked up, catching her stare, and alas, stared back. Heat crept up her neck, spreading to her face. Surely, 'twas the fire's heat causing her flush — she hoped he believed the same lie.

Galeron grinned. His demeanor was infuriating. And endearing. And more confusing than her loss of memory.

"Sit." He continued to tend the fire.

She paid no heed to his demand and thrust her hands toward the fire. To her dismay, the sharp smell of the rabbit caused her stomach to roar with hunger.

Galeron's blue eyes sparked with mischievousness. "I gather 'tis been some time since you ate?"

"Apparently." She plunked down on a fallen log, certain her face turned countless shades of crimson.

He plopped beside her, chuckled and poked at the fire. He was so close she could smell the woodsy scent on his skin. She inhaled deeper, tucking the fragrance into her mind to savor when she was left to her own.

He cleared his throat. "Allow me to tend to that cut."

Inwardly cringing, she changed the subject. "How long before we eat?"

With a quick wink, he leaned back and rummaged in his saddle pack. He cradled her hand and placed an apple in it, keeping one for himself. His smile highlighted the dimple in his chin and she found herself offering a genuine smile in return.

"Ah, glorious," she said, grateful he didn't see how his touch affected her. She waved away his offer to use his dagger, then bit heartily into the fruit. With a moan of pleasure, she relished the explosion of juice across her tongue. "Naught could taste sweeter in this moment."

Oh, one thing might. A sampling of the nectar on his lips would certainly qualify. She sensed his tension when she took a bite. Mayhap he had the same thought? He grunted and crunched into the apple, mumbling something about a damn green-eyed mystery.

Were her eyes green? Damnation. Her mind was truly addled.

* * * *

Had she imagined Galeron's lingering touch when he offered a portion of rabbit? He ate in silence but suddenly chuckled, her nervous prattle the most probable cause. What had she just said? Her mind drifted to the most sinful things. Had she spoken indecently?

"I did not realize how famished I was," she blurted.

He lifted his flask. "A swallow to wash it down?"

She tilted back her head, inviting him to squeeze it into her mouth. As soon as it touched the back of her throat, her eyes watered. "'Tis ale!" she said, choking. "I thought it mead!"

"Nay, fair one. Mead proves too sweet for my taste."

She wrinkled her nose and bolted to the nearby creek.

Water trickled from her cupped hands and onto her tunic. She pulled the damp cloth from her chest, then peered through the branches and caught him looking. He frowned and flung a bone into the fire. Aye, he obviously did not like what he saw. What did she care? He was naught to her. Yet, his dismay troubled her. She patted the corners of her mouth with the arm of her tunic as she left the creek. His gaze was fixed on her as she approached and she wished she had washed her face as well. She sat beside him. Elbowing him hard in the ribs when he offered the flask again, she grinned. "Keep that poison to thyself."

Their laughter startled a flock of crows perched above.

"I do so wish I had my arrows," she whispered.

"Pray, pardon?"

"I am simply musing."

He watched the crows until they were out of sight before tossing the remnants of the meal into the fire. "You mentioned arrows."

"I keep thinking of them." She covered her disquiet with a laugh. "I wonder what happened to my quiver and bow?" It troubled her that she could recall that, but had no explanation as to the way she was clothed. Or, for that matter, anything else.

"What a deliciously twisted maiden," he whispered.

"Pray tell, what are you mumbling about?" She tucked her breeches into her boots.

He didn't answer. She caught him staring at her legs. Her hands paused and his gaze darted to hers. His cheeks flushed and he whisked the saddle pack from the ground, making her jump.

He stooped in front of her, furrows creasing his brow. "There is naught to fear. I did not intend to startle you."

She exhaled, frustrated at her reaction. "I am not afraid, Sir Galeron."

He took her hand. "Yet you tremble."

He did not notice her tremble began at his touch, not before. She pulled from his grasp. "Shall we set off?"

He leaned closer and for a moment, she thought he would embrace her again, but he grabbed the bedroll and went to his steed.

Had she angered him? She tossed dirt onto the fire's remains. "Sir Galer—" His name faltered on her lips. The beauty in his movements made her forget about the handful of dirt still in her palm. It trickled through her fingers, leaving a small mound at her feet. How did such a huge man move with such grace? Gooseflesh tickled her skin and she prayed he did not really possess the ability to read thoughts. She dusted her hands, trying to recall her question.

"Sir Galeron, why have you chosen to bring me to your home instead of the village?" When he didn't answer, she pressed on. "You know naught of me."

His hands stilled above the bedroll. "'Tis my duty." He pulled the pack from his shoulder and threw it over the horse. "Until I am certain nay harm follows, your refuge shall be at Ramstone."

She studied the dusty toe of her boot for a moment before kicking dirt over the coals. "Your duty," she whispered while she watched the last wisp of smoke surrender and die.

He tied back his hair, then motioned to his stallion. "Your ride awaits."

"I am to ride with you?" She ambled closer, Galeron's body growing more desirable with each step.

His eyes crinkled at the corners. "Do your eyes spy another ride among us?" He spun his hand in the air and bowed. "Forgive the oversight, young maiden. A carriage cannot be acquired. You are reduced to riding double with a knight."

She surrendered to a devilish whim to imprison his mocking stance and grabbed for his tunic. But he thwarted the effort when he rose. She snatched her hands back.

He squinted. "What impish deed were you up to?"

A fit of giggles rose in her throat and she covered her mouth.

His confused expression made her laugh harder, her tension melting.

Galeron leaned against a tree, crossed his arms and seemed content to wait for an answer.

With her laughter now unhampered, she twirled, aware she acted as a child. But with each spin, her ever-present tension released, so 'twas quite worth it. Watching the forest canopy rotate, she nearly lost her footing.

"Are you mad?" he called out. "What brings such humor?"

She stopped and fought to keep upright. "The image of your tunic pulled—" Her squeal of laughter blurred the rest of her answer. Mayhap she *was* mad.

"I believe the wound on your brow rendered you senseless." His eyes held mirth. More than anything, she wished to release it fully.

Laughter pitched her words like an out-of-tune gittern. "Aye, you discovered a mindless waif in the woods, dressed as a lad, nay less."

The unleashed gaiety proved to be contagious and although he appeared to be trying to hold back, he was not able to refrain from joining the light moment. He grabbed her arm when she stumbled again. "Careful."

Their laughter quickly filtered into an afterthought. She willed him to say something...anything. She swallowed, faltering under his stare. "Mind you, I intended to pull your tunic over your head." Her voice sounded loud in the wake of silence. She blinked.

"Pray tell, why would you do that?"

The leaves rustled underneath her boots as she took a step back. "'Twas a sp-spontaneous whim." Her eyes locked with his when he moved closer. "'Twas amusing at the time."

His touch on her waist proved gentle, but she could not move. His eyes clouded as he pulled her against him. She should deliver a stinging slap, but couldn't. Inexplicable fulfillment from his nearness deemed such a move impossible. Her fingertips searched as if they knew what she needed. Galeron's face was warm under her caress. A whispering breath brushed her cheek and she closed her eyes. A jolt of warmth shot through her when his lips met hers. She parted her lips, barely enough to allow her moan of surprise, then kissed him back.

A guttural growl began in his throat and vibrated through her body. Galeron's tongue, moist and inviting, entwined with hers. The kiss abruptly ended and a chill replaced his warmth when he stepped back.

"Galeron?" Her gaze lingered on his mouth and she traced the contour of his lips with her finger. He kissed her fingertip, and tremors radiated up her arm from the simple gesture. "Sweet angels in heaven," she whispered, "every part of me responds to you."

She ran her hand along his tunic. The mere thought of touching the skin beneath it caused her breath to quicken. Had she ever been so close to a man? Surely she would recall such splendor. Though sinful, it seemed so natural to be in this one's arms. A willing victim of sorcery, she whispered, "Do that again."

He gently took her hand from his face. "I must—"

"I beg you, daren't breathe a word." The expression on his face threatened to end the moment and her throat closed. The last of her plea was barely audible. "Allow me to savor this magic."

He took a step back. "I should not have…" His breathing grew labored and he raked his hand over his face.

"By the way you are acting, one would think 'twas *I* who kissed *you*." She grinned at him. "You are well?"

"Ah, fair one…" Tiny lines appeared by his eyes when he gave a faint smile. "Nay, I do not believe I am." He looked as if he wanted to say more, but he heaved a sigh.

His muscles tensed when she grasped his shoulder and rose on tiptoe to whisper in his ear, "Spin more magic, Galeron."

"God in heaven, grant me strength." He snatched her in a savage embrace and she grew heady with the power she seemed to have over him. The last she saw before she closed her eyes was his tortured look, or perhaps 'twas the way a man looked before he surrendered to passion. His moan pulsated against her lips, his tongue prodding for entrance. Once again, he explored her mouth, then his lips moved to her cheeks, her eyelids, her brow. Oh, how beautiful and right it was.

She released the leather thong holding back his hair and it fell against her face, the smoke from the fire sweet in his locks. His tongue teased her ear. Her breathing ceased in the moment he drew a lobe into his mouth. When he nibbled her neck, moans blended with her pulse. It took a moment to realize the sounds were her own. Her eyes shot open at the sensation of her liquefying heat pulsating in her undergarment. Memory or not, she certainly would recall such sensation. This was oh so wrong! Tormented by his taut muscles beneath her palms, she pushed away.

His arms relaxed but remained at her waist. Certain he could not mistake the trembling of her body, she refused to meet his eyes. Her forehead pressed against his chest, her own heaving with passion, she grappled for words, yet uttered only one. "Wait."

"I—"

She held up a hand, silencing him. "Galeron, I am not certain of my identity, but I do not believe I am one to act in such a manner." She raised her chin. "However shameful, I…" She looked into his eyes, searching for words to convey the desire swirling through her body, the dismissal of all that was decent, the total need and want of him. Her body responded, yet she uttered not a word. He must realize she was willing. Galeron's eyes looked wild and she wondered if he saw the same abandon in hers.

"There is nay shame other than my own. I regret my actions and beg your forgiveness."

The sting of his comment struck deeper than the wounds she harbored. She pushed his hands from her waist. "I regret naught but for the shame *you* harbor."

"'Tis with good reason."

She shook her head. "What reason may that be?" It seemed an eternity before he answered, and she began to wish she hadn't asked.

"I must confess, I am promised to another."

Her lips parted in a small gasp.

He bridged her silence with another stab of an apology. "I shall never forgive myself for the hurt I see reflected in your eyes."

"'Tis not hurt you see, Galeron." Her fingernails gouged her palms.

"I shamed my duty as a knight by taking advantage of your innocence. For that, I am filled with remorse." He reached out his hands, but she refused the silent invitation.

"Am I simply a distraction along the way?" She touched her cheek, a stark reminder of her ugliness providing an answer. "Was it pity that drew you into a kiss?"

He blinked several times. "Nay. You are far from a distraction."

She did not miss the fact that he left the second question unanswered. "My memory did not erase my heart. Why did you choose to cast such a spell upon me?"

"Wh-what?" Realization played over his face. "Nay! The only magic at play is — it matters not." He cupped her chin. "Can you forgive me?"

Forgive? She could not think with him looking at her like that. She took a step back and answered. "There is naught to forgive." She took his hands and smiled when he rubbed his thumb across the top of hers. Safe in his silence, she continued to expose her heart. "I do not understand the swiftness of my feelings, but when you kissed me, I felt you as a part of myself."

Galeron's eyes darted to hers. Still he said naught.

"I need not an identity to understand that passion reached my soul and nestled into its home. That is where magic plays a part." She squeezed his hand. "Our magic."

He closed his eyes and whispered, "Yet, I am promised to another."

She swung her head as if his words had the force to strike her.

He knelt, pressing her knuckles against his forehead. "I pray pardon. I shall not yield to such a mistake again."

"Mistake." The word came so softly, yet slammed into her. She stared at his bowed head, memorizing each wave, each bit of sunlight reflected in his hair. She held nay right to a man she barely knew. She did not even know herself. She fought to ignore the anger trying to root to protect her feelings and ran her hand across his head.

"Rise, Sir Galeron. If forgiveness is what is required to fulfill your duties, then forgiveness is granted with nay regret." Finding it difficult to meet his eyes, she focused on a lizard clutching a branch, watching it until it scurried into the leaves, knowing he watched her as well. She could feel him, even though he no longer touched her.

He heaved a sigh. "I shall finish packing the horse."

"Please, grant a moment more." Feeling more alone than upon waking in the forest, she carefully chose her words. "I wish every joy bestowed upon your marriage."

He looked over his shoulder. "Your words are kind, fair one."

She dropped her hand to her side, she muttered, "Aye, kind." His stride seemed purposeful, focused and dismissing. Oh, how she wanted to hate him, but she hated herself. She had caused this, though until this moment, she did not realize how her feelings had developed into something deeper than lust. "Nay," she whispered. Yet she realized—he had captured something deep within her.

A branch caught his sleeve. He reduced it to kindling. Feeling just as splintered, she spoke her mind. "May my *kind* words burn in hell's fire! I shan't ease your guilt with lies."

With his jaw set, he kicked through the destroyed branch and came so close his breath touched her face. "Lies?"

"Lies!" She shoved him, sending him a step back. "Lend your ears to the truth, Sir Knight." His bulk seemed to dwarf her and she began to pace to create a distance. "I am unable to grasp that you deem it"—she uttered a growl of frustration—"a mistake. We did naught wrong. You feel as I do." She strode to him and toed his boots, her jaw set rigid. "You cannot deny it." His face showed the flicker of a smile. "Galeron, I do not jest."

"Indeed, fair one."

"Cease calling me that!" At his stunned silence, she continued. "Ah, nay advantage was taken." She ran her fingertip along the dimple in his chin. "I wanted all that was given."

"It cannot happen again."

Tears threatened. She daren't blink and release them. "I shall not speak a w-word of it." A tear escaped.

He wiped it with his thumb, causing more to spill. "I know not what reserve I dig from to avoid kissing these away." She rested her cheek in his palm and he swallowed. Hard. "I pray you find the happiness and joy you deserve."

The painful fact that she had found both in his arms shattered something inside her. The hurt invading her heart proved impossible to douse, yet she placed her turmoil under guard when he prodded her chin. She met his gaze with a smile.

"Now, allow me to tend to your cut before we leave."

"There is nay need." She turned away.

He guided her face to him. She stifled a shiver at his gentle touch. "There is definitely a need," he whispered.

He assured her all would be well while he stitched the slash on her face. She did not make a sound, biting the inside of her cheek until she tasted blood. She would not cry in his presence again.

She relished his tenderness, certain it was the last time she would encounter it. He finished closing the gash and she took a swig of his ale to hide the pain.

"Will it leave much of a scar?" she asked.

"I shall ask my brother for salve to ease the scarring once we arrive, but 'twill leave a mark."

She leaned into him while he led her to the horse and smiled when he didn't step away. Their eyes met as he lifted her into the saddle and she witnessed the shadow of the passion in his eyes—a shadow she was certain would never materialize again.

He placed his foot into the stirrup, hefting himself behind her. "Ready to set off, fair one?"

She almost reminded him to refrain from calling her that, but was too intent on closing off a sob, wishing she could close her feelings for this man as well. Imprisoned in the confines of the saddle, her body tasted his contact and she tried to justify her feelings by cramming reason into her heart. The man was simply following his duty. He must abide by the marriage agreement. She had to forget the way she responded to his… God forgive her for how she wanted him.

No matter what she fashioned to dismiss her feelings, her heart held no part of it. She laid her head against his chest, treasuring every beat of his heart, painfully aware it belonged to someone else. Sadness tore through her when he caressed her cheek.

"Forgive me," he whispered.

"Granted," she answered, leading his hand to the reins. With a prod to the stallion, their journey began.

Chapter Two

Discovered Jewel

Her body relaxed and Galeron wrapped a protective arm around her waist. Sure she was asleep, he allowed his kiss to linger on her temple. A tug of regret stung. The agreement was sealed. He must remember that, but his body's relentless response to her made it difficult to focus on his duty. It did little good to dwell on his heart's reaction. The next hour passed torturously slow. He looked forward to the comfort and lull of normalcy Ramstone offered. He cradled her head, running his thumb against her face. His head began to droop, but the tenseness of her body startled him to wakefulness.

"Well rested?" Her silence made him peer down. The depth of terror on her face shocked him. "What is it?"

She did not answer. Sweat peppered the edge of her tight-fitting hood. She tore his arm from her waist and dismounted before he could fully rein in the horse.

"Whoa!" He grabbed her forearm just in time to break the long drop.

When her boots touched the ground, she slipped from his fingers and stumbled away. He quickly followed. She cried out when he tentatively touched her arm. "'Twas a bad dream?"

Her troubled eyes filled with tears, her lips quivered, but she said naught.

He opened his arms and she stepped into them. "Fret not, you are safe." He could lead an army, but he did not know what to do with her, so he simply held her trembling body.

"The horrid wind. Branches whipping past. So dark. So terribly dark." She swallowed, then drew a ragged breath. "I-I dared not stop."

He cradled her face in his hands, forcing her to look at him. "Easy, fair one. Breathe." He inhaled slowly, as if doing so would help her.

"I could not breathe!" She backed away. "He wished to *kill* me."

A surge of fury coursed through him. "Who dared harm you?"

She seemed to forget mentioning it. "Lightning struck a tree." She bunched the hem of her tunic in her fists. The raw emotion drained from her voice. "I was thrown from the horse."

Galeron took her hands. Her skin was clammy. Wisps of auburn hair stuck to her forehead. This was more than a dream, he was sure of it.

She slipped from his grasp and hugged herself, as if her body would fall apart without her holding it together. He took a step toward her, but she pulled away, her feet shuffling through the leaves. Was she afraid of him?

"'Tis not the memory of the fall that distresses me. It was the pursuit." She twisted around to face him as if she were begging for an explanation.

Afraid she was ready to faint, he readied himself to close the distance lest she step away farther. "Who chased you?" He would strangle the bastard himself. With great effort, he released his fisted hands. "Who?"

"I do not know, Galeron!" She burst into tears. "I wish I did."

In two strides he gathered her into his embrace. This time she allowed his nearness. "You are safe. 'Twas but a night terror."

"A horrid dream." Her words upturned, tripping her statement into question.

He nodded, though he was certain this was more than a dream. "There is naught to fear any longer." She responded, but her words were muffled against his chest. He tilted up her face. "What?"

"I am not afraid." She swiped her tears, but more puddled in her eyes, destroying any validity to her statement.

He could not help but smile. "Nay, you fear naught." He guided her head back to his chest. Her shaky breath whispered against his skin as her trembling slowly subsided. He savored her closeness, nay matter that he should not. Ever. "Damnation," he whispered.

She peered up, her eyes widened as she searched his face. "You are angry," she whispered. It was not a question.

He exhaled slowly. "My anger is directed at the one who haunts you." And the fact that he was faltering in his convictions. He shook his head. "You are safe with me."

"I *feel* safe." She offered a tentative smile.

"As do I — now that you do not have my dagger." Her face turned crimson. *How endearing.* She stepped out of his arms. "Oh, come now, I was teasing, fair one."

"Cease calling me that."

"As you wish, fair one." He offered his arm.

She rolled her eyes and slipped her hand into the crook of his arm. It seemed natural resting there. This maiden seared his heart with the mixture of peace and fire. Would his betrothed? It mattered not. He had made an agreement. And now, he was filled with regret at the fact. Because of her. A maiden without a name.

"Cease brooding about my dream." Her small smile melted his sad thought. "Shall we be off?"

His mind screamed all the reasons they should not stay a moment longer. His heart whispered for a moment more. He pointed to a flat boulder jutting from the landscape. "Let us sit for a while."

She touched her head and sighed as she sat. Her gaze glided up to his when he brushed her fingers aside.

"Lie back." He sat behind her.

She looked over her shoulder. "Why?"

"Woman, just once refrain from your questioning."

To his surprise, she did as he asked. He rubbed her temples. Within moments, she hummed her content. What was he doing? He dropped his hands and scooted away. She lay back in the place he relinquished, closing her eyes against the sun.

"We shall rest here for the remainder of the day." He nearly said *for always.* Did he not have a sane thought when she was near?

"I fare well, Galeron. Do not be foolish."

"Aye, we shall be off then." With no intention of doing so, Galeron cradled his head in his hands and watched the clouds drift. After a few moments of silence he spoke. "I believe your dream holds answers. I do not wish to cause distress but may I ask…" He turned to find her staring at him.

"In this moment, naught can cause distress." She smiled and turned her face to the sky.

Her profile was beautiful. The lock of hair peeking from her hood beckoned his touch. Her nose, sprinkled with faint freckles, turned up a bit at the end. He wished to kiss it.

"What do you need to know about my dream?" she asked.

Oh yes, the dream. He cleared his throat. "Why were you pursued?" Receiving a shrug in response, he continued. "What was your destination? Most important, did anyone in your dream call out? A name mayhap? Furthermore, why would—"

She jumped up and raised her hand. "Wait! 'Tis quite a flurry of questions."

He sat up. "Then answer one at a time."

"Are all knights as daft as you?" She grinned. "Which of the countless queries shall I respond to first?" She tapped her finger on her bottom lip.

He'd nibbled that lip. Kissed that fingertip. He realized he was not listening and focused on her voice. "Thrown from a horse, and most disturbing, I believe someone wishes me dead. I have nay other answers. Even those are not clear."

"I should keep my questions to myself." *And his impure thoughts.*

"Actually, your questions are the same ones I now ask myself." She motioned the length of her body. "As well as to why I am wearing this garb." She laughed.

He felt her laughter within him—and how badly he would miss it when they parted company. "'Twould be fitting for you to possess a name as well." He studied her.

She squinted, warily meeting his inspection. He ran a finger through the strand of hair that had been torturing him. It was as soft as he had imagined. Then he untwisted the cord beneath her chin.

Her breathing quickened as he removed the hood, but he could not stop. Transfixed, he watched the long, auburn locks spill from her hood and onto her shoulders.

He released a breath. "I shall dub you...Ruby." Her jade eyes flickered with yellow specks in the sunlight. "Ruby of the Forest." He widened the mere shadow of space between them. The single step back seemed a chasm of eternity. "Ah, those red tresses are a jewel in themselves."

"Surely you jest." She snatched the hood, but he did not miss how her eyes filled with want. "My true name shall come in time." She tucked it into her belt, her hand shaking.

Galeron's heart drank her in. He must turn away. It was wrong.

Her smile waned. "You are looking at my ugly wound."

"Nay. I am but admiring the jewel before me." Would she believe he noticed naught but her beauty?

"Enough of this silly name game. Let us be off."

He swept his hand and bent in an exaggerated bow. "As you wish, Ruby of the Forest."

"You are insufferable." She clicked her tongue and headed for Galeron's stallion. "Such a fool."

He laughed. A fool for her, mayhap.

* * * *

Though he enjoyed the clear day, Galeron welcomed the cooler air when dusk arrived. He assumed she was unaccustomed to long rides and made certain to stop more often than he would if he rode alone. Once again, she readjusted her bottom in the saddle, arching her back a bit to ease the tension. He wrapped his arm around her waist, sitting her on his lap. "Now, be still." As usual, she paid no heed to his orders and moved. He gritted his teeth. "Comfortable now?"

Seemingly unaware of his sarcasm, she snuggled against him. "Aye, 'tis better." Within moments, she drifted to sleep.

'Twasn't a bit better. Galeron's mounting discomfort accompanied raw emotion. He cursed himself for pulling her closer, as it made the situation even more unbearable. He distracted unsuitable thoughts by counting the horse's steps. The feeble attempt to prevent his body from responding to her was unsuccessful. At least she slept and could not feel his arousal. He swallowed hard and focused on thoughts of home…and his bed. Nay, this would not do at all.

He slipped her back onto the saddle. The sun began to set, but his emotions roiled. Though he had bedded many, none made him care as he did for this one. His heart tangled, twisted and broke. For this was more than want. It was need.

Chapter Three

Breath Taken

"Stop a moment. Allow me to absorb this splendor."

He pulled on the reins.

"What is this place? Look at all the corn roses! The red appears molten. The yellow embraces the last rays of sun." She outstretched her arms. "Ah, the view is pure bliss."

"There is a monastery just over that hill." He pointed, then rested his hand on her waist. "They grow these for medicinal purposes." He paused. "Seeing this through your eyes causes me to discover the beauty I took for granted a mere day ago."

His touch made her smile. "They dance in the tall stalks."

"The monks?"

Her whoop of laughter escaped before she could stifle it. "The corn roses."

"Ah…they simply sway in the breeze."

She twisted in the saddle and he frowned. Intent on easing his surly mood she said, "Nay, Sir Knight, inspect closely, they are dancing."

He chuckled. "The bruise to your head is clouding your sight."

She tilted her head. "Oh? Mayhap I should bruise your head as well, for your imagination is…" The odd grimace he gave made her take pause. "You have but to imagine. Their waxy heads sway then bow to the heavens, like a dance."

"As you wish to believe."

Why was he so… Argh! She shrugged. "Very well, blind knight. Carry on, but surely 'tis a sin to trample through this meadow." She glanced up. "Mayhap you can take a different path?"

His lips neared, and for a moment she thought he would kiss her. "Your poetic *dance* continues for miles, fair one. However, I shall avoid the densest parts." He rubbed his jaw.

"You are right. 'Tis a sight to treasure."

He was the treasure. She sighed, her lighthearted mood punctured, but she continued to smile. "I knew you would see it through my eyes if you looked long enough." She had to turn away. Why did it matter what he saw? Or thought?

"Nay other season holds the beauty of autumn. Ramstone is blessed with flora year round." He stopped for a moment when she turned, seemingly surprised at his own comment. "The gardens are surrounded by thick shrubs of holly." Galeron's mouth upturned, but she detected a hint of sadness. "My mother used it to ease the household's coughs and fever." He cleared his throat. "Just the same, 'tis a sight to behold in the winter."

She wished he would have continued to talk about his mother and wondered what the woman would think of him returning to Ramstone with her in tow. "I thought holly was poisonous."

"Only the berries." He grinned. "The contrast of the berries *dancing* in the snow is striking though."

"Pray tell, a burly knight studies the beauty of flora?"

"Ah, Ruby of the Forest, I know well of the beauty before me."

Beauty. As if on its own volition, her fingers touched the wound on her cheek. "You are blind after all," she muttered as she faced the meadow. "Let us be on our way." His deep chuckle vibrated against her back as he spurred the stallion into a canter. He guided the stallion along the far edges of the meadow, the earthy scent wafting up with the soil the hooves disturbed. The comfortable silence lasted for hours, broken only by the occasional snort of the horse.

The ride less entertaining once it separated them from the meadow of corn roses, she caught herself dwelling on the name Galeron had dubbed her, and how beautiful she felt despite the cut on her face. Still, 'twas not her name and she surely would not go by it. Was it kindness or mere pity that he dubbed her after a precious stone? She squirmed at the thought and he shifted in the saddle.

"Would you prefer to dismount and rest for a while?"

Gods. If they stopped, she would surely lie down and sleep. "Carry on, I am eager to finish this day's journey."

"Then hold still."

This man was fond of orders. To solidify the fact that she was not one to obey, she shifted her bottom one last time. "Surly knight, mayhap you are the one in need of

45

a rest?" He kicked the horse into a canter without answering. "Ah, I suppose not. Just as well, the scenery is beautiful from astride the saddle." Though she sounded foolish, she chattered about the clouds, a stream, sparrows flitting about, to stave off the chance of falling asleep. The dream haunted her thoughts, goaded her fears, and she was not taking a chance of allowing it to reoccur. Eventually naught, even idle conversation—be it one-sided after a while—could stave off exhaustion. She closed her eyes, resting but for a moment.

Ruby woke to darkness—her heart pounding in her throat. Why were they in a full gallop? She gulped several breaths, calming herself. The reason for her unease was not a night terror, but a different dream. One filled with Galeron's lips, his hands upon her body. Still in a gallop, she peered around Galeron. They were alone. No chase. Naught to fear. Why then was her whole body trembling? Her night terror was less confusing. She looked up at Galeron. Calm, like water lapping at her bare feet, washed over her the moment she caught his moonlit profile.

She longed to pull his face to hers and kiss him. Surprise him. But he surprised her by catching her stare. His eyes widened. Again, she wondered if he possessed the ability to read thoughts, and turned away. Not bothering to slow the horse, he chuckled. Her bottom bounced in the saddle and she wished she were still in his lap. What was wrong with her? Her thoughts were those of a harlot! She had dreamed of him like a harlot as well. He was groaning her name. *Ruby... Ruby...Ruby.*

"Ruby?"

Her insides jumped. How many times had he called her? "Aye?"

"We are almost to my home. Ramstone is just ahead."

Home. She peered at the landscape glistening in the full moon. "I see naught. Where?"

The horse whinnied as if to answer. At the crest of the hill, he pulled on the reins. "There." He pointed.

She squinted at the silhouette of Ramstone on the next hill. The moon shone above it, lending an eerie glow to the walls and turrets. "You did not tell me your home was so..." At a loss for words, she sighed. What was Galeron thinking when he decided to bring her here?

"My home was so what?"

"Prominent."

"'Tis simply my boyhood home, Ruby."

She gulped. This was more than that, a manor, the wealth apparent even from this distance. What would they think of her? A mangled ruffian? A mangled memory? And a want that flamed like a blacksmith's fire for the man who was trothed to another? "Mayhap you should leave me in the village."

"You are safer at Ramstone."

"But—" She stiffened when two men on horseback flashed through the gates. She lost the comfort of his arm when he returned both hands to the reins. "They are aware 'tis you, aye?"

"I hope so." He chuckled.

She did not find humor in his jest. An unexplainable fear gripped her.

As if he sensed her unease, he placed a hand on her shoulder. "Ease your mind, fair one."

She licked the salty taste off her lips and drew a breath when the men pulled to a stop in front of them. "Ah, Galeron, I waged a bet 'twas you. Yet could not figure out why you stopped here." The man glanced at her and gave a slight nod. "Greetings."

"I was showing… It matters not. All is well," Galeron said before she could respond.

"That is yet to be seen. We were sore worried." The man turned to the other and it was then she noticed he was younger than the men by quite a few years. "Announce his arrival."

She suffered an uncanny chill as the boy headed down the hill. *What worries them?*

"Alex, was that necessary?" Galeron said.

There was something familiar about the one named Alex. His smile. And the way his eyes glinted with mischievous pleasure. She started to ask if they were brothers but Alex spoke first.

"I would enter armed with an explanation." Alex glanced at her. "And one about your decision to delay…" He glanced at her again.

"Pray thee." She swallowed hard. "I fear I caused his delay."

"I thought as much." Alex smiled wide and winked at Galeron.

Galeron chuckled. "Alex, your wicked smile reflects enjoyment of my predicament."

Alex leaned forward in the saddle. "I cannot wait to hear the story you shall weave this time."

This time? She looked from one man to the other, for once, speechless. Which was just as well, for the men spoke as if she were not there.

Alex cleared his throat. "What became of the lad?"

"I shall divulge everything should you win," Galeron said and kicked his steed into a gallop.

She whooped her surprise and clutched the saddle horn. Alex kept time as they bolted down the hill. She tried to bite back her laughter, but could not refrain from the enjoyment of the race. "Make haste!" She looked back as they ascended the next hill. "He is gaining!" When she turned back, she saw the short distance to the closed gates. She gripped his arms, screaming. "Slow this beast!"

As if Galeron's bellow were a magic key, the gates opened, sparking laughter from both men. They *whooshed* in, the hooves coming to a skid, the snorts of the steeds seeming to mock her as well.

Alex swung out of the saddle and handed his reins to a groom. "I won."

Galeron laughed. "As you wish to believe."

The inner ward came alive with the commotion. The oily smells of the torches mingled with the nearby gardens, lending a sweet, smoky odor to the night air. A squire took the reins as Galeron dismounted, then he helped her dismount as well.

An older man stomped toward them. "Fie upon thee! Where have you been!" She raised her eyebrows higher with each step the man took, resisting the urge to back away. The man was immense.

Galeron squeezed her hand. With her free hand, she grabbed Galeron's sleeve and clamped her gaping mouth. The man continued to shout his displeasure. She darted a peek at the squires, wishing to follow them to the stables.

"For what reason, pray tell, did you delay the journey to your betrothed?" He'd neglected to tell her *that*. Before Galeron could answer, the man stepped closer. "Nay reason, short of death, should have deterred you. They are waiting!" He thrust his hand toward Alex, just missing Ruby. "Alex was perfectly able to stay behind with the wounded lad. Are you void of sense?"

"Father, I beg patience." Galeron pulled her slightly behind him.

Ruby stepped back out. This man, this...this ogre was his *father*? And Galeron believed she was safe here?

Alex stepped forward, locking eyes with her. "You should come with—"

"Step away, Alex," Galeron's father growled. "This is between your brother and me."

Alex left without another word. She took advantage of the distraction and tugged on Galeron's arm. "Tell me the way to the village."

As if time slowed, Galeron's father's attention swerved to her...to Galeron...to her again. "Who—what—" His gaze ran the length of her before glaring at Galeron. "I suppose the reason for your delay stands beside you?"

Galeron's jaw twitched. "There is much to explain, Father. She is my guest."

Ruby stepped forward, cleared her throat and mustered a smile. "However, if you would be so kind as to direct me to the village—" His eyes bore into her. She made to leave, but Galeron held to the back of her tunic. "Surely, I can find it myself." She bit the inside of her cheek when Galeron's father put up a hand. The two were infuriatingly domineering. "Point the direction, Sir Galeron." A part of her—a minuscule part—was thankful Galeron still had hold of her, for she feared venturing out to the middle of...of nowhere. "'Tis wise I take my leave before I speak my mind."

"Enough," Galeron whispered.

"I prefer to—" Galeron's father held up his hand. Again. It took all she had not to storm away. If she but had a place to storm to.

"At least for the night." His frown eased. "I beg forgiveness for my rude behavior." The hulking man bowed slightly. "I am Lord Easton, father of Galeron. Welcome to Ramstone Hall." His gaze darted to Galeron's fingers still twisted in her tunic.

She jerked out of his grasp and smoothed her tunic, wishing she could do the same to her ire. Her plight left nay choice. She would stay for a night. Without the assistance of a skirt, it made her curtsy as awkward as the situation. "I am honored, Lord Easton." She hoped the village was within walking distance.

He motioned toward the door. "Let us join the others. We were ready to dine when you arrived."

"I am thankful for your hospitality." She glanced at the gates. They were closed.

Lord Easton nodded and turned to Galeron. "Son, this is not the end of our discussion."

Galeron's shoulders twitched a vague shrug. He reached for her hand and gave it a reassuring squeeze, but dropped it as they approached the doorway. Her apprehension gave way to distraction while she took in the enormous entry. Her fingertips deftly tucked in and out of the carved grooves on the door while she crossed the threshold. She looked past Galeron and was entranced by the flickering candlelight illuminating the artwork on the ceiling.

"Look, those carvings are —"

He finished her thought. "Dancing?"

Her eyes meeting his, she grinned. This man infuriated her in one moment and eased her soul in the next. "Aye."

Easton looked over his shoulder. "Dancing?" He shook his head and strode away.

"That frightened me as a lad." He motioned to the painted ceiling.

"Are they not angels?" She squinted at the ceiling. "Besides, I cannot imagine you afraid of anything, even as a child."

"I feared they would swoop down and carry my mother to heaven."

He motioned to a portrait near the stairs. Her black hair cascaded far below her shoulders, a wreath of ribbon and flowers adorning like a crown. How young she was. Two young boys clutched her skirts. She supposed they were Galeron and Alex. "I am to meet her as well?"

"She died long ago." His words tumbled quietly.

"Oh." Naught else came to mind. She interlaced her fingers between his, offering comfort. But he wrenched his hand from her hold.

"Dare not attempt that within these walls."

She focused on anything but him to hide her bruised feelings and allowed Galeron to place her hand on his arm to guide her to the next room. A full seating of people looked up from a long oak table. She whispered without moving her lips, "I assumed we would wash first! I am still dusty from the road."

"You are more than dusty, fair one. You are a delightful mess."

She glared at him as they sat, but he seemed too involved in rearranging his linen cloth to notice. She grinned across the table at the blatant stare of the same young man she had seen outside the gates with Alex. He blushed and looked away, but not before his eyes traveled to the cut on her cheek. Ruby pulled at her hair to cover it.

The woman next to her leaned closer. "What lovely hair you have."

She smiled. "My thanks. I only wish I took the time to braid it." And wash. And find something fitting to wear. And flee from their inspection.

"You are Galeron's guest?"

A servant slipped between them and set down finger bowls, ending the exchange. She dipped her fingertips in the bowl, wishing to wash her face as well. Her mouth nearly tasted the aroma of the heavily laden platter when the servant placed a succulent roasted beef on the table. One of the fruits surrounding it dropped to the table. She rescued the apricot before it hit the floor. The servant smiled while placing a loaf of bread between her and Galeron.

"Good reflexes," Galeron whispered, tearing a hunk from the bread. "Now cease your play."

Steam puffed out of the loaf. An odd vision took form in the steam. A child drizzling honey on bread.

"Ruby, you are crushing the fruit." She continued to stare at the loaf a moment, then looked down at her hand. Sure enough, juice seeped through her fingers.

"What ails you?" he whispered.

What ails *him*? The decision to stay was a mistake. She slipped what was left of the apricot into her linen cloth. "I am just weary." She rinsed the stickiness off her hands and a servant whisked away the finger bowl.

"Galeron, would you be kind enough to introduce your guest?" Lord Easton said.

She detected the inflection in his voice when he spat out the word *guest*. She certainly would not stay. The ache in her head throbbed with the threat of blinding her.

Galeron smiled. "Ruby of the Forest, allow me to introduce you to my family."

"I beg you, refrain from using that title," she said.

Lord Easton laughed. "'Tis unusual, I must say."

"Indeed." Ruby glared at Galeron. "Quite unusual."

"Seated beside you are my younger brother, Sir Alex, and his wife, Lady Sarah." Galeron pressed his leg against her. Mayhap he needed more room.

Ruby smiled. "My pleasure, Lady Sarah." With a nod she added, "Sir Alex."

"Before you, my youngest brother, Rafe." She did not detect a resemblance at all. Had Easton fathered him in the years since Galeron's mother's death? Mayhap he was a bastard son.

"I recall meeting you outside the gates." Rafe brushed his blond hair to the side, opened his mouth as if to speak, then gave a small nod instead. Was he mute?

"*I* recall you kept us in suspense, Galeron," Alex said. "I am still trying to fathom how you always end up with a beautiful maiden."

Beautiful maidens? Ruby smiled through a pang of jealousy.

Proving her deduction incorrect, Rafe joined in. "Did you meet the boy? Where is he?"

Galeron sighed. "Rafe, he was — she — I mean the lad —"

"Oh, pay attention quickly. Galeron is stuttering!" Rafe pointed.

Laughter erupted around the table. Ruby did not know whether to join the mirthful conversation or not. She turned to the soft scent of jasmine.

"I am grateful you are here. I tire of being the only female at this table. There is not much use of manners with these men," Lady Sarah said.

"So very true," she whispered.

Rafe leaned forward. "Ruby of the Forest, may I inquire where you are from? I am certain 'tis not the forest." The boy's smile held the same disarming quality as Galeron, a resemblance she missed before. "I would also enjoy hearing how you acquired such an unusual name."

She smiled at Sarah, ending their quiet conversation. "Your eldest brother found humor in dubbing me so," Ruby said, instantly regretting her answer when everyone stared at her.

Galeron interjected a rescue. "I created the name because she has nay recall of her own. She is the wounded soul we mistook for a lad."

Each question blurred into the next, everyone talking at once. *A lad…? How did you end up in the forest…? Whence did you come from…? Who harmed you?*

Mouth agape, she darted from one inquisitive face to the next. "I do not know."

Now talking among themselves, no one paid heed to her answer. *I must say, I did wonder about her attire… I as well, but then again, mayhap 'tis with reason… And the poor child, her wounds… What could have possibly happened?*

She stifled a sigh. "Well, I am not certain. When I woke in the forest—"

"Are you lost?" Rafe asked, then looked to his father. "Mayhap you can help? You are acquainted with owners of the land nearby."

"How did you get hurt?" Sarah placed a hand upon hers. "If 'tis too painful to speak of—"

"She knows naught!" Galeron shouted above them.

Ruby slipped her hands from Sarah's and clutched them in her lap. She stared at the grain of the oak wood table, her cheeks aching with the effort to keep from succumbing to nervous laughter. Of all times to laugh. They would deem her mad on top of all the other things that must be flitting about their imaginings.

Lord Easton cleared his throat. "Enough questions, the poor girl is exhausted."

"Not too exhausted to attack," Galeron muttered. Ruby pinched his side hard enough to guarantee a bruise. Other than shifting out of her grasp, he showed no sign of her assault beneath the table.

Lord Easton raised his mug. "Welcome, Ruby of the Forest!" Everyone toasted. Easton leaned toward Galeron. "Honestly, son, you succeeded in dimming any rudeness I displayed earlier. That slip of a woman could not harm a thing."

Galeron nearly spat out his wine. "Dare not lend her a weapon." She attempted to torture another body part, but he leaned to reach for the bowl of turnips, thwarting her efforts. As soon as he straightened, she tried once again.

"Dare not attempt—" he whispered.

"Cease saying that," she quietly interrupted, stabbing her meat so hard her knife clinked against the pewter plate. The maid refilled their mugs and Ruby wondered if she overheard their exchange.

"Galeron, do entertain us with a tale of this intriguing journey," Sarah said.

Ruby paused mid-bite.

"Despite not completing it." Alex eyed Ruby.

She twisted the linen cloth in her lap as Galeron spoke. "After brandishing my dagger, she kicked me!" Galeron laughed.

Ruby swallowed her bite and added. "And I am sure his nose still aches from the onslaught with my head."

"Oh, that." Galeron shrugged. "I thought a leaf landed between us."

Ruby patted the corners of her mouth with a linen cloth. "By a mere coincidence, you dropped me to the ground in that instant?"

Alex whooped his pleasure and everyone else joined in the banter. She truly began to enjoy herself in that moment—until Galeron spoke of her attempt to leave the forest alone. Moments later, she exhaled a breath. The brute had the sense to omit the times they were in each other's arms. She loved the interaction between these strangers and relaxed.

"Pray tell, what happened next?" Lady Sarah asked when Galeron paused to take a drink.

"Next?" Galeron shrugged. "We arrived at Ramstone."

"That is all?" Sarah smiled at her. "Nay adventures, treachery or even a wild animal to slay?"

"He *did* slay ferocious rabbits," Ruby said. The din rose while the men teased Galeron yet again. Ruby found it quite entertaining.

Sarah leaned closer to her. "Shall I address you as Ruby of the Forest?"

"I am certain my own name cannot be as entertaining as the one Sir Galeron tortures me with."

"I shall simply call you Ruby then."

Ruby liked her instantly. "'Tis at least a real name."

A slow smile spread across Sarah's face. "I believe we could invent a name for Galeron."

Thief of my senses...my heart...my very breath. "I can think of a few," Ruby said. She saw Galeron turn from the corner of her eye. When she met his gaze, he raised an eyebrow. If he uttered his incessant "dare not attempt it," she would certainly scream.

Seemingly intuitive of her thoughts, he patted her leg and returned to the conversation with the men. She nearly jumped at his touch, but hungered for it when he removed his hand.

"Ah! We should name him Galeron of the Dark Night." Sarah grinned.

Ruby stared at her. Whatever was she talking about? Oh. The name. "For him? I do not understand." She nearly suggested Ordering Oaf, but thought not.

"Dark night," Sarah repeated. "Dark mood and he is a *knight*."

"Jester of Ramstone would be more fitting," she said. The fool he was. A fool she hated to love.

"You do not know the man. I assure you Galeron does not jest about anything." The dishes clattered at Galeron's fist upon the table as he burst out laughing with Rafe.

"Nay?" Ruby raised a brow at Sarah and smiled.

"He *is* in an exceptional mood tonight." Sarah's eyes narrowed to a squint. "I do not believe I have ever seen him laugh like that. Or laugh at all, really."

Galeron leaned toward Ruby before she could respond. "Ruby of the Forest." Galeron choked at her expression. With a quick recovery, he pointed at Rafe. "Assure him you attacked me with my own dagger. He believes I am weaving a false tale."

She stopped at each set of expectant eyes, saving Rafe for last. "I have not a notion what the man is talking about."

Rafe laughed so hard he fell to the floor. Flushed with embarrassment, he scrambled into his seat, but he still chuckled. "She mocked you well, brother!"

Galeron smiled and returned the pinch she gave him earlier. She ground her heel into the toe of his boot in response, her satisfaction thwarted when his mirthful eyes peered over his mug.

"Ah, I was sure I smelled pie," Lord Easton said, ending the foolishness. "'Tis the best part of the meal."

"I cannot partake of anymore." She hesitated at the tart aroma of the pie. "Well, mayhap a bite or two."

Easton chuckled. "'Tis the last of the fresh berries of this season, so enjoy a whole slice."

She closed her eyes and savored the creamy bite of pastry, thick with almond milk. A flash of sight spun her away from Easton's voice. A basket of berries. She swallowed, barely getting it down. Berries, splattering into pools of—she glanced at her tunic—blood? The conversation faded to a distant hum. She ran her tongue over the gritty seeds, the disquieting surge of danger stealing the enjoyment of the pie.

Galeron cleared his throat. She realized the conversation at the table had ceased. A flash of heat spread over her face.

"You seem very engrossed in that pie, but I believe Lady Sarah is waiting for an answer," Galeron said, his voice on the edge of laughter.

She turned to Sarah, completely disoriented.

"I love pie as well." Sarah waved the inquisitive looks away from Ruby and repeated in a whisper, "I said I have a perfect bedchamber in mind. Would you like me to have it readied for you?"

She leaned close to Sarah. "I am honored. However, I believe I shall find a place in the village."

"Nonsense, there is nay place to stay. 'Tis filled with wedding guests."

"Oh." *Galeron's wedding.*

"Galeron would not have brought you here if he did not intend you to stay with us."

"I do not believe Lord Easton is very receptive to the idea of a houseguest."

Sarah sighed. "He really is a kind man."

Ruby glanced at Easton. Fully relaxed, he did not seem quite as intimidating. "He does not seem to hold his anger."

"You simply caught him scolding his son. Now, would you like to see the chamber I mentioned?"

The thought of rest punctuated her weariness. "Lady Sarah, I am grateful for your kind offer."

"Delightful. I am certain you shall love Ramstone."

Love Ramstone? Never. Even though she feared she loved the man who resided there. The unbidden thought made her wince. Could she truly care so deeply for Galeron in such a short period of time? She shoved the answer away. It could not be. All enjoyment depleted, she slid her pie aside. He shoved it in his mouth with one bite and winked at her. Ruby shook her head. How could a simple wink thrill her so? She must douse her feelings.

The evening lengthened, the banter filtered into conversing between the men, while she and Sarah became more acquainted. When Lord Easton called for his pipe, Sarah suggested they leave the men to their own devices, then turned to plant a small kiss on Alex's cheek.

Ruby whispered her farewell to Galeron, but he did not turn from his conversation with his father. He chose *now* to ignore her? Of course, she had nay right to expect more than courtesy. His kiss, however, was still sweet on her lips. Damn him.

"We shall take leave," Sarah announced to the others.

Alex and Galeron pulled back the women's chairs as they rose. The nearness of him was comforting while they sat, but now, with him close behind her, Galeron's woodsy scent made her wish for their time in the forest. Far away from here. From reality. Ruby brushed by him, certain he would see her out. She followed Sarah and Alex to the door.

They paused in the doorway and she realized Galeron had stayed behind. Alex kissed Sarah's hand and turned to her. "Rest well, Ruby of the Forest."

"I shall," she whispered, cuffed at the separation from the only comfort she could remember. Alex took the seat beside Galeron. Easton leaned toward his sons, drawing them into conversation. She clutched the edge of the door. As if sensing her gaze, Galeron turned, a mug poised at his lips. Did time pause? *Fare thee well*, he mouthed. His blue eyes held her captive. Easton called his name, freeing her. Ah, but she was a willing prisoner.

Sarah laced arms with her. "Are thee well?"

She blinked. "A bit weary. Shall we be off?" She stole a final glance over her shoulder.

She made sure to nod when appropriate at Lady Sarah's chatter while they ascended the stairs, all the while silently vowing to avoid Galeron during her time at Ramstone. A simple look was all it took to make her swoon. She should never have agreed to stay.

Sarah stopped in front of a pair of carved doors. "I adore this room." She opened them with a flourish. A tub was at the center of the room, a fire blazing nearby. She could hardly wait to soak in the hot water a manservant took from the hearth.

"'Tis the last one, milady." He poured the contents of the cauldron into a huge tub.

"You may take leave, Charles." Sarah took a folded drying cloth and draped it on the edge of the tub. He bowed quickly and left.

A maid finished straightening the coverlet on the bed and whispered her apologies for not having it ready in time. Sarah dismissed the comment with a wave of her hand. "The hour is late, Bridget. You did well." She smiled at the young maid. "You may go."

"Do you like it?" she asked her once they were alone.

The makeshift bed of leaves in the forest came to mind. "Lady Sarah, this room is beyond the comfort my words could convey." She clapped her hands, then ceased, her face heating at the impulse.

"So, I am to believe you approve." Sarah giggled.

Unexpected tears filled her eyes. "Lady Sarah, I wish I could repay such kindness."

"Call me Sarah. The joy you show is payment enough. Enjoy your bath before the water turns cold. I am certain you are weary."

"Indeed. My body feels like a huge bruise."

Sarah examined Ruby's cheek. "You poor soul. Does it hurt?"

She suppressed a wince. "A bit. I am certain I shall recover quickly with a night's rest out of the forest." *And far away from here.*

"Alex should examine it in the morn." Sarah dropped her hand to her side.

"Do not fret. Sir Galeron did a fine job of stitching it."

"As you wish. Rest well." With a wave of her fingers, she closed the doors behind her.

Wasting no time in letting the dusty male garments fall to the floor, she could barely wait to dip into the steaming tub. She scrubbed until her skin tingled, happy to be rid of the grit from the road. The washing sponge proved a worthy pillow and she rested her head on the edge of the tub. The aches and tension of the day floated away, easing the punishment of her escapade. Her gaze drifted to the high ceiling and she mused about the name Galeron had given her. She supposed she would love any name simply because he chose it. However, his teasing must cease. Come morn, she would insist he simply call her Ruby. In the least, until she recalled her own name.

The steam carried the smell of the lavender soap, easing the jab and prod to remember her past. Right now, she did not want to try. The rhythmic crackle of the fire beckoned her to release all thought. Her hands floated weightlessly to the surface. Exhaustion overthrew the turmoil in her mind.

The click of a latch startled her out of a sound sleep. Ruby splashed water onto the floor in her haste to sit. Footsteps faded. Gooseflesh pricked her skin while she bundled in the drying cloth, eying the door. She hurried to the hearth and crouched, leaving a puddle while she blotted water from her hair. She examined her dusty garments, dismayed she had naught clean to wear, then spied clothing draped across a chair. Apparently the footsteps she heard were a servant delivering something to wear to bed.

A sigh escaped as she pulled the night-rail over her body. Gods, it was soft. Her stitches pulled against her yawn. She blotted it with the drying cloth, rinsed it and then hung it over a chair by the fire. After a dismal effort to braid her hair, she decided to let it stay loose. She pulled the hangings around the bed and slipped beneath the coverlet. With a prayer still upon her lips, she fell asleep before her hair had dampened the pillow.

Chapter Four

Out of the Window

Ruby stretched and winced at her twitching muscles. She groaned, wriggled deeper into the feather mattress and tucked the woolen blankets under her chin. Mayhap a short stay at Ramstone was not such a bad suggestion. Still bleary with sleep, she took a moment to focus on the canopy.

She admired the depiction of a fairy, tipping a leaf to catch a drop of dew for a drink, then whispered a giggle at a sprite, frozen in the act of lassoing a hummingbird with a chain of daisies. Sunlight filtered through the embroidered hangings, lending an enchanted aura to her little haven. She drew back the hangings. The tub was gone. She hadn't heard it being removed. Though she was tempted to go back to sleep, her curiosity would not allow the luxury and she slipped out of bed.

Retrieving a robe off the end of her bed, she scrambled into it. Again, someone had thoughtfully left her something. She scurried to the hearth, tossed on an extra log and watched it catch before sitting at the window seat. Outside, the gardens reminded her of the corn roses and her lips parted in a slight smile. Bittersweet, but a smile just the same. She turned away, examining the room.

Along the adjoining wall stood two huge chests, both decorated with fairies. Above, a kirtle hung on a peg. Was it for her? She had not notice it last eve. Ruby jumped at a rap on the door. Would Galeron dare visit her chamber? She ran and pressed her ear against it. "Make thyself known," she whispered.

"Pray pardon. 'Tis I, Sarah."

She let her in, chastising herself for already forgetting her vow. "Enter, milady."

"Call me Sarah," she reminded, handing her a small container. "Salve for your wound."

"My thanks."

Sarah kicked off her slippers, tucked her feet beneath her and patted the cushion on the window seat. "Rest well?"

"I did." The dream had not returned. She pointed to the chests. "Those are quite beautiful. The fairies are so detailed." Ruby set the salve on the table and joined her. Sarah appeared much younger with her hair down and it solidified a kinship somehow. "What brings you this morn?"

"Forgive the early hour. I feared you might be distressed waking in a strange bed."

"Your concern is for naught. This room was of great comfort."

Sarah toyed with the latch on the window. "I cannot imagine the suffering of your plight. Nay memory, you say?"

"The canopy. I love it. 'Tis a wondrous work."

"Oh." Sarah sighed. "I tend to be at a loss whenever he is away, that was but one of my little projects."

"*You* stitched it?"

Sarah fidgeted with the lace on a cushion. "Aye, it seems I have an abundance of idle time with his duties."

"Did you paint the fairies on the chests?"

"Nay, however, 'tis where I gained the idea for the fairies on the canopy." Sarah giggled and pulled a pillow from behind the others. "My first attempt looked more like a troll with wings."

"Still better than I could do." She paused. "I think." Concern etched Sarah's face and she waved her hand to dismiss it. "Mayhap you can impart some lessons?" Why did she suggest such a thing when she had no intention of staying?

"Certainly you but need a reminder. Surely, something so familiar shall bring about your memory."

"Mayhap." She ran her fingernail in the grooved stone by the window. "Pray tell, how did you meet Sir Alex?"

Sarah darted to her feet, her words spilling while she paced. "I was introduced to him when I was ten and five. My heart was captured at once. As if we were meant to be together."

While she talked about her husband, Sarah nearly swooned. Ruby related, all too well, to Sarah's pleasure. "Alex was the most glorious man…so kind, giving, and I must say quite smitten. He did not even try to hide his feelings as most young men do."

Ruby leaned forward to catch each word, reveling in the sweetness of a newfound…friend? She mustn't become too attached…but a part of her longed for another woman to speak to.

"He was training to be a knight. Galeron was by his side when we met." Sarah's eyes widened. "Galeron intimidated me at first, but once he gave Alex his blessing, I forgot all about his scowl."

The brute savors intimidation. Ruby bit back the retort, nay matter that it was in jest. She must be careful not to say the wrong thing. Her first impression had not fared well and she enjoyed this woman's company. For now, she would keep blatant remarks to herself. Ruby grinned, for Sarah's chatter did not pause during her wandering thoughts.

"And Alex and I wished to be wed at once." Sarah blushed. "We both tired of waiting."

"For what, pray tell?" Blatant remark. Alas, was she a complete oaf? Sarah's eyes opened so wide, Ruby almost burst out laughing. "You had to wait…" she prodded.

Sarah nodded. "My father insisted on a long courtship." She shook her head. "You know how fathers can be."

Ruby shook her head. Sarah's expression fell. "I have faltered, yet again. Of course you don't."

Why could she not ignore the innocent question? Ruby scrambled to rekindle the tiny flame of friendship. "Do not fret. How long since you wed?"

"Nearly five years, but we waited three before Father would allow me to marry."

Ruby smoothed out a pillow. "How did you bear it?"

Sarah gave a secretive grin. "We discovered ways." Oh, so this woman could be as blunt as she. "Alex is quite imaginative."

Mayhap Galeron was as well — *nay, daren't think of that now!*

"Ruby, you are blushing! Have I embarrassed you?"

She changed the subject. "Have you been blessed with children?"

Sarah sighed, tucking a lock of hair behind her ear. "Nay, though I pray for it daily."

Ruby detected a sense of sadness and made a mental note to refrain from bringing it up in conversation again. "Tell me more about your life here at Ramstone."

"It is a blessed one…all I have, really. Even after all our years together, my heart still fills when Alex enters a room." Sarah's hand remained poised, caught in the thought. "Much like a spark of flint against steel…"

She swallowed hard, for she experienced the spark. The one that singed, the pain still fresh. "It never fades? Even a little?"

Sarah shook her head. "Never."

At that moment, Ruby realized she was forever cursed.

Sarah ended her story with an exaggerated curtsy. "That, my new friend, is how I fell in love with Alex and made Ramstone my home."

New friend. The words reverberated through her. "You seem well matched, his eyes barely left you last eve."

"We *are* blessed. I hope the forthcoming marriage—"

"I am sure Alex is wondering where you are." *Forthcoming marriage.* Ruby rubbed her temple. "You need not keep me company."

"I am chattering and you are in pain." Sarah sat near her. "Alex can concoct something for such aches."

"I am simply weary." Of Galeron and his damn confession. She would no longer focus on him. Or a friendship with Sarah. Or anything but finding her lost past. Naught was fair, or just, or made any sense.

"I shall send for some tea." Sarah started for the door.

"Nay." Ruby forced a smile, realizing how rude she sounded. "I can have some when we break fast with the others."

Sarah waved her notion away. "Nay, Galeron insists you rest in your chamber."

"He *what*?"

"Do not take it to heart. The men ate at dawn." Sarah walked to the hearth and rubbed her hands before the fire.

"I suppose he expects me to isolate myself here? Follow his orders?" She paced the room. "He has no right!"

Sarah looked up from the fire, her mouth agape. "Ruby...he simply wishes you to rest. You have been through so much. Ease your mind. You can leave this room any time you wish!"

Ruby stopped pacing, dropping her hands to her side. "I am acting like a petulant child." She concentrated on retying her sash, scrambling for a fit apology.

"Pay nay mind, Ruby. My ears were the only ones privy to your comment." She shrugged. "I realize how infuriating he can be, always throwing orders. I married the right brother."

Ruby jutted her chin, thankful for Sarah's kind reprieve. "Indeed."

"Enough about him." Sarah leaned against the bedpost. "You may keep my robe. It fits you well."

"My thanks," she said. "Are you the one who brought it to my room? 'Tis beautiful."

"I had my maid bring it." Sarah sat beside her. "She is sorting through my things and will bring you a few garments before the day wanes." She pointed to the kirtle on the peg. "For now, there is that. I chose yellow, thinking it would accent your brilliant hair. I see why Galeron dubbed you Ruby."

She swallowed past a sudden lump in her throat. "Aye, yellow is…lovely."

"'Tis but a simple frock to wear about the halls. You shall be measured soon enough."

Ruby darted a look from the kirtle to Sarah. "Measured?"

"For your attire, of course." Sarah leaned forward. "I shall divulge a little secret."

"I adore secrets." She tilted her head. "At least, I *believe* I do—" Ruby jerked a nod. "Aye, I do."

"You are the first maiden I have ever met who staves off a secret by trying to decide whether to enjoy them or not." Sarah giggled and beckoned. "Galeron ordered the staff to treat you as a Lady of Ramstone."

"Did he?" She sat back. "That is peculiar." Ruby absently ran her fingers along the stitches on her cheek. "Are you certain?" A scant bit of hope entered her heart.

Sarah nodded. "Galeron may be gruff, but his heart is kind." A huge smile brightened her face. "You shall be taken well care of while he is gone."

Ruby blinked. "He is leaving? Yet I am to stay?" The ever-present ache in her head grew to a throb. She stopped herself before she said any more.

Sarah studied her. "Galeron is an honorable man and wishes to aid in your recovery."

"Of course. And I am grateful," she choked out.

"I must take leave and bid Alex farewell." Sarah started for the door but stopped short of it when Ruby leaped to her feet.

"They have not departed?" Her head swam at the sudden movement but she followed Sarah to the door.

"I shall send that tea up." Sarah patted her hand. "It is best you remain in your chamber. The gaze you shared with Galeron last night did not go unnoticed." She left without waiting for a response.

She plopped, face first, onto the window seat. Fie it all. Sarah knew. *Follow her. Explain.* She punched the cushions on the window seat. *Lie. Then leave this place.* She paced the room, knowing that choice was foolish. She had no place to go. A knock interrupted her worries. "Sarah, I am thankful you came back—" Her smile froze when she swung open the door. "Oh." She nearly ran into a young girl holding a tray. "Who might you be?"

The maid entered with a shy smile, placing a food tray on the table. "Bridget. Your maid." She filled a mug and brought a chair to the table. "I just passed Lady Sarah in the corridor. Would you like me to fetch her or send word?"

"Aye. Nay. I shall speak with her later." Ruby ignored her confused expression and sat, perusing the tray. She grabbed a mug and took a huge swallow. Eyes watering, she gasped. "'Tis *ale*!"

"Aye, Sir Galeron insisted I add it to your tray."

"He did, did he?" She popped a grape into her mouth to counteract the bitter taste. "Alex's tea would serve me better. Is there any of that?" The maid poured from a small pot. She crinkled her nose at the first sip. "Oh my, even ale is more pleasant." Still, she took another sip before placing it on the tray. "Ale indeed." Arse. Still, a smile twitched beneath the surface.

"How else may I assist, milady?"

She crunched into the thin skin of another grape and swallowed. "I am in nay need of assistance."

Bridget cast down her gaze. "I have been ordered to assist you, milady."

Uncomfortable with the fact, Ruby took several bites before responding. "My name is Ruby, not milady, and I am most certain I do not require assistance with anything." Bridget wiped her hands on her apron. Her hands shook slightly and a pang of empathy swelled for the maid's obvious uneasiness. "Surely, you have other duties other than waiting on me?"

First on one foot, then the other, the maid fidgeted for several moments. "I shall tidy the room while you eat!" she blurted, seemingly delighted with the thought.

Ruby tore off a piece of bread and smiled. "So be it."

The young maid hurried to the bed and efficiently made it up. When Bridget gathered the clothing piled in the corner, Ruby saw her confused expression.

"Oh." Ruby swallowed a mouthful. "Those can be disposed of. Though men's attire I, uh…they are mine. Not a man's." Ruby stammered, her voice rising with embarrassment.

The bundle spilled from Bridget's arms. "By your leave, I did not think it otherwise." She stooped, shoving the pile in her arms. "I offended you. Sir Galeron shall hear of this."

Ruby stood, her hands on her hips. "Not from me. All is well, Bridget." What had Galeron said to the poor child?

Bridget deposited the clothes by the door, grabbed a pitcher of water and filled the washbasin. Ruby returned to her meal, glancing at Bridget from time to time and offering a smile. Bridget averted her gaze each time. Her cheek. Of course. She lifted a platter and looked at her reflection, immediately returning it to the table. Gods, surely the swelling was the cause — and the curve of the platter did not create a fair likeness — and — oh, damn it all. She grabbed honey and drizzled it on a hunk of bread. Again, the memory of a child pricked her. She took a bite, lost in thought. Which was worse, the phantom child or her wounds? Out of the corner of her eye, she saw Bridget standing by the table. She swallowed the sticky mouthful. "Bridget. Take some time to yourself. You needn't stay here."

"Pray pardon, milady?"

"Ruby," she corrected. "Are you not finished with your duties?"

"I have yet to assist milady with dressing." Bridget picked out a chemise from a trunk and held it up.

Ruby clutched her mouth, barely suppressing her mirth. "I need nay assistance with *that*."

"As you wish." Bridget hurried to the door and grabbed the bundle of clothes on her way out. "I shall be back to pick up the tray."

Ruby washed her face and undressed. Her hood lay by the door, forgotten, and she picked it up along with her nightclothes. She carefully folded the night-rail and robe but held on to the hood. Gooseflesh spread over her body, yet she stood naked, holding the hood to her chest and reliving the moment Galeron had freed it from her head — the flicker in his eyes when he watched her hair spill from it — the huskiness in his voice when he dubbed her...and the kiss. Ah, the kiss. She must stop thinking of that.

"Ruby of the Forest indeed," she muttered, wadding the hood in her fist. She tossed it on the table and snatched the chemise, wishing she had breeches instead. "The name sounds like a" — her eyes fell upon the design on the trunk — "fairy's name." She shrugged into the kirtle and struggled with the lacings up the back. She loved the name. Fairy or not.

"Ruby, may I enter?" Sarah called from the other side of the door.

She dropped the lacings. "Of course." What should she say? How should she act?

Sarah waved a pair of slippers. "These should fit." She glanced around. "Where is Bridget?"

Ruby tried on the slippers and turned her foot to one side then the other. "They do fit. My thanks." She eyed her boots. "Once those are cleaned, I shall return these to you."

"Those boots?" Sarah wrinkled her nose. "Just keep the slippers. Bridget shall dispose of those."

Ruby made note to stash them under the bed.

"Where *is* that girl?" Sarah peered out of the door. "She should have arrived long before now."

"I sent her away." Ruby sashayed around the room. "These are quite comfortable."

Sarah closed the door and leaned against it. "You sent her away? Before she had you dressed? Why?"

Three questions. Which should she answer first? "She did well, and once she was done, I told her to take leave. Because I was still eating." She drummed her finger on her chin. "Oh. And I do not require assistance to cover my naked body." There, all answered, and not one blunt comment.

Sarah giggled. "Friend, you have a bold way of expressing your thoughts!" She turned Ruby around. "Yet, you *require assistance* in lacing up a kirtle around your" — she lowered her voice — "naked body."

Ruby fell into a comfortable chat with her new companion. No longer adrift, she twirled in the new dress, with Sarah commenting on how well it fit. Sarah giggled when Ruby nearly tripped. Struck with the bittersweet memory of how the same folly preceded Galeron's first kiss, Ruby sat, careful to shield her feelings. Sarah suspected enough as it was. Thankfully, her new friend was decent enough not to mention it this time.

Sarah picked up a brush and started arranging Ruby's hair. "Fasten it up, or leave it down?" She dropped the brush in Ruby's lap. "I have the perfect silk fillet to place in your hair. Stay here," she called over her shoulder.

"Where might I stray?" Ruby strolled to the window seat and pulled the hangings aside. "I have nowhere to go." She spied Galeron and Lord Easton below in the inner ward. Curious, she opened the latch and leaned out for a better view. Galeron's voice was loud, but she could not make out his words. He took a bedroll from the horse and slammed it to the ground. She shook her head. What raised his ire? She leaned out farther when Alex came into view. He spoke in quieter tones. He seemed to be the peacekeeper. After a heated discussion, Lord Easton stormed away. She knew full well she should refrain from spying upon the scene, yet her curiosity held the best of her and she made no effort to tear away her gaze. Alex handed the bedroll to Galeron just as their father approached again. She deciphered Galeron's curses, but little else.

"It seems Galeron acquired the art of intimidation from his father," she muttered. Easton thrust his hand forward. Reminiscent of how she had refused Galeron's apology in the forest, he now ignored his father's offered hand.

"Dare not attempt it." Her laugh pitched the mocking comment. They both looked up. She leaped off the window seat. When she dared peek out again, Easton had stepped back and Galeron was in the saddle. Ruby's mirth soured.

Blast him! He had nay intention of bidding a farewell.

She jumped when a hand touched the small of her back. Too embarrassed to turn around, she gripped the windowsill. "I pray forgiveness."

Sarah knelt on the window seat. "Then pray for me also. I was watching from my chamber as well. It seems Galeron is unhappy with his departure."

Though she witnessed a dispute between father and son, it never occurred to her that he did not wish to leave. She feigned indifference and gripped the sill tighter. "Why would he show such displeasure?"

"I know not. He is a disagreeable man." She shrugged, as if it were explanation enough. Sarah leaned out of the window. "Fare ye well, Alex. God be with you all!"

Alex's smile matched the enthusiasm of his wave. "Fare ye well, love. You shall be in my arms in less than a fortnight."

Galeron's frown transformed into utter shock. She swallowed when he raised his hand, a slow smile erasing the deep furrow on his brow. Her hand remained poised when he looked away. Even from a distance, she saw his jaw clench when his father spoke to him. He did not return his gaze to the window, but called an order to his men and started for the gates.

She sidestepped from the window and pressed her back against the wall. Ruby closed her eyes, but it did not shut out the fact that he was riding away with her heart. Though aware of his destiny, she was ill prepared for the reality of it.

Sarah curled upon the window seat and stared at her, but Ruby did not offer an explanation. The gates slammed. She pulled the window closed, turned the latch, and cursed herself for opening it in the first place.

Sarah patted the cushion. "Ruby, I beg thee to sit. 'Tis imperative I tell you of the reason for the journey."

Ruby clenched her teeth so hard her jaw throbbed. She swallowed and balled the soft fabric of her skirt into her fists, fully realizing her newfound bliss had just burned into ashes of lost hope.

Sarah cleared her throat. "I believe there are circumstances you are not aware of."

"What circumstances might that be?" Ruby began to pace the room. "Shall I tell you?" She took no notice of the handkerchief Sarah offered and wiped her eyes with the back of her hand. "I am certainly not *aware* of my name, or whence I came. I am not *aware* of what my place is here at Ramstone Hall. I am not *aware* of much of anything at all!"

She dug her fingers into the back of a chair and glared at Sarah. "However, I am highly aware that Sir Galeron was on his way to retrieve his betrothed when he came upon me. He told me of his marriage agreement, and…never mind." She fell into the chair, her anger intensifying the pain. "Aye, the brute did not even intend on bidding me a farewell."

The instant Ruby witnessed the shock on Sarah's face, she regretted her harsh attitude. "You have been naught but kind. I repay you with my wrath." She sat beside her. "I beg forgiveness." She nearly wept when Sarah embraced her.

Sarah pulled back, locking eyes with her. "I was not aware Galeron told you himself." Her brow furrowed. "Why *would* he tell you?" She had said too much and now Sarah would not heed her upheld hand. "Did something transpire between the two of you?"

"Nay!" Ruby darted to her feet.

Sarah eyes grew wide. "God in heaven, something did. By the way you are acting—"

She fought back her tears. "Naught happened." Though, God forgive her, she wished more had. Wished everything had.

"You *love* him!" The expression on Sarah's face was more of pity than accusation.

Ruby marched to the window, yanked at the coverings and stood in the shadows. "He is promised to another. Whether I care or not. And I do not. 'Tis of nay consequence." Did she love him? Could it be why it hurt so to see him go?

"What you feel matters to me, Ruby."

She stepped from the refuge of the shadows and offered a strained smile. "I haven't any right to feel anything at all."

"What has he done?"

"I beg of you, let it rest." Ruby guided her to the door.

Sarah took her hands. "I ache for the words to extinguish the sadness in your eyes. Yet, here I stand, unable to find the sentiment to offer you comfort."

With a soft whisper of laughter, Ruby assured her. "Pay me nay mind." She silenced Sarah with a shake of her head when she began to protest. "It makes nay difference now."

"Ruby, we *must* talk about this. If he took advantage—" Her eyes sparked. "Damn him."

"He was a true knight, honorable and just." She dropped Sarah's hand and sighed. "I ask again, let it rest." She guided her into the corridor and waited for her to go.

"If you cannot tell me, mayhap you can rest your tribulation in the Lord's hands," Sarah whispered.

She nodded and closed the door, waiting until Sarah's footsteps receded before releasing her tears.

Chapter Five

Galeron's Confession

"Hell's teeth, Alex, do you ever cease your babble?" Galeron offered a weak smile at his younger brother's insistent attempts to engage him in conversation. "Aye." He had responded the same, countless times.

This time Alex noticed and shook his head. "Are you listening?"

"Forgive me, my thoughts were elsewhere. What were you saying?"

"I am wasting the air I breathe speaking with you."

"It seems so." He squinted at the menacing clouds. "It shall rain soon."

"Why so sullen?"

Galeron glanced at him. "I am caught in a snare."

"A snare?"

"The blasted marriage."

"You had not a qualm before."

"Aye, 'twas nay matter either way." He shifted in the saddle. "Father deemed it time to marry and I was carrying out a duty."

Alex gnawed off a piece of dried fruit. Two lines deepened between his brows as he chewed. Galeron studied the horizon. His younger brother had a way about him, and though others did not seem to notice, Galeron knew Alex analyzed a situation before he spoke his mind.

"Does the maiden you brought to Ramstone have anything to do with your dour mood?"

How was he to answer that? Galeron kicked the horse to a canter, frowning when Alex kept up. "Tell the men to pick up the pace. 'Tis nearly dark."

Alex stole a sidelong glance at him. "Very well." He dropped back, allowing Galeron the solitude he clearly wanted.

The day waned, the crisp air whispered threats of a cold night. Galeron's mood plummeted with the growing darkness. He closed his eyes and inhaled the deadened aroma of autumn leaves disturbed by his stallion's hooves. He should have lain with her on that bed of leaves. He twisted the reins in his hands. He ached. She singed the blood flowing through his heart and now it burned for her.

"Hail, Galeron, now seems a good time to rest these horses, does it not?"

Galeron frowned and blinked away the vision of green eyes and flaming hair. "Soon, brother, we must make up lost time." From the corner of his eye, he saw Alex studying him. "What is it?"

"We should rest."

She awakened him. Rest did not exist. Galeron spurred his horse. "Father is dismayed at the delay as it is. Do not question me."

"The delay is not what concerns Father." The saddle creaked as he leaned toward him. "His main concern is where your duties lay, brother."

Galeron yanked the reins. His stallion pawed the ground in protest.

Alex scurried to ease the rising tension. "Those were Father's words, not my own."

The others caught up, ending the one-sided conversation.

Galeron's words bit into anger. "We shall stop for the night." He urged his horse toward the tree line. The familiar path through the woods clutched the shadows — shadows of a recent memory.

The men glanced uneasily at Galeron when they reached the clearing. Aware they read his discontent, he did naught to mask it. He simply did not care. Rafe dismounted, his smile punctuating his weary stride.

Galeron tried to erase his frown. "Tired?"

"Nay." Rafe grinned and stretched. "Shall I prepare a fire?"

Nodding, Galeron handed the reins to his squire. "When you are done with that, dole out the rations."

The men washed at the creek and settled around the fire. Rafe passed around fruit, dried meat and biscuits. "Had we stopped to hunt, we could feast on—" Galeron's glare cut Rafe's complaint short. "Pray pardon, brother." He crawled into his bedroll, still chewing.

"Get some sleep. We will rise with the sun." Galeron snatched an apple and left the men circled around the fire. He leaned against a nearby tree and hoped the weariness of the day's ride would offer a dreamless night. He turned the apple in his hand. Shall he always envision the nectar wetting Ruby's lips every time he saw the damn fruit?

Alex nudged him as he passed. "Is your intention on eating that, or are you admiring the way the firelight dances upon it?" Galeron could not help but smile. He tossed the apple into Alex's hands. He crunched into it and sat, his back against the tree.

"I shall fulfill my duties. Father made his blasted concern known this morn." Galeron hated the fact.

Alex swallowed and wiped his mouth on his sleeve. "Why was he so angry?"

Galeron sighed, regretting the way he'd shunned him. "I challenged him to find one more suited if he was suspect of my intentions."

"Your intentions?" Alex took another bite and talked through his mouthful. "I do not understand."

"Father accused me of giving Ruby attention I should reserve for my betrothed. I have not even *met* Mara. I fail to see why he sees this as an issue anyway. I am simply assisting Ruby. Does he miss the honor in that?" He did not give him the chance to answer. "Nay, he finds my kindness toward Ruby an act of betrayal."

"He *said* that?"

Galeron gave a sharp nod. "He suggested I take her as my mistress." He lifted his finger to silence Alex. "Even *you* decided against taking a mistress."

"That is because I love Sarah." Alex shrugged. "By the way you are taken by Ruby, 'twould be a fair idea."

Galeron set his jaw. "I am not taken by Ruby." He was thankful the firelight did not illuminate his denial. Everything was changed and he was beginning to realize how much.

"Perhaps Father is able to see what you cannot."

Galeron glared at him. "Indeed?"

"Pray thee, do not take my words as an accusation, for 'tis not." He took a deep breath. "It seems Sarah witnessed a gaze between you and Ruby. She said it was a gaze that…" He took another bite of the apple, deep in thought. "Damn, what were her words?"

"She is being foolish, reading where there is nay story to tell."

Alex ignored the comment. "Ah, I recall. 'A gaze which locked others out yet welcomed each other in.'"

Galeron snorted.

"Sarah was not the only one who witnessed it. I saw it as well," Alex added.

Galeron's eyes narrowed. "Your sight was clouded with an overabundance of ale."

"In the doorway." He sighed at Galeron's raised eyebrow. "Father witnessed your distraction when Ruby left the table. You did not hear him call your name, not once, but several times."

"Perhaps my ears were clouded with ale."

"Damnation!" Alex lowered his voice when several men turned their way. "You are fully aware of the gaze I am referring to."

Galeron silently nodded.

Alex threw the core to the ground. "What have you *done*?"

Weighted silence led the conversation to a halt. Still, Alex would not relent. Galeron sat, facing his brother. He dug his fingers into Alex's shoulders, his voice taking on a throaty growl. "Brother, I shall utter these words but once. I pity the maiden promised to me, for the marriage is doomed to be a loveless one. My heart is held captive by another."

Alex's eyes widened. "Ruby." It was not a question.

Galeron returned to his position, back pressed against the tree.

"Galeron, I am not privy to what transpired in the forest, and I do not wish to know of any tryst."

"'Twas more than a tryst."

"With all due respect, your heart cannot achieve *anything* in such a short time."

"Nay, Alex, my heart never knew anything before. Now it knows too much." He watched the sparks shoot from the nearby fire when Rafe added more wood. Galeron relished the ensuing silence. He closed his eyes and waited for the retreat of Alex's footsteps. He sighed when Alex spoke again.

"You have sown your seed on every journey. Ruby is another one of your conquests, but you are overdue to marry. Mara is the best choice."

Galeron stared straight ahead. "You cannot presume to read my heart. Do you not see? I tried to deny my feelings, to nay avail."

"Ruby is quite beautiful, even with the cut upon her face. 'Tis simply lust."

"*All* I ever experienced is lust. I never gave thought to the fantasy of love for I did not believe it truly existed." He turned to the fire. "It exists."

"Galeron—"

"Nay maiden takes my senses as Ruby does. She is not a mere conquest. I have not bedded her." Galeron frowned. "Do not fret. Shame shall not soil the Ramstone name. I shall wed—" Somehow, saying Mara's name was a betrayal to Ruby. "I shall wed Jastar's daughter, but my heart remains empty. Ruby is the only one to fill it." Galeron stabbed his finger into Alex's chest. "Not a word. Swear."

"Aye, I swear it," Alex whispered. "Does Ruby realize you are betrothed?"

"She does." He winced at the reminder of her reaction.

"Is she aware of your feelings for her?"

"Nay." Galeron peered at the stars through the branches. "The silent farewell proved more painful than I could imagine. She was so…far removed from the lad she was dressed as the night before."

"I saw. At first I did not recognize her." Alex sighed. "'Tis unfortunate your paths did not cross before the marriage agreement was sealed. Perhaps then you could have followed your heart."

"There are sacrifices we endure as knights, dear brother. This is a sacrifice I must bear alone."

Alex straightened. Galeron saw the hope in his eyes as he spoke. "Did you tell Father how you feel? Perhaps he would—"

"Nay, little brother, you know as well as I he considers it foolish to marry for love." Galeron shook his finger in time with his words, mocking his father. "Marriage is an agreement for gain in stature or to join forces between kingdoms. Love shall be granted to the lucky few fate chooses." Galeron's hand curled into a fist. "Fate…humph."

"All shall be well in time, Galeron."

"Time? Time lengthens my yearning for her."

"Nay, it grants healing. Mara shall fulfill your life. I am sure of it."

Galeron nudged him. "For a married man, you have much to learn."

Chapter Six

Remembrance Garden

Ruby watched Ramstone's gates from her window. She wished she could quell the urge to do this each morn. The painful reminder that Galeron would soon come through them with his betrothed did not ease as the days passed. She jutted her chin. She would leave. Today. When the day waned, she lay her head, knowing she had no place else to go. Was her only choice to wander aimlessly, lost as the day Galeron had discovered her in the woodlands? She turned away from the window.

There was nay respite. His absence did naught to ease her longing. 'Twas a wound that refused to heal. Ruby bowed her head, losing faith. She had no defense against her feelings of abandonment, however, each morn she still prayed for his safe return.

The time she spent with Sarah made the days easier to bear. It brought the clarity a true friendship could provide, dimming the despondency of the nights she bore alone. There was not a rise of the new day without one of them seeking out the other. They spent many hours together, sharing long conversations. The two grew into steadfast friends. Ruby, however, became an expert on skirting issues that focused on her love for Galeron. She had told Sarah of her feelings, but could not bear to speak of it often.

Ruby shook off her dark thoughts and set about fulfilling her promise to practice embroidery with Sarah in the garden. She grabbed a basket, shoved in her sewing supplies and hurried to the stairs. When she entered the garden, Sarah was already there. Little time passed before she examined Ruby's work.

"Nay, Ruby. You must twist the thread several more times to create the knot."

Ruby plopped the mangled creation into her lap. "Let us take leave from this and enjoy a horseback ride instead."

"Just work your knot."

"I would rather die."

"Give it time. You will."

"How utterly clever you are." Ruby stabbed the needle into the cloth. Even without a memory, she could not imagine ever enjoying pulling thread through a blasted piece of fabric. "My flower looks horrid. Why even bother with the knot in the center? I would rather be —" Ruby's smoldering frustration sparked into recognition. She caught her breath and dropped the needle.

"You pricked your finger again?" Sarah asked, her needle moving in perfect precision.

"I remember." The corner of Ruby's mouth twitched with a tease of a smile. Her hair was swept into her eyes by the breeze as she watched the children play in the meadow, her hand poised, ready to capture the moment.

Sarah looked up from her work, the needle dangling from the bottom of the cloth. "You remember sewing?"

Ruby absently rubbed the needlework. "A landscape." She sought to scratch the surface of the memory, discover the origin of the meadow, the children trampling through it.

"Whatever are you talking about?"

She nearly shushed Sarah. "I remember…a painting." Ruby closed her eyes, not mentioning the children, certain it would prompt Sarah to ask even more questions. "I can see it."

"Open your eyes. You are frightening me."

Ruby's heart fluttered. "Oh, Sarah…" she whispered. She examined her hands, as if seeing them for the first time. "I am not complete without a brush in my hand."

Sarah jumped up, her work forgotten, as it fell to the ground. "You paint?"

Ruby nodded, fearing the memory would fade if she spoke another word. Sarah pulled her to her feet and hugged her. The memory remained vivid. She could nearly hear the laughter, smell the paint, see the colors and sensation of the stroke of her brush. Then, quick as a wisp of smoke upon snuffing a candle, the memory floated away. Willing it to reignite was for naught. It was gone.

"Ah, Ruby of the Forest, mayhap I should address you as Ruby the *Artist*."

Ruby wrinkled her nose. "Creating silly names for me is becoming a sore habit."

Sarah giggled, seemingly unaware of Ruby's dismay. "Painting could very well be the portal to your past!"

"Mayhap. I am not certain if—" Despite her frustration, she could not help but smile when Sarah began to sing an impromptu verse.

"Ruby cannot sew a stitch," she sang.

"What ever are you doing?"

"Listen!" Sarah repeated the first part again. "Ruby cannot sew a stitch. Her embroidery is atrocious. Place a brush into her hand and she shall paint quite ferocious!"

"Ferocious?" She burst out laughing. "You are *mad*."

Their peals of laughter echoed off the garden walls while Sarah made up more silly songs. Ruby looked up at a deep laugh. Had Galeron returned? It was Lord Easton standing at the end of the walk. Her gaiety dampened and she just missed grabbing Sarah's arm as she ran to him. *Do not tell him.* She wanted a bit more time to decipher the phantom memory.

Sarah's excitement turned her revelation into babble. "Ruby remembered. I thought 'twas her stitching she recalled, but 'twas painting!" She motioned for Ruby to approach. "Tell him!" Sarah didn't wait for Ruby to explain, rushing faster than a winter melt overflowing the edge of a creek. "She paints! She is a Pictor!"

Easton flashed a smile. "That is wonderful! We should call you Ruby the—"

Ruby put up her hand. "I beg, spare the jest."

He clasped his hands behind his back, grinned and gave a slight bow. "As you wish." He sounded so much like Galeron her insides tumbled. "You regained your memory?"

Angels above, if only 'twas true. "'Twas such a small bit."

Sarah's hair bounced with her excited prance. "Small? It is enormous! Ruby did not simply recall painting. She remembered painting a landscape." Her eyes widened. "Mayhap 'twas her home! We simply must visit the art shoppe so she can purchase the means to expand the memory. Today."

"There is such a place?" Ruby scuffed her toe in the stones. "I mean, I never realized a place dedicated to art supplies existed."

"Ah yes, it exists. I cannot wait for you to see it." Easton waved his hand. "And, it so happens I intended to suggest a ride to the village."

Ruby wished to disappear. She had nay means of purchasing supplies. And was unsure if she wished to buy them if she did. What if the memory was a craving to recall, tricking her mind into believing it true? What if she stood with a brush in hand, unable to create anything? Did she dare trust this? Damnation, why, when all she wished was her memory back, did this cause her heart to gallop with fear, distrust, and make her wish she didn't recall it at all?

"The carriage shall be ready soon." Easton said, "The seamstress is expecting you both for a fitting."

Ruby's head snapped up. "A fitting?" The furthest thing from her mind was a fitting. How did the conversation sway from art supplies to fittings?

"Aye, for the wedding." He broke into a proud grin. "You also are in need of daily wear. I assured Galeron 'twould be done."

She concentrated on keeping her smile intact as her heart shattered. "Ah, the wedding." Certainly Galeron did not expect her to attend. "I am certain your son did not mean..." She swallowed hard. "All I need is replacement of my tattered breeches and tunic. Sarah has given me everything else I need."

"As amusing as that is, I am also certain he did not intend to dress you as a lad." Easton chuckled. "Let us visit the art shoppe first." He offered his arm to Sarah. "And you can guide Ruby to proper attire afterward." He paid no mind to Ruby's silence and offered his free arm to her. "I keep my promises, especially when they are for my family. Accept my son's generosity." He patted Ruby's hand the moment she placed it in the crook of his arm. "He does not expect anything in return."

His innocent comment stung like a hornet. How many times must she die? How was she to escape from attending the wedding without Easton realizing she loved his son? Thankful Sarah had steered the conversation away from Galeron, she didn't bother to join in and allowed the two of them to talk as they made their way out of the garden. Her head darted up at the call of her name…the one Galeron gave her.

Easton scrutinized her. "Where were you, child?"

At hell's door. With a conspiratorial wink, she said, "Wondering if I can convince every woman to at least try donning breeches. They are quite comfortable." She smirked, hoping her jest would deter his worry.

"Your wit is…refreshing," he said. "I suggest we enjoy a full day in the village."

"An excellent suggestion." Sarah winked at Ruby. "Plenty of time to spend at the art shoppe."

Easton nodded. "With two beautiful ladies by my side, I shall be the envy of all men in the village."

Ruby displayed a genuine smile. Though her scar deemed her far from beautiful, she thought him kind to say such a thing. Mayhap he was not a tyrant after all.

Chapter Seven

Jastar's Gates

Galeron furrowed his brow. The knights who customarily would have met them as they neared Jastar's gates were nonexistent. Dusk had fallen, adding to the eerie sense of emptiness. Their shadows moved against the walls as they approached. Still no one called from the gates. He dismounted, squinting through the dim light. A cool gust blew dead bits of leaves in circles by his boots.

The silence drummed doom. The men followed his cue and approached the outer wall. They stood on each side of the gates, weapons ready.

"Galeron of Ramstone requests entrance." The ghostly creak of movement pricked his alarm, but he realized it was the gate swaying. He shoved it completely ajar.

Without removing his attention from the empty courtyard, Galeron grasped the hilt of his sword so tightly the grooves etched his palm. He signaled for

Alex and Rafe to follow. Alex motioned for the others to investigate the surrounding area.

Galeron grabbed Rafe's sleeve when he tripped over a body. Determination seemed frozen in the face of the dead knight. He scanned the others — each lay as if waiting for the next strike. All wore the open-eyed fortitude of a fight to the death.

Galeron sprinted through the corpse-littered courtyard, toward the main hall of the castle. His brothers followed. No one had uttered a word since entering the gates, but Galeron's advance spoke volumes. He was ready to slay whoever had created the carnage.

As they neared the main door, the faint smell of smoke permeated the air. Rafe moved to the side while Alex tested the door.

"'Tis unbolted," Alex whispered.

Galeron surged with resolve as he charged through the doorway. Alex and Rafe followed, ready to strike whoever lay in wait.

Not a soul occupied the expansive entry. No breath other than their own was drawn. The debris crunched beneath their boots when they stepped into the next doorway.

An overturned table and chairs lay in shambles across the room. The unmistakable stench of rotting food creased the air. Galeron ducked into the kitchen. The cooking pit, long cold, held a pot full of stew. He walked through the next doorway and peered down the long corridor. The lamps were out, but he could see the halls were deserted. Returning to the main entry, he met Alex and Rafe.

"Anything?" he asked.

"Nay," Rafe whispered, still looking about with wide eyes.

"The place is deserted," Alex said.

"Too deserted." Galeron strode to the main hall and thrust his hand into the eating area. "The attack took place during a meal. Yet, nay bodies are here." The smell of rotting food mingled with something he had not smelled in years—death. He turned, sword drawn when someone ran into the room. Both his brothers had done the same, but lowered their swords when they saw it was one of their own. "Damnation! Do not barge in like that," Galeron snapped. "You are apt to find a sword in your gut."

The squire stood at attention. "Sir Galeron, the men searched the grounds. Only dead remain."

Galeron sheathed his sword and grunted. Alex motioned to a body, half-obscured, beneath the table.

"Heave the table to the side," Galeron ordered.

Rafe took several steps back and gagged at the sight of the butchered body.

Galeron led him to the door. "Stand guard here." He lowered his voice. "Take a few breaths. It gets easier as you become a seasoned knight." He left his brother to recover, then squatted by the man lying across the splintered wood. The entrails spilling from him appeared as if rats had feasted on them. "By his attire, I would say he was of high rank." He lifted an arm and shook it. "Stiffness is relieved."

"At least four days since the attack then." Alex turned the face one way then the other, then guided the man's eyelids closed. "Poor bastard."

Rafe took a few tentative steps closer, holding a cloth over his nose. "How do you know it's been four days since he died?"

"Less than a day passes before the body stiffens. Then about three for it to relax," Alex explained before turning back to Galeron. "Lord Ronan?"

Galeron made a hasty sign of the cross. "It appears so. Mara's father." If she was dead, he was at fault. "Find her." Rage thrummed a steady beat through his body. He pointed at a group of men. "Search the grounds." Without hesitation, the men dispersed. "We shall search in here." Rafe took a step to follow him and Galeron growled, "Not you. Stand guard."

"Against who?" Rafe motioned wildly about the room. "The rats?"

He stormed over to him, barely containing his fury. "Are you defying my orders?"

Rafe blinked hard, then squared his shoulders. "Nay, brother. I am not defying you. I am but asking to be included in the search. "

"I daren't imagine what you may come upon." Galeron pointed at Lord Ronan. "You couldn't even handle that." He regretted his words as soon as he spoke them. It was he who had failed, not Rafe. "I need you here," he added in a civil tone.

"Galeron," Alex said. "He could accompany me."

Never taking his eyes from Rafe, Galeron shook his head. "Nay. He shall do as I ordered."

"How am I to become a seasoned knight if I am left to guard doors, start fires and hand out blasted rations?"

Galeron matched Rafe's glower. He was nay longer a boy. He heaved a sigh. "Very well. Go with Alex."

"I shall search on my own."

"Intent on pushing your stand, are you?"

Rafe grinned.

"Aye, alone then, little brother. Keep your sword drawn." Galeron allowed a slight smile. "Search the lower level." Rafe darted from the room. Galeron rolled his eyes. "Your sword, Rafe!"

Alex chuckled. "He is stubborn. Like you."

Galeron strode to the doorway and peered down the hall. "Watch him, but take care. I do not wish him to be aware you are doing so."

"He is nearly ten and six. Let him learn on his own."

Crossing his arms, he faced Alex. "This is his first journey."

"Allow him be the man he wishes to be."

Alex had never questioned him before. Yet now, with their young sibling in tow, he decided 'twas the best time to do so? Galeron leaned in the doorway Rafe had taken. "Mara may still be here."

"Once again, you steer away from the fact the boy is now a knight," Alex said. "You must give him more responsibility."

"Begin the search." Galeron strode out of the room. Near the staircase, partially obscured by a broken chair, lay a body. A female.

He threw the chair aside. His eyes traveled from the wood protruding from her chest to the broken railing above. Galeron knelt, ran his fingers across her unseeing eyes and whispered a quick prayer. He straightened her skirts, covering her bare legs. On her right hand, he noticed a ring, cutting into her bloated finger.

Alex entered and started for her. "You found Mara?"

Galeron indicated the ring then looked above. "It appears this woman was pushed through the railing."

"Has the upper level been searched?"

Galeron headed for the stairs. "Not yet." At the top, he motioned down the corridor. "Search the east end and I shall see what lies in the west. Call out if you need me."

"Tread carefully." Alex stalked away.

"I tread on naught but guilt." Alex was already too far to hear, but Galeron knew his words held truth. Had he not delayed the trip, Mara would be safe at Ramstone.

Time and again, he found rooms empty, some ruined, others intact as if waiting for their owner to return. Galeron came upon a knight in a doorway with an arrow protruding from his ear. What intrigued him more was the small blanket lying near the body. Galeron snatched it from the ground and brought it to his nose. Though he had only held one babe, he recognized the scent—sweet with lavender soap mixed with the unmistakable smell of urine. Still holding the blanket, he stepped over the dark-clad knight and into the room. His back to the wall, he scanned the area until he was satisfied it was deserted.

"Where are you, little one?" His question smashed the silence in the nursery. He walked to the cradle next to the bed and dropped the blanket in it. His boot caught against something at the edge of the coverlet skirting the floor. He crouched then lifted it.

"Hell's teeth." He dropped the coverlet and sat on his haunches. Heaviness punctuated the air. "Pray thee, let my eyes be lying."

His buckle scraped the floor as he stretched beneath the bed. The young nursemaid's skirt crinkled in his fist as he pulled. The soft sound of the burden as it slid across the floor thundered in the silence.

The maiden's apron, stiff with dried blood, lay in tatters. Her face, stained by tears and blood, reflected a haunted twist of fear.

"My sweet Lord, I beg you." Galeron stopped his plea. His prayer could not change what lay before him. He released the grip the nursemaid held on a young babe. Surprised at the warmth of the tiny body, he cradled it in his hands, holding it at arm's length as he rose. He nearly dropped the bundle when a whisper of a cry escaped the pursed lips.

"Damnation! Damnation!" Too stunned to think of another word, he continued to repeat it. His heart raced as if a battle-axe had struck. Still holding the child, he swung to the doorway. "Alex!" He lowered the babe into the cradle.

Alex's footsteps pounded down the hall, but they did not seem swift enough.

"Make haste!"

Alex leaped over the knight in the doorway and landed, full force, his sword brandished for battle. The wildness in his eyes faded and he sheathed his sword with a nervous grin.

"I feared you were being attacked."

His smile wavered when Galeron directed his attention to the cradle. "I found a babe." Galeron's throat closed at the distressed flicker in his brother's eyes. Though it remained but a space of a moment, he knew the reminder of Alex's stillborn son came to mind.

Alex brushed the strawberry-blond curls from the innocent face before transferring the child to the bed. All his bravado seemed to sweep away as he stripped the child of its bloodied clothing, and soiled cloth from the babe's bottom. Neither brother spoke while he examined the boy. "I am concerned about this." Alex pointed to the mark discoloring the temple. "However, the blood is not his own." He tipped his head toward the nursemaid. "She protected him with her life."

Galeron rummaged through the frocks scattered on the floor and found a cloth to wrap around the babe's bottom. "Here."

Alex redressed the boy, scooped the scant bit of life in his arms and started for the door. "Certainly there is a goat on the grounds. He has gone too long without nourishment," he called over his shoulder as he left the room.

"I shall send word to find one," Galeron said to his brother's back. He picked up the nursemaid, laid her on the bed, then wondered why he did so. He caught up with Alex.

"Make way." Alex nudged him aside.

Rafe stopped Galeron. "Is it alive?"

"Indeed. I need you to start a fire."

"The room facing the inner ward is cleared. Should I build it in there?"

"Aye. What of your search?"

Rafe motioned to the woman on the floor below. "Nay maidens other than her. I do not believe she is young enough to be your trothed."

"There is still hope Mara hides on the grounds. She may be too frightened to make herself known."

Rafe shook his head. "The babe seems to be the only soul who survived this tragedy. I searched with the others. This household has disappeared."

"People do not disappear. They flee, they hide, but they do not disappear."

"They are nonexistent then. Other than the dead knights, there are few others." They looked up at a conversation between two men ascending the stairs.

"Poor lad," one mumbled. He looked up at Galeron. "And very few are found here. The ones who remain are dead."

"And my betrothed is still to be found...along with the people who must have worked here." Galeron descended the steps and followed Alex's voice ordering someone about. He recalled his brother's request and backtracked his steps to the men still talking at the top of the stairs. "Find a damn goat or cow and milk it. Bring it to Alex for the babe." He turned, nearly bumping into Rafe. "If you insist on traipsing my heels—" Regretting his sharpness, he sighed. "Let us join Alex."

Galeron watched from the doorway. The way Alex bent over the basket tore at him. Too stark a reminder, he hoped Alex could save this one.

Rafe gave a nod, but Alex was too intent on his task to notice. Galeron stood over him. "How does he fare?"

Alex sat back on his haunches, his arms clasped about his knees. "I have done all I can."

The babe lay still, the only movement the rise and fall of his chest. Even that was shallow. Galeron lifted the basket, lowering it by the hearth.

Alex moved to a chair, his voice weary. "Without his mother to suckle, this scant bit of life can only be saved by the grace of God."

They turned at the clunk of a bucket on the floor. Rafe dipped a ladle and brought it over. Alex sighed. "He needs milk."

"There is none," one of the squires said from the doorway. "All the animals are dead."

Alex lifted the babe's head, dipped the corner of a cloth and wrung a few drops of water past the tiny parched lips. Then he gently wiped the sleeping face.

Galeron stepped away. "Rafe, gather the men and meet me in the main hall." He turned in the doorway. "Alex, join us when you have finished tending to him."

He could not exit the room fast enough. Galeron pressed his forehead on the outer wall, relishing the coolness of the stone. *Lord God in heaven, spare the babe.* He strode around the corner and into the main hall. He sorted unbroken tables and lined them against the wall — anything to distract from the thought of the boy. He quirked his eyebrow when Alex shadowed the doorway.

"If he survives, I am bringing him home to Sarah." He strode into the room. "Though she refuses to believe she cannot have another child, I am certain of it. I saw the damage after...after the birth." He averted his gaze. "This child will give her what she longs for."

And what his brother longed for as well. Changing the subject, Galeron gestured toward Lord Ronan. "We shall gather the bodies in here until daybreak." As an afterthought, he added, "Except for the blasted attackers. We must dispose of them."

"Shall I call for Rafe? He could organize the men."

Galeron grasped Lord Ronan beneath the arms. "First, let's get him off the floor."

The table creaked with Ronan's weight. His fingers clutched his sword and Galeron heard one snap as he pried it from the hilt. He slipped it into the sheath and laid it ceremoniously on Ronan's chest, crossing his arms over it. Alex called for Rafe. Within moments he entered, but Galeron continued his task as his brothers conversed. He closed his eyes and silently asked the dead man for forgiveness before offering a prayer for the man's soul. He raised his face to meet the expectant stares of his brothers. With his hand sliding off Lord Ronan's body, he doled out orders.

"Rafe, choose six men to gather the bodies." He watched for his reaction. Would he bolt at the idea or embrace it?

"Me?" Rafe's dimples, deep and long, reminded him of his uncle's smile. He missed him, and his long visits when he and Alex were young. "I am to do this?" Rafe's question knocked away the memory, focusing Galeron to the task at hand.

Galeron stifled a grin. "Aye, you are to do this, young one. Anyone void of dark armor lay upon these tables. Then, see to it the intruders are burned tonight."

Rafe's eyes widened. "Burned?"

Mayhap he pushed too far, but he must toughen his little brother. "To the bone." He scratched his jaw. "But first, behead the bastards."

"As you wish." Rafe strode out of the room.

Alex slapped Galeron on the back. "Finally, you give him responsibility."

"The horses and carriage need to be brought to the inner ward." Galeron loosened the lacings of his tunic. "We shall rest here tonight." Without waiting for a response, Galeron stormed out of the room. His guilt followed like a phantom. He could not ignore the itch at the back of his mind, certain a clue must hold the answer to the mystery within Jastar's walls, and searched the upper level again.

He found a crumpled blue dress on the floor of an east wing bedchamber. The lace caught against his calloused hands. Too ornate for daily use, it resembled the garment Sarah had worn when she married Alex. He stood in Mara's room trying to tell himself otherwise, but he could not deny that this dress was fit for a wedding. His wedding. Mara's wedding.

Alex's call filtered through his tortured thoughts.

"In here," he answered.

Alex hesitated in the doorway with a crooked grin. "I already searched this room."

Galeron fingered the garment. "This was hers."

His brother approached. "The carriage is inside the gates. The hands are watering the horses now." He received no response. "Have you found anything of use we may have overlooked?"

Galeron remained focused on the garment in his hand. "Rafe mentioned something that haunts me. These walls housed many. Where are they?" He absently rubbed the embroidered stitches between his fingers. "Where is she?" He shook the garment. "This is my fault."

"Galeron, dare not entertain such a thought." Alex tilted his head toward his brother. "After we bury the dead in the morning, we can ride into the village to find a wet nurse for the child. Hope has it that we shall find someone who knows what occurred here."

Heavy with guilt, Galeron said naught.

Alex cleared his throat. "Our spirits are weary. We should rest." He gently removed the dress from Galeron's hand.

The silken cloth fell from his grasp. "What has become of Mara? Dammit to hell, had I not delayed..."

He tossed the dress on the bed. "Galeron, do not take this upon thyself. Mayhap she escaped to the village."

Galeron raked his hair back. "Jastar protects the village, not the other way around." He strode from the room, but took a last glance at the dress. His steps, in time with Alex's, echoed eerily off the walls of the long corridor, magnifying the emptiness of the castle.

Galeron clumped down the stairs and entered the room where the babe rested. "I shall take first watch over the babe. Get some rest."

Water simmered over the flames. Nearby, lay a bucket with a drying cloth and soap beside it. Galeron questioned Alex with a smile. He shrugged. "A bath to warm the babe."

Galeron swung the pot from the flames. Pulling his leather gloves from his belt, he poured it into a washbasin. Alex added cool water until he was satisfied with the temperature. Galeron left to rummage some food and returned with smoked fish he found stored in the lower level. He stole a bite. The peace on his brother's face brought a reprieve from his dark thoughts. Somehow, caring for this child brought healing to his brother as well. He tore off another bite.

"Cease that. We can boil that for broth." He dropped Galeron's fish into a pot, added water, and hung it above the fire. Still chewing, Galeron peeked into the basket. The stillness of the little body caused his breath to catch. His broad hands dwarfed the bundle when he felt for a heartbeat. He blew a sigh. Alex's expression tore at his heart, but neither made mention of the utmost thought.

Galeron leaned back in his chair and stretched his legs. "Two at the gates—another at each entry," he shouted at one of his men passing by. The babe did not flinch with his shout.

The men shuffled throughout the castle in search of the long awaited comfort of a bed. Alex rolled out his bedroll upon the floor near the fire.

"Why not sleep upstairs?" Galeron asked.

Alex brushed the curls from the tiny face. "I wish to remain near. Wake me for my watch."

Galeron did not wake him. He held the tiny bundle close to his chest deep into the night. 'Twas the first time he had allowed tears to escape since his mother's death.

Agitated after a sleepless night, Galeron gazed down upon the lifeless bundle cradled in his arms. Dim light filtered through the window covering and kissed the babe's face. He brushed his lips across the boy's forehead, inhaling the smell of the lavender soap lingering from his final bath. Galeron quietly carried the child to the inner ward. The fog hugging the ground lent a dismal mood to his words.

"May your soul float to the heavens." His strength drained as if he carried a burden much heavier than the minuscule weight of sorrow in his hands. What rightful place was there to bury a child?

At the outer gate, he stopped. Fog swathed his face, accompanying the lone tear. He carried the boy back into the main hall. With the babe's head tucked beneath his chin, he took the stairs by twos to the upper level. He strode down the corridor and entered the nursery. He pushed open the adjoining door into the parents' chamber. He stopped in front of a portrait. The child belonged to the woman he had found. The life in the smiling face of the painting tore through him. He kicked open the trunk at the foot of the bed and rummaged through it with his free hand until he found what he was searching for. He lowered the babe onto the bed and removed the blanket. The chill of death pricked his palms as he wrapped the infant in his mother's night-rail.

He sped down the stairs with his heart clutching the tiny burden. He stopped in the main hall and stood before the woman's body lying on the table. "Here is your mother, young one."

Galeron placed the babe on a chair. He pulled the stake from her chest. It gave easily, but the stench emitting from her wound made him wish he had thought to cover his mouth. He picked up the babe, its tiny face peaceful in eternal sleep. Unable to utter a prayer past the lump forming in his throat, his words remained in his heart. He drew comfort, certain God heard the prayer just the same.

He covered the gaping wound with her child. The time seemed to crawl as he crossed the woman's arms over her infant. Galeron removed his sash and banded her hands together. They should never be separated again.

He carried them into the fog, intent on digging a grave before Alex awoke.

Chapter Eight

The Art Shoppe

"I expected a table of wares." Near the front was a painting of children frolicking in a meadow. Ruby peered closer. "'Tis…" The shelves in the shoppe drew her attention and rendered her speechless. They were lined with vials, premade brushes, palettes and wood panels in every size and shape.

"Nay village is blessed with a shoppe such as this." The way Easton boasted, one would believe he had built it himself. Easton brushed by and held the door.

Sarah tapped Ruby's chin as she passed. She realized her mouth hung open and giggled, then hurried through the door after her. Ruby examined the array of roots and dried plants. She rubbed a leaf between her fingers. A hint of blue colored her skin. 'Twas the exact shade of Galeron's eyes. A sigh passed her lips while she brushed off her hands. Did a moment of peace exist without him? She craned around the corner looking for Sarah and bumped a row of wood panels. She swallowed a curse and crouched at the panels strewn across the floor. Sarah hurried over to help pick them up.

"Look at Easton," Sarah whispered. They giggled at the obvious dismay in Easton's expression and began to stack the panels.

"He is sorry he brought us." Ruby's effervescing giggle cut short when she saw Easton's boots near the farthest panel. She looked up. His grin brought a bittersweet tug to her heart. "Galeron has your smile."

"Have you chosen your supplies? I shall pay for whatever you need."

She darted a glance to the shelves, heat infusing her cheeks. "I find it hard to decide. 'Tis familiar and foreign at the same time." She eyed the oil, knowing she would need some to mix her paints. "I was thinking of some of that...mayhap."

He chuckled. "You could add it to all the other things you have chosen."

She glanced at her empty basket and rolled her eyes. "Your jest is noted." She returned her attention to the shelf.

Easton opened the container of oil she mentioned, scrunching his nose.

"'Tis supposed to smell like that." She could nearly taste the familiar scent of the oil.

He replaced the cork and plopped it into her basket. "I shall leave you to your own." He gave the maidens a wink and strolled toward the front. "Try not to destroy the place."

She half listened to Sarah chatter while she examined the dried roots. Bringing a small handful to her nose, she closed her eyes and inhaled. Her lips twitched into a smile, the sweet, earthy scent easing her mind. The thought of a meadow, combined with the ring of children's laughter, crashed into her mind. The scent of wildflowers in the breeze mixed with a faint oily smell as she cleaned her brush. So vivid and sharp was the vision, the bristles of the brush nearly pricked her fingertips — a brush she'd made with her own hands.

"There is a young man I would like you to meet."

She jumped at Easton's voice and dropped the brushes. Heat crept into her cheeks. She nearly bumped heads with him when they both stooped to collect the brushes.

"Heavens! You startled me." She blew the stubborn wisps of hair out of her eyes when he rose and bowed before her.

"I pray thy forgiveness." He straightened with a teasing smile. She placed her fists on her hips and gave a wry grimace, fully realizing how alike father and son were. "There is a young man I would like you to meet," he repeated, motioning her to pass.

She made no effort to move. "Pray tell, who?"

"Do not be so wary. He is a family friend. 'Twould be nice to know someone other than my immediate family at the wedding, would it not?"

"I fancy 'twould be nice to know *myself* first."

Easton chuckled and waited for her to pass.

She sensed the stranger's eyes upon her while she made her way through the narrow aisle. She met his gaze. Though she hoped her glare would force him to avert his gaze, she turned her eyes down first.

"Good day, Palmer." Lord Easton smiled at Palmer's blatant admiration.

Palmer pried his eyes away to focus on Easton. He came around the counter with open arms. "I pray thee accept my apologies for my absence upon your arrival.

I had stepped back to sort a few things." He gave a slight bow. "Father was just speaking of Galeron's wedding this morn."

Ruby wished her heart would quit leaping from the rightful place in her chest. Blasted nuptials!

"I am sure many a maiden is sore disappointed at the pronouncement," Palmer droned on.

"Aye, 'tis high time he marries. He has delayed much too long," Easton said.

Ruby grew weary of forcing a smile and made her way back to the task of choosing supplies. When Easton cradled her elbow in the palm of his hand, she looked about for Sarah, knowing where this was leading. Aye, 'twas a fine thing. Any other time she would be underfoot.

"We expect Galeron and his betrothed to arrive any day now," Easton said.

"I understand she is very beautiful." Palmer nudged him. "Word is out, she was sought by many a suitor. What is she like?"

Easton shrugged. "We have yet to meet her."

She wished he would get on with the introduction. Her heart raced, though anticipation was not the reason. Dread, pure dread, filled her, and she didn't know why. All she wished for was an escape.

"Galeron is a fortunate man, just the same. And her family is in high standing," Palmer responded to something Easton said.

"Aye, her father decided Galeron is the only suitable husband for his daughter." Easton's face filled with pride.

She toyed with the brushes in her basket. *Mayhap this pointed handle would do well to stab myself with.*

"Ha!" Easton bellowed. At first she thought she had spoken aloud, but he and Palmer were still talking about Galeron.

"I suppose his reputation with the ladies did not carry to his land then." Palmer stopped short when Ruby cleared her throat.

"I beg forgiveness." Palmer gave a questioning look to Easton. "Are we to be introduced?"

"Ruby of the Forest." Easton chuckled at her despairing grimace. "This, dear maiden, is Palmer. His father, Myles, is my boyhood friend."

Ruby gave a sharp nod. "Palmer."

She nearly sighed with relief when Sarah joined them, a handful of tiny panels in her hand.

"Palmer, 'tis a joy to see you again!" Sarah gestured at the paintings lining the walls. "Are these yours?"

"Lady Sarah, you know full well I cannot paint." He laughed and kissed her hand. Though he spoke to Sarah, his eyes never left Ruby's face. "However, I do recognize exquisite beauty."

She caught herself raising her hand to hide her scar and tucked an errant strand of hair instead. Surely he was speaking of Sarah, but must he stare so blatantly at her scar?

She glanced from Palmer to Ruby and back again. "The works here *are* beautiful." She nudged Ruby and showed her the panels into her hand. "These would be perfect above the window seat."

She dropped them into the basket without looking at them. "Excellent idea."

Palmer took Ruby's hand. "I am pleased you have come to visit my shoppe."

"My pleasure." No pleasure at all, really. She could not fathom why she felt the need to run the moment her hand was in his. Maybe it was his leer. She may as well have been naked.

Palmer kissed her knuckles. "I am blessed to meet such a beautiful maiden." He locked eyes with her and caressed the underside of her hand.

His voice was smooth as the honey she loved to drizzle on her bread. She found naught sweet about his stare. He wrapped his fingers over the top of her hand. Ruby's stomach coiled when his eyes strayed to her cleavage. Out of respect for Easton, she allowed him to hold her hand a moment shy of shameful, then slipped from his grasp, longing for the tenderness of Galeron's touch.

Palmer smiled. "Is there anything I can help you find?"

An escape. "I have found all I need."

"Ruby, you have barely chosen anything. Mayhap Palmer can make a few suggestions," Easton said.

With a terse smile, she looked over her shoulder. "How kind of you to remember my quandary."

Easton gave Ruby a wink and nudged Palmer. Ruby nearly jerked Sarah off her feet when she passed, avoiding taking Palmer's offered arm. "Lead the way."

"As you wish." Palmer started down the aisle and they followed.

She glared at Easton, her ire burning out of control. *Blast him and his meddlesome ways.*

Palmer pointed at the panels. "Were you looking for a certain size?"

"One of each shall do." One after the other, she slapped wood panels into Palmer's waiting arms. This blatant pairing was ludicrous! How dare Easton push this man onto her? She slammed down the basket and scooped a sack of roots without taking the time to see what they were. Did he not realize she had a mind of her own? She grabbed various items off the shelf and dropped it into the basket as well. She placed it precariously on top of the panels.

Palmer peered over the tower of supplies. "You must paint nonstop."

She choked back the urge to shout and returned the majority of the panels to the shelf.

Easton called while hurrying down the aisle, "Nay! Keep it. Allow me to do this for you."

She avoided eye contact with anyone, wishing she had never mentioned her ability to paint. Easton shooed the others to bring the purchases to the front. He waited until they were out of earshot. "Choose what you wish. I only want to give you a link to your past."

She was mortified she had directed her ire at him. "I shall find a way to repay you."

"Is that what troubles you, child?"

"Nay." Ruby glanced at Palmer. "*He* ails me."

"Palmer? I find him to be a suitable companion for the wedding."

"So, you presume I want a companion?" *Or wish to attend at all?*

Easton blinked. "I thought—"

"With all due respect, Lord Easton, you must heed the fact I make my own choices. I do not need *any* man to accompany me *anywhere*." She spoke in half-truths, but she wanted to make it clear she had no interest in Palmer.

The two dueled stares.

"Very well," he finally said. "But call me Easton. I do not understand why you have reverted to my formal address."

She studied the toe of his boot. "Forgive me." She nearly added that she did not understand the anger that consumed her, but stifled the foolish comment. Easton tucked his fingertips under her chin. "Do not bow down, child. 'Tis I who should pray forgiveness."

"We remain friends?" She found it surprising how deeply she needed his acceptance.

"Indeed. Now, shall we collect your purchases?"

She grinned. "Certainly." She slipped her hand in the crook of his arm and met the others at the counter.

Palmer handed the basket of purchases to Ruby. "I trust I shall see you again?" He squeezed her hand when she grasped the handle.

She wondered what Easton saw in him. "Let go," she whispered, pulling the basket away.

Easton tucked the panels under his arm. "Palmer, my thanks for everything."

"Good day, Easton. Sarah." Palmer kissed Sarah's hand and reached for Ruby's, but she looked in her basket, pretending not to notice. "Fare well, Ruby. I hope to see you soon. Very soon."

Ruby answered with a slam of the door on her way out.

The ride home was awkward, for her companions had witnessed the way she treated Palmer. Why did she always act before thinking? Upon arriving back at Ramstone, Ruby gathered all she could and left the carriage. Arms full, Ruby nearly tripped up the stairs. Though Easton ordered a servant to carry it, she insisted on doing it herself. She glanced back, urging Sarah to follow. She picked up the wood panels and followed several steps behind. By the time Sarah entered the chamber, she already had the easel set up.

"Here?" Sarah laid the panels on the table.

Ruby glanced up. "That is fine." She noticed Sarah's glum expression. "What ails you?"

"Naught." Sarah settled in the corner of the window seat. "When this was my room, I always loved sitting here."

"'Tis my favorite corner as well." She glanced above it. "You were right. Those panels would be perfect up there."

"It could remain yours for as long as you wish."

She rummaged through her purchases, intent on avoiding the topic. From the corner of her eye, she saw Sarah staring out of the window. The final rays of the day lit the sadness on her face. Ruby sauntered over and stood beside her.

"The Lord's hands dip into the palette of nature and create such beautiful sunsets," Ruby said.

Sarah did not respond.

"I could paint a sunset for you."

"I would rather watch it with you." Sarah sighed. "From this window."

Ruby pinched the bridge of her nose. "We shall see." She offered false hope, but the sadness on Sarah's face eased a bit. She returned to the table and began mixing a few paints, the oil wafting and meeting slight memories. "I have done this many times." Her breath caught and she looked up. "Of that, there is nay doubt."

Sarah selected a panel. "Here, paint something."

She propped it on the easel and dipped her brush. Their silence locked her in peace. The only sound was an occasional tap against the palette.

"This feels…" She cocked her head, trying to explain.

"Right?" Sarah said.

"Mmm-huh." The paint gliding onto the panel spun a spell, quieting her swirling thoughts.

Sarah grabbed a blanket and curled up on the window seat. Having her nearby felt as right as the movement of the paint strokes.

At first, she simply experimented with color and hue, then the painting seemed to take upon a will of its own. Flurries of time and memories old and new transformed the blank panel into a meadow of vibrant corn roses against a brilliant sky.

The tap of the brush on the palette signaled her final stroke. Ruby's full lips curved, but her smile was tainted. Galeron invaded even this moment. Damn his kiss…his arms…his confession. Tears wet her cheeks before she could fight them back and she discreetly wiped her face.

Sarah moved the hair falling into Ruby's eyes and tucked it behind her ear. "Why are you troubled? The painting is beautiful."

"I love the corn roses, they are my favorite flower."

"You remember more?"

"Nay, but they are my favorite now." The time she had spent alone with Galeron was too dear to share, even with Sarah. "They remind me of something."

"What?"

"A beautiful meadow I saw once." She picked up her brush and added a final touch to her painting. "I do remember that I always found peace with a brush in hand." She smiled. "This is what I need."

"Aye, you had a peaceful expression the whole time you painted."

"I can sell my work." She blushed. "I mean not to boast, but mine is as good as the ones Palmer sells."

"You wish to *sell* this painting?"

She tilted her head and studied the panel. "Nay, this one is a little treasure I shall keep. I shall paint others to sell."

"Why would you sell any of them?"

She imagined using the money to make her way, even acquire a small abode.

"Ruby?" Sarah's voice filled with concern. "Answer me."

Ruby worried her bottom lip.

"Why do you wish to sell your paintings?" Sarah repeated.

"I must make my way."

"You *still* choose to leave?" Sarah sighed. "Pray tell, would you consider a wing here? A whole wing just for you."

Hope burned in Sarah's eyes. Ruby did not have the heart to douse it. Not just yet. "I make not a promise to stay, but I shall consider the offer."

Sarah hugged her. "I am certain we can come to a decision that will make us both happy."

Ramstone harbored heartache. The only escape was to leave. She swallowed hard at the thought. She removed the painting from the easel and placed it in Sarah's hands. "Take care, the paint is still wet." She hoped Sarah didn't notice the crack in her voice.

Sarah's mouth gaped. "For me? Ruby, 'tis a treasure of yours!"

"So are you, dear friend, so are you."

Chapter Nine

Remains

Galeron followed the rough-hewn road leading into the village. He dismounted from time to time, searching for life among the bodies. By the number of the men littering the ground, it was apparent the majority wore the crest of Jastar. A few wore no crest at all and their armor was the same as the ones he saw at Jastar, unbuffed and dark. The helmets were adorned with horns sharpened to deadly points.

"'Tis naught but a death trail. What happened here?" Galeron asked.

Alex sighed. "There is something dark and evil in this place."

Galeron didn't respond to the comment. He knew then it was not his imagination taking liberty with his mind. He had felt the same from the moment they arrived.

The occasional snort of the horses covered the lack of conversation as they traveled up the next hill. The silence only magnified Galeron's anguish. Though he attempted to banish the memory of the babe's last breaths, they continued to echo in his mind. The futility of his efforts haunted him, no matter how he wished for a happier outcome. Sadly, a thousand wishes could not change the fact that he had covered a mother and her babe with the dirt of their homeland.

Though Galeron had carved the words 'Two Together' upon the cross he pounded into the ground, he wished he could have honored them with names. His fingers tingled. He looked down and unfurled his fists twisted in the reins.

"Ho, Galeron. Look ahead!" Alex shouted.

Galeron snapped his head at the tone of his brother's voice. The Ramstone knights halted upon the crest of the hill and stared upon the village. Galeron cursed when the stench reached them on the breeze.

"God's eyes, this place has the weight of hopelessness and the smell of death," he whispered.

Galeron drew his sword and started down the steep hill. He felt as if he were leading his men into the pits of hell. When they reached the valley, he scanned the desolation, tasting the death in the air. Judging by his men's silence, he knew they sensed the evil spirits.

A crease invaded his brow. Something itched at the back of his mind, like a rash from ivy. He raised his gloved hand, halting the men. His leather breeches creaked against his saddle as he turned to them. "Other than the obvious devastation, something is out of place, yet it evades me. Pray tell, does anyone know of what I speak?"

The men stared at the emptiness. Alex's eyes widened. "Where are the villagers?"

Galeron dismounted and the men followed his lead.

"Search everywhere. Do not leave any place untouched." Rafe remained at Galeron's side. "Go search, boy."

"Am I not to go with you?" Rafe's eyes were eager and full of adventure.

"We can cover more ground this way. Keep your sword drawn."

Galeron kept his distance, assuring Rafe did not stray far from his vision. With the exception of the slain knights and a few dead elders, no others were there. Dawn filtered into darkness yet the men still searched.

Just when they believed no survivors remained, Alex shouted, "Over here!" The men found Alex in an alley, pulling the helmet off a wounded knight.

Galeron rested his elbow on Rafe's shoulder. "Well?"

Alex unclasped the chest plate. "He breathes."

Air gurgled, fighting to escape the throat. The knight's pallor held the gray tint of death. Galeron knelt beside the man. "What happened here?"

"He wears Jastar's crest," Rafe said.

"Silence, Rafe," Galeron said, without looking up. "Who attacked the village and Jastar?"

"Captive," the knight whispered through cracked lips.

"What captives?"

"Oh God—our children."

Galeron darted a dismayed glance at Alex. "Where have they been taken?"

"They took them…took them all."

Galeron frowned. "Who?" He moved aside, allowing Alex to staunch the blood.

At Alex's nod, he bent to continue the questioning, but the Jastar knight made the next query. "Survivors?"

"Rest, Sir Knight," Galeron said.

The knight gritted his teeth while Alex bandaged his midsection. With a growl, he grabbed Alex's arm. "Ann! Where are our sons?" The Jastar knight drifted off, his head lolling to the side.

Alex pressed his ear against the knight's chest. "He still lives." He tied the final knot on the bandage.

Galeron looked up at Rafe's pale face. "Take two men and place him in the carriage."

"Brother, travel may take what life this knight still has."

"'Tis a chance we shall take. We must hasten to Ramstone and warn the others. Distance from this dark place can only do him good. Besides, Rafe looks ill." As if on cue, Rafe ran off retching, and spilled his morning rations onto the ground. Alex shook his head when Galeron started toward Rafe. "Leave him be."

"Very well, but keep him close."

"As you wish. However—" He stopped at Galeron's glare. He tied his horse to the carriage and helped transfer the knight. "Rafe, you ride beside the carriage. I need you to stay close in case I need assistance along the way." Alex climbed into the carriage.

Rafe wiped his chin and climbed into his saddle.

Convinced there were no others to rescue, Galeron led the weary knights, resigning himself to the long ride ahead. He gladly bore the sleepless ride to put as much distance as possible between his men and the godforsaken region. He swayed with the movement of his stallion, reflecting on how the journey now held complications and despair. Other than reports from Rafe, little was said. At sundown, Galeron finally allowed the men to stop. They made camp, ate and fell emotionally and physically exhausted into their bedrolls. Soon, the only sounds were the occasional snore, accompanied by the crackle of the fire. Throughout the night, Galeron and Alex took turns tending to the Jastar knight, who clung stubbornly to life.

As Galeron drifted off, he cursed himself for not asking the knight's name. *Lord, spare me the wretched task of burying another nameless soul.*

Chapter Ten

The Decision

"The autumn mornings are becoming cooler."

"Oh!" Engrossed in the butterflies floating through Ramstone's gardens, Ruby did not hear anyone approach before Easton spoke.

Regret played across his face. "I did not mean to startle you, but I saw you shiver from the window. So I brought this." He held out a cloak.

"My thanks. I fear the sunshine of the day fooled me." She allowed him to drape it over her, but was surprised when he tugged the ends to meet under her chin and tied it. Like a father. She swallowed hard. Why could she not recall her own?

"What causes such pain to creep across your face?" Easton tilted his head when she didn't answer. "It shall come to light, Ruby."

"I pray each night, but naught... Aye, you are right, it shall come to light." She focused on the last remnants of the garden. "It seems the flora is surrendering to the cold." The same chill permeated her life, nay matter what. She was no closer to finding her past than on the day Galeron had found her.

"Aye, but soon the holly shall mature."

She almost told him how Galeron spoke about the sight of the holly against the snow. Ruby shifted her stance and clasped her hands behind her. "I regret I shall miss it." Her heart stuttered a beat. "I have been very happy here at Ramstone." She took a breath and turned to face him. "You all mean very much to me."

"What are you trying to say, young one?"

Her eyes focused on the deep lines across his forehead. "I do not wish to appear ungrateful." Her gaze met his and she faltered at the concern she saw in them. "I-I must leave."

He cleared his throat. "You are welcome to stay here indefinitely, you are aware of that?"

"Aye."

"Then why leave? You have nowhere to go."

"It is best I find a dwelling in the village. Pray thee, do not mistake my need for independence as ungratefulness. This decision was not made lightly." She clutched the cloak to stop the tremble of her hands.

After several moments he said, "I do not understand."

"'Tis best I am on my own."

A slow smile crept across Easton's face. "I believe I have the perfect solution."

She quirked a grin. "You have a place in mind?"

"I certainly do. You could have a wing of your own, right here at Ramstone."

She stared at him for several moments, her smile fading. "You spoke to Sarah."

"Aye, she came to me last night, however, I believe it a fitting place for you to stay." He crossed his arms, quite pleased with himself. "As long as you wish."

She flicked a wilting blossom, watching the petals twirl to the ground. "She shouldn't have," she whispered, staring at the petals at her feet. "I must go, Easton."

"In the short time you have graced Ramstone, your companionship brought Sarah joy. Can I do anything to deter your departure?"

Her eyes burned with the effort to keep from weeping. "Nay."

"I shall help you find suitable employment in the village." He spoke so quickly, his words jammed together.

She looked up, wondering what caused such a quick change in his demeanor. A smiling Sarah hurried along the path.

"Oh dear," she whispered.

"I assume you have not told her?"

"We spoke of it, yet I—"

"Good morn! You are out early." Sarah's manner danced with excitement. "Ruby, you must come and see the east wing."

She glanced at Easton while Sarah chatted on. "One of the corner rooms has windows on three walls. The light will be perfect for you." Sarah's final words fell to a whisper while she looked from one to the other. "To paint."

Ruby swallowed hard. "Sarah." It was all she could say.

Sarah's animated mood dissipated.

"I shall take my leave." With a nod, Easton escaped.

She delivered a scowl to his back. Coward. Her ire dampened at the hurt on Sarah's face. "I beg you, lend an ear."

"Nay, I shan't! My wish is that you stay, Ruby. 'Tis not only due to selfishness. I also fear for your safety." She drew a fractured breath then whispered, "Do not go."

Ruby felt she was drowning in guilt. "I caused those tears. That kills me." She took a step, inadvertently catching the toe of her boot in her hem. With a plummet toward Sarah, she brought both of them to the ground.

She winced at the pebbles cutting into her elbows while peering through the tangle of her crimson locks. "Sarah! Are you hurt?" She met Sarah's broad grin. "Oh, I suppose you are not."

"I must say, you are the clumsiest maiden I have ever met," Sarah said. "Help me up."

"Aye, but who shall help *me*? These skirts are naught but a tangled quagmire!"

She burst out laughing while they kept stepping on each other's hems. Nearly up, a loud rip caused her to laugh even harder. "I have torn your skirt!" she said, gasping for air.

"Nay, 'twas *your* skirt—I'm caught in your hem." Sarah joined Ruby's infectious laughter.

"G-get it out," she said, not caring whether she did or not.

Sarah escalated the situation by trying to stand and falling flat on her bottom. Captured in a debilitating fit of laughter, Ruby ended up slamming beside her. No help at all. Any strength or desire to rise from the ground was lost.

Side by side, they sat in the garden throughout the day, leaning against each other as their squeals fed the sadness into unhampered glee. She gathered comfort from Sarah's company, and watched the sun set. Ruby promised herself this was the last day she would mourn the man she never had. Love was a horrid thing.

Later, after securing a promise Ruby was feeling better, Sarah reluctantly left her at the chamber door. Fortunately, Ruby fell asleep immediately. Unfortunately, her dreams did not hold to the promise she made and allowed Galeron in.

With her departure looming, Ruby still counted each day since Galeron had left, hoping she might catch a glimpse of him before she left. Then the thought of a woman beside him made her swallow back such a thought. Until she surrendered to the darkness of the night, and dreamed of Galeron's warm body against her. When morning light illuminated her room, he was her first waking thought. A chilling void brought tears of longing before she even opened her eyes.

This morning proved no different. She snuggled deeper into the blanket, trying to return to her dreams. Frowning at the insistent tap on her door, she pulled herself out of bed to answer it.

Bridget entered with her morning tray and Ruby hurried to move the scattered paintings to make room on the table. "They are beautiful, milady." Bridget craned her neck to examine them closer, still holding the tray.

Ruby fingered the edge of a panel, depicting a scene from the garden. "My thanks, Bridget. The gardens are my inspiration." Ruby tried to ignore the twinge of pain, knowing she would be leaving such beauty.

"I cannot see why they did not choose the garden as a setting for the wedding. But I suppose they must hold with tradition and marry on the church steps."

Ruby frowned. "Aye, I suppose."

Bridget set the tray on the table and clasped her hands. "Will there be anything more, milady?"

"Ruby. Call me Ruby."

"Nay, I mustn't."

Ruby grinned. "To answer your question, you are aware I can dress myself."

Bridget unsuccessfully tried to suppress a giggle. "Good day, milady." She curtsied and scurried out of the room.

Ruby popped a tart in her mouth. Too inspired to linger indoors, she washed and slipped on her favorite yellow kirtle. On the way out, she grabbed a wrap and strolled to the garden, a panel under her arm and a basket of supplies swinging from the crook of her elbow.

A smile, dreamy and a bit disconnected, spread with the morning light among the colors of the garden. It would not be long before they faded in the upcoming frost. Upon nearing the bench in the garden, she stopped short.

Easton did not seem aware of her approach. He was speaking softly. For a fleeting moment, she glimpsed the faraway look upon his face before she turned to leave.

"Ruby, you are welcome to sit."

She hesitated until he patted the spot beside him. The bench was cool against the back of her legs, despite her wrap. "Beautiful morn."

"I visit my wife here every morn."

Ruby quelled the whim to glance about. "Do you?" was all she said.

"'Twas her favorite place, here among the beauty."

Ruby contained her surprise at his openness. "How long has she been gone?"

He tilted his head. "It seems a lifetime ago. Galeron was not quite ten years when she died." He motioned to her basket and smiled slightly. "You came to paint?"

"I imagine 'twas difficult—losing their mother, I mean."

"Galeron watched over his brothers, especially Rafe. He would not let the wet nurse out of his sight when she held him. Once, she fell ill, and he was so upset I thought I would lose him as I did when his mother died." He seemed to be talking more to himself than her.

"Lose him?" She blurted louder than she meant to. "Did he run away when his mother died?"

Easton turned from his reverie. "What?" Realization spread over his face. "I did not mean to burden you."

"I can lend my ears, if you so wish." Guilt tore through her. Though she cared for his well-being, her inquisitive heart craved for more knowledge about Galeron.

"Sometimes 'tis good to talk, aye?"

She smiled and waited.

"Galeron, the poor lad, spoke not a word for months after Ella—" He focused on his hands. "After his mother died. When he did, he confided in Rafe's wet nurse. The woman came to me in tears. She told me Galeron blamed himself for his mother's death." His voice grew quiet. "I do not know why he came to such a thought."

She opened her mouth to speak and then realized she had naught to ease the pain in his voice.

He did not seem to notice. "I figured 'twould be best to remarry for the sake of my young sons, yet I could love nay other." He shook his head. "Ah, 'tis foolish to marry for love, for the void when one passes proves impossible to fill. Sometimes 'tis better not to fall in love at all."

She was tempted to agree.

He placed his hands upon his knees, grief aging his movements. He stood and rubbed his chin. "I shall take leave and allow you to finish what you set out to do."

She took a deep breath. "Milord, may I inquire about something?"

He raised an eyebrow, painfully reminding her of Galeron. "Call me Easton. Pray tell, what would you like to ask?"

Her nervousness tensed her body, as if a rod held her upright. "Sarah mentioned Sir Galeron would be gone but nine or ten days and a fortnight has passed." She stifled the urge to turn from Easton's scrutiny. "I mean, the men should be back by now."

"What is your question?"

She followed his gaze to her fidgeting fingers and stilled them. "The delay is worrisome, do you think not?"

"Galeron shall return soon enough with his betrothed."

His abrupt change in mood flared her ire. "I am certain he shall."

"His betrothed is most likely accompanied by her maids. Women tend to slow travel. I am sure all is well."

She hated that word—betrothed. She propped a wood panel on the easel and rummaged for a brush. Stupid girl, why did she ask? "I see."

"I have a proposal."

Her gaze darted up. "Oh?"

"Once Sarah has wakened, let us ride to the village. 'Twould be a nice distraction from worry."

Was he able to see her heart? She smiled. "Excellent."

"You should bring a few paintings to the art shoppe. Sarah tells me your work is exceptional." He displayed his hands as if holding one. "I may even purchase one myself."

Her cheeks heated at the compliment. She mixed a bit of paint until she was satisfied with the color. "I shall decide before we go." Her mood lifted at his smile.

"While we are there, you should visit the seamstress."

"Visit the seamstress?" She dipped her brush and looked up. "Whatever for? I have all I require."

"But, you are still in need of a fitting for the wedding."

Stones…nay, boulders crashed in her stomach. "A fitting for the wedding." She wished she could quit repeating his words.

"Galeron's wedding." He turned from one side to the other. "At the church. Remember?"

"I wonder what paintings I should bring today." She dipped her brush and studied the tilt of a leaf.

After an awkward pause, Easton walked away. She saw him glance back from time to time, but she pretended to be absorbed with her painting until his footsteps faded.

The morning light danced upon the last of the blooms, so beautiful a moment ago. Tears blended the colorful flora into a shattered mosaic. The paint dripped to the ground. The garden lost its luster. She wept.

Ruby fought a yawn as they rode to the village, and she did not make any attempt to join in the conversation. Utterly disgusted with herself, she realized she was already breaking her vow to cease her self-pity.

Though Easton did not realize how his words wounded, his suggestion to take a ride to the village was a good one. The early-afternoon sun did not hint at the coming months of cold, and she raised her face to the warmth. Even Easton's inadvertent reminders about the wedding could not daunt her enthusiasm for visiting the art shoppe.

Sarah steered the conversation away from the nuptials. "How many paintings did you bring?"

Ruby looked up from a cart full of fruit, an apple still in her hand. "Four." She paid the vendor and fell into rhythm of Easton and Sarah's stride. "Are we going to the art shoppe now?"

Easton pointed. "Our first stop."

When they reached their destination, she hesitated but a moment, then decided to face Palmer. When her eyes adjusted to the dimness, she discovered the place empty. Sarah led her to the far wall and pointed. "Mayhap you could hang your paintings back here."

"Easton, my friend!" She spun around at the rambunctious voice. A smile, missing several teeth, shone through the stranger's bearded face. "I regret I missed your last visit."

Easton grinned and gave him a hearty handshake. The spoke in hushed tones, the stranger glancing several times in their direction. "Who is that?" she whispered to Sarah. "They seem to be talking about us." Or more likely the stranger had noticed her unsightly scar. The thought had not passed her mind since the last time she was in the village and she hated the reminder.

Before Sarah could respond, the elderly man strode toward them. "Lady Sarah, greetings! You must have entered while I was in the back." He smiled at Ruby.

"Ah, Myles," Sarah took his hands. "It has been too long." The man brushed his lips on Sarah's cheek. "Your presence brings my heart joy." He turned to Ruby. "Ah, you must be Ramstone's guest."

She gave a small smile. "Indeed."

He leaned back so far Ruby feared he would topple. "Ah, Ruby of the Forest. My son surely did not exaggerate your divine beauty. If your paintings are half as exquisite, they shall sell well indeed."

Ruby's stomach coiled. Beauty indeed. "'Tis an honor to meet you, Sir Myles."

"Sir Myles," he mused, standing a bit taller. "Might I see the paintings Easton told me about?"

So *that* was what Easton was discussing with him. "Aye, if I may, I would like to display them for sale."

"But of course. Palmer hoped you would bring them."

"They are in the carriage. I shall fetch them." Easton stepped outside.

"Sir Myles, your shoppe is well stocked. I have never seen such a grouping of art supplies in one place." She frowned, amazed she recalled anything about the contents of any other art shoppe.

With a sharp tug on his shirt, he chuckled. "*Sir* Myles," he repeated. "My name is Myles, simply Myles." He motioned for Easton to place the paintings on the counter as he came in. "One of a kind, 'tis said. This establishment belongs to my son, but I tend it when my wife cannot watch after our grandson. Are you in need of supplies, Lady Ruby?"

"My name is Ruby, simply Ruby." She grinned at Myles' laughter. She wondered about the grandson Myles mentioned, and why his mother could not watch after him, but refrained from asking.

"Where is Palmer now?" Easton tilted his head, squinting at one of her paintings. "I like this one."

"He shall be about soon enough." Myles turned his attention back to Ruby. "Are you here to attend Galeron's wedding? It seems the village has filled with wedding guests. Even some of the villagers have taken in some of them."

She blinked at the sudden change in conversation. "Aye, the occasion seems to be quite the event." She toyed with the brushes arranged in a little clay pot on the counter.

"Myles, how *is* Jadon?" Easton sauntered to them.

"Ah, he is a handful of joy. Julia finds it difficult to keep up with the little one. He is at the age of mischief." He toyed with his mustache. "When she told Palmer he needs to acquire a permanent nursemaid, he decided to stay home with the lad today." He chuckled. "He has not had much luck."

Lord Easton leaned close to Ruby. "There is a perfect opportunity."

She bumped the pot of brushes, toppling it over. "Myles, may I inquire about the job of nursemaid? I am in need of employment and a place to dwell." She scrambled to retrieve the brushes while shooting a crooked grin of apology at Myles.

Myles winked at Easton. "Palmer said he would stop by with Jadon around dusk. Will you be in the village then?"

"Aye, we have yet to begin shopping. I would like to speak with him." Why had she been so rude at their first meeting? She may have lost this opportunity due to it.

Sarah nearly wrenched her neck looking from Myles to Ruby. Her mouth dropped open, then clamped shut.

Ruby noticed, yet could not allow such fortune to pass. "I should return to talk with Palmer then?"

"Indeed. Continue shopping. If you cannot find what you are looking for, we may have it in the back room." Myles' smile, so unlike his son's, spread warmth. "Your paintings would show best in the window." Myles peered closely at them. "I am certain my son shall be impressed."

She could hardly contain her excitement. "The chance of selling them is a kind offer." He glanced up, offered a smile, then set about to connecting wire to the panels.

For the first time in weeks, a bit of hope blossomed. She pulled Sarah with her. "Let us see what ingredients are available." She called out to Myles, "Are they fresh?"

"Aye, Palmer ground those roots this week." He pointed to a shelf near the back.

She grinned at Sarah. She sighed in return. "Come, cease that pout." She led her to the shelves, ignoring Sarah's heavy sigh.

She picked at a variety of roots, placing some in pieces of oiled cloth. Another sigh. She folded the cloth, laid it in her basket, and filled another with the oddly familiar blue-tinged roots. Another sigh. She gave Sarah a warning glare and picked up a cut-glass vial. "This would be pretty to hold oil." At the next, much louder sigh, she resisted slamming the vial back on the shelf.

"I am grateful for such an opportunity presenting itself. You, as my friend, should be happy for me."

"I am!"

Ruby turned to her, a smile twitching the edge of her frown.

"Well, I am *trying* to be happy for you," Sarah muttered.

Ruby gave Sarah's hand a squeeze. "Try a bit harder, friend. You look as if you may cry at any moment."

Sarah sighed, caught herself and glanced at Ruby. "Pray pardon." She examined a palette, then returned it to the shelf. Ruby ran her finger across the edge of the paintings hanging along the wall. Her hand came away with a heavy coating of dust. Had her hope to sell been a foolish one?

Sarah shook her head. "Yours are much better." The woman had an uncanny way of reading thoughts. Ruby smiled her appreciation.

She recalled the painting she'd seen as she entered and headed for it. Ruby's smile dissipated as she neared. The depiction of the children frolicking in the meadow produced sorrow so deep tears stung her eyes. Why did this one stir her so? Consumed with the odd realization there must be a child in her past, she did not see Sarah's eyes fill with concern.

"What is wrong?" she whispered.

She turned, the far away memory still in her heart. "I wish I knew." She was close enough to overhear Easton and Myles' conversation, and listened to it instead of her unsettled thoughts.

"She shall make a perfect nursemaid for your grandson."

Myles nudged him. "Palmer's choice would entail much more than a nursemaid. He is completely taken by her. Do you suppose there is a chance it could develop into something more?"

Easton heaved a sigh. "Not in the least. She told me herself she needs nay man in her life."

"A shame," said Myles. "Jadon needs a mother."

She wanted to hug Easton. She hoped Myles would relay the fact to Palmer before she saw him again.

Chapter Eleven

Journey of Guilt

The ends of Ruby's hair tickled his bare chest. Her lips parted in a slight smile. He loved her smile. His breath quickened at her nearness. The warmth of her body beckoned his passion. His loins tightened and he fell willingly under her spell, his heart slipping into bliss. His body lurched at her hot breath whispering into his ear. He strained to listen and cursed the heartbeat drumming out her words.

Her warmth turned into icy alarm. With impending doom choking him, he wiped the sweat trickling from his brow. His vision blurred. The shattering sound of his boots on the forest floor blended with her scream. He hacked the overgrowth from his path. His breath seared his lungs yet he could not draw nearer to her. The snapping branches grew in volume, so deafening it drowned out his own voice shouting her name.

Galeron woke with Ruby's name on his lips. He glanced around, relieved no one looked his way. He stared at the forest's canopy, shoved the recurring dream back to the icy depths of his mind, and kicked out of his bedroll. Pulling on his boots, he met Alex's eyes and gave a nod. By the darkness around Alex's eyes, it appeared he had not slept.

"Have you watched over him all night? You should have woken me." Galeron crouched beside him. The knight's face had regained some color. "Alex, once again, you rescue a man from the edge of death."

"He is fevered. 'Tis not a good sign." The knight began to mutter. Alex leaned closer then shook his head. "He called out during the night, but I could not make out his words."

"Will he wake anytime soon?"

Alex shrugged and placed a poultice under the bandage.

Galeron looked around, spotting Rafe by the creek. "Wake the others, Rafe. We are leaving."

Rafe was working his way across the camp when the wounded knight began to thrash. Alex and Galeron held him down.

"Release me!"

Rafe fetched a drink from the stream and brought it to them.

"We are not your foe. You shall do harm to your wound. Lie still!" Alex shouted.

The knight took a breath and winced. "Who the hell are you?"

"Alex. Sir Alex of Ramstone. Now, quench your thirst." He supported the knight's head and helped him drink.

The knight licked his cracked lips and propped himself up on his elbow. Pain washed the color from his face and he dropped to the bedroll. "Wh-where am I?"

"Rest now. You are among friends," Galeron said.

"What of Jastar?"

Alex and Galeron glanced at each other.

The knight grabbed Galeron's tunic. "What have you done with them?"

Galeron pried his tunic from the knight's grasp, meeting little resistance. "Lie still. I shall tell what I found." He hesitated, trying to cushion the truth. "Brother Knight, when we arrived at Jastar, it was deserted." When he didn't speak, Galeron asked, "What is your name?"

"Jac…Sir Jac of Jastar." He moaned, his eyes fluttered, but he stubbornly focused on Galeron. "Tell me of my family."

"We found a few in the castle. None survived."

"I am aware of my father's demise," Jac whispered, his voice cracking. "Who else was there?"

Sweat gathered underneath Galeron's tunic. "I found a nursemaid's body in the nursery." Jac's eyes held such terror Galeron avoided his gaze. "There were many knights with the Jastar crest, and some with the black armor you spoke of. As I said, none survived."

Sir Jac moved his lips several times before uttering, "What of my Lady Ann?" the reverence of the way he spoke her name cut through, his love apparent. "She was fleeing with our sons. Certainly you found them safe?"

Galeron glanced away. "'Twould be best to rest now."

"They must have escaped. What of my sister? A young maiden? Her name is Mara. Did you find her?"

Galeron's breath stuttered at the name of his betrothed. "We shall speak of this later."

Weakness permeated his voice, but Jac's demand spoke volumes. "Tell me now!"

Galeron swallowed. "A woman, fair of face and golden hair, was found." He decided not to mention the gold band on her finger.

"Ann? My Lady Ann?" He stared past Galeron, the loss washing across his face.

"Sir Jac?" Galeron waited until he focused on him. "I found an infant—a boy."

"Was he with Jacson? His brother would have watched over him. He is small, but quite a brave lad." Jac smiled, his eyes taking on what he wished to believe.

Galeron shook his head.

"So, they are here? With us...here?"

Galeron could not tear away from the hope in his eyes. Alex placed a hand on his shoulder, but it brought no ease to the painful word he had to utter. "Nay."

Jac stared at him. "They are here," he repeated, his grasp on hope unraveling.

"We found the babe. He lies in his mother's arms for eternity. I buried them myself." Galeron clenched his fists.

Sir Jac uttered an inhuman scream before relinquishing to unconsciousness. Alex, bowed in prayer for the knight, jerked up his head at Galeron's shout, "Fucking mercy? You claim to be a merciful God?"

Several men looked up. Others, packing their bedrolls, let them drop. Rafe, with a water skin still dripping, stared wide-eyed. Mouths gaped with not a word.

"I swear vengeance." Galeron shook his fist toward the heavens, his muscles pulsating with each thrust. "You allow a babe to die? An innocent babe? What other cruelties have Your sacred eyes been blind to? You allow evil to ravage innocence?"

He strode through the clearing, cursing anyone who failed to clear his path fast enough. "The leader of the vile demon's armor shall burn in hell, but first I shall make them pay for what You ignore!" The horses snorted their discontent as Galeron stormed past, leaving an eerie silence in his wake.

Galeron stared at his upturned palms for what seemed an eternity. Unable to pray to God, he prayed to the woman he never met…probably never would. "Mara, forgive me. So much of your family's pain could have been avoided had I arrived in time." He bowed, interlocking his fingers, hoping God had not forsaken him. "I beg forgiveness, Lord."

Moments later, he ignored the wary looks and ordered his men to pack up. Before the day was half over, the skies opened, hampering their journey. The storm refused to wane for days, and several times, Galeron wondered if it was the Lord's punishment.

The suction of the hooves plodding through the mud lent an eerie echo to the air. Galeron eyed the menacing skies, rain streaming onto his face.

"'Tis offering nay respite." Alex brought his steed beside Galeron's.

"We have endured rain for three days. What is one more?" Turning in his saddle, Galeron grimaced and dismounted. He stood shin-deep in mud by the carriage. "Free the blasted wheels from the trench!" He had lost count of the times they repeated the chore. "Heave!" he yelled, pushing with his men. "Heave!" He barely heard the creak of the carriage above the thunder.

The spoked wheels sank into the ground. Galeron stopped and wiped his soaked locks from his face. "Dammit to hell. Cease!" Blinking the wetness from his lashes, he contemplated the next move.

Alex slopped through the mud. The wind swept his words away, but Galeron could read his lips. "Hopeless."

He craned, speaking near Alex's ear. "We must abandon it." He motioned to Rafe to relieve the horses from the carriage. Nodding and snorting, the pair seemed happy to be free of their burden. Rafe, still holding the reins, led them to Galeron. "What of Sir Jac?"

Galeron grinned, despite his frustration. "Well, little brother, do you fear we shall leave him behind? We shall secure him to a horse."

Rafe scrambled in the carriage, guiding Jac's body while his older brothers slipped him out into the rain. In an effort to catch up to them, Rafe tripped out of the carriage, plummeting face-first into the mud. Galeron burst out laughing. Alex wiped the rain from his face to hide his smile.

"May the both of you make a cozy home with the devil," Rafe said, nearly slipping again when he stomped away.

"Aw, Rafe, do not leave angry." He turned to Alex. "Poor lad. I could not help but laugh."

"He was mortified, Galeron," Alex said, helping him secure Jac to the horse. "The white of his bewildered eyes against his muddy face was a sight I shan't soon forget."

"We must swallow our teasing before he decides to shove us into the same mess." One of the men retrieved Jac's armor from the carriage.

"Galeron." Alex pulled him aside. "Ramstone is still a day's ride. We could wait out the storm." He pointed toward the trees. "'Tis the last shelter 'tween here and home."

Galeron said naught. Alex waited. Thunder crackled through the silence.

"Galeron? What say you?"

"Damnation, have your way!" Galeron turned, avoiding the shock on Alex's face. "Mount up!" he shouted to the men.

Alex followed Galeron's path to his horse. "*My way*? You are acting like a cornered boar."

Galeron tied the horse bearing Jac to his own. Without responding to Alex, he kicked his foot in the stirrup and swung into his saddle. Galeron raised his arm, his muscles twitching with unspent energy. Pointing wordlessly toward the shelter of the forest, he kicked his steed into motion. He bowed against the storm. 'Twas the very place he wished to avoid. He entered the trees and welcomed the relief from the downpour. The men's good-natured banter halted each time Alex called out to him. To his relief, his brother finally gave up as they delved deeper into the forest. Rafe approached him as he dismounted in the clearing.

"Galeron, what shall I do first?"

"What do you think? Build a blasted fire!" Galeron kicked the soggy leaves. Ruby's makeshift bed was but a matted spot now. He was cursed. 'Twas a vain task to banish the reminders of his forest nymph. He glanced up at Alex's arrival and untied the sheepskin keeping Jac dry. "Help me get him down."

Alex eyed him as they lowered Jac onto the bedroll. "What ails you?" he asked, checking Jac's bandages. "Your temper has free rein as of late."

Blowing a great breath, Galeron offered his hand and pulled Alex to his feet. "Am I forgiven?"

"Aye, from the first curse to the last."

Galeron forced a chuckle and ignored the reminder of how he had kissed Ruby on the spot they now stood. "Where is Rafe?"

"I am stoking a fire, as you ordered."

"Is he still angry about how we laughed at him?"

"Nay, your foul mood shocked it out of him." With that, the brothers chuckled.

Rafe arrived with an armload of branches and began arranging them.

"Mind you are not too close to the bed of leaves," Galeron said. "They still could catch despite the rain. It's dry here." He stated the obvious, but hoped to start a conversation with Rafe to ease the tension.

Rafe frowned. "All you have me do is build fires. I suppose I am the expert. You need not direct on how to go about it."

"Very well, Knight of Fire. It seems the rain washed the mud off your face. 'Tis a shame it did not do the same for the scowl." Galeron walked away with Rafe's jovial curses and Alex's laughter fading behind him. Instead of spending time with his brothers, he kicked off his boots and stretched out on his bedroll, far away from Ruby's tree. Damn, he was reduced to naming things after her. Though his muscles jittered and longed for rest, Galeron knew his avoidance was due to his troubled mind. With fingers laced behind his head, he gave into the memory the fire's warmth evoked. Closing his eyes, he relaxed at the thought of Ruby snuggling beside him. He prayed for a dreamless sleep.

Chapter Twelve

Alterations and Sighs

Ruby and Sarah followed Easton out of the shoppe. The painting of children still haunted her. Could it be she had a child? Perchance she had painted a likeness? Easton interrupted her thoughts.

"You shall make an excellent nursemaid."

Ruby hid her confusion with a smile. "I haven't the position yet, Easton."

"Dear child, you acquired the position with the first sparkle in Myles' eyes earlier. There is but the formality of meeting with Palmer."

Ruby absently nodded, trying to force the incessant bud of memory to full bloom. A child. She was sure of it. Well, almost.

"Palmer shall welcome the offer, Ruby. 'Tis not a reason to frown," Easton said.

Ruby shrugged, grateful Easton did not notice her distraction, though Sarah delivered a squint filled with concern. "Where are we off to now?" she asked, starting down the lane.

"There is little time before the wedding and still you have not been measured, so I suppose that should be the next stop," Easton said.

Her footsteps faltered.

"Ruby fell in love with one of my dresses. I already had my maid take up the hem. Therefore, nay fitting today!" Sarah said, full of false cheer.

Again, Easton did not seem to notice. Ruby figured his focus lay in more pressing matters, for he was eyeing the tavern while they walked.

"Very well, but stop to inquire about yours, Sarah. It should be ready." He stopped at the door of the seamstress, still looking down the lane. "I have business to tend to. I shall see you when we meet Palmer." Hands in pockets, he strolled on. A tavern maid waved from the doorway of the establishment.

"Let us get this done with," Sarah said.

While Sarah tried on her garment, Ruby whispered through the hanging. "I regret you fabricated a tale for me. You are a dear friend."

She stepped out and turned so Ruby could lace up the back. "I could not bear to see you suffer through a fitting for the wedding. 'Tis the least I can do to ease your heartache."

"Naught but the passing of time shall ease that. I have nay choice but to accept Galeron's upcoming nuptials." Ruby smiled, but the thought stung her heart like an angry wasp. The pain echoed in Sarah's eyes. She must cease her self-pity. 'Twas hurting her friend as well. Ruby took a deep breath. "You must not speak of my love for Galeron."

"I shan't."

"My heart shall heal. Do not fret. I shall stand strong." Just the same, a tear escaped. She quickly wiped it.

"But 'tis so unfair." She pouted at Ruby's stern frown. "Very well, your secret shall remain safe."

"We must cease this nonsense. Here comes the seamstress. She is sure to report our tears to Easton—sniff it up!" She hoped Sarah couldn't detect the strain in her laughter.

After the final adjustments, Ruby waited while Sarah changed. Sarah excused the seamstress and turned in front of Ruby. "Fasten me up?" She wrinkled her nose. "She tightens them too much."

Ruby pulled on the lacings. "Tell me when it is to your liking."

She looked over her shoulder. "Do you think Easton is at the art shoppe yet?"

"He is probably still at the tavern."

"The *tavern*?"

Ruby wiggled her eyebrows. "A woman, quite beautiful I might add, greeted him at the door." Her grin blossomed. "Whatever could he be up to?"

"Business to tend to indeed!" Sarah sniffed. "He wastes his money on harlots." She looked over her shoulder again. "A bit tighter, if you please."

Ruby yanked on the lacings.

"Too much." She grunted. "Loosen them!"

Laughing, Ruby made a final adjustment. "Shall we have a peek in the tavern doors?"

"Perish the thought!" Sarah stepped outside. "Mayhap Palmer is back."

Ruby walked in the opposite direction, thoroughly enjoying teasing her friend. "'Tis a bit early. Let us visit Easton." Her laughter made several villagers take notice when Sarah hooked on to her arm and swung her full circle in the direction of the art shoppe.

Ruby did not miss Palmer's wink while he hung one of her paintings in the window. The child in the meadow. She had almost decided not to bring it. The day she'd painted it brought mixed feelings, all of them unsettling.

Sarah poked her head in the doorway. "We hoped to find you here."

"Did you now?" Palmer's grin lit his face. "You just missed my father. He left to meet Easton at the tavern." He tipped his head a bit to meet Ruby's eyes. "I, however, never visit the establishment."

"'Tis of nay consequence to me where you visit." Ruby winced at a sharp jab from Sarah. "I see one of my paintings is in the window. My thanks."

Palmer smiled. "My pleasure, Ruby of the Forest."

"Ruby will do."

"I plan on hanging the others, but that is my favorite," he said, pointing, "You captured the essence of the child's joy without showing the little one's face."

Aye, only because she failed to recall it. "My thanks." The familiarity still tore at her, remaining just out of reach.

"Ah, 'tis one of my favorites as well," Sarah said. "It amazes me how you can create a soulful feeling with just a few strokes of your brush."

Heat flooded her face. "I never know what I am going to create until I begin to paint. 'Tis as if I am a tool to a higher power." She switched the subject to business. "Do you believe they will sell? I hope to earn my way here in the village."

"I do not think *any* of your paintings shall stay in my shoppe for long." He cleared his throat. "Father mentioned your interest in moving to the village. That pleases me."

"I only have an interest in the position of nursemaid." She sidestepped, narrowly missing another jab from Sarah.

Palmer chuckled. "How fortunate! I am in dire need of someone to watch over my son, Jadon."

"Stop teasing, Palmer," Sarah said. "Myles told you, did he not?"

"Aye, that he did." He directed them to sit at a table along the wall. "I have a dwelling to make up the meager pay."

"You dare not suggest I live with you." Ruby's hope vanished.

"Of course not." His cheeks colored as he shifted in his seat. "In there. I mean, you would—there is a room in the back." He glanced at the door along the back wall. "It has the luxury of an inner fire pit."

Sarah stilled Ruby's drumming fingers. "How secure is a back room for a maiden, alone, nay less?"

"Your worry is for naught. The seamstress, Dianna, has lived alone since her husband died."

"Dianna? The oldest woman in the village?" Sarah ignored Ruby's kick under the table.

"She is not that old." Palmer leaned forward. "What of *young* Mary? She has been living above the draper's shoppe for nearly two years. She has never encountered trouble."

"That may be so, but still." She took Ruby's hand. "You should tell him."

Ruby blinked "About Mary? I have never met her."

Sarah rolled her eyes. "About your, um…loss."

"Oh, *that*." She wanted to cuff her for the blatant attempt to thwart her chances. She sighed. "Palmer, I do not know of my past."

Before Palmer could respond, Sarah added, "She has nay memory."

"If that poses a problem, then I shan't take any more of your time." Ruby stood to go.

"Easton already relayed that fact to my father." His slow smile eased her tension and she sat back down. "My father spoke highly of you. His word is all I require to assure that you are fit for the position."

"Excellent!" Ruby clasped her hands on her lap to keep from applauding. She made it a point to ignore Sarah. "One final matter, Palmer. I wish to apologize for my rudeness the last time we met."

"Oh, for the way you met my honorable advances with the slam of my own door?" Palmer finished for her.

"Aye, for that."

"Your eyes, though beautiful, were full of ire." He shook his head. "What caused you to direct it toward me?"

"I did not direct it at you." 'Twas a blatant lie and she had not a doubt he was aware of it. She swallowed hard, picked a drip of wax from the candle and rolled it between her fingers. "Forgiven?"

"Certainly." He smiled.

Ruby placed her hands in her lap. "Very well." And it was. Unfortunately, Sarah would need to be convinced.

"Are you certain she will be safe?" Sarah said.

"Ruby is a known friend of your family, Sarah. Nay a soul would dare step past *that* boundary." Palmer did not wait for a response and drummed his finger on the table. "Ruby, the position entails caring for Jadon until he retires for the night. All evenings shall be free to do as you please."

"Would you escort her back here at the end of each day?" Sarah asked.

"Nay need for that," Ruby said, at the same time Palmer said he would.

Palmer cleared his throat. "Well, just the same. I shall ensure you are home safe." She took a breath and slowly let it out, itching to tell him she could take care of herself. Something in his eyes told her it was no use. Assuming her silence as agreement, he continued. "Should you decide to take on the task, I ask you to start as soon as possible."

They all looked up to the door opening. Palmer came to his feet. Easton and Myles entered with a young child in tow.

"I stopped by but the seamstress informed me you had already left." Easton kissed the top of Sarah's head. "We thought we might find you here."

Ruby hardly heard him. The timid glance the child gave her broke her heart. She smiled, but he clutched Myles' hand tighter. Hair the color of summer corn brushed his brow, obscuring the blue eyes peering from beneath. She made a silly face and the corners of his mouth twitched into an uncertain smile.

Palmer opened his arms and the child rushed into them. He sat, positioning the lad on his lap. "Jadon, this is Ruby."

She sensed his shyness and spoke first. "Sir Jadon, 'tis a pleasure to meet such a gallant young man."

His bashfulness cracked, then shattered into an impish grin. "Sir Jadon! 'Tis like a knight! I am to be a knight, Papa says so."

Ruby glanced up at Palmer. "Well, Papa is always right, is he not? I am most certain you shall make a brave knight."

"I am four years." Looking down, he whispered, "I am not brave yet."

Ruby focused on winning the lad's smile again. "Well, Sir Jadon, there are many types of bravery. I can see you have a brave heart."

Jadon's eyes grew wide. "You can *see* my brave heart?"

She stifled a grin. "I can indeed."

"I already see you shall be good for him." Palmer took her hand. For the first time, she did not even wish to pull it away. "When shall I clear the back room?"

Ruby looked at everyone, giving the longest gaze to Sarah. "I have yet to accept the position, Palmer." She rose. Though she wished to accept on the spot, she wanted to give Sarah a bit of time to warm to the idea.

"You shall make a wonderful nursemaid, Ruby," Sarah whispered.

Heaven rained down, sprinkling Sarah's blessing over her. Despite how badly she craved this, she knew she would not take it if it tore their friendship. "You think so?"

One shake of her head. Two. Then a smile. "Aye. I do."

"Consider the position filled, Palmer." Her pulse quickened at the finality of the change in her fate. *Angels above, remind me why I am doing this.*

Myles swung Jadon out of Palmer's lap and into the air. "What do you think of that, little one? Ruby is to be your nursemaid." Jadon gave a sidelong glance at her while whispering in his grandfather's ear. Myles burst into a hearty laugh. "Aye, she is a beautiful nursemaid indeed!"

More and more, she found herself touching her scar anytime someone mentioned her looks, now being no exception. She pulled a bit of hair to cover it.

"I shall close early to celebrate!" Palmer latched the door. "Let me show you your new abode." He opened the door to the back room.

Ruby peered in, wrinkling her nose at the dusty shelves. A rat. Was it staring at her? She hurriedly closed the door. "I shall clean it straight away."

"I will not hear of it!" Palmer said. "I shall have it ready by morn."

"The morrow then." She accepted a mug of mead from Myles. Her new home. For now. Her heart shall remain unrequited, but it seemed she would make her way nonetheless. Ruby raised her mug. "To the greeting of a new life!" And mayhap, the recollection of her old one. She took a huge swallow in hopes the sweet mead would dull her pain.

Ruby dozed on the way back to Ramstone, never thinking the second mug of mead would make her so woozy. She went upstairs as soon as they arrived and brushed the dust off her clothes before the evening meal. After splashing the cool water on her face, she placed her hands on each side of the washbasin and stared at her reflection. "Stand strong, woman, you have nay choice but to move on."

Though excitement pulsed through her, a certain dread lingered near. With a flounce of hair over her shoulder, she headed downstairs.

She watched Sarah roll a parsnip across her plate while Easton talked about something… She wanted to stab her fork into the incessant rolling vegetable to cease Sarah's dark mood.

"Do you plan on eating that?" Easton asked. She grinned at the fact that she was not the only one who noticed Sarah toying with her food.

Sarah shrugged. "The empty seats around this table are beginning to wear on me." She put down her fork. "The men have been gone too long. Why haven't they sent a rider to tell of any delay?"

Easton took a swig of ale and wiped his mouth. "Delay could be for many a good reason. Do not fret." He stabbed a piece of roast pig with his knife and stuffed it in his mouth.

Sarah nodded. Ruby looked from Easton to Sarah several times. "Sarah, you are satisfied with such an answer?"

Easton choked on his mouthful and quickly washed it down with another swig. Sarah stared at her for a moment then resumed rolling the parsnip.

She slowly rose, clutching the table to keep from throwing something, preferably the parsnip. "Very well, keep your silence, but 'tis not satisfactory to me." She placed her palms on the table and leaned closer to Easton. "I am not blind to the worry in your eyes. I do not expect you to know the reason for the delay, but do not deny it has been too long. Most of all, refrain from telling us *not to fret*." She threw her linen cloth next to her plate. "'Tis insulting."

Tears filled her eyes. Mixed emotions — the newness of venturing outside Ramstone, worries about Galeron and now her outburst, crumbled her brave front. She fled the room, ignoring their calls. She did not stop until her back pressed against her chamber door. A tub, steaming with invitation, sat in the middle of the room. Easton. Remorse filled her.

"I am horrid." She jumped at a knock on the door. "I do not deserve such kindness." Ignoring the insistent tap as long as she could, she finally opened it. Sarah laid a comforting hand on her shoulder.

"Easton is concerned for you. I told him 'twas because you are leaving, but I have a notion the reason you are so upset lies elsewhere."

Ruby stared at the trunk sitting in the middle of the room. One trunk, filled with expectations of a new life. One heart, empty and broken when she departs. "Too much has transpired."

Sarah nodded slowly. "Your heart shall rest in time." She changed the subject. "I was horrid to Easton."

"You were *right*. Easton said so."

She shook her head. "I doubt that."

"Indeed. He even pointed out several possible reasons for the delay. Galeron's—his, um…"

"Betrothed? Simply say it."

Sarah spoke quickly, as if doing so would make it less painful. "She may have hindered the progress by bringing others with her."

"Aye, he mentioned that before." Ruby picked up the lavender soap and sniffed it. "Do you think I can take some of this with me?"

"Easton also said Rafe may have slowed them. This is the first time he has accompanied them."

Ruby grimaced.

"That is a lame excuse," Sarah admitted.

"Which is why I became so frustrated when he said not to fret. Something is wrong."

Sarah took the bar of soap from Ruby and sat it on the edge of the tub. "I believe he was impressed with your little speech."

Ruby bit back worry for her sake. "I had nay right to speak to him like that. A lord! I tend to forget that. Oh, Sarah, I am mortified."

"*He* isn't, for *Lord* Easton insisted I come and assure you are well. Oh, and that he shall see you once you have rested." Sarah pointed to the steaming tub. "That seems the perfect place to do so."

"Well, if I *must*." Ruby offered a weak grin.

Sarah nodded and tossed a drying cloth to her. "Enjoy. The morrow shall bring many changes for us both." She turned to leave, then looked over her shoulder, worry creasing her brow. "Pray for them."

"Every single night," Ruby said.

As soon as Sarah left, Ruby shrugged out of her clothes then stepped into the tub. She lowered slowly, hissing at the heat, but soon her skin got used to it. The water rippled between her fingers while she rested her head on the edge. Her whisper permeated the air. "Once more, I wish to feel your warmth when you kiss me. Ah, but one more heartbeat, Galeron, one chance at a lifetime with you." Ruby watched the firelight flickering across the ceiling until the water chilled.

Soon, her hair dry from the fire, her night-rail wrapped about her knees, she struggled with her prayer. "Lord, I dare not ask for Galeron's return to me...but bring him home—bring them *all* home safe. Ease Sarah's worries and grant dreams of comfort through the night." She blew a long breath. "I know not if I have a right to pray for myself, however, I ask but for a portion of memory, be it small or grand." Anger, fear and frustration coursed through her, and her hands unfolded, only to fist. "Is it your will that I remain adrift? Is it a punishment for something I have done? Is it?" She looked about the room, almost waiting to be struck for her blasphemous behavior. "I pray forgiveness. Amen," she hastily added before climbing into the bed.

She embraced the comfort of the darkness and pulled the hangings closed. Arms wrapped about her legs, she allowed a final cry before fleeing heartache in the respite of sleep.

Chapter Thirteen

Lament

Alex touched Sir Jac's brow. "Damnation, he is still fevered."

Rafe and Galeron abandoned the task of loading the horse and went to them. Galeron brought a drink to Jac's mouth. Delirious with fever, Jac slapped away Galeron's hand. "Find them! Go!" Jac shouted.

"His thrashing is causing the wound to bleed anew," Alex said, above Jac's shouts.

Galeron held Jac down. "Get on with it."

Alex tore at the knight's tunic, cleaned the pus oozing from the wound, all the while, Jac's tortured shouts echoed. "Flee *now*. Dare not stop!" He grabbed Alex. "God in heaven, Mara, you cannot fight them any longer." Jac's voice, though weakened, screamed of terror.

Galeron suffered a twist of remorse at his betrothed's name. Jac's eyes glazed and he fluttered into unconsciousness. Alex applied a cool cloth to his brow and rewrapped Jac's wounds.

Rafe gripped Alex's shoulder. "He clings to life. 'Tis due to you, brother."

Alex shook his head. "Credit belongs to the Lord above."

"He always says that. 'Tis due to Alex." Galeron ruffled Rafe's hair. He snatched up the knight's bloodied tunic, dunked it in the water and draped it over a bush. Pulling one of his own tunics from his pack, he called to Alex, "Here, this should fit him."

The two of them maneuvered Jac's limp body, helping Rafe pull the tunic on him.

"Careful, do not disturb his bandages," Alex said.

Rafe frowned. "I am not a fool. I would not do that."

"You were not dubbed a fool," Galeron said. "Alex, he survived seven days of this journey. How do you think he shall fare the remainder? We can be at Ramstone within a day's time."

Alex shook his head. "He cannot survive another day across the back of a horse."

Galeron rose and looked around the clearing. "We could construct a travois."

"Too rough a ride," Alex said.

"Hmph." Galeron stared at Rafe, deep in thought.

"What?" Rafe scrambled up and faced him.

Gods, the lad tried too hard to please. "I am mulling over whether to leave you with Alex or bring you with me."

Rafe shifted from one foot to the other. "I choose to come with you."

He grinned at the hopeful expression on his young face. "I need muscle to free the carriage from the mud. I shall only choose the burliest of men," Galeron teased.

"I am as strong as you."

His smile widened.

"Nearly," Rafe said.

Galeron gave a sharp nod, his mind made up. "Tell the men to ready."

Rafe set off. He tripped on tree roots and glanced back to see if anyone witnessed it.

Galeron was quick to hide his mirth. "He is as clumsy as you were at a young age," he whispered to Alex. "I fail to recall…when did you finally grow into your feet?"

"The day of my first battle."

"Aye…well." He raked his hair from his brow. "I do not wish to leave you here alone with Jac, but I haven't a choice. 'Twill take the muscle of the few men we do have."

"Fret not. You shall be back soon enough." Alex followed him to his steed. "God carry thee, brother."

"May He be with you also," Galeron said, his eye on Rafe mounting his horse, his blond hair untethered and swishing into his eyes.

Galeron swung into the saddle and motioned for his youngest brother to sidle up beside him. He laughed outright when he cantered toward him with a beam of pride on his face.

"Give the order to proceed."

Rafe's eyebrows shot up. "Me?"

Galeron nodded. He stifled the whim to laugh when Rafe had to shout twice to get the men's attention. "I *said* proceed! We are to retrieve the carriage."

With a stern look ahead, Galeron led them to the trampled path they had forged the night before.

* * * *

Alex heaved a chuckle and Galeron realized what a sight they must be with mud-plastered faces. Their clothing was crusted with more of the same, residual clumps that matched the horses' legs, but they had pulled the carriage free of the muck. Alex shook his head. "Stop smiling, Galeron. Your teeth are blinding against your mud mask."

"Smells like you're burning it," Galeron pointed to the food and strode to the creek.

"Just your portion, brother," Alex shouted after him.

With a stream of water trickling from his fingers, Galeron washed his face and nudged Rafe. "You did well. I am proud of you." Rafe flashed a smile and shot a scoop of water at him. "For that, you shall pay, water rat!" Galeron shoved him into the creek. He ignored his little brother's shouts and dunked his own head into the water. Rafe was still uttering a stream of curses through his laughter when Galeron left the creek, shaking water from his long locks.

"You're a bastard brute, Galeron. You shake like a wet cur!"

"Why do you find it necessary to do that?" Alex grinned, brushing the drops away when Galeron stood above him. Galeron wiped his sleeve across his face and answered with only a chuckle. "I say, is your light mood due to the greeting of a meal?" Alex asked, handing him a portion of the rabbit.

"Aye, could very well be." Galeron sat, ripped it from the bone, and stuffed it in his mouth. He had dined on the same feast with Ruby at this very spot.

Rafe sat beside his brothers with a soggy thud. "You arse. That water is freezing."

Galeron nudged him off the log.

Alex grinned. "Here, have some rabbit, boy."

Galeron shook his flask at Rafe. "This should warm you."

Rafe got back on the log and accepted the rabbit. He chewed, eyeing the flask. Finally he snatched it and pulled a long swig. Though his eyes watered, he did not give Galeron the satisfaction of choking on it. "How do you *drink that*?"

"In moderation. Do not get used to it, Rafe."

"Nay danger in that," he said.

Alex took the flask and downed a swallow. "He is too young, anyway." He held it out to Galeron. Rafe intercepted it. Galeron snatched it before Rafe could squeeze out a mouthful. "Enough. Fetch a drink from the creek."

Rafe strode off. "'Tis horrid anyway."

Once the men had eaten their fill, they carefully transferred Sir Jac to the carriage. Galeron mounted and looked up when the sun filtered through the branches. "Finally! The skies have blessed us with a kiss of warmth."

"Ah, the great poet speaks," Alex mumbled, climbing into the carriage.

Galeron shot a frown before calling back to the men. "Move out!"

By the time they reached the hilly terrain, the sun had quelled the dampness of the ground.

"I began to doubt the carriage would make it," Rafe said.

"I, as well." Galeron glanced at the carriage. "Fall back and check how our brother is faring with the knight." Left to himself, Galeron allowed thoughts of Ruby to fill him. The idea of simply seeing her again carried hope. Heartache bobbed to the surface and sneered at him. He supposed 'twas more of a burden of hopeless yearning. He turned at the whinny of Rafe's horse.

"Sir Jac remains the same."

Dead or not, Rafe sounded so much like their uncle Zane, Galeron took pause. It had been many years since he thought of him. "Is your voice deepening?"

Rafe steadied his horse. "W-what?"

Galeron shook his head. "You reminded me of...never mind. What did you just say about Sir Jac?"

Rafe rested his forearms on the horse's mane. "I said, he is the same, nay better, nay worse. Are you...well?"

He ignored the question. "We shall head to the comfort of Ramstone. Rafe, you have done well. You shall ride with me now."

Rafe's eyes widened. "Not in the back with the men? I am to finally become a leader?"

"Easy there, Rafe. You still need to earn that position...long after I am gone." Galeron stared straight ahead. "But you can ride with Alex and me from time to time."

Rafe shook his head. "Damnation!"

Galeron gave him a sideways glance. He had grown into a fine young man. Why did he not realize it before now?

"Galeron?" Rafe's brow furrowed. "'Tis not fitting to call me young one anymore."

"I suppose not." The corners of Galeron's mouth twitched. Rafe reined back and turned his horse. Had he insulted him? "Rafe, wait. Where are you headed?"

"Back to ride with Alex for a bit."

Galeron shrugged. "Be off then."

"Ah, I shall return." Rafe flashed a straight row of teeth. "To ride alongside you."

Chapter Fourteen

Settlement

Ruby ceased her nervous chatter when the carriage stopped in front of them. She looked at the single trunk at her feet and glanced up at Sarah. "The time has come."

"Is that all you are bringing?"

"Aye, my friend, 'tis all I own." She smiled. "Most is what you gave me."

"Your art supplies." Sarah started for the door. "I shall fetch them."

"I have everything." Yet, she had naught. She dared not meet Sarah's eyes. She watched the servants load her chest atop the carriage, blinking to dam her tears.

"All set, milord." The male servant bowed before Easton and left.

Easton opened the door and motioned to Ruby. She pulled up the hem of her skirt and stepped into the carriage. When Easton and Sarah settled in, Ruby frowned at their brooding faces. She grabbed hold when the carriage lurched. "Oh! The horses surely anticipate the freedom of the road."

Easton nodded. Sarah stared out of the window. For a time, Ruby watched the scene of the countryside unfold. The trees joined in the colors of autumn, and some even bared their branches to the upcoming winter. The soft orange leaves contrasted against the evergreens. She tucked each shade into memory and hoped to recreate them with her paints.

"The countryside is beautiful." Though she had not asked a question, the lack of response from the others struck her. She could not tolerate the silence any longer. "Pray tell, why the somber mood? I shan't be but a short ride away." She sighed at their blank looks. "I am prone to read more into your silence than what is on your minds." She looked from one to the other. "Hell's teeth! Speak out. Your silence weighs heavy on me."

Easton's face brightened, his eyes crinkling with a smile. "Aye, dear Ruby, you may wish to refrain from such curses in the village."

"I am not one to refrain."

Sarah's slow smile encouraged Ruby. "'Tis what I shall miss the most."

Easton placed his hand over Sarah's. "I as well." He looked away, his voice barely carrying over the creaks of the carriage. "I shall miss the laughter you brought to Ramstone."

Sarah began to weep. Holding her tear-streaked face in her hands, Ruby fought the urge to cry. "You are my chosen sister, my truest friend. Nay distance can alter that. We can see each other *anytime* we choose."

Sarah accepted the handkerchief Easton offered, patted the corners of her eyes, then gave Ruby a faint smile. "You are my only sister, only sibling at all really.

In my early years, loneliness followed me, for I was an only child. The constant reminder of not being the son my father craved certainly did not help." Sarah sighed. "I do not mean that as it sounds. He loved me fiercely, but I know he wanted a son as well. Secretly, I wished for a sister, though, someone I could share secrets with." She cleared her throat. "What I am trying to say is, 'twas worth the delay to have such a dear sister now."

"Ah, dear sibling, I do so love your rambling." Ruby squeezed her hand.

The remainder of the ride passed quickly, filled with unfettered conversation. Upon arriving at the outskirts of the village, Sarah pressed something into her palm. She began to question it, but Sarah silenced her with a hard squeeze. She slipped the parcel into her pocket and gave a furtive wink.

Myles and Palmer met them when they stepped from the carriage. Palmer scrambled to the top and lowered the trunk to the driver and Myles. He wiped his brow and called down. "We would like to offer the evening meal at Father and Mother's."

Lord Easton retrieved the wool blanket Sarah insisted on bringing. "Once Ruby is settled, we shall join you. Our thanks for the kind offer."

The men grasped the handles of the trunk and motioned the woman ahead. They weaved to the back of the shoppe. Ruby paused in front of the door. With a quirk of her eyebrow, she grinned. "You ready?"

"Aye," Sarah said. "Get on with it."

Ruby threw open the door with a flourish. "Oh." She scanned the room. "Palmer certainly cleared the room as promised! It looks...roomier."

"'Tis due to the lack of furnishings." Sarah ignored Easton's whispered warning and pointed as she spoke. "There is but that tiny table and two chairs along that wall and a chair over there. And I believe that one is broken."

Ruby rolled her eyes. "I have eyes of my own, Sarah. And it is not broken. It's cracked a bit, that is all."

"*This* is to be your bed?" Sarah sat on the cot and stared at Ruby.

"How thoughtful of Palmer to bring it in." She frowned at the click of Sarah's tongue. "The bed is sufficient."

"Oh my, we are going to have a time readying this for you to live in. 'Tis so barren."

"All I require is a bed to lay my head and a fire for warmth." She outstretched her arms and smiled. "I have both."

Sarah looked at the splintered floor and wrinkled her nose. "You have naught."

What had happened to her belief in this venture? Her blessing for the opportunity for Ruby to live on her own? She opened the shutters. "Ah, fresh air."

"'Twill not lend proper light at all. How will you paint?" Sarah picked up the washbasin on the small table by the bed. "Not quite the tub for soaking in, is it?"

Ruby sat upon the mattress of wrapped straw and crossed her arms.

"You shall require a proper feather mattress and a fur to place upon your floor." Sarah finally noticed Ruby's scowl. "What?"

"Can you not find one positive thing to comment on?"

Sarah looked around. "I am hard-pressed to find much." She pointed to the hearth. "At least you have the luxury of warmth and a place to cook."

She delivered a crooked grin while Sarah swung out the hook. "You could hang your pot over the fire."

"Pray tell, what pot? I do not own one." She smiled at Sarah's nervous giggle and hurried over with a hug. "All is well. I have a gift of making even the drab seem beautiful." She frowned, wondering what made her say such a thing. Was it true? Did she have an impatient memory waiting to be discovered, then arising on its own?

"This?" Sarah outstretched her arms. "This dusty, old abode beautiful? Please, just come home to Ramstone. We can transport you here each day."

"*This* is my home, Sarah."

Both of them turned at the rap on the door. "I understand you want the best for me," she said, her hand on the handle. "This is the best...for now." She opened the door leading to the art shoppe.

"May we enter?" Easton peered in. "Is there room?"

Argh. Ruby bit the inside of her cheek and motioned them in.

Myles and Palmer placed the trunk by the cot. Easton tossed the wool blanket on the mattress and placed his hands on his hips.

Palmer finally broke the silence crowding the small quarters. "There is an easel in the shoppe. As agreed, you are welcome to use any supplies you will require for your painting." He walked to the fireplace. "I cleaned this out for you. There is a pot behind that hanging." He pointed to the corner.

"A pot to cook in." Ruby glanced at Sarah. "The dwelling is perfect."

Sarah delivered an unladylike snort.

Easton glared at her. "You will stay to help Ruby unpack?"

"Of course." Sarah offered a weak smile.

Palmer stepped closer. "I shall close for the day so you will not be interrupted. I anticipate seeing you again at the evening meal." He bowed, his lips on her hand.

Disgusted at the warmth of his tongue, Ruby shoved her hand against his teeth. "Until then." *He dares that again and he shall wear the meal.*

Still nursing his mouth, Palmer left the room. "I shall lock up."

"Myles, shall we share a drink at the tavern?" Easton asked.

"Ah, my friend, I should get home. However, there is ample time before the meal for you to go."

Easton smiled. "Until then."

Sarah glared at their backs until they were out of sight. "Enjoy himself indeed. 'Tis not only a drink he shall partake in. He is—"

"A man. He is partaking in nay wrong. Unlike a cad with a wandering eye and devilish tongue." Ruby glanced at the movement in the doorway. Palmer raised his brow. Ruby's face warmed at her gaffe. "Could you close the shutters out front?" She noticed faces peering in the shoppe. "I seem to be the topic among their minds."

"Mine as well." Palmer stepped into her room and shut the door. "One man was bold enough to come into the shoppe to catch a glimpse of you. I escorted him out and latched the door."

"The shutters?" she reminded.

"Ruby!" Sarah shook her head. "What is it you need, Palmer?"

"I wanted to show you a few things before I go." Palmer gave a makeshift tour, pointing out the use for each area of the room.

Ruby pitched her eyes to the ceiling. Sarah giggled, quickly covering her mouth when Palmer glanced over. He proceeded to show how to secure the back door, all the while assuring Ruby she would be safe. "Come here, Ruby, this tends to stick." He pulled on the latch. "I can show you how to undo them."

Ruby stayed put. "I am quite capable, Palmer. We shall join you for the evening meal."

Palmer took her dismissal graciously. "As you wish." He bowed and left.

"I thought he would never leave," Ruby whispered. She twirled into the middle of the room, bringing a laugh to Sarah. A bit dizzy, she plopped on the bed, her gaiety frayed by the reminder of Galeron catching her in the forest. The finality of leaving Ramstone, and Galeron along with it, became reality. Had she fooled herself? The departure from Ramstone should free her from the reminder of Galeron. Ah, yet distance failed to blind her mind's eye. Ruby envisioned weathered crinkles at the corner of his blue eyes when he laughed.

"Aye," Ruby said, realizing Sarah was speaking.

"As well as some hangings for the window. I am certain we have some."

Ruby looked at the window. "Some hangings, aye." What she wished for, she could not have. What she searched for remained out of reach. There was nay choice but to make her own way. She detected another pause and turned to Sarah. "Aye."

"Oh, Ruby, you have not listened to a word I have said. If you say aye again, I shall be forced to...to do something."

She grinned. "Pray tell, what might you do?"

Sarah began unpacking the trunk. "You must focus on something besides Galeron."

"I am not even thinking of him."

With a wave of her hand, she continued. "I realize 'tis difficult, but you must stop. Though I did not wish you to leave Ramstone, 'twas a wise decision."

The lump in Ruby's throat stopped any response.

"I could never be as independent as you. You have a strong spirit, even though your heart is—"

"Cease this talk." Ruby swallowed.

"I wish Galeron wasn't betrothed."

"Yet, he is." She took a cloak from Sarah's arms and hung it on a peg near the bed. "I cannot control how I feel about him, nay matter what strength I possess."

Sarah handed her a painting, wrapped in linen. "Which one is this?"

Ruby propped it on the chipped mantle. "You have not seen this one. It depicts the morn we tangled ourselves in a mess of skirts. I believe I captured the laughter and friendship." She turned. Sarah's eyes were brimming with tears. "Each morn, I shall wake to this painting and begin my day with a smile."

"You are a gem, dear friend. The name Ruby fits you well. My doubts about this dwelling." She held an imaginary wand. "Vanished. The humor this painting casts makes it brighter. I absolutely love the way you captured our silliness."

* * * *

Hours of toil reflected in the new abode. The setting sun bathed the room in a soft light. "Ah, the back room is now transformed into my home." Ruby turned at the loud rapping on the back door.

Sarah grabbed Ruby's arm. "Dare not answer that."

The rap became more insistent. Ruby pulled a pitcher from the shelf, looked at it then traded it for a carving knife. "Dearest, please stop leaving your sword lying about. Oh, and will you answer the door? I am busy carving this meat with that big knife you sharpened."

Easton's laughter rose above her shout. "My hands are full, open the door!"

Ruby giggled and unlatched the door. "Easton, you could have said that to start with." Eyeing the baskets on his arms, she clapped her hands. "Ah! Fruit, vegetables, even a loaf of *bread*!"

He placed the baskets on the table. "You have done well with the room!"

"Fine indeed," Sarah said.

Easton shook his finger in a mock scold. "Send word if you are in need of anything, Ruby." His grin faded. "You are one of the family. We have grown to love you."

It was Ruby's turn to be speechless.

Easton cleared his throat. "Shall we take leave for Myles' abode?"

"Certainly!" He handed Ruby her cloak. She paused in the doorway and looked into the room. A smile of contentment spread through her. Mayhap she could be happy here.

* * * *

The meal went well, and after a tearful goodbye, Ruby was alone in front of the shoppe, waving at the departing carriage until it was out of sight. Upon latching her door, she shuttered her window and lit a candle. The flicker dispelled the shadows around the table, but not her mood. Keeping her promise to wait to unwrap the parcel Sarah had given her, she pulled it from her pocket. Corner by corner, she folded back the silk wrapping.

"Ah!" The candlelight shone through the ruby gemstone. Tears blurred the sparkle while she slipped the ring on her finger. It was a perfect fit.

Chapter Fifteen

Return to Ramstone

Sarah watched the sparks from the fire zigzag and float up. She sat on the hearth, hugging the nightshirt he had worn the night before his departure. "I cannot bear another night without you beside me." She paced the length of her chamber, wrapping the nightshirt around her shoulders. "Where are you? Why haven't you sent a message?"

Without Ruby as a distraction, she filled her days worrying incessantly about Alex. She quit inquiring about his delay and Easton refrained from talking of it. Sarah opened the window and whispered into the cool night air. "Lord, when I was young, I believed my prayers would hasten when I sent them from my window. I am nay longer that child, but I have tried all else." Her fingers interlocked, pressing divots into her hand. The nightshirt slipped to the ground as she knelt on the window seat and began to pray.

"Open the gates!"

She recognized Galeron's voice and ceased her prayer. The inner ward filled with men. She searched for her husband among them. The sill pressed hard against her waist, for nearly half of her body was straining out of the window. Then she spied Alex's empty saddle.

"Nay. Oh God, nay." Her feet tangled in the nightshirt in her haste to leave. She fell on one knee, ignored the bruising from the stone floor and lurched for the door. Panic pulsed through her while she fled toward the stairs. She grabbed the banister and took a deep breath before making her way to the lower level.

Certain her fears would become real if she uttered another prayer, she only whispered Alex's name. Easton called out to her when she ran through the doorway but she did not wait.

The men had already dismounted when she reached the inner ward. Her breath came in gasps while she elbowed her way through the squires. She felt the warmth of the horses, hoping to see past them. As if in a dream, the moonlight illuminated Alex stepping from the carriage.

"Alex!" Tears of relief blended with her call. She ran, full force, into his arms.

He fell against the carriage, laughing. He placed his lips upon hers before she could utter a word and greedily drank in her welcome.

* * * *

Galeron's eyes rested upon them. He shoved back the memory of the kisses he had shared with Ruby. When a servant lit the torches, Galeron scanned the crowd to find her.

Lord Easton intercepted him in a clasping hug. "Thank God in heaven you have returned unharmed!" His huge grin, replaced by wide-eyed confusion as soon as he peered into the carriage. "Where is your betrothed, Galeron? Who is *that*?"

"Sir Jac." Galeron blew a breath between his lips, the stress of the journey heavy upon him. "Father, there is much to tell." He eyed Sarah. "Mayhap 'tis wise to wait inside."

"Nay, I bore enough waiting." Sarah linked arms with Alex. Galeron knew he should turn away when his brother ran a tongue along Sarah's ear, but it made him smile and lightened his heart.

"Heed his wishes, fair lady, and go inside. I shall be there shortly." Alex nuzzled her neck. "You smell of jasmine. I cannot wait to bed you, woman." Did Alex fail to realize how loud he spoke? It seemed Sarah did, for she gave a playful shove and hurried off.

Galeron watched Sarah until she was out of earshot. Angels above, how he prayed for a life such as theirs. With a mental shake, he focused on the task at hand. "Father, pure evil has thwarted our plans." Weariness infiltrated his voice. "Jac is Mara's brother. Explanations are forthcoming. My principal concern is to tend to him. He still battles death."

"Of course, of course." Easton swung open the door. Glimpsing the mangled Jastar armor on the floor of the carriage, he realized the explanation held no promise of ease. "Where is Rafe?"

"Here, Father," Rafe said, from behind. He nudged his father. "I rode in front with Galeron most of the day."

"Indeed? Very well, son." He met Rafe's eyes. "I am relieved you are unharmed. We worried over the time it took to return."

The inner ward became a flurry of activity. It took no time to bring Jac inside and stable the horses. Everything in order, Easton started when Galeron shouted. "Bolt and guard the gates!"

"Why the extra precaution?"

"Though we have not seen the others on our journey home, I dare not assume our safety." Galeron paced, his father keeping step.

"Others?"

"Aye, with ill will." Galeron watched the inner ward empty. "Go on ahead, I shall join you shortly."

"Very well, but make haste." Easton patted his shoulder and left.

Galeron tried to soak in the contentment of being home, but found it difficult to calm his uneasiness. He gulped the crisp night air. He had nay right to desire her presence, yet he took for granted she would greet him. Galeron wiped his hand over his face and placed his helmet at his feet. The clink of the metal shouted against the silence in the abandoned inner ward.

The emptiness sucked at his soul. His weariness did not allow him to contend with the disappointment flowing over him when he realized Ruby chose to remain indoors. Torn by the responsibility of Mara's demise, he could not deny the days spent away from Ruby failed to diminish the way he felt about her.

The crunch of the pebbled ground beneath his boots echoed in the inner yard. He stopped pacing and looked up at the star-filled sky. Galeron prayed, "I beseech thee Lord, close my heart."

Sarah walked by the open doorway then back-stepped. Galeron faced the night sky, hoping she would leave him on his own. He offered a weak smile when she approached.

"Galeron?" She stooped to pick up his helmet, concern mirrored in her expression. "What are you doing out here alone?"

He took the helmet and propped it under his arm. "Alex must be tending to the knight, or you would not concern thyself with my whereabouts."

"He is. However, I am concerned about something Rafe said."

"Do not fret over Rafe's ranting." Damn lad needed to refrain from speaking around the women.

"He said that knight was the only survivor at Jastar."

"Did he?"

"Aye, but Easton silenced him."

"Did he?" Galeron repeated. He crooked his eyebrow and grinned, but Sarah did not return his smile.

"I see you did not arrive with your betrothed."

Galeron looked up at the stars. "Aye, 'tis apparent."

"Well, 'tis *also* apparent you shall remain as secretive as Alex. I cannot get an explanation out of him either. I suppose he thinks I should be satisfied with the blessing of the safe return, but if you returned without her, does that mean —"

"I trust all was well while we were gone?"

She sighed and stepped closer, but he still did not face her. "You were sorely missed, Galeron. By *all* of us. We were worried."

He looked down at her hand tugging his sleeve. She motioned to the great hall. "Your father awaits. Are you coming inside?"

"You go. I shall join all of you in a moment."

Sarah stomped a foot. "What ails you?"

"I am well, Sarah." He slowly turned his head. "I am enjoying the peacefulness of the night. That is all." Galeron scratched the growth on his face. "I could not help but notice the absence of our houseguest. Has she already retired for the night?"

"You mean Ruby?" She shifted her stance. "She left."

Galeron let his helmet drop to his side. He tapped it several times against his leg. "Why did you and my father allow her to leave?"

"Allow her? Phfft. That woman is as stubborn as you." She met his burning stare. "Do not try that with me, Galeron." She looked away, defeated. "So much happened while you were gone." She paused for a moment, seeming to gather her thoughts. When she spoke again, her voice was tight. "Ruby paints beautifully. Is that not a surprise?" She glanced at him and looked to the stars. "She is now a nursemaid for Palmer's son and lives in the back room of the art shoppe."

He had no words. No breath. He followed her gaze, the stars seemed as far away from him as Ruby did.

Sarah cleared her throat. "You must be exhausted."

Not trusting his voice, he nodded.

"I intend to visit her in the morning." She nudged him. "Galeron?"

Galeron offered a bit of a smile and focused behind her. She turned to see who was venturing into the inner ward, then lifted a questioning brow when no one was there.

"Mayhap we should go inside as you suggest. I long for this night to end." He took Sarah's elbow and led her indoors.

Sarah's words echoed with each foot step, each breath. *She left. She left. She left.* The chorus haunted him, causing his heart to lock everything else out. Damn green-eyed curse. He left Sarah in the doorway and stormed into the great hall.

* * * *

Lord Easton looked up from the table. "We have been—"

"My men still have the dirt from the long journey caked on their clothing. I am eager for the night to end." Galeron poured a drink and passed the pitcher. "Let's get on with this." A flood of reports later, Galeron turned to leave.

"This is not over." Easton sighed. "I know you are weary, but there is more to address." He waited until Galeron sat. "Many neighboring families have arrived for the wedding."

"The blasted wedding is not of concern here," Galeron droned.

Easton frowned. "Many of them are accompanied by knights for protection on their journey. We should not overlook the advantage of their presence among us."

"I suppose we must explain why I arrived without my betrothed," Galeron said. "As well as why they cannot leave here." He glanced at Alex. "How many saw us carry in the wounded knight?"

Alex shrugged. "Not many, but those who did not heard about it. Word spread quickly. They are worried."

Lord Easton rose and paced about the room. "Galeron, send your messengers to the neighboring lands to gather the leaders and their knights here at

Ramstone. Though our ranks are the most powerful in the vicinity, we shall combine armies and make whatever pacts we must to acquire the cooperation of others. It seems Jastar and their neighboring village were taken by surprise. That shall not happen here."

"Do you believe they are headed here?" Rafe shifted in his seat. "We did not come across anyone on the way home."

Galeron's face softened. "Ease your mind, Rafe. Father, I would take this opportunity to say Rafe was of great assistance." Though his uncle Zane was seldom spoken of, Galeron added. "At times he reminded me of your brother."

Easton sat by him and leaned forward, so close his forehead nearly touched Galeron's, his whisper hissing against his face like a viper. "He is naught like him. The man is dead and a good riddance too." He leaned back, his face concealing the hatred. "Rafe, I am proud of you."

Rafe, his smile so big it nearly split his face, puffed his chest. "Father, I learned much. Galeron eventually — "

Easton raised his voice. "As I was saying, we shall build our army. 'Tis our duty to avenge the innocent who were unfortunate enough to fall under their might. We shall hunt them down."

"When will we set out?" Rafe said.

"Soon enough, but tonight you shall rest," Easton said. "Be off, men. We shall commence talk in the morn."

Galeron threw open the doors. He fought the whim to roll his eyes when he saw many of the houseguests milling in the main entry.

"They are looking for answers," Alex said.

Easton addressed the gathering. "I assure your safety. You may remain our guests until 'tis safe to travel." Easton smiled and signaled for the servants to show them to their respective chambers.

"When is the wedding to take place?" a woman's voice called out.

Galeron intercepted the question. "It shan't. Due to the fact there is nay bride. And the man who signed the agreement is since dead." He looked up at a movement. Sarah was descending the stairs. He half expected Ruby to follow. Struck with her absence, he strode outside, ignoring his father's call. The garden hedges took a beating as he passed and he did not stop until he stood in the middle of the path, his breath ragged. He tensed at his father's voice.

"Did you fail to hear me?"

Galeron swung around. "Why did Ruby leave?"

Easton stopped short. "Ruby? What does her departure have to do with anything?"

"Are you responsible for her leaving?"

"What? Nay!" He strode a breath away. "How dare you say what you did in there? You cannot assume—"

"I am leaving to fetch her."

"Who? Ruby?" Easton guided Galeron to the gardens. "Sit. I cannot fathom how you still stand."

Galeron sat, his body aching. "Father, you must understand. I—"

"*You* must understand. You have duties to attend." Easton sat, motioning with his hands. "Dispatch messengers. Send men to guard the village if you must, but you shall stay here tonight. You haven't rested in days."

Galeron gritted his teeth so hard they ached. "I cannot rest until Ruby is safe behind our gates."

Easton sighed, placed his hands on his knees and rose. "If I thought she was in danger, I would have stopped her from going. Allow Ruby to lead her life, Galeron. 'Twas her choice to leave."

Galeron's stomach lurched. "She wished to leave?" Without so much as a fare thee well. He looked across the path when the door opened. Alex waved and started toward them.

"Ah! Here you are. Have you dispatched the messengers yet?" Alex asked.

"Nay." Galeron stormed off without another word, but caught his father order the dispatching of guards to the village.

Chapter Sixteen

Blended Visions

"These colors are for painting, Sir Jadon. They shall make you ill if you eat them." Ruby took his paint-smeared fingers from his mouth and wiped them. "Let us focus on the colors once again, shall we?"

Jadon batted his long lashes and smiled at his new nursemaid. He watched her drip paint onto the parchment and splashed his fingers into each one, proudly identifying them.

"Blue. Green. Red." He pointed at Ruby with drippy fingers. "Like you!"

Ruby laughed and hugged him, disregarding the paint he smeared upon her smock. "Sweet lad, how are those colors like me?"

He pointed a dimpled hand at her smock and said, "Blue." Next, he wrapped one of her curls around his finger. "Red." He cradled her cheeks and placed his forehead to hers. "Green. You have green eyes."

"Little knight, you are very wise. Let us use some of those colors to paint a picture."

She smiled when he handed her a cloth to wipe his handprints from her cheeks. True joy tingled for a moment before the familiar itch of uncertainty stole it away. The boy reminded her of someone. She laid the wadded cloth on the table she'd set up in Palmer's garden. "What would you like to paint?"

Jadon looked about the garden. "Mama loves flowers. The ones I bring her always die. Painted flowers shall live forever." Jadon smiled while tears filled his light blue eyes. "Mama couldn't live forever."

Ruby sighed and cradled Jadon's sad little body in her lap. "Your mama lives forever in another way, right here." She placed her hand upon his chest. "Your heart is filled with all the kisses she gave to you when she was alive."

Jadon burrowed his curly head in the crook of her neck. His breath mixed with the dampness of his tears. "Forever?"

"Aye, Jadon, forever. Your love blends with hers, like this." Ruby picked up a brush and mixed the dots of colors he was working on. She formed it into the shape of a heart. "See? That love *blends* into your heart."

Jadon looked up, tears clinging to his long lashes. "In my *brave* heart?" He smiled. "Like a knight, aye?"

"Aye, Sir Jadon."

Ruby placed him in his seat. A child's scream echoed in her mind. Reeling at the odd memory, it took a moment to compose herself. "Here, try this." Her hand shook when she dipped one of his fingers in the paint then guided it to the parchment. "Press, here…and here." She stared at the fingerprint flower. This, she had done before. Angels above, who was the child haunting her?

Ruby paced the length of the small garden and watched him paint, smiling whenever he searched her out. All the while, she toyed with the wisp of memory and tried to expand it into something she could grasp. A child of her own? She kept arriving at that conclusion. Was she wed?

"Ruby!" Sarah entered the rustic garden. "I was told I could find you here." She tousled Jadon's curls. "We must talk."

Ruby banished her dark thoughts. She planted a kiss on both of Sarah's cheeks. "Oh, you have been sorely missed, my friend."

"I did not come alone."

Ruby yanked off her paint smock. "Where is Easton then?" She pulled her into an embrace. "Ah, your gift! I have not been able to thank you." She held out her hand, allowing the sunlight to reflect against the ring.

"I knew you would like it, however—"

"Oh, but I do. I shall treasure it forever." She glanced up then fisted her hand, dropping it to her side. She gave Sarah a questioning look.

"I tried to tell you," Sarah whispered.

Ruby clenched her teeth into a smile as Galeron and Alex approached.

"'Tis a relief to see you returned safe. How was your journey?" The details certainly did not interest her, and she wondered why she asked.

Galeron looked as if he were about to answer, but she did not wish to talk about his woman.

"In the least, all of you returned safe. Sarah was worried." She fumbled with the painting. "I am Jadon's nursemaid." She blushed, knowing she babbled like a fool.

Galeron's stare seemed to burn through her. "It seems many things changed in my absence."

The back door opened into the garden. For once, she welcomed Palmer's arrival.

"Palmer, why have you arrived so early?" Ruby knocked over a container of paint in her haste to do something with her hands.

"Papa, look!" Jadon pointed at the flower painting.

"Very good!" Palmer gave Ruby a wink. "You have done well."

"For Mama. These flowers shall live forever." Jadon smiled at Ruby. "Like the love you talked about."

Palmer picked up Jadon. "Ruby, he smiles so much now. You are all he speaks of."

Ruby sensed Galeron's eyes upon her. She blotted the paint on the table. "I adore him as well." Unable to help herself, she glanced at Galeron. Confusion played across his face. Good. She grinned at Palmer. "Have you come for a midday break?"

"Nay, I have closed the shoppe for the day." Palmer nodded at the others. "So, I shall leave you to it."

"To what?"

Ruby sensed something was amiss.

"Ruby, we must talk," Sarah said.

She placed her hand on Palmer's arm. Surely Galeron would notice it. "Nay need to close your shoppe. I still can tend to the child while Sarah and I talk." She glared at Galeron. "And the men do whatever they came to do."

Galeron blew a huge breath. "We rode here with one intention."

She met his eyes. "What may that be, to bring your betrothed shopping?" She ignored the clench of his jaw, and delivered a forced smile.

"Jadon, bid Ruby farewell." Palmer lowered him to the ground.

Jadon hugged her legs. "On the morrow then?"

"Mayhap even tonight." She smiled at Palmer.

Palmer stuttered something unintelligible when Galeron stepped forward and crossed his arms.

Sarah grabbed Ruby's arm. "I beg thee, cease your infuriating game."

Ruby swallowed hard. How could she embarrass her like that? She planted a soft kiss on Jadon's cheek. "I shall return in the morn."

Galeron walked a few steps then turned. "Shall we go?"

Ruby nodded and took Sarah's arm. She stole a glance over her shoulder. Something inexplicable tore at her and she wished to gather Jadon in her arms and run. The short distance between Jadon's garden to the back entrance of her home seemed to stretch into miles. Ruby kept the conversation focused on her new life. She wished she could ask Sarah why she had brought Galeron, however they were but a step behind him.

"Forgive the untidiness of the garden. I have not had the time to clear it. In the spring, I shall start anew. I already have decided what to plant." She must cease rambling. "Sarah, I have changed a few things. Wait till you see. I moved the table to the window." She shot a crooked grin at her companions while she pushed on the door. "It sticks sometimes." She shoved a bit harder. "The inside is much tidier than out here." She resembled a lunatic, but could not seem to stop. A frown creased her brow while she slammed her shoulder against the door.

Galeron's arm brushed her when he pointed to the door. "'Tis locked."

Ruby focused on anything but him. "Oh." She retrieved the key from her pocket then placed it in the lock.

The men were still snickering when she entered. She did her best to ignore them and opened the shutters. "I have some fresh fruit." She slapped the basket on the table between them. "Sarah, come sit…" She looked at the table, dwarfed by the men settling in the chairs by it. "On the bed with me."

"We could pull the chairs about the table." Galeron's chair scooted on the splintered floor to make room.

"We could." Ruby sat on the bed and motioned for Sarah. "Well, you have me worried. Why have you come?"

Galeron chuckled. "That's our maiden of the forest, straight to the point."

She was no one's maiden. Ruby calmed a bit when Sarah laid her hand over hers.

"The men finally arrived last night. There is so much to tell you, but I will come to that later," Sarah said.

"Come to it now."

Ruby feared the news was worrisome by the crease on Sarah's brow. "We do not wish to alarm you, however…"

"You just have, so out with it."

Sarah looked at the men and Ruby followed her gaze. Galeron cleared his throat. "You must return to Ramstone."

Ruby bristled. "Must I?"

Alex frowned at Galeron. "Ruby, there is potential danger afoot. Safety is assured behind Ramstone's gates."

"I am safe here." Ruby followed the length of Galeron as he rose.

Sarah spoke up. "Perhaps 'twould be best if you two took leave. Ruby and I can discuss the matter."

Alex nudged Galeron. "We shall be just outside."

Ruby released a breath and stood. "Very well." The door closed. She swung toward Sarah, sending her braid from its clasp. "What were you thinking, bringing him here? You betrayed me!"

"Pray thee allow the opportunity to explain before you place your wrath upon me. I would never betray you!"

"Oh, Sarah." She plopped onto the bed. Her skirts billowed and fell against her legs. "I pray forgiveness. Seeing him shattered my guard. You are right. I should hold trust in you." She took Sarah's hands. "Why does Galeron find it imperative I leave my home, and why do you agree?"

"We can explain it all on the way back. Time is of the essence. Trust me, danger exists and you must return with us."

"I thought you understood. I cannot ever go back there."

"But listen —"

"I am not going back."

"His betrothed did not return with him."

Ruby could not sit still. Did he come back for her? She snatched some kindling and added it to the smoldering coals. "She refused him?"

"Nay, she is missing. The men shall be leaving soon to find her."

"He is leaving to find her," she repeated.

"And fight some evil army, from what I have overheard." Sarah shrugged. "I am ill-informed about what happened, but I sense their worry. Galeron is posting guards about the village while they are gone."

"Why then, do I need to return to Ramstone?"

Sarah slapped her hand upon the bed. "Apparently, I was mistaken in my belief you would return without question."

"Nay, you were mistaken in your belief I would return at all."

"I am at fault for everything."

Ruby recoiled at the slapping comment. "You do not have *anything* to do with this."

Sarah lit one of the candles on the table. "I must confess, 'tis my doing Galeron's marriage agreement was forged."

She balked at the change of subject. She joined Sarah at the table. "Sit." Once Sarah sat, Ruby placed her chin in her hands and sighed, sending the candle flickering for survival. "You are not making one bit of sense."

"Galeron would never have agreed to marry had Easton not told him it was his duty as the eldest son."

She shook her head. "I do not understand."

"Had I been stronger, my babe would have been born a strong lad."

She gasped. "Your babe? You never told me."

"'I rarely speak of it." Sarah's eyes pooled. "Galeron would not have been forced to marry and bring an heir to Ramstone."

"Sarah." Her throat closed. "You must not take this blame." She handed Sarah a handkerchief. "We should have spoken of this sooner."

Sarah offered a weak smile. "Indeed. You always ease my burdens."

"'Tis what our friendship is about. We help each other." Ruby picked at the skin of an orange in the bowl.

"As I wish to do for you now. We have already talked with Palmer." Sarah smiled through her tears. "He has agreed 'tis best for you to return to Ramstone until 'tis deemed safe to return."

"You *what*?"

Both of them focused on the knock at the door. Ruby stormed over, swung it open and motioned for the brothers to enter. Just as they sat, Ruby slammed the door on her way out.

Chapter Seventeen

Garden Fate

Ruby stormed about the small garden, then kicked a bucket and sent it clunking against the dusty ground. Angry she injured her toe, she limped to the bench and rubbed her foot. "Fie and fie again!"

She swung at a sound, her hair swirled out of its braid with the force. Framed by the dusky evening stood Galeron.

"Be gone, knight." Angry tears threatened.

"Why are you so stubborn?"

She ignored her injury and stomped toward him. "How dare you!"

Galeron splayed his hands. "How dare I what?"

"You had nay right to go to Palmer behind my back and interfere in my life." Her anger at the sordid twist of events made her tremble. "'Tis *my* life."

"Ruby, 'tis your life we are trying to protect."

"What of Jadon and his family? What of the rest of this village? Are they in danger as well?" Her words were spewed in gasps of rage. "I refuse to abandon that little boy." With her voice cracking, she turned away and tended to a shriveled plant. "I beg thee, be off." She heard his footsteps in the graveled walk as he neared.

"Why did you leave?"

"The same reason I am asking you to do the same." She pricked her finger on a dead stem and placed it in her mouth.

"I am not fond of riddles. Why did you leave Ramstone?"

"To remain..." She swung around. "Far from you."

He closed the distance between them.

She stood a breath away and looked into his eyes. "I do not need you or anyone else to think for me. Fight your own battles, and leave me to mine."

Galeron took her by the arms. "Damnation, you are the most stubborn maiden I ever met. Bring the boy and his family along if you must, but return to Ramstone!"

She shrugged from his grasp and shoved him. She was shouting now. "Take your leave, Sir Galeron. I am not one of your *duties* anymore. You are free of me. You have your betrothed and I belong to another."

"I am not so easily convinced, fair one. There is naught between you and Palmer." He gently took her arms and pulled her closer. "Come back."

She shrugged away. "Not him, but someone. What other reason would I think I have a child of my own? I *must* belong to another."

Galeron sat on the bench. "You have a child?"

"Leave. Just leave."

He strode to her, pulling her into his arms. "Not without you. If you have a child, we shall find the young one. As far as belonging to another, he is less than a man. If you were missing, I would not rest until I found you."

She clenched her jaw. "You say this as you set out to find your betrothed?"

She leaned back as his gruff whisper brushed her cheek. "If I have to carry you over my shoulder to do so, I shall bring you back to Ramstone."

She slapped him fully on the cheek. His head turned with the force of her blow. For a moment their breaths intermingled, while they stared each other down.

She blew at the wayward lock falling in her eyes and jerked her head to the side when he reached to push it from her face. "I am not free and neither are you." She shuddered when he cradled her chin in his hand and placed the tendril behind her ear. Her eyes met his when he wiped the tears on her cheek. "Damn you."

He kissed her.

She shoved him away. "You are about to be wed. I refuse to be your wench."

"I would never ask you to be my wench. I simply wish to assure your safety while I am gone."

"Gone? Go to the devil, brute."

"Come inside. There is much to explain." He neared and brushed his lips against hers. "I have missed you, Ruby."

The torture of doubt ripped at her. Anger collided with warmth, sinful cravings with confusion, and she spent all of her emotions on him.

The stubble of his beard scraped her chin. She grabbed his neck as he kissed her and hoisted herself, wrapping her legs around his waist. Galeron's moan twisted around her heart while their tongues intertwined in a frantic dance. His broad hands roamed down her back and cradled her bottom. She pressed against him and reached into his tunic, relishing the warmth of his body. His chest rose and fell beneath her fingertips while she reeled in the darkness he brightened. She cried out at the sensation of his lips following the low neckline of her bodice. She sensed a tremble when she pressed hard against him.

"Woman, refrain from doing that."

"This?" She grinned and wrapped her legs tighter around his waist.

"You know not what you do, milady." He slowly lowered her feet to the ground. Stilted breath flowed from his lips while he kissed her temple. "God in heaven," he whispered. "I did not intend to…"

"Neither did I. Shhh." Ruby closed her eyes and listened to his heartbeat pounding as hard as her own. *Let this be.* Allow the haunting reminders of her past to release their grasp. Would fate deem she belonged to another? She wanted to believe fate would be kind for once.

Her eyes flew open at the nearby gasp and she shoved out of Galeron's embrace. Ruby busied herself straightening her skirts. She scowled at Galeron. "Look what you have done!"

Galeron chuckled.

"I suppose you witnessed that…did you?" Ruby questioned Alex and Sarah.

"We did—well, most of it." Alex burst out laughing. "The heat of your blush would bake bread."

Sarah punched him in the arm.

She swished past them, thoroughly scorched with shame, but most of all, she was torn in two. The others followed her inside. Sarah fidgeted by the table while the men sat. She finally sat on the edge of the bed against the opposite wall.

She choked Sarah's giggle with a scornful stare. She wanted to march over and slap the smiles from the men's faces as well. Instead, she sat on her fisted hands and glanced at Sarah beside her.

Alex broke the silence. "I dare say this outcome was not what I expected when we came to fetch you. Sarah, help Ruby with her belongings. Galeron and I shall wait outside. Call out when you need us to lift the trunk." The men started for the door.

"I shan't be returning to Ramstone." Ruby fingered the creases in her skirt.

Galeron's deep gasp punctuated her declaration. She met his incredulous stare. Her explanation choked in her throat, fully aware she was responsible for the pain in Galeron's eyes.

He muttered something unintelligible and walked out without a backward glance.

Alex whipped his gaze from Ruby to the open doorway and followed his brother. Ruby's insides shook at the force of the slamming door. She stared at the exit, the tap of the swinging lock ticking off his farewell.

Sarah grabbed Ruby's shoulders. "What holds you here? Galeron has made his feelings known. Isn't this what you wanted?" She shook her. "Look at me!"

Ruby tore her eyes from the door.

"Is your hesitation because of Jadon? I am certain Easton will welcome Palmer and his family. Is that what you wish? I simply do not understand."

Ruby shattered her silence with an intake of a stifled sob. "I should never have given in to my passion. Everything is happening with the haste of a storm ripping through my life."

"All shall be well, Ruby. Just come back to Ramstone."

She paced the room, wringing her hands. "My wishes have been granted, yet, I cannot partake of it again. I fear my love for Galeron may be a betrayal on another."

Sarah's mouth dropped open and she gripped the table as she sat. Ruby turned away from her friend's disbelieving face and chucked another log into the fire, watching the sparks fade at her feet. Sarah whispered behind her. "Another?"

"I have memories of a child." She brushed the wisps of hair sticking to her damp cheeks. "What if I am a *mother*? God's eyes, Sarah, I may have a family who waits and worries for me." Ruby spoke past the choking sobs. "I selfishly followed my heart in the garden. 'Tis not fair to Galeron — or me."

"Ruby, do not do this."

Ruby looked away from her friend's pleading eyes. "I *obviously* cannot trust myself when I am close to him. Until I am sure of who I am and where I belong, I must stay in the village. 'Twould be a mistake to return to Ramstone." She ground her tears with the heels of her hands. "Our love is cursed."

Sarah led her to the table. "You recall a child. What of a man?"

Ruby sighed and sat. She took an apple from the bowl. Would she ever partake of this fruit without thinking of the day he placed one in her hand? The day in the forest would forever live. A cruel reminder.

"What of a man?" Sarah repeated.

She blinked at the impatience in Sarah's voice and dropped the apple into the bowl. "I do not recall. The only man I — " She stared at Sarah. "Galeron is the only man my heart follows. Damnation, why?"

"There is nay answer to that, Ruby."

They sat. The only sound was the crackling of the fire and occasional sniffle from Ruby. Ruby scratched at a splinter on the table. "I would have given myself fully to Galeron. I *crave* him. Already, I have sinned."

Sarah's hand stilled her own. "Come, your past is done with. Let us be your future."

She snatched away her hands. "Are you mad? I may be wed and he still searches for his betrothed." Nearly toppling the chair, she bolted. "Do not bring him here again."

Sarah jumped to her feet. "I did not bring him —"

"Then take him from here." She placed her face in her hands. "I am poison to him."

Sarah gently pulled her hands down. "You must try to make him understand before we depart."

She glanced at the door. "*How*? I told him in the garden, yet found myself in his arms. I lack the strength to turn him away when he is standing before me." A tense shiver teased her spine. "All I want is to be in Galeron's arms. Now I must hurt us both by running from them. He shall grow to hate me. I cannot place blame on that."

"The look in his eyes is not hate."

"It shall be after tonight." She could swear her heart shattered at the promise of those words. "They are waiting. Go."

"I shall do as you wish. Be it known, I believe you are making a terrible choice." Sarah stood. "Ramstone's gates are always open to you."

She slipped out of her grasp and ground her nails into the palm of her hand. "Go."

Sarah gave her a hug. Ruby caught the last glimpse of Galeron's scowl as Sarah pulled the door closed behind her.

* * * *

Galeron held the door while Alex assisted Sarah into the carriage. He held up his hand when Sarah began to speak. Galeron squinted at her, daring her to continue. The carriage set off and Sarah leaned forward. "Galeron, you must understand—"

"I fully understand." Galeron stared at the shadows passing by.

"She needs to—"

"I care not what she needs."

"Cease interrupting. I must tell you what Ruby said!"

Alex brushed his lips across the top of Sarah's hand. "My love, her words carried through the door. A repeat shall bring needless pain."

Galeron scowled. "Indeed. Ruby is naught but a pain."

Sarah began to protest, but was silenced by Galeron's growl. She wiped at the tears, and for the slightest moment, he was repentant. Then she spoke of Ruby again, which began another argument. On the journey to Ramstone, Galeron cursed, Sarah wept, and Alex tried to comfort them both. By the time they reached the gates of home, they all sat in silence. Galeron stepped out of the carriage before it came to a complete stop and strode inside. He heaved a sigh. The main entry was filled with wedding guests. He ignored the clutches on his sleeve while he weaved through the crowd. By the questions asked, everyone knew about the attack on Jastar. The warmth of the room stifled him and he couldn't wait to rid the guests from his sight.

He made eye contact with his father and finally met him at the doorway of the great hall. "Hell's teeth, what's the meaning of this?"

"I told them of Jastar's demise."

Galeron leaned against the doorway. "You did what?"

"Many still chose to travel to their homes and they needed an explanation as to why they should remain here." Easton peered past Galeron. "We've awaited your return, come and speak with the men gathered in the next room. They have agreed to join our army." He smiled at Sarah as they approached. "The knight is conscious. Mayhap you could see how he fares?"

"I shall be off then." Sarah gave Alex a quick kiss. She waved to Easton and purposely ignored Galeron while turning into the crowd. His remorse apparently came too late, for he saw the contempt in her eyes before she left.

Chapter Eighteen

Intentions

Sarah had to nudge her way to the stairs and stopped on the landing. The smooth railing was cool beneath her twisting grip while the double doors of the great hall shut her out. She hurried up the rest of the way. Upon arriving at Sir Jac's door, she happened upon Bridget.

"I was simply bringing him a bit of nourishment." Bridget blushed and avoided her gaze.

The girl was apparently taken with the man. She chuckled. "Ah, I see." She knocked on the wounded knight's door.

"Enter!" a deep voice called.

The maid followed her to his bedside and Sarah took the tray from Bridget. "Sir Jac, I am Lady Sarah, wife of Sir Alex." She offered the tray, waiting until he took the mug of broth from it.

"Lady Sarah, may the Lord bless you all for your kindness." He took a sip. "Lord Easton paid me a visit and spoke of how your husband's intervention saved me. I would like to thank him. Is he here?"

"He is in a meeting with his father. I shall inform him of your request. How do you fare? You seem much better."

"I am." Jac swallowed the rest of the broth, the silence heavy in the room. "I gather Sir Alex and Sir Galeron both are in the meeting."

"They are." She looked back at a sound. Bridget was busying herself...or scurrying around the room doing naught, Sarah was certain it was the latter. She turned back to Jac. "I shall take—" Sarah tried to pull her gaze from his eyes. What was she saying? His eyes unnerved her. Nay, it was her nerves alone. It had naught to do with the man. "Shall I take your mug?"

Jac smiled and handed it to her. His smile. Gods, had she met him before? She went to place it on the table without turning away from him. The mug clanged against the floor, startling her out of the odd hold he seemed to have on her.

"Milady!" The maid rescued the rocking mug and sat it upon the tray.

Heat shot into her face. She thanked Bridget and glanced at Jac to offer an apology. He was grinning. "Rest well, Sir Jac." She started for the door. "The meetings usually last throughout the night."

Apparently, he enjoyed her unease, for Jac's smile grew wider. "Very well, I shall speak with the men in the morn. My thanks for the broth...and the kind company."

"Mayhap the meeting is over after all. I shall go downstairs and see. If it is—or not, as I said, sometimes they talk all night." Still speaking, she directed Bridget out of the room and stopped at the doorway. Though she often rambled, nerves were the cause this time. She could not seem to stop. "Well, I shall notify you either way. Of the meeting—" She swept the door closed on his rambunctious whoop of laughter. An odd sense of relief cascaded over her the moment she did.

Not bothering to go downstairs, she leaned over the railing and saw the doors to the meeting were still closed. Upon hearing Jac's laughter stop—then start again—she huffed past his door and stormed to her chamber. "Let him wait," she muttered.

* * * *

Downstairs, sequestered from the others, Easton questioned his sons about their journey into the village. Galeron scowled, leaving Alex to explain.

Thankfully, he excluded what he witnessed in Ruby's garden.

"Ah, a strong will that one has. Post extra guards outside Ruby's home then," Easton said.

"I pity the guards," Galeron muttered.

Easton glanced at him. "Messengers have been dispatched to the neighboring lands. Are you ready to commence the meeting with the leaders who are here now?"

Alex and Galeron gave a nod. Rafe grinned and shifted from one foot to the other. Galeron could not resist a smile. "Sit, Rafe."

Easton raised his voice. "My thanks to all who have gathered here tonight." The buzz of conversation silenced. "The knights from the neighboring lands shall be arriving soon enough, however, 'tis imperative we begin planning the search and attack now."

Galeron leaned forward. "They attacked Jastar. We believe they captured the survivors and the fellow villagers."

"Along with Galeron's betrothed," Easton added.

Galeron, Alex and even Rafe delved into the plans, each of them fielding the suggestions from the other knights. The night lengthened and the meeting finally ended. Galeron's own plans materialized as he made way to his chamber.

Hours later, Galeron noticed the sun peeking through the cracks of the shutters and blew out the stub of a candle. The air filled his lungs and he took a few moments to enjoy the rosy glow of the sunrise. Though he felt the effects of no sleep, his heart found peace with the letter he'd penned. He shook his head at Ruby's words echoing in his mind and interrupting his solitude.

The chair scraped against the polished-stone floor as he sat. Picking up the quill, still fresh with ink, he read over the words one last time then signed with a flourish. He sprinkled sand to dry it and sealed the parchment with a bit of wax. Leaning the chair precariously, he stretched as he planned the duties he needed to carry out to deliver the letter himself. Though he had not discussed it with his father, he intended to accompany the additional guards he would dispatch to the village. He pulled on his breeches and answered the heavy rap on the door.

"What are you grinning at?" Galeron peered down the hall and looked back at Alex. "I suppose Sarah assured your night was well spent."

He answered with his smile and strode into the room. "Get dressed. I have something to show you."

Galeron yanked a tunic over his head. "What may that be?"

"I went to redress Sir Jac's wound." He handed Galeron his boots. "He was dressed and walking on his own."

He crooked his eyebrow. "Should he be doing that?"

Alex shrugged. "Nay, but he is determined to anyway." He followed Galeron to the washbasin. "I told him we would defeat the men who destroyed his family. He asked to join us in the quest."

Galeron looked up, water still dripping from his face. "Impossible."

"I told him you would be the one to make the decision."

"Do *you* deem him able? We shall be leaving soon."

"I do not see how he could be ready to travel, much less battle, in such a short period of time." Alex followed him into the corridor.

Galeron thought for a few moments. "I shall offer him the responsibility to guard with the other knights in the village when he is stronger." He combed his fingers through his wavy hair. "Damn, I forgot a strap."

Alex took his own and cut it in half with his dagger. "Here."

Galeron grinned and tied his hair back. "Let's meet with him before we go downstairs."

He nudged Galeron as they walked down the corridor. "I see the darkness below your eyes. You must get some sleep."

Galeron smiled even wider. "Aye, soon enough."

"I must say, your mood certainly has lifted since I saw you last."

"You mean since Ruby."

"Why such a change?"

Galeron motioned to Sarah, coming down the corridor. "There's your woman."

Sarah's expression changed to a smile and she nearly flew into Alex's arms. Rising on tiptoe, she gave him a quick kiss. Her smile faded when she turned to him. "Did he inform you about Sir Jac? Is it not great news?"

"'Tis welcome news, indeed. We are on our way to meet with him now." Galeron offered a smile, but she did not return it.

"I just came from there. He is waiting." She frowned. "What is it about that man?"

"Who? Sir Jac?" Alex glanced at him. "What do you mean?"

"He is...unsettling." She sighed and shook her head.

"Sarah, if he has made advances—" Galeron grabbed Alex's shoulder to keep him from storming down the corridor.

"Nay, ease your mind! Ignore my foolish whims." Sarah caressed Alex's twitching jaw. "I wish I kept my thoughts to myself. The poor man has been naught but respectful."

"Sarah, enough about Jac. I want to offer an apology." Galeron smelled the scent of jasmine as he kissed her hand. "Am I forgiven?"

Sarah swallowed hard. "I would still like to speak with you about Ruby."

Galeron sighed. "Later?"

"Very well, until then." Sarah planted a quick kiss on Alex's cheek. "Forgiveness granted, Galeron," she said, walking away.

Alex watched until she was out of sight. "She smiles in daylight and sobs at night." Prodded by Galeron, he continued toward Jac's chamber. "She is very worried about Ruby."

"All shall be settled very soon," Galeron said with a wink.

"Wait." Alex stopped. "What are you up to?" He shook his head and hurried to catch up, meeting Galeron at Jac's door. "What is it?"

Galeron looked down the corridor and lowered his voice. "Very well, I shall tell you now."

Alex chuckled and mocked Galeron's stance. "I assume it is highly secretive by the way you are scouring the corridor."

Galeron scowled. "Lend me your ears, brother, this is important." He led him farther away from the door.

Alex rested his shoulder against the stone wall. "Go on."

"I spent hours contemplating all that came about in Ruby's garden last night."

"That explains the lack of sleep on your face."

Galeron sighed at the interruption. "I shall wait an eternity for her if I must, but 'tis my aim to tell her of my intentions when we go station the guards at the village today."

Alex's brows rose. "Intentions?"

"I intend to marry her, Alex. I stayed up most of the night composing a letter, professing how I feel."

"That is well and good, brother, but she —"

"She shall return once she reads it."

Alex nudged away from the wall. "You are serious! How do you intend on telling Father? How can you nullify the agreement to marry Mara?"

"One thing at a time. First, I need to see Ruby."

Alex grinned. "She shall leave you with battle wounds."

"Ah, I had a taste of that last night."

Alex chuckled. "Aye?"

Galeron rubbed his cheek. "I'm surprised her handprint isn't still there."

Alex burst out laughing and Galeron nudged him. "She delivers quite a sting." He joined in the laughter, his heartache lifting with their renewed banter.

Their shared mirth cut short at the creak of Jac's door opening.

"Fie it all! Did he hear us?" Alex whispered.

Jac stepped into the corridor, nodding a greeting. "Sir Alex." He grasped Galeron's outstretched hand. "You must be Sir Galeron. I wish to offer thanks for" — he threw up his hands — "everything." He winced at the sudden movement. "I owe you both my life."

"You are a brother knight. I am certain you would do the same." A twinge of guilt led Galeron to search Jac's manner to see if he had overheard the conversation.

"I have much to discuss with you. Draw up a chair. I shall inform you of the plans I have made." Jac led them into the room.

Galeron and Alex caught each other's glances and hesitated in the doorway. Galeron's ire rose at Jac's insolence. As if deciphering their stances, Sir Jac heaved a sigh. "I have forgotten myself. I am accustomed to being the knights' commander at Jastar. I have shown disrespect. I ask forgiveness."

Galeron's mind raced with realization. "I was not aware you held such rank at Jastar. I gather you are the eldest son of Lord Ronan?"

Sadness flickered in Sir Jac's eyes. "The *only* son, we lost my older brother years ago to sickness." The last of his words fell to a whisper. "Now Father has fallen at the sword of evil."

Galeron succumbed to the nagging questions on his mind. "I haven't an intention to cause unnecessary pain." He positioned a chair across from Jac. "However, I must ask you to push past the grief and tell me what you know."

"You mean about Mara?"

Alex sat. "We mean about anything."

Sir Jac limped to the table and poured a mug of water. "'Tis not what I intended to discuss with you." He eyed Galeron, the chair creaking as he sat. "I am aware you are Mara's betrothed."

"Aye." Galeron shifted in his seat and raised his eyebrow at Alex.

"Lady Sarah, the wonderful woman, sat and spoke with me." Jac swallowed hard. "Sir Galeron, you are not responsible for what happened to my sister, Mara."

"It seems you had quite the conversation." Galeron's jaw twitched.

"Be at peace. I hold nay ill will toward you. The attack happened before you were expected. There was naught you could have done to change the events which fell upon us." Jac cleared his throat. "'Tis fair you are told all, regarding the agreement between your father and mine."

"Pray tell?"

"Mara never intended to honor the agreement of the betrothal."

Galeron sat back, stunned.

Jac shook his head, but a slight twitch at the corner of his mouth foretold a smile. "She told our father she would sleep with death himself before lying in your bed."

Galeron found his voice. "She would betray your father?"

"She has a mind and a spirit one would not even try to tame." Jac flashed his teeth at the look on Galeron's face. "Aye, she is quite a determined maiden, that one."

Damnation, what had his father matched him with?

Jac's grin faded. "Your face speaks volumes, Sir Galeron. She was—is—a wonderful maiden. Any man would be blessed to have her."

"As you conveyed." Galeron stood as Jac rose.

Jac squinted at Galeron. He blew a breath between his teeth and began to pace. "The last I saw of her…" Jac's voice broke and he waited a moment before attempting to speak. "I know not where to begin."

Galeron sat, his body weary, his mind alert. "Where did you see her last?"

"The last time I saw Mara, she was fighting. Damn fool child. I killed the knight intent on taking her and ordered her to run. She refused."

"She refused to run from a battle?" Galeron kept his face blank.

"She was pulling on me and screaming."

Alex leaned forward. "Why would she stay?"

"I believe she was trying to tell me something."

Only a maiden would nag in the middle of a battle. Galeron bit back the comment. "What was of such importance?"

Jac's voice lowered to a whisper. "Chaos was all about. There were so many, over the walls, infiltrating my home. I am not certain what she was saying." Anger infiltrated his voice. "What more must you know?"

"Who were the attackers? They ride with nay crest."

Jac closed his eyes. His skin paled even more. "Nay, we did not know them or where they came from. Or why they… Damnation. Why did they snatch them away?"

Alex joined the questioning. "Did Jastar have any known enemies?"

"Nay, not a one. It has been a peaceful land for many years."

Galeron pondered a few moments while Alex and Jac discussed the lands about Jastar. Galeron cleared his throat to interrupt the conversation. "I have one last question, Sir Jac. I understand you wish to join our quest and become a knight among our army. Would you be willing to stand guard over the village and defend it if the need arises?"

Jac took pause.

Galeron peered at his pale complexion, relieved that he seemed to be considering the duty. "You seem to be healing quickly, but you are not ready for what could be a lengthy search."

"I have been through worse," Jac said.

Galeron sighed. "You fought them once, when you were able-bodied." He refrained from reminding him the battle was lost. "I cannot allow you to join the search and battle with the army's stronghold once it is found. Not like that." Galeron pointed to his wound.

Jac leaned out of the window. He cocked his head into the room. "Sir Alex, are those your children?"

Alex frowned. "Nay."

Galeron squeezed Alex's shoulder and walked to Jac. "Those are children of the guests gathered for the wedding."

"Would you defend them if they were yours?"

"Of course." Galeron and Alex said in unison.

"Then you understand."

"You cannot go."

Jac seemed to give up on his request. "Why haven't you married until now, Galeron?"

Galeron squinted at the change of subject. "The need did not arise."

"Ah, I suppose many a maiden was willing to warm thy bed without marriage?"

Galeron clenched his jaw, and Alex darted between them. "Wait—"

Galeron nudged him aside, stepping within a breath of Jac. "You tread heavy on my patience. Had I married your sister, she would have been treated well."

Alex jutted his chin at Galeron's glare. "You both want the same outcome. Cease the swordplay."

Jac ran his hand over his face. "I pray forgiveness. I wished to raise your ire to match my own."

Galeron crossed his arms. "You succeeded."

Jac's expression fell. "I must avenge my father, find my son and sister. Can you not see that?"

Galeron could see the pain in Jac's eyes. "I told how you can be a part of it."

"I cannot do as you ask."

"That is your choice."

Jac sighed. "I intend to slay the ones who killed my family. I shall do this alone if I must." He put out his hand. "However, I would be honored to fight as a knight bachelor, under your banner. You would have my utmost loyalty and respect."

"You would be willing to join as a knight bachelor — nay question of my orders?"

Alex frowned. "This does not change the fact he is wounded, Galeron."

Before Galeron could speak, Jac responded. "Rest assured, I shall be strong enough to ride within a few days. 'Tis the breath of fire that burns within me. The flame of revenge shall not die until the ones responsible for the attack lie dead beneath my sword." Jac's face did not expose anything but determination.

"Jac—" Galeron stepped closer.

"You would have the same need to avenge wrongdoing toward your family. I cannot guard a quiet village while my son and sister remain in peril." Jac put out his hand again. "I beseech you, do not deny my request."

Galeron locked eyes with Alex. They outstretched their hands toward Jac.

"I nay longer carry doubt," Galeron said. "Sheer will shall quench your thirst for revenge and determination shall nourish until you are sated."

Jac smiled as they stacked their hands. "Loyalty in brotherhood."

"Loyalty in brotherhood," Galeron and Alex repeated.

With a newfound goodwill and respect between the three, Galeron and Alex left the room, leaving Jac to contemplate the task before them.

"You are sure of this decision of yours?" Alex said as they headed for the stairs.

"Jac shall do well."

"Nay, I mean Ruby."

Galeron sighed. "I suppose I must tell Father before we set off for the village."

"Mayhap you should assure Ruby will have you. You apparently have a penchant for rejection."

"Aye, but the one who rejected me left me free to pursue the one I love."

Alex punched his arm. "You jest with fate, brother. Careful."

Guilt gripped him. How dare he make light of Mara's demise? 'Twas his fault after all. Alex seemed to read his thoughts. "Ease your mind, brother. Though Mara must be found, 'tis fortunate Jac told you of your freedom. All will work out in the end."

"That remains to be seen. I have yet to convince Father." Galeron chuckled, his mood lifting at the thought of Ruby. "And that stubborn little warrior of mine."

Rafe turned the corner, his blond hair still tousled from sleep. "Father is looking for you. He— Damnation, Galeron!"

Galeron did not release the headlock. "Who assigned you as messenger?"

Rafe ducked out of his grasp and grinned with pride. "He's downstairs waiting." He avoided Galeron's next attempt to wrestle him and ran off.

Alex and Galeron chuckled on their way to the stairs. Their lighthearted mood ceased when they saw who waited at the bottom of the landing.

Easton leaned against the banister, talking with a man. A man he had despised since childhood. Craven Calen they had dubbed him, though the man was far from cowardly, but as young lads, they found the insult amusing. Easton and Calen did not notice them standing at the top of the stairway, but the woman with them did. With slightest rise of her eyebrow, she noted them and looked away.

The light shining from the window illuminated her face, giving it an angelic hue. Could it be? He had not seen Lord Calen's daughter in years.

Easton locked his gaze on Galeron. "Ah, here they are now!" He called up the stairs. "Alex, Galeron, surely you remember Lord Calen?"

"Aye." Galeron frowned, then gave the maiden a quick smile. What was her name? Ellie? Edna? She certainly had changed from the wench he had met years ago. Calen, however, had grown in girth, though he was quite heavy before. "Swine," he whispered to Alex. "What is Calen doing here?"

"Shh." Alex descended the stairs. "Greetings, Lord Calen."

Calen grasped Alex's hand as he took the final step. "Galeron, it has been a long time."

Alex laughed. "Apparently so, for I am Alex." He motioned to Galeron, a few steps behind. "This is Galeron."

Calen took a step back. "Ah, forgive me, you resemble each other." He reached for Galeron's hand.

Galeron crossed his arms. "Lord Calen."

"Aye, the last I saw of you, my, you were but a scrap of a lad!"

Galeron squinted. "The last I saw of *you* was at the other end of your whip after I dared touch your horse." He disregarded the glare from his father.

Alex cleared his throat. He bowed at the young maiden. "Lord Calen, pray tell, who is your companion?"

"Why, do you not recognize my daughter, Elizabeth?"

"Ah! Of course!" Alex took her hand and brushed his lips on it. "Pray tell, what brings you to Ramstone?"

Elizabeth gave a slight nod, looked past Alex and stared at Galeron.

Lord Calen spoke up. "She has the beauty of her mother. God rest her soul." He bowed his head as if in prayer, then smiled at his daughter. "Elizabeth, do you recall Sir Galeron and Sir Alex?"

She raised her chin, studied the two brothers for a moment and sighed. "Does it matter?"

Lord Calen's jowls jiggled as he stumbled over his words. "Forgive her impertinence. She is exhausted from the journey." Nearly knocking his daughter back with a glare, he said, "Elizabeth, it may be best to take your leave."

Elizabeth raised her chin, eyeing Easton while he called for a maid. Chin raised, Elizabeth gathered her skirts and followed the maid up the stairs. She paused halfway and turned to face them. "Perchance, we may become better acquainted later tonight?" She pointed her gaze to Galeron.

"We shall dine at dusk." Easton gave a slight bow. "Rest well."

Galeron noticed the way she licked her lips and smiled at him before continuing up the stairs. He wondered who else had noticed her shameless action.

Calen grinned. "Easton, shall the meeting commence?"

"We shall leave you to it then." Galeron started for the door, nudging Alex to join him.

Lord Calen called out, "Galeron, I already met with your father. I hoped you would join us. We have much to discuss."

Galeron rolled his eyes at Alex before turning around. "Lord Calen, I would be honored to be included in your discussions. However, my brother and I have duties to attend." Facing Easton, he continued, "The additional knights need to be posted at the village. Alex and I shall be accompanying them. Perhaps we can meet on the morrow?"

"Alex is fully capable of carrying out the dispatching of the knights to the village. We have a matter to discuss with you that cannot wait."

Galeron nearly crushed the doorknob. "Father, if I leave now, I can return by dusk. We shall meet then?"

"Wait here, son." Easton guided Calen into the next room and called for some refreshments served. He returned to Galeron, still lingering by the door. "Do not disobey me. Get in there."

Galeron stifled a sigh. "Very well. Give me but a moment." He yanked Alex outside, trying to numb his frustration. "What is that swine doing here? I cannot imagine why he could possibly want from me." He strode to the stone path lined with the last of the blooms of autumn.

Alex followed. "I am as surprised as you. I did not even know he was invited to the wedding."

"He wasn't. Perhaps Father sent a message about joining armies to him as well."

"Still, Father would have settled that. It seems Lord Calen has the intention of speaking with *you*."

Galeron propped his foot on the bench and scowled when he spotted Calen peering out the window. He turned his back. "I never have cared for the way Calen conducts himself. He is a sly snake."

Alex shrugged. "His army is needed."

Galeron rubbed his temples and walked toward the rickety gate. "The thought of spending time with the man makes my head ache." He peered at the knight's quarters and slumped against the tree, releasing the precarious hold the dying leaves had on the nearly bare branch. "I shall learn of his intentions soon enough. However, my instincts guide me not to trust the pig."

"Hell's teeth, how we hated him as lads. If Father only knew of his cruelty. Remember how Elizabeth laughed when he struck you?"

Galeron stopped in the middle of his nod. "Elizabeth. Why is she here?"

"Perhaps Calen did not wish to leave her alone."

"With good reason." Galeron rested his arm on the gate and slipped the letter he had written the night before from his belt. "Ensure this is delivered to Ruby." The creak of the gate protested at his kick. "Damnation! This was my last chance to see her before we depart."

"I shall deliver it myself." Alex tucked it in his belt. "Fill me in on the meeting when I return."

Galeron watched Alex until he reached the knight's quarters, then strode through the garden back to the main doors.

Calen stood in the doorway of the adjoining room. "Come, we are waiting."

Galeron scowled. "Dare not direct me in my home." He followed him into the main hall and nudged Calen away from his seat at the head of the table. He glared the length of the table at his father and poured a mug of ale. He gulped all but a swallow and slammed it down. The remnants shot out and sprinkled Calen's face.

"Well, Father, what is this about?"

Chapter Nineteen

The Delivery

Ruby recognized the crest of Ramstone on the guards about the village. She kept her stride as long as her skirts would allow.

Palmer caught up, slipping his hand in hers. "You left too soon. Jadon and I wish to walk you home."

She snatched away her hand and tucked a strand of hair behind her ear to soften the movement. "'Tis but a few doors down."

"Galeron instructed—"

"Galeron is not my keeper, Palmer." Damnation, even Palmer followed his orders? Did the man have nay boundary of power?

"What is a keeper?" Jadon asked, trotting to keep up.

"Well, the knights in the village are keepers of peace." She scanned the lane. "Do you see Sir Galeron or Sir Alex among them?"

Jadon peered about. "Nay."

She shrugged. "I am surprised. It seems the whole army is here."

"Not quite." Palmer ignored her sarcastic smile and pointed to several men. "However, 'tis a comfort to have their protection, is it not?"

Protection. She nodded, still searching through the faces as they passed. The danger Galeron, Alex and Sarah had come to warn her about became a reality. She looked at Jadon and tried to compartmentalize her fear while silently sending a prayer for no harm to befall the child.

"Do not fret. I am certain 'tis simply a precaution, sweet Ruby," Palmer whispered.

She dug her nails into her palms. She was not his sweet anything.

Palmer waited outside while Jadon helped her carry her art supplies into her room. She scooped him up. "I had a wonderful time with you today, little knight."

"As did I." Jadon wriggled free and gave her a quick kiss before returning to his father.

Palmer came to her doorway. "Would you like me to accompany you to the well?" He peered into the room, laying his hand on her shoulder. "Or light the fire?"

"Good eve, Palmer."

Palmer leaned close. Had Jadon not been present, she would have shoved him. Instead, she bore his hot breath on her neck. "If you fear spending the night alone, I am willing to come after Jadon is asleep."

She stooped, just missing Palmer's kiss. "Sleep well, little knight." She rose, meeting Palmer's eyes. "I have something for you to do."

"Aye?" A huge grin spread over Palmer's face.

She grabbed two apples from the basket on the table. "Give these to the *guards* outside my door."

Palmer shifted his stance. "As you wish."

"Step back. I must secure the door now." She smiled at Jadon before throwing the latch. Her fury eased at Jadon's little voice trailing, telling his father about his day.

She pulled open the shutters and enjoyed the brilliant hues of the sunset. Waiting a few moments longer to ensure Palmer returned home, she went outside to collect water from the village well.

Lugging two full buckets proved quite a task. The water sloshed onto her skirt with each step. She placed the buckets on the ground and shook her weary arms. She blew a breath then grasped the handles once again.

"It seems you are in need of assistance."

She jumped, upset the buckets and sent the water pooling at her feet. Still choking on her startled gasp, she peered through watering eyes at the knight who had seemingly materialized. He removed his helmet and burst out laughing.

"Pray tell, Alex, are you an expert in creeping up on women?" She raised her voice over his bellowing laughter. "You frightened me!" Alex was now bent over with laughter. She thrust her hands upon her hips and tried to be stern, but could only smile at how ridiculous the view must be to anyone witnessing the scene. "Refrain from this foolishness. Others are peering out at us."

"Watching you wrestle with the buckets brought a smile. However, I couldn't help but laugh when you jumped." He laughed again, proving his point.

"Ah, it pleases me immensely to keep you entertained." She snatched his helmet. "Assistance?"

Alex ignored her sarcasm and picked up the buckets. "It seems another trip to the well is warranted. You are wearing most of the water you fetched."

She looked at her skirt and laughed. "I am indeed. In the stead of two separate trips to the well, I chose to fill two buckets. It seems the idea was for naught." She looked up at him, a certain happiness filling her. "Will you be staying in the village tonight?" Ruby looked about, hoping Galeron accompanied him.

"Nay, I came to oversee the additional guards. I also need to speak with you before heading to Ramstone." Leaning forward, he whispered, "He is not here, Ruby. He has been summoned to an important meeting with Father and could not accompany me."

"I know not who you refer to." She shrugged. "Why should it matter anyway?"

"Be on your way. I shall fetch water and deliver it shortly."

She gave a small curtsy and placed his helmet on her head. "My thanks, Sir Knight," she said from behind the faceplate. His renewed laughter faded while she hurried to her home. Once inside, she bolted the door, placed Alex's helmet on the table and changed into dry garments. With a quick snap, she knocked out the wrinkles and draped her damp kirtle across the back of the chair to dry.

Chastising herself for allowing the coals to burn down completely, she began the task of starting a new fire. On her third attempt, an aggravating wisp of smoke teased her.

Upon the rap on the door, she assured it was Alex, and unbolted it. He entered, a bucket in each hand and a sack under his arm.

"What is in the sack?"

Alex put down the buckets and dangled the sack in the air. "Rabbit. This one is for you."

All she could afford were vegetables, fruit and sometimes a half loaf of bread. Every once in a while, the butcher saved a few bits of meat for her, but naught could compare to a whole rabbit. She clapped her hands, her laughter bubbling in her throat. "Oh my, what a generous gift. Bless you, Alex!"

Alex placed the sack upon the table with a thump. "'Tis but rabbit, Ruby." He retrieved the buckets from the doorway, set them before the hearth and peered into the cauldron. "Only vegetables and barley. Now I understand why a rabbit brings you such joy."

He regarded the small pile of kindling lying in the ashes and raised an eyebrow. The simple gesture pulled at her heart. "Do all the men in your family do that?"

"Do what?" He toed the ashes. "Are you having difficulty lighting the fire?"

"Not at all. Why do you ask?"

Alex chuckled, stooped and grabbed the flint and bit of rough steel. "I shall start it for you."

She snatched the flint. "I am not helpless, Alex. I am fully capable of lighting my own hearth."

Alex sat on his haunches. "I never thought of you as helpless. What happened to your smile just a moment ago?"

She pressed the flint into his palm. "I beg forgiveness." She sighed and ladled the water into the pot. "I have not been sleeping well. Palmer is being a cad, and now this." She thrust her hand toward the ashes. "I foolishly allowed the coals to cool while I lingered too long in the meadow with Jadon. Now it shall be a late meal because of it." She took a breath after blurting out her complaints.

Alex reached into a leather pouch for a bit of oiled linen and started to shred the edges with his fingers. "Ruby, say nay more. I understand." He stooped and returned to the task of starting the fire. "What is Palmer doing to distress you?"

"He is simply a cad."

"Is he making advances?"

The kindling caught immediately. Soon, the fire was licking the cauldron above it. Alex sat cross-legged on the floor and looked at her for an answer.

"Very impressive, Sir Knight. Pray tell, how did you do that so quickly?"

"A knight can build a fire in a rainstorm, milady." He stood and showed her the linen in his pouch. "Just take a few scraps and soak it in oil and leave it to dry. Keep it in a leather pouch to protect it from the elements and use it to start the fire. 'Tis quite simple."

She smiled when Alex gave her a few scraps of the oiled linen. She swung the pot above the fire.

"Tell me what Palmer has done and I will ensure it ceases." Alex slipped his dagger from his belt and began to skin the rabbit at the table.

"He has taken nay liberties, Alex. Let it rest."

Alex peered at her. "Very well. You seem to enjoy your job as nursemaid. Are you happy here in the village?"

"Aye, I enjoy each day with Jadon." She wasn't sure how to answer the query as to whether she was happy, so she changed the subject. "When does Sarah intend on visiting? I miss her."

"'Twill be some time. Our men have joined with other armies and we shall be leaving within a day's time. She shall stay at Ramstone during our absence."

He waited a moment while she grabbed some rags to protect her hands from the heat of the pot and then handed her chunks of rabbit to add to it.

"Ruby, I do not wish to upset you, but I have come to speak my mind. You must return to Ramstone until all threat has passed."

Ruby's mind reeled at the sudden change in his manner. She took a moment to think while she stirred the meat into the vegetables. Turning, she placed her hands on the table and leaned toward him.

"Alex, please do not waste the little time you have left trying to sway my decision. Go home to Sarah. Deliver word that I shall visit soon. Give Galeron—" She blanched, realizing she nearly said to give him her love. She picked up several more pieces of rabbit and added them to the pot. "Tell him I wish him Godspeed and protection on the journey."

Alex poured water into the basin and washed his hands. She stared into the pot, watching the carrots float to the top, while his boots sounded on the wooden floor and stopped behind her. "Ruby, turn around."

She hooked the ladle and walked to the table, grabbed a cloth and scrubbed nonexistent spills.

"Galeron asked me to deliver this. He wished to do so himself."

She tossed the rag aside then tried to take it, but he kept hold. "First, you shall lend an ear."

She tugged, but he did not release it. "'Tis a conditional message, then?" Alex did not react to her insolence, keeping a grasp on it as well.

Alex sighed. "I am aware of treading past my boundaries, yet I must chance speaking the words you must heed."

"What words might those be? What can you possibly say that will change a thing?" She regretted her words when anger swept his face.

"Hell's teeth! How can you fall into my brother's arms and then push him away? The pain in your eyes matches his. I am afraid your decisions have wounded both of you. What is it you want? God in heaven, why do you deny thyself *and* Galeron?" His jaw clenched. He pressed the letter into her palm. "Good eve, Ruby." Alex grabbed his helmet and headed for the door.

She crushed the parchment in her fist. His stinging words rang of truth. Still, they angered her.

"Is it so difficult to understand, Alex?" she shouted. "Do you truly believe 'tis my choice to live my days with questions of who I am?" She choked back an angry sob while he closed the door and turned to face her. "I am trying to let go of my past, for I fear my memory will never come to light. As for your brother, I find it impossible to deny my love. I want—" She slapped her hands to her sides. "I wish to simply begin life anew in his arms." She pled with him, confessing through her tears. "Yet, 'tis not that simple, Alex. Nay matter what I set my mind to do, I find myself searching and picking up the pieces of a shattered life with naught to hold to."

Alex stomped to her. "Nay, Ruby, you do have something to hold to. You simply have chosen to push Galeron away with each step he takes toward you. I pray you read his letter and retrace your steps to Ramstone. Release the agony of your past. You must face the future. You both deserve a happy life."

His eyes met hers when she began to sob. "Do not weep. I beg you." He kissed her brow. "You have one lifetime, embrace it." He stroked her trembling fist clutching the letter. "Take every word to heart, dear maiden. I have never known my brother to write a letter to anyone. I trust it was done with a pure heart."

Ruby placed her hand on her chest. "His words *are* my heart, Alex. I turned him away because I may belong to another. That does not mean I do not love Galeron." Ruby bowed her head, watching her tears splash at her feet. "Because I do, Alex, with all I have."

Alex tilted her face to meet his gaze. "I realize that. 'Tis nay a love you can hide. However, 'tis not I you should confess to. Galeron has the right to know."

She stared at the letter while Alex kissed the top of her head. "Will you return with me?"

"I shall stay here."

Alex hugged her. "Be safe, dear friend. The knights are here for your protection. Do not hesitate to ask any one of them to escort you to Ramstone should you reconsider."

She released a shaky breath, looked at Alex and choked out a whisper, "I cannot promise a change of heart." *I can only promise a broken one.*

Alex stood in the doorway. "Read his words and you shall read his heart." He closed the door and called from the other side. "Secure it."

She latched the door, leaned heavily against it and listened to Alex's muffled footsteps until they faded away. With her back still against the door, she broke the wax seal and read the words Galeron had inscribed upon it.

My dearest Ruby,

The thought of you brings joy.
The flames reflecting in your hair,
the certain way your eyes enjoy mirth,
penetrate my soul.
The softness of your skin is but a memory,
yet passion cuts a path through my veins.
Every breath becomes torture.
Each beat of my heart yearns for your nearness.
Absence is reality when my arms reach for you.
My nights are empty with unfulfilled dreams.
I plant imaginary kisses upon each point your heart beats.
The sun rises to taunt my agony of knowing you are nay
longer here.
You have slain my heart, yet it lays waiting within the
softness of your hands,
fluttering and whispering of my love.
Hold it close.
Keep it safe until my return.
My heart surrenders to you.
My allegiance is to you.
Your past remains a mystery and your future remains to
unfold.
Allow it to unfold in my arms.
Nay longer deny our fate.
My dearest Ruby of the Forest,
'Tis you I desire,
'Tis you I cherish,
'Tis only you I choose to wed.
My love eternally waits for you.
~~~Your Galeron~~~

Ruby tucked the letter in her kirtle and spun around the room, singing, dancing, grabbing a ladle and kissing it—then froze with apprehension. Was this fair to him? To her? She was no closer to finding her past than she had been when they last spoke. Naught had been resolved. And what of his betrothed? The agreement? Did she dare believe? Trust?

"'Tis only you I choose to wed. My love eternally waits for you." She whispered his words. Inspired yet torn, she grabbed her art supplies and propped a fresh panel on her easel.

Hours later, the mouthwatering aroma of the simmering rabbit stew permeated the small room. Ruby washed her brushes as she examined her painting. The growling of her stomach reminded her of the time that she had been engrossed in her art, her comfort.

She swung out the pot and retrieved a chunk of rabbit, then frowned and allowed it to cook a bit longer. Her stomach growled as she secured the shutters and doors against the chill and darkness of the night.

The woolen blanket billowed in the air when she whipped it from the bed and lowered it onto the cold floor. She slipped off her boots and stockings, then propped her feet on the hearth, enjoying the fire's warmth. A thrill ran through her the moment she reached into her pocket and touched the letter for what seemed the hundredth time. Though the words were etched permanently upon her heart, she yearned to read Galeron's message once again. With a furrow of her brow and a conflicting smile, she slipped it out. Her lips moved silently while she relived the first moment of joy when her eyes fell upon his letter.

With a smile, Ruby tucked his words into the creases and caressed the folds, finding comfort in knowing his fingers touched the same edges. She slid it into her pocket, lay on her stomach and gazed into the fire.

Resting her head on her arms, she watched the blues and reds intermingle and shoot from the hot coals.

She slowly relinquished the pursuit of her past and listened to the unexpected song playing in her heart. It sang of promises. No matter what discoveries she made of her past, Galeron was sure to be part of her future. It played a tune, which brought the peace and contentment that evaded her for so long.

"The scratches of your quill upon this parchment shall be my treasure." The happiness in her voice sounded alien to her. She turned to her back, her hair falling across the blanket. "Dear Lord in heaven, keep him under your protection. Deliver Galeron from harm and bring him back to fulfill our life."

When she rose, the slight weight of the letter in her pocket made her smile. Impatient to eat, she ladled out a mug of broth, allowing the meat to cook a bit longer.

She settled on the blanket and finished the broth, welcoming the warmth and relaxation it offered. She sat the mug on the hearth and stretched out on the blanket. With the heat against her face, she waited for the stew to finish cooking and drifted to sleep with Galeron holding her in her dreams.

Chapter Twenty

Disagreement

In the main hall of Ramstone, Calen rescued his mug when Galeron pounded his fist against the table.

"Nay!" Galeron locked eyes with Easton. A splinter of fear pierced his heart. "'Tis a shame you had not informed me of this *notion* in private, Father." His jaw ached from the tension when he shot a threatening look at Calen. "Take your leave. I must speak with my father."

Calen's face transformed into a syrupy scowl. He turned from Galeron's glare and focused on Easton. "Shall you send me and my army away?"

"Nay, Calen. Stay seated."

Galeron gripped the edge of the table and towered over them. The time seemed to slow and grow stagnant, making it difficult for him to draw a breath. He bristled when Calen raised his mug. "Shall we toast?"

Galeron snatched Calen's mug, slamming it on the table. The heat of the room made him queasy. "Father, I have a matter to discuss which shall render this asinine idea useless."

Calen raised his portly body from the chair. "An agreement is — "

"Swine! Be off."

"Galeron!" Easton strode to Galeron and took him by the tunic. "The agreement is sealed."

When his father released him, Galeron thought his legs would buckle. Calen raised his mug once again and Galeron wrenched it from his hand. Easton's eyes widened when the mug crashed into the fire, sending sparks into the room.

"I refuse to be a pawn in this agreement!" Galeron grabbed Calen and threw him out the door, then turned to his bewildered father.

Galeron staggered when his father shoved past him and dragged the red-faced Calen back into the main hall. "Forgive my son's insolence."

Easton glared at Galeron, still in the doorway. "Be seated." Though his father's voice was low, Galeron heard the fury in his voice, so he sat without another word.

"The marriage agreement between you and Calen's daughter, Elizabeth, is sealed." Easton pressed his forehead against Galeron's and whispered, "You dare dispute me again, son, and the punishment shall be severe. We need his army."

Galeron glanced at Calen as he sat several chairs down. Desperate for an opportunity to escape such a fate, Galeron blurted out the first thing that entered his mind. "Father, I meant nay disrespect." He looked at Calen, his contempt well hidden. "I beg forgiveness.

You must understand this agreement is for naught." He ignored the sigh from his father.

"Nay?" Calen pointed to the rolled parchment in the middle of the table. "It seems to have your father's signature."

Galeron gripped his thighs to keep from slamming his fist in Calen's taunting smile. He realized the attempt was feeble, but until he could speak with his father in private… He looked across the table at his father. "Why would you sign? An agreement has already been sealed with Lord Ronan for the marriage to his daughter Mara."

Easton gave Galeron a questioning look. Moments passed in silence. Lord Calen spoke up, breaking the locked battle between Galeron and his father. "If I may speak—"

Galeron kept his eyes focused on his father. "With all due respect, Lord Calen, this is between my father and me."

"I shall not be dismissed. After all, it is *I* who suggested this agreement." Lord Calen leaned back in his chair and hooked his fat fingers in the sash around his sagging belly. "Be assured, my daughter is sought by many. Consider this an honor."

Beads of sweat trickled down his temple. He took a deep breath before speaking to Calen. "Pray tell, do you desire to keep that tongue you wag?"

"Galeron!"

Galeron glanced at his father. "Lord Calen, I am certain there is another way to repay you for your army's assistance." Turning to Easton, he continued. "Surely there is a parcel of land or a sack of gold coins to line his pockets?" He ignored the glare from his father. "'Tis a shame you have attempted to seal such an agreement when I am already indebted to Jastar."

Lord Calen cleared his throat. *"With all due respect,* Galeron, from what I gather, Jastar's daughter, Mara, is nowhere to be found and feared dead."

Betrayer. Galeron was certain his pulse visibly pounded at his temple. He hoped his father read the thought in his eyes. By the change from anger to confusion on his face, he had the whim he could. Galeron quietly responded to Calen while continuing to stare down his father.

"Until Mara is found, I am bound in the agreement with her father." Galeron wished to banish the man from the room so he could speak freely without the leering eyes of the vermin before him. Lord Calen continued to annoy him with his arrogant attitude when he placed his elbows on the table and dripped his sarcasm into the air.

"You are bound to the agreement? Where, pray tell, can Lord Ronan be found? Is he not among the ones you buried at Jastar?"

Galeron answered calmly. "It seems you have discussed the matter at length with my father. Now, *I* request to discuss it further." Slowly turning his head, he squinted at Calen. "Alone!"

"Galeron," Easton said. "Enough."

Lord Calen nervously pulled back from Galeron's menacing stance and looked to Lord Easton for support. He received a nod.

Calen waddled to the door, his stylish clothes pinching his rolls of fat. With his hand upon the handle, he turned back, red-faced irritation apparent in his sputtering protest. "'Tis imperative this agreement be honored, or my men shall leave Ramstone tonight."

"Understood. I shall send for you shortly," Easton said.

Lord Calen scowled and slammed the door behind him.

Before Galeron could utter a word, Lord Easton held up his hand. "What has given you the notion to show such disrespect?"

"Disrespect? Yet, you show no hesitation to disrespect me! You made an agreement that concerns my…" Galeron raked his hands through his hair. "You dare hurl the word disrespect? That, Father, is the stone you cast!"

Easton sighed. "Son, I regret I did not come to you first, but time did not allow the luxury. His army is strong, larger than our own, and combining them assures a future—"

"You need not explain. I know the power you crave, the control you always hold, the wealth that never seems to be enough." Galeron's fury unfurled like a flag in battle, and even if he wished to, he couldn't stop spewing his anger. "Even after mother died, you did not falter for a moment to grieve, but threw yourself into building this army, leaving your young sons to fend—" Upon witnessing the color drain from his father's face, he stopped. Galeron averted his gaze and paced about the room, the words dripping from the walls like oil. He finally stood with his back to his father, his hands clutching the mantel above the hearth. He spoke barely above a whisper, "I did not come to speak about that. Or a goddamn agreement, and certainly not to vomit words of hatred as I have. And for that, I beg forgiveness." He took a deep breath to quell his shaking. "I came to speak to you about Ruby."

"A knight has been posted outside her dwelling. Now, lend your attention to the matter at hand. Calen's army shall help our cause immensely. We need the power of many if we are to find and defeat the men who destroyed Jastar."

Did he not listen to a word he said? Galeron nudged a stray coal into the fire with his boot. "Find another way."

"Elizabeth is a fitting wife. You understand the politics of the situation. He is threatening to leave with his army. I cannot believe you choose to allow that to happen." Lord Easton raised his voice. "Turn and face me! I refuse to reason with your back to me."

Galeron swung around. "Find. Another. Way."

"The rampage shan't cease on its own. They do not know we are aware of their attack on Jastar. 'Tis an advantage we must act upon now. Your hesitation shall put many in peril. Galeron, I regret I lay such a burden upon your shoulders, yet it must be done. A marriage was to take place anyway. At least you are acquainted with this maiden."

"I shall not marry her."

"You never questioned your duty in the past. I shan't tolerate it now."

Galeron plopped in the chair by the fire. Resting his head in his hands, he stared at the floor, envisioning his dreams slipping through the wooden planks. "Father, I dare not question my duty as a knight. I fight to defend the innocent. I am willing to do whatever you ask of me, but I cannot marry Elizabeth. There must be another way." He raised his head, his gaze boring into his father's for several moments while he tried to find the words to convey all he needed to tell.

"What ails thee, son?" Easton whispered.

Galeron's mind crowded with emotion. The possibility of losing the joy he had experienced when he composed the letter to Ruby becoming a reality. He wanted to explain everything to his father, but he simply whispered his confession instead.

"I love Ruby."

"Ah. I see."

Easton rubbed his palm across the table. "You have fancied a fair amount of maidens in the past. Now, you believe your heart fancies Ruby."

"A coin for a wench does not compare to something so pure." His face heated with anger. "Tread softly, Father."

Easton smiled at Galeron, seemingly composing his thoughts. A pop from the damp wood crackled loudly from the fireplace, echoing through the silence. He finally spoke after what seemed an eternity to them both.

"I daren't minimize the feelings you believe you hold for Ruby. She is a beautiful maiden." He picked up his chair, moving it closer to Galeron. "However, she knows naught of her past and holds nay future to speak of. Though being a commoner is nay fault of her own, 'tis where she stands. It shall haunt you both someday. In time you shall realize a future together is pure fantasy."

Galeron tried to ignore his father's attitude toward social standing. He had no time to argue but one fact. "I am sure of my heart."

Easton placed his hands on Galeron's shoulders. Looking him straight in the eyes, he spoke softly, but firmly. "Your duties lie here, not with a waif you found in the forest. Ramstone requires your agreement to take Elizabeth as your betrothed. I have allowed you to sow your seed about the country while I watched your younger brother marry before you. The time has come for you to fulfill *your* duty as a knight of Ramstone with this agreement. You shall fulfill the need for a mightier army, as well as producing an heir to carry on the Ramstone name."

"Ruby shall bear my babes. Nay other."

"A simple village maiden does not have the social standing Elizabeth meets. An agreement has been sealed and you shall hold to it."

"She is —"

"Galeron, you shall do this."

"I love her. Only her."

Easton dragged Galeron out of his chair and slammed him against the wall. "*Love* has naught to do with this. *Love* brings destruction. Your mother looks down on you and sees this insolence. Grant her a bit of happiness and honor your duty as her eldest son!" Breathing in gasps, he looked at his fist, about to strike his son. "Oh my God." He dropped his hand. "Forgive me."

Galeron shrugged from his grasp. "Mother has naught to do with this."

Easton shook his head, his voice barely audible. "You shall follow your duty, not the whimsy of what you believe is love." He rested his hand on Galeron's back. "You shall see that in time, son. Until that time comes, I trust you daren't question your duty as a knight…and your mother's son."

Emptiness took harbor in his soul while his heart evaporated into a vapor. Galeron shrugged away. "Inform Lord Calen he must have his men ready by dawn," he whispered. "You shall always regret this, Father." Striding off, he disregarded his father's plea to wait. With his mind scrambling to find a way out of the hell he had pitched into, he flung open the doors and headed outside. He stood, nearly at attention, in the gardens where he had played as a boy with Alex and his mother.

His hands shook as he raked his fingers through his hair, slumping on his mother's garden bench — the very bench he and Alex had built for her when she was with child. He cradled his face in his hands. The letter he had sent to Ruby, so full of promise, now remained tainted with heartache. Though he held no regret for the words he wrote, he regretted the fact Ruby's eyes fell upon them while their future dreams spun out of reach. Hot tears dripped into his palms.

Chapter Twenty-One

Nightmare

Ruby clutched her chest and bolted from sleep. With her heart slamming, she tried to fathom what the commotion was. The continuing screams shredded her nerves. Her bare feet tangled in the blankets when she scrambled from the floor, and she kicked them away. She tried to clear her head and struggled to unlatch the shuttered window with shaky hands. She peered out the small crack she allowed, but all she saw was the moonless night. A terrifying cry was so close she jumped, slamming the shutter on her fingers. She backed away. Her hair whipped her cheek while she searched for something — anything, to use as a weapon. She grabbed a carving knife and stood, frozen, wondering what she must do. Oh God, Jadon! She ran to the back entrance, the love for the child lending her the courage to unbolt the door. She grabbed a breath, then, with darkness as her savior, she slid into the night.

She pressed against the wall, the cold wood permeating her thin kirtle. The acrid smoke snatched any freshness of the crisp night. Flinching at the sound of the screams and clashing swords, she crept in the darkness. A sharp stone cut her foot and she considered backtracking to retrieve her boots. More screams. Closer now. With the jab of stones pricking her feet, she continued to the corner of her dwelling and peered around.

The smoke made it difficult to discern between the silhouettes of knights in horned helmets fighting with those from Ramstone. Despite the cold, her skin was hot.

"Nay, dear sir. Take me! I shall give you anything. Spare my son!"

Ruby could do no more than stare at the woman begging for her child. The horned knight kicked the woman to the ground and rode off.

Ruby shook uncontrollably and wept while the woman ran after the knight, screaming the child's name. She shouted to warn her of another knight bearing down behind the woman, but her voice did not carry over the commotion. Without slowing his pace, he whisked the pleading woman into the saddle and fled from the village, her screams fading into the night. Were they stealing everyone? Why? She must stop them from taking Jadon. But how?

Lightheaded and nauseated, she slid down the wall and hugged her knees. Hot beads of sweat cooled against her skin. She scratched the uneven surface of the wall behind her until her fingers ached. She suffered pain, so 'twas not a nightmare. This was happening. Her lips moved silently in prayer while tears coursed down her face. The cries from the villagers grew closer with each shattered breath she took. She would soon be discovered if she continued to cower. Though fear immobilized her, it terrified her even more to think of Jadon in peril.

The darkness quickly surrendered to the light of the spreading flames. Knowing time was of the essence, Ruby saw her way clear, then fled as if the devil himself was in pursuit.

Stones and twigs tore at her bare feet while she crossed the narrow alley that took her to the rear wall of Jadon and Palmer's home. She nearly ran full force into their back entrance. Her lungs burned. Jadon's sobs and Palmer's shouts pierced her sanity.

"Papa, nay!"

The knife secure in her fist, she tried the door. Locked. Tears of frustration sprang to her eyes. She froze at the sound of hateful, mocking laughter. The hair on her arms stood.

She inched to the window and gave a tug on the shutter, again thwarted by a latch. Bile rose in her throat. Every fiber of her being ached to reach Jadon. She slid the knife between the shutters and lifted the latch. She waited a moment, then, with her breath frozen in panic, she pushed open the shutter.

Firelight filtered in from the adjoining room but she was unable to see anyone. Jadon whimpered. Palmer wept. Fear paralyzed her with each word of his plea.

"I beg thee, sir, release my son."

"Stand back or I shall slice his throat," a deep voice said.

Jadon's scream relinquished her fear and courage filled the void. Ruby hoisted herself up and scrambled in. She crawled across the room on all fours, careful to keep the knife from tapping the floor. She kept to the shadows and peered out the edge of the doorway. She pressed her hand against her mouth, stifling an involuntary scream.

A dark armored knight held Jadon, draped like a sack on his arm. His massive hands dug into the child's side while Jadon's small arms reached for his father.

Palmer stood, pleading at the point of the knight's sword. "Take all I have. I shall give you anything. You have nay need of a child. He is but an innocent babe."

A deep laugh echoed from within the horned helmet. "I shall take all ye have anyway. The boy shall leave with me."

Palmer ran to a chest against the wall, flinging it open. The knight swung Jadon in front of him, his little feet dangling in the air. When he placed his blade on the child's throat, Jadon's face paled.

A gasp escaped her lips, but Palmer's shout covered any noise she made.

"Nay! I was retrieving this sack of gold coins." Tears streamed down Palmer's face. "I beg mercy." He held out the coins. "Take it. Take all I have. I b-beg thee. I shall do anything you want." Palmer fell to his knees. "You can take my life, just daren't harm my s-son."

The knight sheathed his sword and kicked Palmer to the floor. He pressed his boot at Palmer's neck. "I shall not harm the lad. What use do I have for a dead child? 'Tis a live boy I require."

Ruby frowned. What requirement could a child fulfill for him?

With Jadon still in his arms, the knight snatched the sack of coins from Palmer's grasp. "However, I thank ye for yer generosity."

Palmer took the chance of his closeness, grabbing hold of Jadon's nightshirt. The knight kicked him in the face. Even from the distance, Ruby heard Palmer's bones crack.

"Papa! Do not let him take me!" Jadon screamed while the knight carried him to the door.

She took a step, ready to run out of the shadows after him, but hesitated when Palmer retrieved his sword by the fireplace. Unsheathing it as he ran, he lunged for the knight.

The knight threw Jadon and drew his sword in one fluid movement. Jadon landed with a sickening thump, against the wall. Blood flowed into the child's terrified eyes as he caught sight of her. She pressed a finger to her lips, scooted on her belly and grabbed his outstretched fingers. She slid him through the doorway, at the same moment witnessing the evil knight's sword slip out of Palmer's chest.

She tucked the knife into her sash and gathered Jadon into her arms, shielding him from the sight of his father's body. To her dismay, the knight turned. He growled upon seeing her flee to the window. She lowered Jadon to the ground. "Run, little knight! Run!"

The knight grabbed her skirt and yanked her backward. Her stomach scraped the sill. With all her strength, she kicked at him. The fabric tore, leaving him holding a remnant of her skirt as she fell out of the window. Still trying to regain her breath after the hard fall, she realized Jadon hadn't moved from where she'd dropped him. Ruby scooped Jadon into her arms and fled.

The pound of the knight's boots fueled her resolve. She dashed into her back entrance, dumped Jadon on his feet and secured the door.

"Where's Papa?" His eyes rounded. "We must save him!"

Ruby handed him the carving knife. "I beg thee, be a brave knight." She dragged him to the bed. "Hide under here until I fetch you. If anyone else comes, use the knife."

"But—"

Crashes filtered from the art shoppe. "Make haste! Hide!" She slid him under the bed and rearranged the rushes on the floor to hide his tracks. Though her dwelling was tiny, it seemed an eternity before she reached the door adjoining the art shoppe. The commotion on the other side confirmed her fear. He had found the other way in.

"Go—go—go." Ruby willed her fingers to cooperate with the task of bolting the door. Before she could secure the latch, the door splintered. It took a moment to grasp how she ended on the floor.

She saw movement underneath the bed and feared Jadon would cry out. Still on her bottom, she scooted backward, trying to get to her feet. His gauntlet slammed into her cheek, nearly rendering her senseless.

"Wench! Where is my boy?"

"S-Sir, he ran off."

Hot, rotting breath blasted her face while he effortlessly raised her by her neck. She clawed at his arm in blind panic. She kicked against his armor, then froze while his face distorted into another's—a gaping hole where his eye should be—a dagger pulsating in its place. The vision disappeared when the knight pinched her breast.

"Ahh, ye be a tender poppet."

With her lungs begging for relief, she pulled off his helmet and bashed it into his face.

He wrenched it from her and tossed it aside. "Bitch!" He slammed his forehead against hers. "Ye best tell me now." His bloodshot eyes were all she could see.

Her dagger. Ruby reached for it, hidden in her boot. Nay. She was barefoot, yet her dagger's hiding place seemed so real. She drew a laborious breath, certain it was her last, and began losing sight of the knight. She sucked a bit of air. "You. Must. Come. With. Me!" Her eyes rolled back.

The knight loosened his grasp on her neck. "Why must I come, wench? Ah, ye have decided to show me where he is?"

"N-nay, he is d-dead." Naught made sense anymore. Who was dead? What was she saying?

"He be alive. What did ye do with the lad?"

"The lad," Ruby repeated, fighting to remain sane.

His voice broke through her haze. "I saw ye take him. Now I see why ye did such a thing." The knight lowered her to the ground, his voice quiet and syrupy.

She drew a painful breath and winced when he smoothed her hair.

He smiled. "Ye see, the boy be mine. I was rescuing him when ye took him away." He ran his hand against her cheek. "Ye poor soul, ye thought 'twas helping."

"He is not yours, filthy brute." Her legs threatened to buckle when he backhanded her. "H-he ran. I-I know not where." Her neck wrenched when he delivered another blow. She spat blood. "W-wasting precious time, sir. The ungrateful snip will be far off if you do not hasten."

With a snarling growl, he flung her across the room, nearly sending her into the fire.

Another child must not die because of her. She would die defending him. Ruby crawled away from the advancing knight and pulled herself upright. His laugh blended with the ring in her ears. She stumbled through the shoppe doorway.

He wrapped his arm around her waist and pulled her back. Splinters embedded her fingertips when she tried to hold on.

"Do you not see? I shall help you find the ingrate."

"I shall find him soon enough, me lovely." He pulled her hair, forcing her to face him. "I ache for a rutting."

She denied him the satisfaction of fear and clenched her eyes. "What of the boy?"

He licked her face. "I have a way of torturing tender bodies. First, we have a friendly little rut, then ye shall tell of the lad's whereabouts." His whisper struck her harder than any of his blows.

She blinked, trying her best to focus. "Sir, I speak the truth. The ungrateful child ran from here before I could enter my door. I did not even see which way he went." She did not break his stare. "You followed me for naught." *Go back to the depths of hell you came from.*

He struck her with the back of his hand. Her world went black. She sensed she was floating…until she slammed against the floor. Through her haze, she heard something metal drop near her head.

"Wake up, lying whore!" He straddled her waist, grabbed her bodice and shook her. "Where he be?"

"Nay." Tears dripped into her ears. She closed her eyes, welcoming death. It had to be death. Naught could hurt her there.

"Bless my seed, Lord." His whisper muffled against her neck.

Her body seemed separate and her pain ebbed. He stank. The smell piqued her senses, bringing her fully conscious. She felt his body against her. It made no sense. Another metallic clunk and his chest plate, chainmail and other parts of his armor *thunked* on the floor. "God in heaven, deliver me."

"God cannot deliver anything, me sweet whore." His knuckles dug against her while he unclasped the flap of his breeches.

She realized then he had not yet begun to torture her. She grabbed the closest piece of armor and slammed it against his head.

He didn't flinch—only yanked her hands above her head and held them to the floor with his weight. "Do not try me patience, wench."

Her clothing twisted between her legs as she tried to avoid the teeth tearing her bodice. She stared at the bed, hoping Jadon did not peer out. The knight squeezed two fingers between her jaws. Ruby tried but couldn't keep her mouth closed. He thrust his tongue in her mouth. She bit down, taking fingers and tongue, and gagging on his blood.

He slapped her. "Yer fire shall be well received by the others." He tore her skirt to her waist. Terror paralyzed her scream as his clawing bruised her tender skin.

"Breeches?" For a moment he seemed confused, then laughed and ripped them to the crotch.

"Nay!" She bit his shoulder, thrashing like a mad dog defending his kill. She spat out the chunk of his flesh, aiming for his face but missing.

He grappled at his wound and rose to his knees, still straddling her. As he pulled back to deliver another blow, she scooted from beneath him. Sparks, colors and a loud hum filled her head. She barely felt the next blow. Her mind screamed, the terror unable to pass her lips while his filthy finger molested her maidenhood. She choked and tasted vomit.

"Stand back! Daren't hurt my Ruby!" Was that a voice?

The hand stopped its invasion. Ruby shouted for Galeron. Or mayhap she simply thought his name. She swiped the blood from her eyes. Nay, it wasn't Galeron standing there, it was Jadon, brandishing a knife over his head.

"Run!" she screamed. "Oh God, run!"

Still trapping her with his knees, the knight sat up and glanced at the fresh gash on his arm. He grinned at the boy. "Ye scrap, there ye are. Now give me that knife fore I take it from ye."

She slammed both hands into his chest, but it didn't budge him an inch. Nor did it take his attention from Jadon, standing there in all his knightly glory. "Jadon! Run!"

Too late, the knight sent a backhand across one small cheek. The blow opened a gash on Jadon's face.

Blood trickled from his temple. "A knight does not run." He lunged, aiming the blade at the face of her attacker.

She wailed and squirmed, pounded and thrashed. Anything to detract the knight's attention from the child. "Ja-a-don!"

Her attacker leaped off, wiping the blood from his face. "Ye cut me!" He intercepted the next jab and picked up Jadon.

She pushed to her knees, squeezing her eyes against the nausea, willing herself to remain conscious. She shook her head, but only sprinkled the floor with blood.

"Ruby!" Jadon screamed.

The knight struck him. "Yer worth is all that keeps me from killing ye."

With pure fury, she threw herself at them. One of his arms flashed out. He effortlessly sent her airborne. Jadon's cries gave her the determination once again to stand. With terror imprisoning her mind, movement seemed to slow.

"Wench. Do not think ye be spared." The knight's laughter rumbled. He tossed the knife aside and secured his manhood into his breeches.

Jadon resembled a corpse standing.

The knight shook Jadon by the back of his nightshirt. "Here be me sack of gold."

The room seemed immense, almost like a long corridor which did not end.

"The lad shall be mine after all, eh, wench? Now *both* ye shall bring Master's praises." His voice was ragged as he stalked her, dragging Jadon behind him. "Yer a vessel. The lad interrupted the blessing. Perhaps 'tis the Lord's will to wait. Much sweeter ye be a virgin for the Master."

She could not understand his ranting. Neither did she care. Her only concern — the child she loved, held in his filthy grasp.

"Jadon?" Her voice echoed in the corridor. She shook her head. No corridor. Her room. This was her home. "Jadon, speak to me."

The knight released Jadon then nudged him with his boot when he fell to the floor. "There be more lads in this village, eh?" He began to dress.

Hate, hot as hell fire, stripped what was left of her sanity. The pop and gurgle of the stew drew her attention. A turnip bobbed with the boil.

An idea surfaced. "I believe this fight has left me wanting of you." That would get the bastard's attention. Now he would pay.

With his chainmail still in his hand, his jagged toothed smile met hers. "Aye, ye be a dirty girl." He tossed the chainmail aside and came toward her.

She reached into the fire, the stench of burned skin licking her senses. It took a moment to register she held the pot, and another to suffer the searing pain.

With every bit of strength she possessed, she heaved it.

Her scream mingled with his wails. He held his face, falling to his knees.

It seemed an eternity for her foot to meet his chest. He fell back, blindly reaching for her. She grabbed a chair and swung. The sound of a bone cracking made her smile. She wished she could shatter every bone in his body.

Ruby snatched Jadon by the wrist and dragged the limp body through the doorway. She stood in the middle of the art shoppe. Lost. She walked toward flames, drawn by the burning, beautiful paintings. The smoke closed her lungs. The fire lapped closer.

Jadon coughed.

"J-Jadon?" She fell to her knees. His hot breath on her cheek woke her sanity. She lifted him and stumbled outside. She moved unsteadily, as if she were a puppet under someone else's control.

Stand strong. The voice seemed to come from inside her head.

Jadon was a dead weight in her arms.

Stand strong. Was she mad? She welcomed it, for it diminished the screams in the village, easing her fear. Though surrounded by death and fighting, she was alone. The smoke, so thick she tasted it, stung her eyes. Her nostrils filled with the stench of burning flesh and she wondered if it was her hands. Flames licked the darkness, the heavy heat bearing down on her.

"Stand strong." She repeated the words aloud, strength the furthest from her grasp. Her arms seemed broken twigs. Jadon weighed a ton.

Tears blurred the chaos. She stumbled through black smoke and into the alley. Galeron's stallion stood waiting. Oh dear God, was he hurt? Dead?

The horse's nostrils flared, its eyes controlled with years of training. The reins dragged the ground, the war saddle empty. She blinked, sure the vision would disappear. The horse remained.

She lowered Jadon by an overturned cart, afraid to turn away. The boy slumped to the ground. "Easy," she said. The horse sidestepped. She limped closer. Hell's teeth, what did Galeron name his horse? She realized she had never asked. "Dare not flee, I beg you."

The stallion snorted as if he understood. She grabbed the reins. Jolts of pain throbbed in her hands, as if they'd been dipped in pitch and made into torches, but she did not let go. The battle seemed disconnected and oddly cloudlike.

The stallion's eyes bulged and its ears laid back on its head. The animal reared, nearly wrenching her shoulder from the socket. "Easy, you demon!" The horse calmed a bit, but snorted its distaste. "Demon," she said again. "Is that your name?" Ruby gasped at the flash of white. She tugged the horse's head down. Aye, thank the heavens, one ear *was* white. Galeron's steed was dark as sin, naught a speck of anything but black. She glanced at Jadon. His chest moved.

"Come, Demon." She moved on, leading it through the alley. "I swear, I shall slay you myself if you fight me again." Her voice dripped with gentleness.

She tied the reins to a twisted knurl of a tree that looked evil and alive. Swords clashed, screams of dying and wounded, shouts, orders, crackle of burning timber…everything flooded in. She backed away, tree branches like claws reaching for her. Her palm slipped against her neck. Pain and insanity collided.

She held to the wall bordering the alley. Each step led to another and another until she reached Jadon. She gathered him in her arms, their blood mingling, the pain shared. His head lolled back. A moan, long and drawn, passed his gaping mouth. She clutched him to her breast and stumbled to the horse, praying for strength.

She grunted as she eased Jadon over the saddle. Her stomach lurched with each attempt to hoist herself behind him. The war saddle seemed to cradle her. The horn bit into her waist as she leaned forward to gather the reins, but could not free them.

"Nay," she whimpered. Certain they were about to be found, she slid down and freed them from the tree. She clawed at the horn, all strength turning liquid, and she doubted she could mount again. A sword against another clashed nearby. The encroaching knights loaned the strength she lacked.

She ducked low in the saddle and with the stirrups cool against her tattered feet, she kicked the snorting beast into a full gallop, holding tight to Jadon with one hand, the reins with the other. Heartbeats and prayers to stay aboard drummed in time with the hooves, the sanctuary of Ramstone a reality. Tears blew from her face. Her throat ached whenever she tried to draw a full breath.

Free of the village, she dared her first relieved breath. Hoofbeats drew near.

"Nay, a foe!" came a shout.

Digging her heels into Demon, she glanced back. A scant group of villagers caught up and together they fled under the cloak of darkness. A bit more secure accompanied by the few fortunate enough to find a way out of the pillage, she led the way out.

A flash of lightning illuminated the sky. Was she forever cursed? A storm dared make the night even worse? As if in answer, the sky opened, crying for the dead. She draped herself over Jadon, but the bitter cold and unrelenting rain saturated the remnants of her clothing. In the least, 'twould douse the fires devouring the village.

She tried to wake Jadon, and though dark, she could see his head wound had stopped bleeding. Why then, did he not wake? She kept her fingers on his pulse. It was weak, but steady. After what seemed hours in the storm, she slowed her pace and shifted Jadon. "All is well, child. You are safe now." How she wished she could believe her words.

He slumped against her chest. "Speak to me, my little knight." She couldn't even cry. "Jadon, you must wake. For me. Please!" Urging the horse forward, she repeated pleas of Jadon's name into the night.

Chapter Twenty-Two

Speak to Me

"Riders approach!" The call echoed from the turrets. Galeron and Alex strapped on their swords and ran to the inner ward with Rafe and Easton on their heels. Already, many of his men were armed and running to the gates.

"Galeron!" A shout rang from the other side, far in the distance. An awful boding wrenched Galeron's gut, stopping him in his tracks. It was her voice.

"Ga-ler-on!" Ruby's drawn out plea rose above the others. Then a great pounding, as if a million fists clamored against the gates, overpowered every sound.

"Open the gates!" Galeron shouted, racing ahead.

The night took on a dreamlike quality. The villagers fled through, many of them weeping, but one woman stood silent just outside the gates, her face to the skies, holding a child. Was it Ruby? Or did he imagine her voice?

"The villagers say horned knights—" Alex shouted, but Galeron was already in a full run.

"Ruby!" She did not answer as he raced to her. Something about her stance struck him. She was hurt.

She dropped to her knees, cradling Jadon as the last few villagers pushed by. Her eyes looked to be open, but they did not seem to see anything. The brothers reached her at the same time.

"Damn the one who did this." Galeron knelt beside her. "I shall kill him."

She blinked at his shout. "Jadon. Hurt."

"I have him, Ruby." Alex took him from her arms.

Galeron lifted her battered frame and carried her inside the gates. Ruby's trembling grasp nearly tore his tunic when the heavy plank slid across the gates.

"They at-attacked."

Her voice was so thin, he could barely make out her words. "Rest, fair one. Do not try to talk." He noticed her wince when he shifted his grasp.

Easton rushed to them. "The peasants say the village is— Ruby! What happened?"

"Someone has beaten her. Are you blind?" He rushed by but Easton and Alex followed, asking questions.

"Who did this?"

"Ruby, how did Jadon get hurt?"

"Where is Palmer?"

"Is *he* the one who attacked you?" Galeron glanced at Alex. "Arse. He shall pay."

Her eyes looked wild. Had he lost her to madness? "Ruby? Who hurt you?"

She raised her hands. "Cease shouting!"

Galeron grabbed her by the wrist. "Dear God! What happened to your hand?"

Ruby seemed distant. "He hurt Jadon."

"Palmer?"

"Dead." She pushed against his chest. "I am ill. Release me. "

He lowered her. Shakes ravaged her whole body and she swallowed several times, but did not empty her stomach. He did not ask any more questions. "Come now. Let me take you out of this rain."

She turned away and shook her head. "She is splashing right through the puddles."

Galeron followed her gaze. Sarah ran toward them, shouting Ruby's name.

"Her skirts shall muddy." Ruby sighed. "A shame."

Galeron realized then that her tattered hands were the least worry. He uttered a silent prayer.

Sarah removed her cloak and wrapped it around Ruby's shoulders. "You are safe now."

"Jadon…" Ruby blinked several times, her expression one of waking from a dream. "Where is he!"

"Right here." Jadon's head fell back when Alex placed the child in Sarah's arms. "Sarah shall tend him."

Galeron glimpsed Jadon's face, pale and drenched a contrast to his blood-soaked hair. "You tend him, Alex."

"We must go." Alex nodded at Sarah. "She knows what to do. I taught her well."

Ruby smiled and kissed Jadon's brow. "Sweet knight, you are safe." She looked up at Sarah. "T-take him inside."

"Of course, but you are hurt as well. Come with us."

"Soon." Ruby peered at Galeron. In the darkness, he could not see her clearly, but her hands almost clawed through his tunic. "Everything is burning. Fire everywhere."

"I shall carry you in now, Ruby."

Ruby's hand shook as she pointed. "Take him now."

"Only with you." Sarah tugged her arm.

"No, I shall only bring harm!" Her shout silenced Sarah, who hurried Jadon out of the rain, but hesitated when she reached the doorway.

"Go!"

Galeron pulled her into his arms, stifling her scream. "Easy." He wanted to take her inside, but did not want to distress her further. "They took leave. See? Alex is going as well. He shall tend Jadon."

"I killed him."

For a moment Galeron believed he heard wrong, but then she pulled away. "I killed him."

"Who? The enemy?"

"Nay." She gasped. "The boy..." The sudden tilt of her head made him ache. She did not make any sense. He drew her back into his arms, trying to shield her from madness.

Galeron wiped the rain from his face. "You must get out of this storm."

"Dare not take me in there." Ruby's eyes sought his. "*He* is there. Dead. 'Twas my fault."

Galeron nearly touched his nose to hers. "Focus. He lives."

"He is—he is *hanging* in there." Ruby pounded his chest. "You do not listen!"

Did she not notice pain? He held her wrists to stop any further damage to her hands. For a moment, neither spoke. She pulled back. Even in the shadows, he saw her recognition. "G-Galeron?"

When he heard the confusion in her voice, Galeron led her to an overhang, shielding her from the rain. They were close enough to the torches to take advantage of the warmth. Though he sensed her reluctance, he led her into the light.

She refused to look at him.

"Time is of the essence, fair one. Tell of the attack." Mayhap she would describe her own attacker. Galeron prayed he still lived, for he wished his own sort of revenge.

Her haunted expression was barely discernible. There were more wounds than healthy skin on her face. Her lips, once so beautiful, were split and swollen. He wanted to slaughter the one who had inflicted the wounds, but he kept silent, waiting for her to speak.

"He…" She looked back down. "Spirits save me."

Galeron traced his finger along her chin and lifted her face. His ire boiled at the marks on her neck, but he swallowed his rage. "Sweet Ruby, speak to me." He concentrated on keeping his hands from fisting while Ruby spoke numbly about the attack on the village. She told how the knight had killed Palmer and attempted to kidnap Jadon. When she spoke of the knight in her dwelling, she shook uncontrollably, no matter how he tried to comfort her.

"J-Jadon tried to s-save me. The stew. Alex brought rabbit." She peered up at him. "I have not had rabbit in such a long while."

He regretted asking. "Enough."

"It was boiling. I threw…he…the knight—we escaped." Her wide eyes, cavernous with shock, filled with tears.

"Jadon saw." She stared through him, as if seeing the whole horrific scene again. "I killed a man."

"Fear not, the stew would do nay more than burn the bastard." Galeron silently vowed he would run a sword through his gut. "Jadon witnessed naught but your bravery, sweet one." He coaxed her out of the light of the torches.

"Did Alex tend to Jadon?" She blinked. "The lance rammed through him."

Galeron hesitated for a moment. "Ruby, Jadon was not harmed in such a way."

She looked across the inner ward and whipped her gaze to Galeron. "I was there. I saw!" She burst into tears and pushed away from him. "Nay, I am mixing memories of madness."

He held her, fearing for her sanity. Knowing he must go, he broke it gently. "Sarah shall stay with you while I am gone."

A glint of her strength shone through. The jut of her chin, the one he loved, gave him hope. "You must go, but I daren't leave anything unsaid." Her voice tinted with rage.

"We shall speak of it when I return from battle." Galeron feathered his fingers against her hair. When he pulled away his hand, blood smeared his palm. "No more talk. You must be seen to."

She clenched her eyes, sending the tears straight to his heart. Galeron wiped them away before they stung her wounds. He gently kissed her lashes. A small sob escaped her lips and nearly broke his resolve.

"Shhh…" He continued to kiss her face, ending at the corner of her lips, afraid to touch them lest he hurt her further. He cradled her for several moments. Ruby spoke while burrowing her head beneath his chin.

"I tried to fight." Her sobs shook them both.

Galeron paused the stroking of her hair. He took a deep breath and gently placed his finger against her swollen lips. "Speak nay more." He swallowed hard. "The devil's spawn shall pay with his life, Ruby. I promise you this." Though he spoke softly, his fury pulsed through thoughts of revenge. "My love, the torture you endured shall not go unpunished."

He sealed his promise with a gentle kiss. She parted her lips and though it pained her, he matched her probing tongue, lifting her in his arms. Her body relaxed and she nuzzled into his neck. "He did not—"

"Shh, fair one."

"He did not take me fully."

It took all Galeron had not to scream his fury. "All that matters is your life. You are safe now," he whispered.

He held her wounded soul in his arms. She wrapped her arms around his neck and burrowed deeper. Gods, how his very core ached. Galeron had no intention of letting her out of his arms just yet and stepped into the inner ward, shouting orders to the men.

Lord Calen arrived at the scene and quickly dispatched his own men, shooting a hateful glare toward Galeron. Galeron ignored him, too occupied to care why he scowled.

She tensed and clutched her mouth. He lowered her to the ground and knelt beside her, holding back her hair while she heaved. With the last of her strength depleted, Ruby closed her eyes. "Your letter…"

Galeron scooped the unconscious Ruby into his arms. Mud splashed his legs while he ran, his heart ripping from him. He searched the crowd and found his father. "Take over my duties."

"What happened?"

Galeron rushed past, his father's shout echoing in his ears, "Make haste, Galeron. 'Tis imperative you leave within moments!"

"Alex," he screamed as he ran up the stairs.

Sarah met him at the top. "Galeron, what is— Oh dear Lord!"

"Is Alex with Jadon?"

"Nay, Jadon woke screaming. Alex gave the child milk of poppy to ease his pain, then left him sleeping. 'Twas where I was when I heard your shouts."

"I do not need a full account, woman. Find him. Now."

"He is with his squire, readying for battle."

"Damnation!" Galeron sprinted toward Ruby's former bedchamber. Nearly splintering the door with a kick, he laid her upon the bed.

Alex called from the lower level. "Galeron, Father has the men ready. We must depart!" His boots sounded on the stairs. "Galeron!"

"Ruby's chamber!" Galeron shouted.

"'Tis Ruby." Sarah's voice grew nearer. "The men can wait."

"Nay, Sarah, they cannot." Alex's footsteps quickened, then stopped.

Sarah began to sob. "I just saw her in full light. She is horribly beaten."

"Alex!" Galeron watched Ruby's shallow breaths, afraid they would cease should he leave her side. "Now!"

'Twas then an argument started nearby. "Where the hell is my armor?"

"You shan't battle tonight."

Sarah came into the room. "Alex is on his way."

"Is that Jac?" Before Sarah could answer, shouts echoed through the corridor.

"Are you mad? The word is of dark knights with horns upon their helmets. Sound familiar? I *shall* battle tonight."

Galeron strode to the doorway. "Leave him be!"

Alex shoved past Jac. "Very well, if you choose to be a fool, then do so."

"She fell unconscious." Galeron did not tell of her momentary madness. In the least, he hoped it would pass. "Do something."

Alex examined the angry cuts on her face. "Good God."

"The back of her head, Alex. Her blood is already turning the pillow red."

"Stand back, Galeron." Galeron was very familiar with Alex's healing expertise and thanked the Lord for his brother in that moment. "Head wounds bleed freely. This is but a small cut, not as bad as it looks." Alex took the bandages from Sarah and wrapped Ruby's head. "Go prepare for battle." He glanced up when Galeron made no move to leave. "Her clothing is torn." He quickly looked away and tied off the head bandage. Galeron clenched his jaw when Alex moved aside what was left of her tattered skirt. The sight of her torn breeches brought bile to his throat.

"Bruising. Dammit it all to hell."

"Nay." Sarah's hand flew to her chest.

Alex swallowed hard. "I can give her something to stop a child from growing within her."

Galeron snatched the blanket and covered Ruby's nakedness. "She was left innocent. She said as much."

Alex pushed the blanket aside and Galeron covered her again. "Galeron, I am not done examining her legs. They could be broken."

"She stood on them. They are fine."

"Do you wish me to examine her or not?"

Galeron lifted her hand. "Examine these!"

Alex peered at the scorched skin hanging from her palm, then examined the other one. "How did this happen? Did she say?"

"She threw a boiling pot of stew in her attacker's face."

Alex looked away from the darkness in Galeron's eyes. "Sarah, send for the healer. He is in the west wing, tending the wounded villagers."

Galeron grabbed Alex, who winced. "You shall tend her! You are the best of them. Even our own healer searches you out for advice."

Alex spoke quietly but firmly. "You think I do not wish to? Damnation, Galeron, we must battle. Now. So lead your fucking men."

Galeron knew he was right. Ruby's condition shook him. He released Alex. He hated his panic. Never had anyone made him care so much. Ruby must live. He cared not if he returned from battle with a breath left in him if she did not survive.

"Sarah and the house doctor shall do a fine job of tending to her." Alex gripped his shoulder. "Her spirit is strong." Alex prodded him to leave Ruby's side. "Your squire awaits and your mount is saddled and armored."

Sarah took Galeron's face in her hands. "Ease your mind. I shan't leave her side. Return safe." She kissed Alex. "Both of you."

"Watch over them *both*," Galeron said. "She cannot survive any harm to Jadon. I fear her spirit is broken."

Sarah, choked with emotion, simply nodded. He allowed Sarah a moment alone with Alex and turned from their intense kiss. The kiss of battle.

Galeron's tear fell on Ruby. A single tear. No more. He blocked his heartache and nuzzled his face into her rain-soaked hair. With Alex encouraging him to depart, he whispered in her ear. "I shall avenge the demon who caused you harm, my sweet jewel. Hold fast to the words in my letter. Hold fast to our love."

He turned on his heel, a curtain of resolve falling over his soul. With a silent nod to his brother, and a last glance at Ruby, Galeron strode out of the chamber to prepare for a vengeful battle.

Chapter Twenty-Three

Battle on Two Fronts

Due to bubbles in the glass and streaks of rain, Sarah could not see clearly from Ruby's chamber. She unlatched the window and opened it. The wind carried the rain inside, but she watched the army file through the gates nonetheless. "Lord Almighty, grant strength and courage—" She dropped her face into her hands. "I beg thee, bring them home safe." Sobs butchered her words. "Grant the s-strength for Ruby and Jadon to survive all they have endured." She looked to the heavens and begged for an answer. "Lord, how am I to aid them?"

Taking a steadying breath, she battled the urge to surrender to her fears and returned to Ruby's bedside. She applied the salve and saw the ring. The ring she had given Ruby the day she'd left Ramstone. Instead of resting on a graceful finger, it was embedded in raw flesh. Sarah carefully removed it, cringing as a piece of flesh hung off it. Gingerly applying more salve to the groove, she worried over Ruby's deep sleep.

"Ruby, can you hear me? You are safe. Jadon is safe." Ruby's cuts no longer bled, but the bruising seemed to appear worse with each passing moment. Sarah worried over her. Though Ruby had not been raped, the assailant's handprint marked her thigh. Her breeches were torn to the waist. Would her mind survive such an attack? Though a sin, she wished the man dead. Preferably by rape with a sword. She shook her head to dispel the horrid thought.

Unable to bear seeing Ruby in tattered clothing, Sarah rifled through the trunks. She slammed it shut when she only found underclothes and winter wear, then hurried to the door.

"Bridget!" After waiting a moment, she raised her voice and called again.

Bridget opened the door across the corridor. "Is all well, milady? Does Ruby fare well?"

Sarah sighed at the flustered maid. "She has not wakened. Is Jadon sleeping?"

"Aye, Lady Sarah." She glanced back. "But he keeps crying out for Ruby in his sleep."

"What did you tell the lad?"

"I told him she was resting. The healer arrived while I tried to calm him and gave him more milk of poppy." The maid had never spoken so much. Sarah waited for her to continue. "Before he drifted off, he asked if the knight hurt Ruby." Bridget wiped a tear. "Poor babe, he spoke about what happened."

"You shan't speak of it, Bridget."

"Certainly not." Bridget pointed across the hall. "My mother moved Jadon closer to you." She wrung her hands. "But mayhap we should have asked first? Forgive me, milady. I trust 'tis fitting?"

Sarah had not stepped foot in the nursery since the death of her baby. Even now, it caused pain. "Aye, 'tis nay more fitting place for the troubled child to rest his head. You have done well." She gave Bridget a weary smile. "Tend to Ruby. I shan't be long. I must retrieve some things for her."

Bridget gave a slight bow. "If you so wish, I could fetch whatever you require."

"Retrieve a night-rail from my chamber, then return to Jadon's bedside."

"To save you leaving her bedside, I could see to Sir Jac as well."

Ah, so Galeron had turned him away after all. Good. Sarah grinned. "Ah, I see you have noticed the handsome knight."

"I simply—"

"Banish the thought."

Even the candlelight could not disguise the maid's deepened blush. Bridget started for the door. "I-I never— Aye, milady."

"Fetch a robe as well," Sarah called.

With a quick nod, the nursemaid hurried to bid Sarah's request.

Sarah found a bit of solace by keeping busy. She rolled the bandages Alex had left strewn on the bed, changed the bloodstained pillow and placed the water basin by the door. With an impatient huff, she peered into the empty corridor. Where was Bridget? It was apparent she had eyes on Jac. Had she visited his room? She must put a stop to that at once...before Bridget ended up with child.

Sarah braided Ruby's hair. "All is well, my friend." She gently brushed the stray tendrils from Ruby's brow. Ruby moaned but did not open her eyes. Why did she not wake? Were her demons keeping her hostage? She jumped at a sound and turned to the doorway.

"Forgive the delay. I thought it best to fetch water as well." Bridget placed the basin on the bedside table. "My mother suggested I add a bit of lavender oil to the water."

Sarah realized there was not a soul at Ramstone who did not show love for Ruby. "My thanks. 'Tis thoughtful of her."

"Milady?"

"Aye?"

Bridget twisted the apron in her hands. "Milady... Sir Jac's chamber doors are open. As I passed I could not help but notice that his room is empty."

"I see." Sarah sighed. Men and their vengeance. For the first time, she understood. "Fret not, the man apparently went to battle as well."

"Is there anything more, milady?"

"You shall sleep in the nursery with Jadon."

"Aye, your bidding be done." Bridget paused by the bed and placed something on the table. She picked up the basin by the door, she said, "I shall pray for her."

A soft smile lingered on Sarah's lips. She lifted the handmade cross, lashed together with pliable strips of bark, and showed it to the sleeping Ruby. "Bridget brought this." She placed it closer to her friend. "She is praying for you. Everyone is." Ruby did not react, but speaking to her brought a semblance of comfort.

Sarah removed Ruby's torn clothing and washed the blood and mud from her bruised body. When she came to the injured soles of Ruby's feet, Sarah paused. "Why didn't you return with us? Your stubbornness is a curse!" Guilt ripped through her. Her anger simmered, just below the surface of her tears. She applied salve and bandaged Ruby's feet. "Forgive me." Her shoulders sagged, her strength spent.

"You are clean and warm, chosen sister. Rest well."

Sarah gathered the shredded clothing and checked the pockets of Ruby's kirtle. She removed a parchment and placed it on the bedside table with the ring. The smell of sweat and blood rose from the clothing, a sore reminder of torture. She ran to the hearth and flung it into the fire. The flames nearly smothered against the dampness, but finally caught, sending into the ashes the remains of what once was whole.

Chapter Twenty-Four

Fury

The Knights of Ramstone and the joining flanks divided into four groups on the outskirts of the village. Galeron was thankful the storm had abated, but the smoke engulfing the village impeded his vision and made him glad he had denied Rafe's request. He would never have been able to watch over the boy. *He is a man.* Galeron shoved away the unbidden thought.

The screams of the villagers and clashing of weapons against armor muffled any sound of their armor. They kept to the shadows and surrounded the village. When everyone was in place, Galeron and Alex signaled. The battle cry ensued as Ramstone's army advanced.

More than half the village, disintegrating in flames, had fallen to the enemy. The Ramstone knights posted to the village were fighting bravely, but they were obviously too few to make a difference. Thanks to the reinforcements sweeping in from all sides, the unfair balance of the enemy upturned. Most of the horned knights were fighting on foot, providing Ramstone the added advantage of battling on horseback.

With his legs guiding his horse, Galeron swung a battle-axe, dismembering the arm of a knight trying to mount his horse with a lad in tow. The wide-eyed child disappeared into the smoke. Galeron prayed he made it to safety. With his arm raised to finish off his opponent, he swayed at the strike against his head, the echoing from within his helmet deafening. He lost his grip on the axe and fell. Thankful he had strapped his shield to his arm, he slammed into the muddy ground. His helmet scraped against the chainmail and rolled away. A fleeting wish he had secured it as well flashed in his mind.

Galeron found his footing and unsheathed his sword. The dark-armored knight advanced ominously, raising a war hammer with one hand, a morning star circling in the other. "You shall pay for my brother's death," the knight shouted, the flames reflecting off the swinging morning star.

It just missed his head. Galeron leaped out of the way. His ears still rang from the blow of the hammer. In one swift motion, he blocked the spiked weapon with his shield and lunged with his sword. The knight avoided it and threw the hammer. It somersaulted in the air. Galeron sidestepped in time and it only brushed his arm. What warrior would miss?

The horned knight ceased the constant swing of his star and smiled. Why toy with him? The man tucked the star's handle in his belt, then drew the longsword strapped on his back, its steel ringing against the scabbard. How fitting. A bastard's sword. However, this bastard held it as a small dagger, in one fist instead of two.

Galeron turned to the side, all the less of a target, but now in his element. "Come now and taste my blade." Fluid and sure, Galeron's sword clashed with the knight's. If only the bastard would raise his arm a bit higher. However, it was not to be. Any man was aware of the weak spot. Galeron caught the lip of the horned helmet, knocking it from his head. Nay, 'twas not the burned face he sought—the man who had molested Ruby—but this one would do, for now. Galeron sliced the air, taking the knight's nose with his blade.

The man screamed, but his wound only seemed to give new life to his attack—his fury becoming more pronounced, his intent more deadly. Their swords danced, thrust, jab, parry, Galeron grunted with satisfaction when his sword swept past to slice the man's face again. Before he could savor the moment, he caught a blow hard enough to dent his armor and bruise the flesh beneath it despite his mail and leather.

Though Galeron was immense, this man seemed the seed of giants and each blow became more difficult to fend off. Galeron reeled, falling to one knee then bursting back to his feet. He swung hard, the man's mail ringing against his blow. He must have found purchase, for blood dripped down the man's armor, yet the knight did not sway. Again the morning star swung, this time as if it wielded the power of a god. It splintered Galeron's shield. How could this dark knight keep coming time after time?

The knight readied for the next swing. Ah, fate turned in Galeron's favor. He thrust into the attacker's vulnerable armpit, his blade scraping past the chainmail.

The knight roared like a wild beast from hell and hurled yet another blow at Galeron's chest. Gods! His breath was molten, as if the heat of the blow turned his lungs to fire. How could this be? Galeron tried in vain to regain his footing, fending the blows with what was left of his shield. It was like fighting a ghost. Galeron cursed his missed blows. He must find a weakness — must fight on. His shoulder throbbed with the effort of deflecting as he sank into the mud. He rolled away and came to his feet to face not the single knight, but another with a poleaxe. Thoughts resembled an archer's attack, raining down and piercing him. Do not let the bastard win. Cut off the hands that took children. For Ruby. Slice the tongue that dared threaten. For Ruby. Kill him. For Ruby. For Ruby. His mind caught up. The poleaxe! He flipped back, avoiding the first blow. Prior to hitting land, the sound of steel reached his ears before the impact fully registered. He flew — lingering for a breath of time — then landed in the midst of flames, the embers spraying in his wake. Heat licked his face. The odor of singed hair filled his nostrils. He blinked several times to clear his vision. A damaged roof flamed above, checkered and glowing. Chills swept through him despite the heat. He had landed inside. He grasped his chest plate. Though damaged heavily, it was still intact. His sword. Damnation, he had lost his sword. Flames licked his legs as he searched around him. The ceiling groaned, screaming for mercy, and showered upon him. He grabbed his dagger and dove from the collapsing dwelling.

The unwelcome sight of his attacker was but a few paces away, another too involved pulling his poleaxe from a dead man to notice him. He spotted his sword, the jewels on the pommel half obscured in the mud. Too late. Eyes trained on Galeron, blood dripping from his opponent's face. One lip hung from his chin and his jagged, rotten teeth bared in a smile. "It seems ye misplaced yer sword. Mayhap you need a wooden one, *boy*?"

Galeron dove for it. Agony swept from every muscle as he wrapped his fingers around the hilt. The knight laughed. *Laughed*. Galeron lunged for him, dagger in one hand, sword in the other, and half a shield still strapped to his arm.

With a mighty swing, the devil wrapped the chain of the morning star around Galeron's leg, slamming him down. Never had Galeron been outmatched. It would not be so tonight. He shook muddy hair from his vision and fought the chain.

"You bastard!" Breaking loose, he ducked the next swipe, then ignoring his wrenched leg, he leaped — twisting midair and swiping his sword against his neck. The resistance waned — he broke the mail. Galeron landed on his feet behind the man, brandishing both weapons.

Gut-wrenching laughter echoed from the gargantuan knight as he turned. The wound seeped through his damaged mail, black and thick in the darkness. Galeron's sword and dagger proved an ill match against the morning star. His shoulder ripped at the next blow and Galeron bellowed at the excruciating pain. He caught sight of Alex galloping toward him as he fell to the ground. The angels watched over him. With devilish speed, the knight freed the morning star and swung it to gain the momentum. Galeron shielded his face with his wounded arm and tried to stand as Alex neared.

His brother's battle cry rang, the others echoed throughout the village. "Ramstone!" The vibration of hoof beats drummed beneath him, shaking the ground.

Alex raised his battle-axe. The knight hesitated, breaking the swing — then his eyes widened and Galeron witnessed his realization of such a mistake. It lasted not a blink of an eye, but 'twas all the time Alex needed. The knight's shoulders shook with the impact. The arm, still clutching the morning star, splashed in the mud beside Galeron's body.

Galeron ripped the morning star from the dismembered arm and hurled it into the screaming knight's forehead. He fell with a muffled thud, face up, into a murky puddle. Galeron leaned over the knight, assuring the dying man did not miss a word. "This is for the innocents you torture." He slid his dagger, sluicing his eyes. "You shall not see them again." He grabbed his tongue. "This is for the ones you threaten." The pulse of his cries stopped as he cut it off. "Your words shall not strike fear anymore. This" — he twisted the dagger in the hollow of his throat until he hit bone — "devil's spawn, is for laughing." The knight grabbed his wrist, as blood frothed from his mouth. "Your blister-faced comrade shall not die so easily."

Galeron took his helmet from Alex, shoved it on his head. His eyes seemed filled with blood, so focused was his fury. Alex gave a nod and galloped into the melee, swinging the battle-axe that had saved him. Sheathing his sword, he shoved the knight over and hefted the longsword with both hands. "Ramstone!" he shouted, swinging with the might of vengeance. Galeron fed the longsword with the blood of enemies — and nourished his fury with revenge upon Ruby's attacker.

Chapter Twenty-Five

Aftermath and Closure

Dawn broke, its waves of color deepening the gloom of the remains. The moans of the wounded replaced the screams of battle. Galeron stood among the carnage, watching Alex bandaging yet another wound. He stood and wiped his brow, meeting Galeron's gaze. The gleam of sunrise reflected against Alex's armor, giving the appearance of a god, quite fitting. However, Galeron's soul seemed controlled by the devil, for his fury had not calmed with the battle's end.

Alex strapped his medicinal sack and strode to him.

"You saved my life, little brother. May you be blessed." Galeron clasped his brother's shoulder.

Alex shrugged. "You have done the same." He motioned toward the blood dripping from the cuff of Galeron's armor. "How do you fare?"

"I have not found him." Galeron wiped his brow, leaving a smudge of blood.

"Your wound, not your damn search." Alex unclasped his brother's armor.

Galeron growled. "Damnation, Alex. Leave it be."

"You should have come to me. This is bad. Sit." Alex opened his sack and pulled out bandages and salve. "I asked you to sit for a reason."

"I fear I shan't be able to stand again if I do." Galeron laughed to cover the truth of his words.

Alex strode to the well, dipped the bucket and hefted it up. "Then come here."

Galeron ambled over and held out his arm. "Be done, I have work to— Hell's teeth!" He yanked his arm out of the flow of water.

"You cried less when the morning star struck you." Alex chuckled at Galeron's scowl. "Now, hold still. I must flush it."

Galeron gritted his teeth and watched the watery blood flow to the ground. Alex packed and wrapped the wound, finally strapping Galeron's arm against his chest. "I shall stitch it when we return home."

"Nay need." Galeron pulled off the strap. He caught Alex's grimace. "What? I cannot work with it on. We have yet to load our dead."

Alex pushed damp hair out of his eyes. "I saw Calen's men ride out with a cart. Did you send them to Ramstone?"

"Aye, I sent the worst of the wounded with them. I intend to have the others help the villagers bury their dead." Galeron scanned the ruins, stopping to meet eyes with Jac. He had removed his armor. He looked exhausted. From the way he moved, he favored his right side, but Galeron did not spot any blood on his tunic. He nodded a greeting and turned his attention to Alex. "How does he fare?"

"His stitches are intact, for now."

Screams shattered their conversation. Galeron sprinted to his horse with Alex close behind. Galeron motioned to Jac. "Make haste and follow us!"

They galloped toward the forest wall, the horse's hooves sending clumps of mud sailing through the air. A maiden broke into the clearing. She ran, her eyes wild with terror, her hands grasping air as if it could support her stumbling gait.

The horses reared at the pull of the reins. As soon as the hooves hit the ground, Galeron dismounted, sword in hand. Still focusing on the forest wall, he ran toward the terrified maiden, hearing Alex and Jac a pace behind.

She uttered a pitiful cry. Her matted hair swung, freeing the leaves clinging to her locks as she searched for a means of escape.

Galeron and Alex stopped their approach, but Jac continued to run. She froze, her chest heaving. Then she whimpered and outstretched her hands, defending his approach.

"Easy, Jac!" Galeron shouted.

Jac stopped, then resumed a slower approach. "Do not fear—" She threw herself at Jac, clawing at his face. Jac dodged her hands. "All is well! I shan't—"

Pounding her fists against his armored chest, she shook with heart wrenching sobs. "Nay, horrid vermin, you shan't!" She turned to flee, but stumbled to the ground. "Pray thee, have mercy and kill me instead."

Jac knelt beside her.

Galeron called out. "Let him help you. We are of Ramstone."

She fell into Jac's arms. He brushed her hair from her eyes, and for a moment, Galeron thought Jac would kiss her brow. She must have sensed his tenderness because her sobs slowly ebbed and she rested her head on his shoulder. Then silence. As if she had not wept. Eerie and complete silence. God, it was happening before his eyes. Ruby's terror matched hers exactly. It killed Galeron, but at the same time, something in him came alive. Something dark and cold.

"All is well." Jac touched her cheek.

Blood trickled into her eyes. She didn't even blink to clear it. "Nay, naught is well."

Galeron glanced toward the forest but no one else broke the treeline. Mayhap she had been hiding there. "Are there any other villagers hiding in the trees?"

She tore at her clothes, wailing. "I was hiding in the forest during the attack, but then…" Her lips moved but the rest of her words caught in the prison of her terror. Her eyes widened as she peered over her shoulder at the forest edge again.

Jac wiped the blood from her brow with the cloth Alex offered. "Easy, you are safe now."

Still focused at the trees, her cries ended with a sigh. "I shan't ever be safe."

Galeron started for the forest. "Who else is in there? Your attacker?"

She tore her eyes from the trees, the haunt of pain accenting her whisper. "The devil himself dwells there." She eyed Jac's dagger, her expression turning from terror to detachment. "Sir Knight, 'tis your duty to protect, is it not?"

All three men answered. "Aye."

"Then you must slay me to protect us all from the devil."

Galeron's steps halted. He turned and met eyes with his brother. "Give her something to ease her pain."

She reached for Jac's dagger, but he placed his hand over the sheath.

"You fail to see, Sir Knights! He said his master would offer a reward for placing a child within me. He has done so. A devil like him. I must die. This seed...it settles within me. Kill me!" she shrieked. "Kill me!"

Galeron strode to her. "Live a full life, young one. Whoever this *master* is — is powerless now. We killed his army. There is nay devil. And if a child shall come of this, it shall be but an innocent babe." He saw doubt in her tear-filled eyes. "I give my word. Though the man who attacked you is evil, he is simply a man... less than a man."

Jac lifted her into his arms. "He shall pay for what he has done."

Galeron remembered saying the same thing to Ruby. How many others had been harmed?

"You cannot kill a demon. Undead. Even his helmet is horned."

"'Tis merely a helmet, nay more," Jac said, lumbering toward his horse.

"Nay! I cannot go back!" She shoved out of his arms. "Do you not *see*? I am a curse to all!" She sank to her knees. "You must take my word. He *is* the devil! His evil face is blistered from the flames of hell."

Blistered. Blistered and burned by Ruby. Galeron swung into his saddle and tore out toward the direction she had come. Behind him, Alex called to Jac. "Stay with her!" Galeron heard him catching up, but did not slow.

They dismounted at the edge of the trees and led the horses into the gray shadows of the interlocking branches. With his sword drawn, Galeron grabbed a coil of rope from his saddle and slung it over his shoulder. Neither spoke as they hobbled the horses. They stalked past twisted branches, deep into the woods. Galeron saw a shadow through the dense trees and held out his hand. Alex stopped several paces away. Galeron ducked, waiting for his advance, but he suddenly turned, heading in Alex's direction.

"Come hither, wench, the rutting is not over yet. Nay use in hiding, I—" His mouth gaped when he saw Alex. His confused expression flashed into rage. He lunged at Alex with his dagger, but he was ready, and fended him with his own blade.

"Do not kill him." Galeron rammed the knight with his shoulder and both slammed to the ground. Alex crushed the wrist holding the dagger with his boot.

Galeron pressed the point of his sword at the hollow of the half-clothed enemy's throat. "Be still, swine." Galeron shrugged the rope off his shoulder and threw it to Alex. "Tie him." He sheathed his sword and fought the whim to send the knight to the hell the maiden fancied he came from.

"We have captured the devil himself, nay?" Alex secured the last knot.

The blood pumping in Galeron's ears deafened him to any humor. Fury cut a jagged path through him. He ground the heel of his boot on the knight's crotch. The man screamed for mercy. *Blistered arse, this is just the beginning.* Galeron continued to accost the knight, kicking him in the temple, the chin, the nose. The man shielded his face with bound hands. "I am a simple villager!"

"Liar." Galeron kicked him again. The man's eyes rolled back.

Alex grabbed his arm. "Enough!"

Galeron clenched his jaw. "Dare not question my actions, brother. This putrid swine deserves nay mercy." A crack resounded with his swift kick into the knight's ribs. "See at his face? His neck? Blistered from the stew Ruby threw at him."

"Gods." Alex stepped back. "Do as you must—but we need answers first."

"I beg mercy, dear sir." He cupped his manhood when Galeron lifted his foot. "Have pity upon this man's soul. I but followed my master's orders."

"You call yourself a man? You beat and tried—" He could not even say it. "*My* woman suffered at your hands last eve." Galeron raised his dagger, turning it in front of the man's widening eyes. "You shall pay."

He glanced at Alex. "This blistered fool is the parasite who wounded Jadon and killed Palmer." Galeron moved the point and traced a thin, bloody line from the neck to the knight's heaving chest. "I daren't doubt he's also the one who left Myles and Julia to die on their doorstep." He slammed the hilt on the man's nose, smiling at his screams.

Alex frowned. "We need him *conscious*. With the wounds you are inflicting, he shall not remain so for long."

"Long enough." Galeron grabbed the prisoner's hair and pulled him to his feet, nearly tearing his scalp in the process.

"Mercy."

Galeron pressed the dagger against his neck. The knight fell silent. Galeron spewed hatred into the bloodied and blistered face. "You dare beg for mercy? How merciful is raping a maiden as you did?"

"'Twas not I!"

"You are still half-clothed, fool!" Without releasing his hold, he motioned for Alex to cut the ropes binding the knight's feet. Galeron violently shoved the knight ahead of them.

The knight stumbled over the undergrowth repeatedly, but Galeron lifted him, set him on his feet and again shoved him toward the clearing.

When the maiden caught the sight of the knight, she screamed. What was she doing here? He glowered at Jac.

"She refused to go to the village," he explained.

Galeron blew a breath. "Just as well. Now she can witness his death."

She clutched Jac, weeping into his chest. "You fail to listen. Devils do not fall at your sword."

Ruby could easily have been the one tormented and crying with no one to turn to but a stranger. He regretted bringing the knight into the clearing. He motioned toward Jac's horse. "Take her to the village."

"I cannot...the devil's spawn."

Alex handed him a small vial. "Milk of poppy shall make her sleep," he whispered.

Galeron knelt beside her. "Go with him. I shall avenge the wrongs this man committed against you. There are nay demons."

Jac carried her to the horse and lifted her into his saddle. She appeared diminutive against Sir Jac's musculature when he swung behind her.

"Just kill me." The maiden's words pierced the air, her slight body drooping with unfair burden. Her eyes gaped at Galeron as Jac prodded the horse.

Galeron remembered the exact same tortured stare in Ruby's eyes before she had fallen silently into his arms. Outraged, he brandished his dagger. In one swift stroke, he slashed the knight's face, opening a gaping wound from forehead to cheek. The knight fell to the ground with a scream.

Alex grabbed Galeron before he could strike another blow. "Galeron!" He leaped back, barely avoiding his brother's unleashed fury.

Jac reined in and waited.

Galeron looked at the dagger in his fist as if it was the first he saw of it. He embraced Alex. "God forgive me."

"Brother, I know your heart. 'Tis your blade I am not sure of."

"I am a leader of men, yet anger overtakes me when my eyes fall upon this"—he stared at the knight, moaning on the ground—"this waste of humanity."

Jac called out, shielding the maiden's face against his chest. "Do you…require assistance?"

Galeron shook his head. "All is well, Jac. We shall meet up when we are done."

Jac left without another word.

Alex examined the knight and opened his pack. He knelt and bandaged the gash.

"Why do you tend to him, Alex?" Galeron snatched at the bandage.

Alex sighed. "We must keep him alive. It seems you deemed it wise to finish off any others."

"Return to the village, now." Galeron struggled to keep his temper to a simmer and placed his hands on Alex's shoulders. "I shall do this myself."

Alex finished bandaging the wound, squared his shoulders, and rose. Galeron took a step closer, towering Alex by nearly two heads, but his brother set his jaw. "I shall stay."

Galeron lifted an eyebrow. "Aye?"

"Aye, I shall, Galeron," Alex dropped his voice to a whisper. "'Tis apparent your perspective is hampered by vengeance for Ruby." Alex shifted his stance, but made no move to leave.

Galeron bristled, but Alex spoke true. "Your words are just." He jerked the knight to his knees. "However, vengeance shall be gained in the end."

The evil knight tried to scoot back, his eyes trained on Galeron's dagger glinting in the sunlight.

"Speak, pig." Galeron carved a niche in a blister, releasing the pus. Then started on another. "Did you sleep in hell?" He met his eyes, his dagger poised. "Or did a woman overtake you with her wits?"

The knight grunted but remained steadfast and defiant.

"Very well, with each unanswered question..." Galeron turned the edge of his dagger, methodically carving an R into his cheek. "Who leads your army?" Galeron waited but a moment. "What? Nay cry for mercy?" He carved a U. "Where is your *master*?" Blood gushed from the B. How fitting. "Tell me all." Not a word. "Very well." Galeron smiled. The Y looked perfect between his eyes.

Within a short time, many slashes added to Ruby's name, yet he failed to offer a single word. Galeron backhanded him, spattering blood into the air. The man's eyes glazed in pain, but he bared his teeth like a trapped animal and spat in Galeron's face.

Galeron kicked the knight backward into the mud. Alex pulled the knight up by the hair. "You *shall* divulge all. This man will not relent until you do."

The knight remained silent.

Galeron drew a line of blood up the knight's arm. Then dug deeper until the man cried out. "Answer, vermin." He backhanded the bloodied face his voice turned cold. "Where have they gone with the children and maidens?" With a growl at the lack of cooperation, Galeron dragged the knight to the forest edge, calling over his shoulder. "Alex, bring more rope."

The knight shouted obscenities while they cut away what was left of his clothing and tied him to the tree.

Galeron circled him, showing him his bloodied dagger before placing it against the prisoner's head. "Do you wish to keep your ear?" He drew satisfaction at the knight's grunt when he nicked it. "Provide the answers I seek, or continue to pay at the edge of my blade."

The knight pushed his head toward the blade. "I shall not betray my master. I speak naught but curses, you bastard." His screams told otherwise when his ear slapped to his shoulder and fell to the ground.

"I suppose I must spare the other. After all, you must hear the questions you are about to answer, eh?"

Repeatedly, the blade invaded the flesh of any extremities that might have tried to touch Ruby. The sun dipped behind the trees and at long last, the knight divulged his secrets in torturous screams while Galeron worked the blade at his crotch. Galeron finally silenced him by stuffing his mouth with the spoils of his labor.

The brothers dragged the lifeless knight into the trees, leaving an offering to the hungry creatures dwelling within the forest.

He caught Alex staring at him as they strode to their steeds. He did not see any peace on his brother's face. Without a word, he mounted and headed for the village.

Galeron's mood remained dark long after they returned to the village. He shouted orders, sending his men scurrying to help the remaining villagers gain some sense of order to the upheaval in their quiet lives.

As the colors of the sky swept into a pink and gray sunset, the men gathered their wounded knights onto one cart and their dead on another. With a final order, they set off for the ride to Ramstone's gates.

Though a single day had passed, it seemed a lifetime of weariness rode on Galeron's shoulders. He swayed with the gait of his steed, finally allowing relaxation into his body. He forced a smile when Jac rode up beside him.

"Galeron, is all well with you?"

"Aye. Fall back."

Jac nodded and did as he ordered. Galeron suffered a bit of remorse for being crass, but he did not wish to explain his earlier actions. He barely understood the loss of control himself. Hoofbeats cantered close. Did Jac dare approach again? Alex gave a nod and slowed his horse to remain abreast. They rode in silence for a while before Galeron said, "Father shall be pleased with what we gleaned from the knight."

"That is so."

"However, it pains me that I must taint that victory with my refusal." He tensed at Alex's silence. "I cannot honor it, Alex."

Alex led his horse closer. "Surely you do not mean the agreement with Sir Calen? I understand your reluctance, Galeron, but you must honor your duty."

Galeron focused ahead, hiding the pain. "I cannot turn from Ruby. I refuse to abandon her after telling her of my intentions."

"The letter…"

Galeron motioned to Alex as he spurred his horse to pull him from the others.

"You speak of honor? How can I turn from all that is good? I asked her to be my wife. How can I deny *our* happiness? Is that honorable?"

Alex blew a breath at the barrage of questions. "I have nay answers, brother. Though Ruby seems to struggle with her love for you, I haven't a doubt her feelings are as deep and true as yours." Galeron smiled at the telling flush of embarrassment on his brother's face. Alex looked away. "I cannot fathom how you shall avoid fulfilling the agreement, but I shall stand by you when the time comes to tell Father."

"I shall speak with him tonight."

"Nay. You are too weary to face this with a clear mind. Daren't speak of your intentions with Father *or* Lord Calen. Not yet. I ask your word on this."

Galeron rode silently, his eyes focused straight ahead.

"Galeron."

"You have my word." He clenched the reins and urged his horse ahead. "Yet Ruby has my promise."

Chapter Twenty-Six

Return

A shout to open the gates startled Sarah from her restless slumber. She sat up in bed, checked on Ruby then ran to the window. Her earlier disappointment when Calen's army had returned sent her to bed weeping, but now she cried tears of joy as Ramstone's army finally passed through the gates. With another check on Ruby, she rushed out of the room, smoothing her mussed hair as she ran.

A flurry of activity swept over her when she threw open the doors into the inner ward. The clamor of the armies echoed off the stone walls while she zigzagged through the masses. The fact that she was so much shorter than the men hampered her vision, and several times she hopped to see over them. Blinking back tears of frustration, Sarah whispered a curse under her breath. At a touch upon her shoulder, she spun around with Alex's name on her lips.

"Oh, 'tis *you*," she said.

Sir Jac smiled and extended his hand. She hesitated for a moment, then with her hand in his, followed him through the throng.

"Where is Alex?" she shouted. "Is he unharmed?" She realized her voice did not carry and nearly ran to keep up with his stride. He stopped and she collided into his back. He looked back, his closeness causing the odd feeling she had experienced the first time she met him.

"I — you — " She was mortified at the heat of her blush when she looked into his unsettling eyes. "Why did you stop so suddenly?"

Jac stepped aside. "There you be, milady."

A few steps away, Galeron and Alex stood together, deep in conversation. Sarah forgot all about her odd sensations and flung herself into Alex's arms. She kissed him, full on the mouth, paying no mind to who was about.

* * * *

Galeron waited a moment, then tapped Sarah's shoulder. "I beg the interruption," he said with a grin. "But, how does Ruby — " Before Galeron could finish his question, Alex scooped Sarah into his arms and strode forward, shouting something about telling their father he would meet with him later. Sarah's laughter faded as they were swallowed into the crowd.

"Very well." Galeron jerked a nod and turned to Jac. He could see the pain on his face with each labored breath. "Jac, you should retire as well. You pushed too far as it is. You are welcome to remain in the main house."

"With all due respect, I shall stay in the knights' quarters." He shook his hair from his eyes. "I overheard discontented mumblings about my stay with your family."

Galeron frowned. "Ignore them."

Jac shrugged. "I *prefer* to be with the other knights. I am grateful for your offer, but 'tis where I belong. Besides, I do not wish to miss the victory celebration with the men."

Galeron nudged him. "Or the mead to ease your aching side?"

"Aye." Jac chuckled. "Shall you be joining us?"

Galeron started for the main house. "Nay. Rest well, Jac." He wondered if the reason Jac chose to spend time in the knights' quarters was the obvious love abounding in the main house. Several times in the past, he caught a glimpse of Jac's sadness at an embrace or simple laughter, and suspected it reminded Jac of his family before tragedy stole it away. He watched Jac as he started down the hill and hoped the mead would dull his pain. Deep inside, Galeron knew it would not. Though it could not compare with losing a family, he could relate to Jac's pain from the pure ache he had suffered for Ruby while they were gone.

A squire met him as he crossed the inner ward. He dismissed the offer to relieve him of his armor with a wave of his hand. As he cleared the doorway, his father stepped into his path. "God granted victory. Aye, my son, I prayed for your safe return." He embraced him for a moment then cleared his throat. "Galeron, make haste, Calen awaits —"

"How does Ruby fare?"

Easton frowned, following him to the stairway. "Sarah has not left her side. Where is Alex?"

"It seems she left Ruby's side after all." Galeron grinned in spite of his worry. "The last I saw of Alex, he was carrying his wife to bed."

"Damnation! Fetch the boy. Calen relayed the battle report when he arrived, but I need to speak with *both* of you."

"Our battles have not ended, Father." Galeron glanced up the stairs. "We shall meet soon enough." Lord Calen and Elizabeth were heading their way. "Allow Alex time with his wife." He placed his hand on the railing, bristling at Calen's grasp on his sore arm.

"Galeron, my boy!" Calen took a step back from the scowl he received. "Word is you acquired important insight about the attack. We must discuss this." He smiled at Elizabeth. "'Tis also time to arrange for upcoming nuptials."

Elizabeth heaved a sigh. "Father, a wedding is the least of our worries with all that is about us. I am perfectly willing to wait for him to ready himself." She stole a long glance the full length of Galeron's body and smiled.

Galeron did not miss her gaze, but he was too weary and distracted to give any attention to it. His only aim was to make his way to Ruby. "I shall meet with you later. I have an important matter to tend to." He left the bewildered group, not caring what his rudeness reflected.

Elizabeth followed him up the stairs, calling his name. He pretended not to hear and continued down the corridor. When Elizabeth rushed ahead and blocked his path, he gave a weary sigh and raised a questioning brow.

"Why shun me? I shall make a fine wife." She stepped closer and whispered, "Perhaps you would put aside your important matter for a sweet sampling? I am free of undergarments." She raised her skirt.

Galeron stepped back. "Step aside. I am weary."

"That I see, my betrothed. The grime of battle still is upon thee." She fingered his armored chest. "'Tis nay shame in my bathing your firm muscles," she whispered, looking down the corridor. "I cannot wait to touch your bare skin. Which door leads to your chamber?"

Galeron clenched his jaw. "I have nay interest in a bath."

Anger sparked in her eyes. "You foul-smelling pig! I shan't allow you near me until you have bathed."

"That sets well with me." Galeron bowed and left her, open-mouthed, in the corridor. He could not help but grin when she turned and stomped down the stairs.

The distance to Ruby's chambers seemed to take an eternity to close. Every part of his body ached and each footstep kept time with the pounding of his head. The victory of battle was an empty one, for the cost had proved too great. After the confrontation with Elizabeth, he yearned even more for an escape from the imprisoning marriage agreement.

He knocked softly and smiled, thinking of Ruby waiting on the other side. His heart quickened when the door opened. "Sir Galeron, welcome back," the young maid whispered. "Lady Sarah shall return shortly."

"'Tis Ruby I come to visit." He tried to peer into the room, but the maid stepped into the corridor, closing the door behind her.

"Sir Galeron, she is sleeping. 'Tis my duty to watch over her until I am relieved."

"Consider thyself relieved." Galeron bestowed his most charming smile.

The maid blushed. "I beg you, the maiden is in nay state to receive a visitor. She is in *bedclothes*."

Galeron suppressed a grin and clasped his hands behind him, trying to recall her name. "Bridget, is it?"

"Aye, sir."

"I shall stand guard at the door until Lady Sarah arrives."

Bridget opened her mouth to protest, but was silenced by Galeron's glare. She started across the hall. "I shall be in the nursery."

"Pray tell, did you say *the nursery*?" Galeron's surprise caused him to speak much louder than he meant and he offered an apologetic shrug when she jumped.

"Aye, the lad, Jadon, sleeps there."

Galeron lowered his voice. "How does he fare?"

Bridget thought for a moment before answering. "He is recovering physically from his wounds, however, one cannot help but wonder if he will completely recover from the tragic events. Every time he wakes, he cries for his father. Lady Sarah instructed me not to tell him of his death." Bridget walked across the hall while finishing her answer. "When I distract him from the thoughts of his father, he cries for Ruby. He does not understand why she does not come."

Fear struck deep. Galeron flung open the doors to Ruby's chamber. "God in heaven," he whispered.

"Sir Galeron! You shouldn't—"

He slammed the door on Bridget's protests and rushed to Ruby's bedside. Her crimson hair contrasted with her pale complexion and her battered face showed even more of the punishment from the night before.

He brushed his fingers along her cheek, avoiding the most bruised areas. "Ruby, 'tis I, Galeron." Pressing his lips on hers, he missed her heated response. He drank in the soft scent of her, hoping sheer will would cause her to waken. "Open your eyes, fair one."

Her stillness ripped into him. He pressed his ear upon her chest, then uttered a prayer of thanks at the assurance of her heartbeat. Surprised at the tremble of his hand when he reached for the bedpost, he pulled himself to his feet. He paced the room. Sweat broke his brow and he stumbled with exhaustion, grabbing onto the mantle. The warmth of the fire did naught to quell the chill sweeping through him.

Unable to stay away, he returned to Ruby's bedside and knelt, his armor chiming against the stone floor. With his folded hands against his brow, he prayed. "Almighty Lord, I beg thee, release her from the depths holding her captive."

Sarah's voice seemed to come from deep in a tunnel. She kept calling his name. Then he fell into the mud, the fire, trampled by horses, then he was torturing the knight, over…and over.

"Galeron!"

He woke with his head in Sarah's lap and Alex applying salve to his forehead.

"You fell over when I tried to wake you and hit your head on the bedpost."

Galeron chuckled.

Sarah shoved his head off her lap. "You find humor in this? I thought you were dead."

"Sarah, Galeron has always been a stubborn sleeper, especially after a battle."

Galeron sat up, fully awake. "Ruby."

Alex spoke in a loud whisper. "She sleeps. Remove your armor and wash. Father does not wish to wait until morn for the meeting."

"Have you seen to her?" Galeron asked, motioning to Ruby.

Alex's face softened. "I have." He touched Ruby's brow. "She is not fevered. Allow her to rest."

Galeron strained to clear his head as he rose, wincing at the stiffness of his wounded arm. He smiled at Sarah. "Thanks be to you for watching over her. Was Ruby in pain when she woke?"

Sarah's eyes darted to Alex before she answered. "She has not wakened."

"At *all*?"

Tears spotted her bodice as she turned to Alex. "I have done just as the healer instructed, but…" The stress of sleepless hours played on her face. She threw her arms around Alex's neck and fell into racking sobs.

Stress emitted from every pore while Galeron paced the room, shouting questions over Sarah's cries. "Why has she slumbered so long?" He thrust his hand toward Ruby. "Why does she remain unresponsive with all the commotion and noise about her? Good Lord in heaven, Alex, what is wrong? Why isn't she answering when I call her name?" Galeron wiped at the sweat on his brow. "*Do something!*"

Twin lines furrowed between Alex's eyes and several times he tried to answer Galeron's barrage of questions. Finally, he shouted at the both of them. "Enough! I am not a damn wizard. What do you expect me to do?" He gave Sarah a hug. "My love, stop crying."

"Why doesn't she wake?" Galeron asked. "Did you —"

"It pains me to see her this way, Galeron. Cease the incessant questions!"

Galeron's mouth gaped, his next query frozen in shock.

Alex raked his hand through his hair. "'Tis my belief the attack in the village traumatized her more than the burns and wounds she suffered. All we can do is wait."

"Wait?" Sarah asked.

Galeron sighed, patted Alex's shoulder and kissed Sarah upon the brow. He had no choice. "Then, we shall wait." He walked to the bed and kissed Ruby's unresponsive lips. "I love you," he whispered.

Galeron snatched his helmet on his way to the door, then turned to Alex. "We shall inform Father of all we gleaned from the knight and plan for the annihilation of the army that took so many lives."

Alex closed his gaping mouth and nodded. "Why the sudden change of manner?"

"Alex, you ask me to wait. I am willing to wait an eternity for Ruby to recover, however, I shan't tarry another moment to tell Father of my intentions to marry her."

Sarah whooped with glee, earning an amused glare from Alex. She clasped her hand over her laughter, happiness reflecting in her eyes.

Alex threw up his hands. "Galeron, I beg thee, keep the talks focused on the battle plans. Tonight is not the time to divulge your intentions with Ruby."

"When is the time, Alex?"

"You gave your *word*!"

Galeron stopped at the door, his helmet propped under his arm. "Very well, I shall keep my word, but may the Lord save Calen if he makes another mention of nuptials with his whore daughter."

Alex heaved a sigh. "I shall meet you downstairs."

Galeron left. Halfway down the corridor, he turned at running footfalls, catching Sarah as she slammed into him.

"Oh!" Covering her nervous giggle, she blushed.

"Is someone chasing you?" He watched Alex amble down the hall. "I suppose not."

"You left before I could offer my well wishes." Sarah hugged him. "The two of you are destined to be as one. Her heart always longed for you, Galeron."

He held Sarah at arm's length and gave a weary smile. "Sarah, I wasn't sure of her feelings, but now the longing shall be sated for us both."

Alex caught up to them. "Daren't speak a word of this."

She tossed her hair back and grinned. "Speak a word of what, pray tell?"

Galeron lumbered down the corridor, leaving the two alone. He almost laughed aloud when he overhead their words.

"Make haste and meet with your father. When you are done, you can find me either in Ruby's or Jadon's chamber."

"Aye, and *you* shall find thyself in our bed with me upon you." Alex's voice was muffled and Galeron did not dare turn around. He wondered if Alex would make it to the meeting at all. He also wondered about the glorious day that he could hold Ruby the same way.

Chapter Twenty-Seven

Demands

Alex rushed into the room just as the meeting started. Why the hurry, Galeron did not know. Minutes turned into an hour and naught was settled. Galeron's eyes grew heavy while Lord Calen droned about having to postpone the wedding. He ignored Alex's nudge and allowed his eyes a moment's rest.

"I do not agree, Easton. It only takes a day to join my daughter to your son. We do not even have a battle plan in place. One more day will not make a difference at this point."

Galeron jerked fully alert at his father's kick under the table.

"The battle plan you speak of," Easton responded, "is nonexistent due to your insistence on discussing naught but the wedding. I suggest we place priority where it belongs."

Calen gripped the arms of the carved seat. "Priority? You speak of priority? Without *my* armies, your knights would be rotting on the ground. Without *my* armies, defeat of the dark knights in the village would have never happened."

Galeron summoned all attention away from Calen's whining when he shoved back his chair and towered over the table. His temple throbbed at the sudden movement.

"Your men are not the only ones who spilled their blood, Calen."

"*Lord* Calen," the pudgy lord corrected.

Galeron's voice rose as he thumped the table with his finger. "Women are without husbands. Parents without children. Maidens' innocence has been ripped from them." He thrust a finger to the ceiling. "And upstairs a child sleeps hoping to find his father when he wakes—one he shall live without because of the battle." He motioned at the men gathered around the table. "The sacrifices of our knights were just as noble as yours. I suggest you watch your tongue, *Lord* Calen." Galeron nearly spat out his name and then lowered his voice before he went on. "I admit we are indebted to your army. For that, we are grateful. We are all weary and wish to discuss important matters of life and death. This prattle about marriage must cease. There is nay need to scurry the marriage before it is time." Galeron sat with a thump of finality.

Lord Easton cleared his throat, taking the opportunity to steer the discussion in the rightful direction. "Galeron, Alex—you gleaned facts from a surviving knight before he died. Please carry on with what you learned."

Everyone's attention focused on the brothers, but Lord Calen would have no part in being dismissed so easily. Galeron rolled his eyes when he slammed his fat hands on the table.

Beads of sweat trailed from Calen's forehead and his jowls shook with his shouts. "An agreement has been sealed! Galeron and Elizabeth are to be wed before any knight under my banner offers assistance from this day forth."

Galeron's chair crashed against the wall and he reached Calen in two strides. The sash around his ample waist proved a perfect handhold. Galeron yanked him from his seat. With his father's shouts ringing in his ears, Galeron ripped the sash from the bewildered man and shoved him so hard into his chair that it nearly toppled back.

Alex joined his brother as Easton continued to shout for order. The men howled with laughter at the scuffle and Easton threw up his hands, knowing Galeron was far too angry to stop.

Alex held the cowering man's hands behind the chair while Galeron gagged Lord Calen with the sash. With the cheers reaching a crescendo, Galeron's shout raised over the chaos. "Perhaps *this* shall silence thee."

"Quite enough!" Easton thumped his sons' chests and sent them to their seats with a thrust of his arm.

Calen swatted Easton's hand away when he tried to assist him, which only fueled everyone's mirth. The laughing stopped immediately when Easton spun around. However, a few sniggers erupted while Calen's fat fingers pawed at the knots of the makeshift gag.

Alex cleared his throat loudly and winced at the grimace his father gave. "Father, perhaps we should delay the meeting until morn. 'Tis obvious tempers are short."

"Short? Tempers are out of control, Alex!" Easton shouted.

"Aye, Father. 'Tis due to pure exhaustion of mind and body. 'Twould be more productive if Galeron and I met with you before—"

Calen yanked the sash from his mouth, gasping and sputtering. "Easton, what kind of household do you run? Is this the treatment I receive for my generosity?"

Before Easton could reply, Lord Calen continued his tirade. Spittle sprayed the air with each word, Calen stood. "What kind of leader are you? You have nay control over your own sons."

Easton splayed his hands and calmly sat back. "Lord Calen, I deeply regret my sons' behavior. You have my deepest apologies." He shot a warning glance at his two sons then continued to try to appease the blubbering Calen. "Proper discipline shall be doled out. You can expect a formal apology. 'Tis best we retire and start anew on the morrow. We shall send word when you can meet with us." Calen opened his mouth. Easton put up a finger to silence him. "*After* my sons and I have a private meeting in the morn." Lord Easton clamped his lips tight.

"I shall *not* be shut out of any meeting. I insist the marriage take place tonight. Expect the consequence of my departure if you do not meet my demands. You need my men and—"

Easton spoke softly, yet his words dripped with conviction. "Lord Calen, I refuse to entertain your crude interruptions any longer." The creaking of the chairs announced every knight's undivided attention. "You sit at my table, but have shown little respect. Yet you demand respect from everyone here. You have been offensive and demanding since the moment you entered my gates. This behavior, Lord Calen, is intolerable. I shall hold nay part of your demands. You shall wait patiently for Elizabeth to be joined with my son. Until then, you shall clamp your mouth shut."

Calen's mouth dropped. Easton placed his hands on the table and stood to face him. "Though I do not condone my sons' behavior, I find it easy to understand why they silenced you. You listen *only* to your words and follow your own interests. It seems you threaten to take your men from here at every turn. Make a choice. I shall give you until the morrow to announce your decision to stay or take leave."

Calen opened and closed his mouth several times without uttering a word. Galeron smiled at the picture in his mind...of a toad in the garden.

Easton filled the gap of silence. "If your choice is to leave, I assure you the utmost cooperation from my stable hands to assist in any duties to ready your men for the long journey."

Lord Calen threw his sash to the ground. Turning on his heel, he stomped to the door. Galeron rushed ahead and pulled open the heavy door, gladly showing him out.

Calen eyed the full length of Galeron's body. Standing as tall as his portly body would allow, Calen crinkled his nose. "You are a disgrace."

Galeron chuckled, irritating Lord Calen even more. He watched with a smile of amusement while Calen's face turned red and then a tinge of purple while he spewed several obscenities. Finally, Calen uttered the glorious release to Galeron's ears. "I shall not give my blessing to a joining of my daughter to such a brute of a man. Burn the damn agreement. You are swine!" Flinging his words across the room with his spittle, he directed his final words to Lord Easton. "I do not require time to decide. We shall all be rid of this place by the time the sun rises."

With that, Galeron slammed the door on the sputtering weasel. Turning, he swallowed his satisfaction upon spotting the scowl his father was directing at him.

Lord Easton shouted for everyone to clear the room — everyone, except his sons.

Galeron nudged by the retreating men, coming to a stand beside Alex at the rear of the room. His cheeks hurt from smiling so wide and his chest hurt from holding back laughter. Reminiscent of mischievous boyhood days, he saw Alex shift from one foot to the other, waiting for his father's wrath, but it took all Galeron had not to whoop with a battle cry. Ruby! Ruby! He had won.

Easton kept his back to his sons long after he closed the doors. Alex motioned toward him. Galeron shrugged and grinned, ignoring his brother's glare of disdain.

Lord Easton's shoulders began to shake and he leaned heavily against the door. Alarmed, they started for their father and stopped in their tracks when he whirled around.

Easton's face crinkled with laughter. Gasping for breath, he stumbled toward them. "I have tolerated that man since you were lads. Oh, when you — when he was gagged!" His voiced pitched high with laughter. After Easton caught his breath, he poured the mead and the three men shared a drink, reliving the last comical moments.

The men of Ramstone shared the closeness, which would be ingrained in their memories for the rest of their days. However, the high spirits they shared tonight would be replaced in the morning with the head-pounding ache of planning a battle against so many, with so few. But naught could dim the happiness Galeron held in his heart. He could hardly wait for Ruby accept his proposal.

Chapter Twenty-Eight

Awakening

Ruby pawed her chest. "Pull it out!" Her chest ached with her plea. "Oh God! Pull it out!" There was two of her, one tugging the lance from her chest. Her screams echoed, mocking her. Blood, black in the darkness, slithered down her body. Her heart pounded so hard her fingertips tingled. Lances in her hands, in her chest, in her head. Why did no one help her? Her heart drummed, deafening her to nearby shouts. Is it the knight? Her mouth opened in a silent scream. No matter how she tried, naught would come out. Naught but blood. Her pleas bubbled and dripped onto her body. So alone. So alone.

"Ruby — awake!" Hands were cool against her face. The heat of pain ebbed. Ruby unclenched her eyes. "My sweet love, cease your struggling. 'Tis I, Galeron."

"The lance..." Ruby gasped for breath.

Sarah knelt by her, Alex a footstep away. "Oh, Ruby." Sarah smoothed her hair. "Shhh..."

The thickness of her dream pulled her, but Ruby swallowed the terror.

"Let go of your dream. All is well," Galeron whispered.

She nuzzled into Galeron's chest. His heartbeat raced, nearly matching her own. She pressed her lips against his flesh. Tasted his essence. Inhaled his scent. Embraced his comfort. The thick dredge of her fear ebbed, but naught could ease the feel of a lance through her chest. She glanced down, though she knew it a dream. No blood. No scream. No *thunk* of wood behind her. *Breathe*. Naught mattered but Galeron's arms around her. Someone kept whispering his name. It was her own voice. Sweet angels, was she growing mad? Even her lashes seemed heavy as she looked up at his blue eyes. "Galeron."

"Ruby, tell me."

"He killed me... He killed me." The sound of the lance against the cask kept sounding in her head. The shock of it piercing her chest — still real.

A child cried out. Ruby wanted to run to him. Save him. "He is dead." The whisper felt warm on her lips, as if blood ran from her words.

"Sarah, fret not, I am with her. Tend to the lad," Galeron said.

She stared into the fire. The flames had tongues to lick and singe her skin. The village, the fires, the knight... "Galeron?"

"Aye, my fair one. I am here." His blue eyes seemed to wash away the fear. Almost.

Sarah entered the chamber. "Jadon has been asking about you."

Was the battle hours ago? Days? A fortnight? "Jadon, he is well?" She sat up.

"His wounds shall heal, but he…well, he has dreams like yours, I suppose."

Sarah draped a blanket over her. 'Twas then she realized she wore a night-rail and Galeron hardly anything at all. She flinched when someone called from outside the room. Had she wakened the whole house? She glimpsed Galeron's bare chest. "Look at you. Did you rush here without dressing?" Ruby did her best to smile.

Galeron winked but she saw the raw concern in his eyes.

"'Twas a dream, Galeron. Cease your worry." She could not weaken, or her screams would return.

She jumped at Alex's knock on the door jamb. "Father, those two *guests* are concerned. It is best you tend to this. I have not a doubt Galeron will throttle them both."

"The sun cannot rise soon enough." Easton bowed slightly. "Rest well, Ruby."

Galeron carried her to the bed and tucked the blanket around her. "I shall return in a moment." With a quick kiss on her brow, he strode to the doorway. "Stay here. Both of you."

As soon as his back was turned, Ruby slipped on a robe and made for the door. Sarah stepped in her path. "Ruby, please, you just had a horrid scare."

"I had a dream, and now I am awake—and very curious. Why would Galeron throttle anyone?" She hurried to the doorway to see. Halfway down the corridor, Easton and Alex intercepted a portly man and young maiden.

Galeron caught up to them and the woman immediately went to his side. She had not even bothered to cover her lace night-rail with a robe.

"Is that the one Galeron shall throttle?" By the way she eyed Galeron's bare chest, Ruby wanted to do it herself. Pain shot through her bandaged hands when she tried to fist them.

Sarah ignored her.

"All is well." Easton cleared his throat. "Elizabeth, return to your chamber."

Elizabeth smiled and placed her hands on her hips, outlining her body even more. "I was so very frightened."

Elizabeth's smile...every woman knew that smile. Ruby's stomach roiled. Had Galeron found his betrothed? Had Alex delivered the letter before or after this woman arrived at Ramstone? Just how long had she slept before waking from one nightmare to another? Ruby needed answers.

Ruby regretted stepping into the corridor. Everyone focused on her. She faced them with bandaged hands and beaten face, stubborn tendrils of hair hanging across one eye. Galeron raised his brow and cocked his head. Ruby jutted her chin. She had a right to...do whatever she was doing.

Elizabeth took a step, glaring at Ruby. "Servant, dare not intrude on us."

"You are mistaken, Elizabeth." The man sneered. "That is nay servant. She is the village harlot Galeron brazenly embraced in the inner ward earlier. I saw them. Thank the heavens you are delivered from the fate of marrying a man who cavorts with someone of such low standing."

Galeron knocked the man to the floor. Elizabeth's scream masked Ruby's cry of surprise. Sarah darted from the room and tried to pull Ruby inside.

The despicable man stood, spitting blood onto the stone floor. He swung his fist, but Galeron blocked it, turning his arm about and bringing his opponent to his knees.

"The only harlot is your daughter," Galeron said through clenched teeth. "And you are the one in low standing."

Elizabeth ran to Easton. "Make him cease! He is hurting my father!" Neither Easton or Alex made a move to help. "Bastards! The both of you!" She clawed at Galeron's arm. "Unhand him!"

He shrugged her off. "Calen, listen well. You shall apologize for your false accusations. How *dare* you tarnish the honor of a maiden as brave and pure as she?" Beads of sweat trickled from Galeron's brow as his voice dropped to a growl. "Without her warning, we could have all been slaughtered." Galeron wrenched his arm, forcing Calen's face to kiss the stone floor. "Apologize!"

"I beg forgiveness!" Calen turned his head. "Now, release me!"

Ruby was ill and proud at the same time.

"You shall rue this day," Calen sputtered as Elizabeth heaved his heavy bulk from the floor. "All of you shall pay."

"You shan't delay your departure until morn. Take leave this moment." Easton stomped toward him. Calen took several steps back. "Never darken our gates with your presence again."

Calen waddled away, Elizabeth still clinging to his arm.

"Alex, assure our men. Escort his army past the gates."

Galeron and Easton started her way. Gods, did all Ramstone men have the same dark expression?

"Oh dear," Sarah whispered. "I hope that anger is directed at them and not us."

Galeron pointed. "I told you to stay."

Ruby and Sarah scattered like frightened mice, bumping into one another in order to make it back into the bedchamber.

"I shall check on Jadon." Sarah hurried down the corridor.

"I shall come as well." Ruby hurried to catch up but Galeron stepped in her way. "Your words were kind, Galeron. I thank you for defending me." She swallowed hard when he didn't answer. "I-I did not mean to cause trouble."

Easton approached with the biggest smile she had ever seen on the man. "I think you did."

Galeron frowned. "Take your leave, Father." Ruby wished he would dismiss her as well.

"Until the morrow then," Ruby stepped into her chamber and attempted to close the door. Unfortunately, they were double doors and Galeron stood in the second one.

"I told you to stay," he repeated.

"Oh? Why is that?" Ruby blew a wisp of hair from her eye. "Did you not wish me to see that...that lace whore?"

Galeron raked his hand over his face. "She means naught." The corners of his mouth twitched. "Lace whore?" His sudden laughter made her jump.

She pursed her lips until she could not hold back, then enjoyed the moment with him—until he silenced her with a kiss. It devoured and claimed. She came alive with his kiss—nay, she arose from the death of her nightmare. "So safe." Her thought swept from her lips when they parted.

"Aye, you are." He pulled back. "Your screams tore my heart."

Why did he have to remind her? "I do not wish to speak of it." This cycle of emotions exhausted her. Everything from terror to laughter ended with an unsettled ghost of a dream. It haunted the corner of her mind with a lance. She was weary of standing strong. Tonight she would simply cry herself dry. She crawled beneath her coverlet. "Until the morrow, Galeron."

He lay atop the blankets next to her. "I shall stay until you fall asleep."

Well, mayhap one more night of standing strong. She shifted into his warmth. She smiled at a vague reflection… Galeron's arms her shield, his nearness a sword to slay the night terrors. Still, sleep evaded her, or mayhap she evaded sleep.

Galeron wrung the cloth over the water bowl and bathed her brow. She tried to smile and he forced a smile back. After returning the cloth to the table, he caressed her face, and she pressed her cheek into his palm. Not a word was uttered and she drew comfort from the silence. He shifted beside her and she molded to him, promptly drifting to sleep in the safe haven of his arms.

* * * *

Easton stood, transfixed in Ruby's doorway. The light from the room highlighted the contours of his jaw. Alex stood by the nursery door and watched him, wondering what caused such concentration on his father's face. He strode to the door. His father remained focused on Galeron and Ruby. A smile, though a bit sad, covered his countenance and Alex wondered if he even realized he was there.

"Father?"

He glanced at him and looked into the room. "I now realize what a grave mistake I made," he whispered.

"Mistake?" Alex studied his father's profile. "About what?"

"I insisted Galeron sacrifice his love for Ruby and hold to the marriage agreement I forged with Calen."

"That is done with." Alex pulled his father from the doorway. "Yet I must ask, one thing. The agreement with Jastar's lord was barely null and you rushed into an agreement with Calen. Why?"

"We needed his men."

"At Galeron's expense?"

Easton took a step back. "I was not aware that he loved Ruby until the agreement was signed."

"You chose not to see what was before you."

"I chose not to listen."

Alex turned away. "At least he is free of Elizabeth. She was not a fitting wife for him, or anyone else for that matter."

"Why do you say that? She would have made a fitting wife."

Alex shifted his stance, glancing behind him. "When we were young, Galeron and I caught her naked with a couple of stable boys."

Easton crossed his arms. "There is more to this, isn't there?"

Alex looked behind him again. "What does it matter? It took place years ago—long before I met Sarah."

"Good lord, boy! You *bedded* Elizabeth!"

Alex was always amazed how his father's whispers carried farther than a shout. He looked around before glaring at him. "Quiet. Galeron did as well."

"*What*?"

"And every stable boy nearby." Unable to stop himself Alex made the sign of the cross. "The mead was flowing freely." Alex kept glancing behind him. "It seems Elizabeth is the harlot Calen speaks of and he doesn't even see it."

"Damnation!" Easton shook his head and chuckled. He took a step toward Ruby's chamber. Easton grasped the double doors, backed out of the chamber and latched them. "I erred and shan't repeat it. The choice of a bride is his." He looked over Alex's shoulder. "Speaking of brides, yours is a step away."

Alex's eyes widened and he spun around. "I love you," he said a bit too loud.

"He certainly does!" Easton chuckled.

"Aye…" Her eyes went from one to the other. "What are you two about?"

"Ruby fares much better," Alex said.

"It appears Galeron spun a web of comfort around her." With a final wink at Alex, Easton left, his whistle punctuating the air.

Alex cleared his throat. "It seems Galeron has calmed her."

"Well, whatever shall I do with my time?" Sarah batted her eyelashes. "Bridget watches over Jadon and Galeron has taken over my duty with Ruby."

"I shall think of something." Kissing her neck, he led her to their chamber.

Chapter Twenty-Nine

Divulge

She pulled back the hanging and uncovered the hidden passage to the lower level. Not wasting a moment, she ducked behind it and began the descent. Sensing a warm hand, she grasped it tightly, wondering if the hand had been there all along.

Ruby clamped her eyes shut as soon as the morning light hit her face. The awareness that she'd been dreaming did not quell the urgency to flee, for memories continued to chase her. She snuggled, savoring the warmth of his body. *His body?* Her eyes flew open and she stared, unbelieving, at her fingertips invading unfamiliar territory across his rippled stomach. She snatched her hand away and shot a glance at Galeron's face then his bare chest. Was he naked? She listened to his breathing, assuring herself he was deep asleep. With a quick intake of breath, she lifted the sheet, peered beneath it and exhaled. Breeches. Relieved, she crept out of bed and gasped at the pain when she stood. Unable to keep from smiling, she watched him grab her pillow while murmuring her name. When did he join her under the covers? She blushed and turned away from his half-clothed body. Something caught her eye.

"My letter!" she whispered. She fumbled with the parchment, cursing the impeding bandages. With the letter in hand, she sat on the window seat and drew comfort from his words. Her breath caught at Galeron's snore. She watched him sleep, clutching the letter to her chest. He certainly had nay place in her bed, but she loved having him near.

She shook away the remnants of yet another dream and lifted her face to the sun, enjoying its warmth from the window. The furrow on her brow deepened while she tortured her bottom lip. A memory tried to surface. She chose to ignore it and attempted to relax.

"This bed grows cold without you in it."

She startled, then a slow smile eased her worry. He looked sinful propped on one elbow, his hair tousled from sleep. "Galeron, pray tell, whatever are you doing in my chamber?" She put the letter on the window seat and leaned forward. "Scandalous household chatter has probably already begun."

"It pays nay mind to me."

"It does to me." She drew up her legs, wrapping her arms about her knees.

The covers fluttered in his wake as Galeron scrambled from the bed and sat beside her. "The household dare not breathe a word. Your worry is for naught." He took her hands. "Are you in pain?"

"The pain is not what worries me." She looked to him for answers. "I woke in your arms."

Galeron arched his brows. "That worries you?" His jest was intended to draw a smile, but tears welled in her eyes.

He rested her back against his chest, wrapping his arms around her drawn up knees. "What troubles you? Do you recall anything?"

"Recall?" she whispered, growing even more agitated. She slipped away and tottered to the hearth to sit. "What have I *done*?" Tingles penetrated every part of her body despite her confusion. Though he sat across the room, his bare chest beckoned her touch. She shivered and tossed a bit of kindling into the fire while waiting for him to answer. His eyes followed her every move. "Are you going to answer me?"

"I am not certain of the answer, Ruby."

"I shall be forthright." She swallowed hard, tears welling in her eyes. "Did we…?" She couldn't bear to finish the question. "How could I forget *sharing my bed with you*?"

Galeron strode across the room and cradled her face in his hands. "Dry your tears, for each drop sears my heart." He sighed when she pressed her cheek into his hand. "I fell asleep."

Her brow furrowed. The dream. She remained silent while Galeron brushed his lips against her forehead. Terror beat the reminder of a child's hand in hers. She closed her eyes, banishing the thought.

"I stayed the night to watch over you, naught more," he whispered.

Ruby turned her face into his hand, embarrassed at her earlier deduction. "I woke with you under my sheets. You are half-clothed, what else was I—"

"I was chilled."

She grinned. "I am such a fool!"

Galeron chuckled. "Aye, that you are, sweet maiden."

She pulled away. "Galeron!"

Galeron's lips lightly teased her ear. "For if I was to lay with thee as your lover, 'twould not be an experience you could banish from your mind." His lips, close enough to torture, yet far enough to evade, made her shiver. He ran his finger from the nape of her neck to her abdomen, but stopped just short of her maidenhood. "Nay, you would not forget."

She trembled at the path of his hands and said, "Then end this torture and show me what you speak of." The pulse in his throat quickened as she kissed it. "Give me something to remember." Loving their playful teasing, she ran her hand against the small of his back.

"You speak of remembering," he whispered. "Whatever woke you may be a key to your past."

Her lightheartedness vanished. She returned to the hearth and stabbed at the coals. "You want me to divulge my dream."

"If you wish to." Galeron waited several moments. Still, she refused to look his way. "The terror in your screams was tangible. 'Twas the reason I could not bear to leave you. I feared you could not face your fears alone."

She offered a slight smile. "For that, I am grateful." She thought for a moment. "'Tis not clear what I must face. The dream made nay sense at all."

"Bits of memory rarely do."

"'Twas not a memory." She slumped into a chair and tried to escape the remnant of the dream. "Just leave it be."

Galeron crouched in front of her and took her hands. "I can help you deal with whatever it is."

"There is naught to deal with."

"There is something you are keeping from me — or thyself. What have you remembered?"

She stood, snatching away her hands. "Damnation, have you been rendered deaf? 'Tis not a memory."

"Hell's teeth, woman, how can you be so certain? What is it you fear? Do you wish to remain lost?"

"*Lost*? Is that how you think of me? Take your leave." She pointed to the door. "Now!"

"Why? So you can continue to deny what your memories have finally — "

"I die," she shouted, her arms stiff at her sides.

Galeron stared at her.

"I am murdered!" She clenched her teeth and fought tears. "In the blasted dream you insist is a memory, I *die*. You oaf! Do I look dead to you?"

Overcome with sobs, she allowed Galeron to embrace her, unable to hold the terrifying visions inside any longer. "The c-corridor." She pulled back and stared into Galeron's blue eyes, fearing to blink, should she continue to relive it. It didn't do a bit of good.

"I-I pulled a child behind me — groping along a line of...of casks. Casks of ale." She swallowed, nearly tasting the dank lower level. "I feared I was wasting precious moments."

"Were you running from someone?"

She nodded. "I found the door and tried to push him through — proved too narrow for us both." Galeron gestured for her to continue.

"He cried for me, refusing to go through the doorway. I placed him on my hip and covered his mouth when footsteps fell — oh God, he is coming for us." She tore at her bandages, her voice rising higher. "Take these blasted things off!"

Galeron clutched her hands to keep her from hurting herself. "Go on."

"The knight—he killed me."

"Knight? What of the child you spoke of?"

"I...do not know." She shivered, remembering the thump against the cask, swearing the sound rang out, even now. Her breath came in gasps. She her bandaged hands against her chest and whispered how the lance had torn through it. Galeron listened intently to her reiteration, while she relived each moment.

"Ruby, forgive me. I pushed you too hard." He kissed her eyes closed and nuzzled the top of her head. "Wait until 'tis clearer and you are stronger."

Ruby's body shook so hard her teeth chattered. The more she tried to control it, the harder she trembled.

Galeron's eyes widened. "God in heaven, Ruby, what is it?"

She tried to answer, but the vision of warm blood dripping upon her arms was so tangible, she feared a perpetual scream would escape instead. She tried not to expose her fear when he searched her expression, but he read her too well. She wrapped her arms around his waist and drew a whisper of comfort, waiting for the terror to subside.

"I killed a child." Ruby could not believe she uttered those words aloud. Her biggest fear, spat out and full of sin. She realized now why she chose to forget.

Galeron shook his head slowly. "Nay, I refuse to believe you could kill a child. Allow your mind to settle. There is something more to this."

Ruby curled into her favorite corner of the window seat. "What horrors await?" She pounded the cushions. The letter fluttered to the floor.

Galeron handed it to her. "I see you read it."

Despite her turmoil, she found herself smiling. "That I did." She rose on tiptoe and kissed him. She enjoyed the way his bare chest rose and fell beneath her palms, and each time it grew more familiar. Apparently, he did as well, for his heart quickened.

He took a step back and sat upon the nearest chair. "Is it too soon to request an answer?"

She eased behind him and kissed his neck. "Is this not an answer?"

"I need —" He closed his eyes when she sat on his lap, continuing to kiss him. "Damnation, woman!" He planted her on her feet and paced the length of the room. "I only have so much strength, Ruby."

"Ah, I see." She grinned. "You lay in my sheets — half-naked, mind you — yet you stop my advances? Hmm, perhaps I *have* forgotten what happened underneath the covers?"

Despite the aches throughout her body, she let out a whoop of laughter when he swept her into his arms.

"Nay, jewel of my heart, as I told you. My touch upon your skin would be remembered."

She gasped as he ran the tip of his tongue across her mouth, pulling back just a bit at the soreness. "I would taste each part of your tender body." A shiver followed the trace of his tongue along her neck. "Every breath, filled with throbs of passion to steal your senses." He toyed with the stray tendrils along her face. "You most certainly would remember, my love."

She forgot about her pain for that moment. She certainly was aware of a weakness in her legs though. The man had a way of turning her to liquid.

"I need an answer from your lips, not just your body responding to mine."

She wished to tease the waistband of his breeches — wished for the escape of all that haunted her. Instead, she eased out of his arms and walked to the door. She nearly giggled when his eyes widened as she latched it and slowly returned.

"Ruby," Galeron warned.

She nudged him back into the chair. "I shall answer with my words *and* my body." She nuzzled his cheek, his stubble tickling her. "I accept your proposal." She slid her tongue from his neck to his ear then paused, his ragged breath brushing her cheek. "My heart cannot refuse you."

His hardness met her hip as she lowered into his lap. She laughed softly, slightly embarrassed at the power she had over him. "Neither can my body."

Taking her exposed neck as an invitation, Galeron obliged by planting kisses upon it. He followed with another on her lips, so deep it stormed throughout her whole body. The promise was sealed, and in turn, their life would begin.

"This day shall be the beginning of our forever." His kisses had a frantic edge. "I feared I had lost you," he whispered, bowing his head.

Ruby steered his face with a tender prod of his dimpled chin. "You always had me, my love." She gazed into his eyes, surprised to see a hint of tears. "I shall treasure your letter forever and I shall love you even longer."

"I know."

"You *know*?"

"Never held a doubt." He examined his nails, then grinned at her.

She smirked, loving the way his eyes crinkled. "You are quite sure of thyself, Sir Knight."

"I am *sure* I shall lose all control if you do not remove your lovely bottom off my lap."

A knock at the door sent her leaping to her feet. She shouted her reply due to the pain of the torn flesh on her soles. "Make thyself known!"

Galeron was by her side in an instant. "Sit —"

She covered his mouth.

"'Tis I!" Sarah jiggled the handle. "Why is the door latched?"

She darted a gawk of panic from the door to Galeron.

"They are aware I'm here, fair one," he said with a grin.

She tried to unlatch the door, but the bandages hampered her grasp. She bit back giggles when Galeron purposely pressed from behind while assisting her. Her flushed face met Sarah and Alex's smiling ones.

Sarah hugged Ruby then grinned at Alex. "Would you be so kind as to give your brother something suitable to wear?"

"I figured you would still be here. Take this." Alex pitched a tunic at Galeron's face. "Ruby, you should be in bed."

"I agree!" Galeron slipped the tunic over his head.

Ruby intended on delivering a scowl, but was distracted by his defined muscles disappearing beneath the tunic.

"God in heaven, Alex, are all men as chiseled as you and your brother?" Sarah laughed. "Honestly, Ruby, you must insist your man cease running about half-clothed."

Her man. Ruby smiled.

Sarah pointed to the door. "Galeron, Alex, cease that laughing and be off," she said with a smile. "The household is full of gossip."

Ruby swung toward Galeron. "I *told* you they—" He crushed his lips against hers.

Alex cleared his throat, breaking the kiss, much to Ruby's chagrin and Galeron's amusement.

"Father is waiting." Alex nudged Galeron out the door and kissed Sarah's brow. "The meeting shall last the day, my love."

Ruby stepped forward. "All day?"

Galeron chuckled. "You are soon to become a knight's lady. Get accustomed to it, Jewel." With a quick wink, he left.

Ruby stared at the carved double doors for a moment then turned her attention to Sarah.

"I am to wed that man."

* * * *

Alex teased Galeron when squeals of glee traveled down the corridor. "I take it Ruby accepted your proposal."

A huge grin flooded Galeron's face. "Aye, indeed she has."

Alex slapped his back. "When shall you wed?"

Galeron sighed. "As you well know, time does not allow it now."

"Did you tell her you took care of the man who attacked her?"

"Nay."

"Did you tell her we must depart soon?"

"Nay."

"Did you—"

"Alex!" Galeron shrugged. "Conversing was not the priority."

Alex's eyes widened. "You *bedded* her?"

"Of course not!"

Alex chuckled. "That is a first," he muttered, starting down the staircase. When Galeron did not follow, he turned to find him frowning at the top of the stairs. "Galeron, I was jesting. Do not fall into a foul mood just before the meeting."

Galeron took a couple of steps. "It is not that. I must tell Father I intend to wed Ruby. He is not keen on me marrying one he *assumes* is a commoner."

Brushing his fingers through his hair, Alex grinned. "I believe Father has opened his heart on the matter."

Galeron quirked his eyebrow. "Indeed?"

"Indeed! You have my blessing." The answer came from the landing below, where Easton stood with his arm resting on Rafe's shoulder.

"So, she agreed to wed such an ugly brute?" Rafe laughed when Galeron bounded down the stairs after him.

The Ramstone men set off to the meeting. Galeron's lighthearted mood dwindled with each step, knowing what he must divulge once the meeting commenced.

* * * *

Galeron cleared his throat and took a swig of the ale before speaking. "There is much to discuss, so listen closely. First, I shall begin with the quest of this dark army. 'Tis the leader's objective to grow his army to be the largest in all the lands. He has been pillaging villages for some time now."

Rafe raised his finger to interrupt. "How is it he could demolish so much without detection?"

Alex intercepted the question. "Nay one remains behind to warn any neighboring lands. They are either stolen away or killed. We were fortunate Ruby and the few villagers made it to Ramstone to give warning of the attack."

Galeron studied Jac while Alex spoke. The man needed to be prepared, but he hated to be the one to tell of Mara's probable demise. He cleared his throat again. "This leader trains some of the kidnapped lads while they are impressionable, making them into his knights at a young age." Galeron thought of his youngest brother, Rafe. "Very young." He sighed. "Others are forced into a life of slavery, serving what they call the Master. Any who refuse are thrown into a flaming moat."

"You acquired this from the knight you captured?" Easton asked.

"Aye, the vermin said nay lad has refused for years. Some have even become his most faithful knights."

"You speak of the lads. What of the maidens?" Jac stood to reach for the pitcher of ale, poured a mug, looking at Galeron the whole time.

Galeron shifted in his seat. "The knight spoke of a maiden who recently defied the leader. It was assured nay other would follow her lead." And of her horrid end. If thought came to him that it could be Mara, would Jac feel the same?

Jac peered over his mug. "What could a mere woman do to defy him? Mayhap 'tis a myth, a story told to frighten others."

"It is true, obedience is instilled with fear, but the man who told me this was fearful himself, eventually offering information I did not ask for." He turned his mug on the table, studying Jac. "And he described how she was tortured and burned while everyone was forced to witness."

His knuckles whitened and he lowered his ale. "Burned?" Jac shook his head. "This putrid leader. What was it the maiden refused to do?"

"Enough said, Jac. There is nay need to dwell with so much more information to cover." He sounded cross, but he had said too much already.

Jac glanced at those around the table then raised his chin. "What did the knight divulge, Galeron? What exactly was she defying?"

Very well, if the man insisted on this line of questioning, he would tell him. "She refused to obey the rules all maidens were expected to follow." Galeron paused. "Breed. They are expected to breed, Jac."

The chair clattered to the floor as Jac darted. "Nay! If he has...nay, not Mara."

Rafe blanched. "Mara—Sir Jac's *sister* is among them?"

Galeron inhaled deeply, his nostrils flaring. "Rafe, there is nay way of knowing that."

Jac's hand shook and he gripped the edge of the table. "Who fathers the bastard offspring?" He stared at Galeron. "Tell me everything. If she is there, I want to comprehend what she has faced."

Alex ignored Galeron's reluctance and answered. "Chosen knights. His men's minds are twisted to believe 'tis just and honorable to impregnate the women. Something was mentioned about a kingdom's heir...but he died before finishing what that might have meant."

Galeron hoped it was enough but Jac did not seem satisfied. When he continued his questioning, Galeron nearly pounded the table to silence him. Any other man, he would, but if Mara was a prisoner, 'twas his fault. If she were even alive anymore. So he let Jac go on.

Alex had answered several questions, and after a moment Jac asked, "What of the young? The ones too young to fight, too small to lift a weapon? What of them?"

Galeron laid a hand on Alex's shoulder to silence him. Rafe looked at his brothers. "Do not tell me they also—"

"Silence!" Galeron leaned forward and whispered, "I shall tear you from your seat and throw you from this meeting. Learn to keep silent."

Rafe nodded in wide-eyed agreement.

Easton poured another mug of ale, deftly changing the subject at hand. "How do they keep this moat in flames?"

"Quite ingenious, really," Alex said with false enthusiasm. "They pour oil upon it—the oil floats on top—and light it."

"What of the young?" Jac repeated.

Galeron had hoped the change of subject would hold a bit longer. "One would assume the flames would burn the drawbridge, but they protect the underside with hammered steel."

"Answer me!" Jac shouted.

Alex spoke quietly. "Even the youngest males are trained as knights as we told you, Jac."

The veins in Jac's face stood out. "The child I have is but three years. What does he do with them?"

Galeron slammed his fist upon the table. "Enough." He blew a long breath. "Jac, why do you torture thyself with details?"

"Because I must! Mara was trying to tell me something when I saved her from one of the knights."

Jac shook his head. "I threw her onto a horse, but she fought to stay when I turned back to the battle." Jac's hands curled into fists. "I did not see her after that. I do not even know if she found her escape." He wiped his hand over his face, lost in his thoughts. "They must have taken my son. Mayhap 'twas what she tried to tell me." He cleared his throat and his voice grew stronger. "Gads, so many young that served our household, some I have known since they were born."

"We shall find them," Galeron promised. "You have my word." He was thankful Jac did not question any further.

Lord Easton cleared his throat. "We must leave a few men behind to rebuild the village." The men nodded. "Galeron, were you able to delve deep enough to learn the location of the castle?"

"Aye, 'tis at least thirty days travel."

"What is the name of this…prison?" Rafe asked.

"Talbot Gates."

"Never heard of it," Easton said, deep in thought. "How odd."

Galeron sat back to allow a moment's silence, studying Jac's countenance. The man looked ready for battle. When Jac seemed to calm a bit, he went on. "Apparently, they have been building the castle — or as he called it, kingdom — for years. We must take it and destroy the entire enemy within while rescuing the prisoners, that is obvious." He ran his hand over his face. "However, even with the vicinity the knight provided, 'twill be a huge undertaking to find."

"I am open to suggestions." Easton sighed.

"The vicinity the knight gave…" A map drawn in the dirt with blood from a severed finger. But Galeron did not divulge that. Galeron scanned the table, every eye waited for his next words. "The map is embedded in my mind. I shall draw one up. Now, the moat of fire is not one we can cross. Unlike most places, this one has nay passage other than the heavily guarded drawbridge. Our best chance would be to stun them with *their* type of attack. Without mercy."

Easton nodded. "I agree, but how will we remain undetected? Will they not see us coming?"

"They built in a forest, felling the center. Not a wise choice in my eyes. Though hidden, it is cover for any attack." Galeron smiled, but his eyes filled with fury. "We left none of his men alive. Therefore, any message to Talbot Gates was undeliverable."

"Talbot Gates," Jac muttered. "Even the name reeks of wickedness." He slammed his fist on the table. "Who is the demon who leads such an evil crusade? Does *he* have a name?"

"It seems he dubbed the castle after himself...or the other way around. We are not sure." Alex spat out his name, "Lord Talbot."

Easton leaned back in his chair. "Our battle plan must be precise. We must cease the brutal pillage this man has brought upon so many."

"Father, forgive my question, but how?" Rafe shook his head. "Now that Lord Calen has pulled his men, we do not number more than five hundred."

Easton grimaced. "Aye, lest you forget, we were outnumbered the other night in the village. 'Tis not always the number that wins a battle." He turned to Galeron. "How can you be certain none of their knights left the village during the last one?"

"The villagers who came to Ramstone the night of the attack told of knights leaving with the kidnapped, however, 'twas before we arrived." Galeron placed his clasped hands on the table. "Not a breath was left in the others." His gaze met each man in turn, finally resting on Rafe. He must find a way to assure that. Galeron raised his voice for all to hear. "As we did in the village attack, we shall continue to show nay mercy to these demons from hell. Are we agreed on that point?" He smiled at the cheers.

Lord Easton unrolled a parchment and slid it over to Rafe. "I give you the responsibility to map out the journey."

Rafe looked at Galeron and back at his father. "I believe Galeron is better equipped. He is the one who knows the way."

Galeron smiled. "We shall work on it together. 'Tis something you must learn." And 'twas a useful task without going into battle. He nearly ruffled Rafe's blond hair as he had when he was younger. Instead, he weighted the edges of the parchment and pointed to show Rafe where to start. Easton continued to dole out orders. "Alex, assure any weapons damaged during battle are repaired." He hesitated when Galeron motioned toward Jac. Easton took a swig of ale and said, "Sir Jac, are you willing to fight under our banner?"

The mumblings about the table silenced. A loud crack emitted from the fireplace at the end of the room.

Jac's smile held naught but contempt and revenge. "Lord Easton, I would be honored to fight under your banner, however, may I suggest not flying the Ramstone colors?"

Galeron's head darted up. Then Jac's meaning shot like an arrow. "Brilliant!" At his father's blank stare, he added, "We shall fly *their* banner."

"Excellent idea, Sir Jac!" Rafe hopped up. "I am certain there is a banner in the pile of rubbish at the end of the village. I could fetch it."

Lord Easton chuckled. "Eager as you are to do that, I believe it can wait until morn. However, banners alone shan't gain us entrance into their gates."

"We could retrieve the armor we left with the blacksmith," Rafe suggested. "I trust the blacksmith hasn't the opportunity to melt it down." He shifted from one foot to the other. "There will not be enough for us all, but I believe it shall help gain our entrance."

"*Our* entrance?" Galeron said. "You shall not be coming, Rafe. Your idea is a sound one, though."

Rafe sat straighter. "I dare not question you, for you are the leader of our army. An army I belong to." Uncomfortable silence stifled Rafe. For a moment, Rafe ran his finger along a grooved edge of the table. "After we have passed their gates, I could ensure the drawbridge stays down to allow the rest of our army to cross."

Galeron stared at him. "How would you assure that?"

"By cutting the ropes." Rafe gulped from the nearest mug of ale. His eyes watered. "You trained me well."

Galeron grimaced, decision made, but he would stave off any more questioning, for it looked as if he were convincing every man at the table but himself. "For now, you shall prepare the map."

Easton chuckled when Rafe slugged another swallow of ale and choked. "There is much more strategy than flying a banner. There is a secret pass to the gates," Alex interjected with a smile. "The knight relayed nay a soul is allowed in Talbot's gates without a shout of one word."

Galeron noted the glint in his father's eye. It seemed Easton enjoyed the suspense and made no move to question what the word was.

Rafe, true to his inquisitive nature, did it for him. "Pray tell, what is the word?" he asked, his words choking on yet another swig from his mug.

Galeron snatched the mug from Rafe and gulped its contents. "We shall defeat Lord Talbot and bring a new life to all who have been captured by shouting" — he cocked his head and grinned — "of all things, the thing I relate to the most. Rage."

Easton knocked the pitcher of ale, tried to catch it, and failed. "Rage?" He shot to his feet and shouted, "Rage?"

Galeron and Alex's smiles disappeared. Easton focused on the rivulet of ale dripping off the edge of the table. He lowered his voice. "Ah, Rage, quite…fitting I suppose. This mad man must be full of rage to lead the life he does." He stood aside, allowing a servant to sop the mess. "Rage is a fitting word," he repeated. He seemed to sense Galeron's stare and looked up. "Cease your concern, son," Easton whispered.

After the servant brought more ale, Galeron took his time refilling his drink. He even poured one for Rafe to shut his gaping mouth. Raising his mug, Galeron encouraged everyone to do the same. "To victory!" He noticed the tremble of his father's hand when he toasted. What upset him so?

The meeting lasted the rest of the morning. The men were finally satisfied and left the room — all except for Easton and his sons. They huddled over the table, discussing the journey. Servants came and went, filling the empty pitchers and bringing each meal. The sun set as Rafe added the final touches to the map.

Galeron gave him a hearty slap on the back. "You have done well, young one."

Rafe grinned. "Enough with the young one. 'Tis *Sir* Rafe," he said as he sprinkled sand on the parchment to dry the ink.

Easton looked up from the map. "Galeron, have you told Ruby about departing for battle?"

Galeron's jovial mood dimmed. "'Tis where I am headed now."

"I believe Sarah is upstairs with her." Alex met him at the door. "Tell her easy, brother."

Galeron shook his head. "There are nay easy words to tell how I must leave her. Again." He opened the door and looked back at Alex. For the first time he realized how his brother constantly had to deal with the situation of leaving a loved one behind. "How have *you* done it?"

Alex sighed. "Galeron, I wish I could tell you it gets easier, however, 'twould be a lie." With Alex's dark words echoing in his mind, Galeron closed the door, then set out to fight the latest battle of his heart.

Chapter Thirty

A Knight's Lady

"Ruby, are you awake?" Galeron spoke softly from the corridor. She had thought he would be detained through the night. Ruby nearly tripped in her haste to the door.

"But a moment!" She smoothed her dress. "How do I look?" she whispered to Sarah.

Sarah, her eyes dancing with delight, tilted her head. "Like an angel. Oh my, that is a contradiction." At Ruby's wry smile, she added, "He shall love it."

Ruby opened the door. Would this joy ever fade at the sight of the man? "Ah, I see the meeting is finally over." Ruby stepped aside.

His intense stare hid naught of his surprise. "Ah. Did I miss an invite to a special occasion?"

Ruby lifted her chin and sashayed to the fire, taking a seat beside Sarah. "Nay, I simply wished to dress like a knight's lady."

Sarah giggled. "Much better than breeches."

Ruby begged to differ, but she certainly loved the appreciation in Galeron's expression. He'd hardly said a word. Had her attire rendered him speechless? When Sarah gestured for him to join them, he did not move. "Where is Alex?" Ruby asked, but still he seemed distracted. Ruby tilted her head. "Galeron?"

He added a log to the fire. "I suppose he is retiring for the night."

Sarah's eyes flickered. "Certainly he did not forget!"

Forget what? Ruby was about to ask, but at that moment, Alex knocked on the door jamb and called out. "Dare not tell!" Alex poked his head in. "Tell me you waited for me to arrive."

Galeron and Sarah spoke at once. "Nay, I did not."

Ruby did not miss Galeron and Sarah exchange a glance. Both surprised.

"Alex, did *you* tell him?" Sarah asked. Alex shook his head. With her hands clasped with his, she blurted. "We have decided to keep Jadon as our own."

Ruby blinked. "As your own? Is he aware his father is dead?" She tried to smile at the good news, but the vision of Palmer being slain prevented it. "I was to tell him."

Sarah took her hands. "You were unconscious for days after the attack. He kept asking for you and his father. I *had* to tell him. He took it as well as could be expected. I thought it best to wait until your bruises healed before he saw you."

Ruby's hand flew to her face. "I must look frightening."

Galeron lowered her hand and whispered, "You are beautiful." He smiled and then turned to Alex. "You shall make a fine father."

"I cannot think of better parents for him." Ruby's smile blossomed. "I worried what would come of Jadon." She wished him her own, but was happy he would remain at Ramstone.

"He is thrilled with the idea of living here at Ramstone and wishes to remain close to you," Sarah said. "He asked if you would still be his nursemaid."

Ruby's heart ached at the thought of losing him as a son. "What did you tell him?"

Sarah furrowed her brow. "I told him you would be his aunt, of course."

She blew out a breath. An aunt. Of course. She was still unused to the idea of actually being family. "The son you have longed for is now a reality. I am happy for you."

They spent the next few hours sharing dreams. She was heady from the sweet mead yet Galeron filled another mug for them all. Absorbing the joy she drew from her new family, her heart warmed at the true belonging and found peace in the acceptance. An incessant tug at the back of her mind reminded how her memory evaded her, snatching a bit of happiness.

"Ruby, what is it?" Galeron asked.

She pressed a crease on her skirt, giving her a moment to refocus. "There is much to prepare for." Turning to Sarah, she said, "Such as plans for my upcoming nuptials."

"Will you choose to be married on the church steps in the village? It should be rebuilt soon enough."

She thought a moment. "The garden. I would love to be married in the gardens."

"Not the steps?" Sarah shrugged. "Leave it to you to think of something unconventional. The gardens are in full bloom in the spring. I suppose you and Galeron shall have to wait until then."

Alex chuckled. "I pray the wedding is sooner, or we shall be expecting a babe by the way Galeron nearly reeks for the want of her."

Ruby nearly spat her mead, her face afire. She glared at Galeron when he slapped her knee and roared with laughter.

Sarah smacked Alex's shoulder. "You drunken oaf!"

Galeron stopped laughing but did not clear his grin. "Here, have some more." He refilled Ruby's mug. "You seem to need it."

Ruby took a large gulp of the sweet mead, wishing she could disappear. Though he could very well bed her now that they were betrothed, he still wished to wait. Why did he torture her so? By the way Alex spoke, Galeron was just as tortured.

"Actually, the gardens are a special sight in the winter. Why wait?" Sarah leaned forward. "The season is almost upon us. We could have a ball afterward in the main hall complete with a wedding feast."

Galeron shifted in his seat and cleared his throat. His smile had vanished.

"What is it?" Ruby's heart quickened. By the way he was acting, she feared the answer was not welcome news. She wished for the lighthearted mood of moments before. At the touch on her cheek, she met Galeron's eyes. He caressed her face as he spilled the news. "We must depart before the weather becomes worse. Late autumn is upon us and our journey is long."

"We?" Ruby swallowed hard. "Journey? Where? When?" She focused on uttering more than one word at a time. "By we, you mean your men. You are going to battle." Her heart sank at his expression.

"I am."

"How long shall you be gone?"

His fingertips caressed her wrists, sending a tremor up her arm. "We expect to be gone for three months."

She answered with a breathless gasp.

"Perhaps longer," he quietly added.

Ruby tore from his gaze and stood. She spied the tears in Sarah's eyes and patted her shoulder on the way to the hearth. She watched the flames, trying to gain a brave composure. Ruby tamped down her fury. Tears stung and she swiped at them. Galeron came to her, his expression full of regret. They faced each other, while Alex and Sarah left.

Finally, Ruby shattered the silence. "I fear for your safety." Burying her face into his chest, she inhaled, placing his woodsy scent into her memory. She raised her face, her hair spilling down her back. "You neglected to tell when you depart."

"Your tears wound me more than any weapon. I beg thee, do not weep when I tell you."

"When."

"We shall leave in three days' time."

She would not cry. "Pray tell, a life with you entails days like this?"

Galeron nodded. "Are you still willing to be my lady?"

She played with the lacing on his tunic, kissed the hollow of his neck, and smiled. "I am willing to be your everything."

They sat on the window seat, whispering promises of their future. His kisses eased her sadness and she slipped easily into the comfort of his caress. She detected a shiver when she traced the dimple in his chin with the tip of her tongue.

"Devil woman," he whispered, "you bring sinful thoughts to mind."

"Mmm. So act upon them before you leave me," she murmured. "We *are* betrothed."

Galeron growled his response. She closed her eyes, relishing the tangled dance of their tongues. Her body melded into his touch when his kisses seared down her neck. She held her breath at his slight pause and exhaled his name when he kissed the cleavage between her breasts. The contrast of the heat of his lips and the cool air caused her to shiver when he slowly ran his hand under her skirt. Galeron's callused fingers worked a fever so foreign she sat upright. She lost focus and welcomed the darkness of her wanton response. The room spun and she could not discern if it was due to the mead or his touch, nor did she care. Thoughts scattered, remaining unattainable as Galeron slid his hand up her leg. The force of her need sent a gasp of his name once again as she arched to meet his touch. When he caressed her through her undergarment, her body relinquished all control. Colors vibrated in her head, shutting out any semblance of reality as a torrent of warmth shot through her.

Galeron silenced her cries with his kiss, his surprised eyes stared into her own. He brushed her hair back and smiled. "Your reaction to my touch nearly made me lose control as well." He swallowed hard and moved his trembling hand away.

She curled in his lap and reached her hand beneath his tunic, relishing the fast rise and fall of his chest.

"Galeron." Words were lost to her. All that made sense was his name. "Galeron," she repeated. Her body seemed to shoot fire into her blood with no relief of extinguishing it. Stutters of his breath along her neckline only heightened her sensitivity. His breath swept over her like a pendulum and his low moan melted what was left of her inhibitions. The tug at her corset released the lacings and the sudden coolness teased her nipples erect. His tender kiss upon each one warmed them as she allowed him to lay her back on the window seat. Delicate flutters spurned a quake when his mouth covered her breast, leaving one always wanting the comfort of his tongue while his kisses traveled to the other.

He gathered her in his arms and carried her to the bed. All gentleness seemed to disappear. He ripped off his tunic. She deftly traced each ripple on his chest, then to the waistband of his breeches. He freed her corset completely and tossed it aside. She drew him to her, trembling when his bare chest touched her own. She arched against him while he continued to kiss and caress her body beneath him.

She cried out his name. He whispered hers between gasps. His embrace, pulsating and welcome, sent wetness from within, readying her for him. He pulled at her skirts while she unlaced his breeches. Her eyes flew open, shocking them with the light from the fire when he rolled off her.

"God in heaven, we must *cease*!" He pushed his hair from his sweaty brow.

Still trembling from the spell of his touch, she said, "Nay!"

Galeron silenced her protest with a tender kiss while he rose from the bed. He traced his fingers along her shoulder and pulled up her bodice. "Ruby, my sweet love." His words were ragged and stilted. "'Tis with regret and all the control I possess that I must leave."

Ruby blinked hard. She scurried from the bed, struggling into her sleeves. She spotted her corset and kicked it under the bed. Tears blurring her vision, she tried to lace her bodice. With her fingers tangled as her thoughts, she wondered what she had done to displease him.

Galeron quickly gathered her in his arms. "Ruby, all is well."

Ruby shrugged away from him. "'Tis sinful the way my body betrayed me. I am shameful."

"Nay, my love."

She spun around, torture spilling from her eyes. She drew a shaky breath and tried to slow the jolt of fear. She cast her gaze to the disheveled bedcovers. "What have I done?"

Galeron coughed into his hand but she suspected he wanted to laugh. "You have done naught. 'Tis I. I am guilty of forgetting your innocence."

She had no doubt that she would have given herself to him completely. There was not a bit of innocence about that. "I felt natural in your arms, yet I acted as a *harlot*."

"Sweet Ruby, dare not utter such things. The only shame is mine for taking advantage." He smiled. "So…natural in my arms, eh?"

She averted her eyes. "My body betrayed me."

"What you experienced was not a betrayal of your body, but a *surrender* of your body to mine—a natural sharing, pure and just." He sighed heavily. "Woman, you shake me to my core. Our wedding bed shall awaken passion reserved for the gods."

Ruby swallowed hard. "I cannot imagine awakening anything more, Galeron. I do not think I could bear it."

Galeron threw his head back and laughed. His joy echoed on the stone walls of her chamber, lighting up her heart. She grinned when he rested his chin on top of her head.

"Your passion brings me joy and your love..." Galeron's voice broke.

She looked at him, surprised to see his eyes brimming with tears. His whisper drew a certain softness inside her.

"I have never needed or loved anyone before you. Nay, even death could not weaken the strength of my love."

Ruby's heart soared then landed onto his. "My heart belonged to you from the first day in the forest." She traced the cleft in his chin. "You shall take it with you when you leave."

Galeron winced. "Let us not dwell on my departure." He turned her around. "Allow me to lace you up."

She turned back, blushing at the reminder. "'Tis past time for you to take leave."

Galeron grinned sheepishly, bowed, and backed away. She rolled her eyes, thoroughly enjoying his jest while she guided him toward the door.

"Ruby of the Forest. I leave with the promise of you in my dreams." He cracked open the door and whispered, "Aye, a sinful dream it shall be."

"Just the same, leave quietly."

"Woman, plan our wedding while I am gone."

She muffled her laugh with her hand.

Galeron nuzzled his face into her hair. "I do not jest, my jewel. The wait to bed you as your husband is torture."

She shivered at the intensity of his words. "I cannot wait to be your lady." She cast a mischievous smile. "Be off, Sir Knight!"

"Grant one more kiss."

She giggled. "We both know where that path leads. Now, be off." She shoved him into the corridor and closed the door.

"Fare thee well, jewel of my heart."

His final whispered words of love echoed in her thoughts while she undressed. She crept into bed, drawing the coverlet close. She inhaled the scent of him. *You always smell of the forest.* She nestled deeper and closed her eyes.

"I am to be a knight's lady." She could hardly believe the reality of her words. "Galeron's lady," she whispered, slipping into slumber with a trace of a smile on her lips.

Chapter Thirty-One

Alex's Concern

Alex leaned out of the window, his grip hard upon the sill, and watched Galeron walk away. "We were to go over the map, brother," he whispered.

With each passing day, Alex grew more uneasy at Galeron's distracted manner. The night before, when they were going over the plans, he looked up to find Galeron had not been listening — at all. Though he did not mind taking on duties, it seemed more and more fell on his shoulders. He shrugged into a cloak and slipped out of the chamber.

He found Galeron, working alongside Rafe and Jac outside the knights' quarters. Their breath steamed against the chill, creating a fog around their faces.

Alex leaned against the cart. "Now where are you headed?"

Galeron darted a grin. "The village, to collect the armor." He looked down and tied the strap to the cart.

Alex examined the knot.

Galeron glanced up. "Shouldn't you be going over the plans of our journey with the men?"

Alex blew warmth into his hands, hiding his irritation. "Aye, but first I hoped to have a word before you left for the day."

Galeron tied the final knot, propped his boot against the cart and pulled tight. He grasped his cloak against the cold and motioned toward the knights' quarters. "'Tis warmer in there."

"Privately, Galeron."

"The stables then." On their way he asked, "What is it?"

"Wait until we are inside." Alex nodded a greeting to a stable boy holding open the door. He yanked the cloak to his nostrils when the steamy scent of the horses mixed with the manure. He spied several stable boys and steered his brother to an empty stall.

"Why the secrecy? All is well, is it not?" Galeron asked.

Alex studied him for a moment. "Nay, 'tis not."

"What is the trouble?"

"Remember the first battle we fought after I brought Sarah to Ramstone?" Alex dropped his cloak from his face, the full stench reaching his nostrils. "Remember the injuries I suffered?"

Galeron leaned against the stable wall and squinted. "Why do you bring this to light now?"

"Do you recall it or not?"

"The memory is seared into my soul. I bargained with God to allow your survival." Galeron cleared his throat and grinned. "Come to think of it, 'tis a wonder he spared the life I bargained with."

"You bargained with your life?"

"This is what you wished to speak about? It pains me to even think of that day." Galeron frowned. "'Tis a horrid reminder, Alex."

Alex shifted his stance. "The reason I was wounded so badly—"

"This talk is inappropriate before battle."

He didn't notice he grabbed Galeron's tunic until it was in his fist. "Damnation, listen to me," he whispered through gritted teeth.

Galeron looked at Alex's hands, then met his eyes. "Enough."

Alex released his hold and blew a slow breath. "'Twas the first time I left for battle after Sarah and I wed." He rolled his eyes at Galeron's raised eyebrow. "As you well know, brother, when we fight, there can be nay other focus but battle and our trust of victory."

Galeron slowly nodded. Alex stepped closer, whispering emphatically. "Do you not *see*, Galeron? You have lost your focus. You cannot concern thyself with Ruby. We have a battle before us."

Galeron cocked his head, but made no response.

"I understand your struggle. I go through the pain of separation every time I leave Sarah."

Galeron crossed his arms, nudging away the horse nibbling on his cloak.

Alex wondered if he was listening. He heaved a sigh and continued anyway. "That day forth, I realized I must pass through our gates with my mind staying to task." Alex waited for a response and then shook his head at his brother's silence. "I must place Sarah in the safety of my heart and close it. I disengage thoughts of her until my return home. You must do the same with Ruby."

By the scowl on Galeron's face, his attention didn't stray after all. "God's eyes, Galeron, if you fail to heed my concerns I fear 'twill be *I* carrying *you* through the gates. I could not bear such a burden. Neither could Ruby." Frustrated with Galeron's insistent glare, he looked down and slid the toe of his boot in the hay.

A horse neighed when Galeron strode away.

Alex glimpsed his brother through the constant wave of the door in the wind. He paced the length of the stable, rifling his fingers through his wavy locks. He rammed his fist into the stable wall and glanced apologetically at the startled horse. Cursing under his breath, he sprinted after his brother.

Alex found Galeron sitting on the low stone wall surrounding the field. He straddled it and watched the horses grazing on the last bits of grass. He studied Galeron's profile, the frown now gone. Alex waited for him to speak first, but still jumped when Galeron broke the long silence. "You speak the truth."

Alex's discontent faded at the pain etched in Galeron's face. "I would never lie to you."

Galeron rested his hand upon Alex's shoulder. "How do I place her from my mind? She burns in my every thought." Galeron let his hand slide back to his lap and twisted his gloves in his hands. "Are you still taken by Sarah like this?"

"Aye, more so with each passing day."

"You do not know —"

"Galeron, I *do* know…" Alex became silent.

The men sat for several moments. Galeron finally stood. "We have much to do. Let us get to it."

"I shall see you when you return from the village. I have things to do as well." Alex hopped down and walked away, turning when Galeron called for him to wait.

Galeron sprinted over and slapped him on the back. "You are a fine brother."

"As are you." Alex cracked a smile. "Now, go lead your men. I tire of doing it for you."

"We shall go over the map after I return." Galeron hit his forehead with his palm. "I was supposed to do that this morn."

"Be off, brother. The men are waiting."

Galeron nodded sharply and strode toward the knights' quarters.

Alex watched Galeron until he was out of sight. Pulling his cloak against the sudden gust, he smiled broadly when the wind carried his brother's voice, barking orders once again.

Chapter Thirty-Two

The Gift

Dawn was breaking and already Ruby could hear the commotion in the inner ward. She wrapped her robe tight and hurried to the window. The fog slumbered close to the ground, masking the activity below.

She grabbed a kirtle and nearly tore it in her haste to dress. Tears of frustration burned as she ran down the corridor, her cloak flapping behind her. She skidded to a stop at the head of the stairs and grabbed the banister, nearly tripping.

"Careful, forest nymph."

Her breath caught while her eyes drank in the beauty of the knight at the bottom of the stairs.

"Galeron."

The torches lining the wall reflected off his armor, giving a dreamlike vision of his ascent on the stairs. Ruby pulled his face to hers and kissed him, the tremor of fear still pumping through her.

"Why the tears?" Galeron asked.

"I feared I missed your departure."

"Ah, Ruby, I dare not leave without this." He swung her into his arms and growled against her neck while carrying her back to her chamber. As he slowly lowered her to the floor, he let his hands slide down the length of her lithe body. "Ah, how I shall miss you," he whispered.

She shivered at the intensity of his words and her heart lurched when she saw tears glistening in his eyes.

"Be at peace, Galeron." Her brave front nearly cracked and she took a moment before continuing. "I am safe here at Ramstone. Not a night shall pass without a prayer for your safe return."

Galeron nodded. "Just the same. Here is something to keep my heart linked to yours." He pulled a small parcel from underneath his chest plate.

Her fingers skimmed over the satin cloth, as she wondered what it held. He placed his hand over hers. How she would miss his touch!

"Open it." Galeron took his hand away. "I shall smile each time I imagine it resting against your heart."

His words nearly did her in, but she had promised herself she would not see him off with sadness. She took a deep breath and glanced up at him before she untied the bit of ribbon. The corners of the cloth slid away, revealing a silver orb on a chain.

"'Tis beautiful, Galeron."

"It belonged to my mother."

Ruby's eyes shot up. "I cannot accept such a treasure!"

Galeron silenced her protest with a tender kiss. "'Tis meant for you, my sweet Ruby." Taking the necklace, he pressed a small button on the side. The orb opened and he placed it in her palm. "My promise when I return." Galeron laid his forehead against her bowed head, inhaling what she assured was the scent of lavender soap. "I shall place it upon your finger the day we are wed."

She fought tears while she fingered the gold band. She closed the orb with a sigh. "Seal your promise with a kiss, Sir Knight."

"The sweetness displayed on your upturned face I shall place, steadfast into my heart." He took her face in his hands and caressed her cheek before he kissed her. "Never does it cease to amaze me how the intensity of my love heightens each time I hold you."

She sensed he was staring directly into her soul. She cocked her head to the side and smiled, unable to speak, lest she begin to cry.

He took the necklace and stepped behind her. "Gem of my heart, I love it when you tilt your head with that expression."

"I adore the names you give me." Now. But oh, how she had loathed them at the start.

He clasped the necklace, then allowed his hand to linger on her neck. Her throat tightened. Unexplainable fear nearly took away her happiness.

"Galeron, I shall wear this for the rest of my days." She turned to face him, hoping he could not detect her wariness. "Well, at least until I hand it down to our firstborn."

Galeron took her by the waist and pulled her to him. "I dream of the night we create the son you speak of."

She gave a wide grin. "Or daughter." She jumped at a loud noise coming from the inner ward. "They are ready."

Galeron strode over and slammed the window, yanking the coverings for good measure.

"'Tis time, Galeron," she said quietly. She met his gaze while she pulled her hood over her head.

The cloak raked her shoulders as he yanked it off and threw it to the ground. She shuddered at the chill. Her tender bruises throbbed, but her heart ached even more as he leaned her back and kissed her with his fury and love intermingled into one. She returned the urgency of his passion without a thought. Galeron quietly moaned his anguish into their kiss until Ruby pounded her fist against his armored chest.

"Blast this armor." Her voice cracked. "I cannot touch you...I need to have you against me."

Galeron stepped back while unclasping his chest plate. He held it at arm's length, grinned, and let it drop with a shattering clang against the stone floor. She giggled nervously at the noise while he pulled off his mail and hauberk and tossed them aside.

With a playful chuckle, she leaped up and wrapped her legs around his waist. "I need you," she said again, not caring how wanton she sounded. She slid her body down the length of his. "Relieve thyself of the rest of your armor," she whispered between kisses while leading him to the bed. "Take me fully before you go. Leave me with a part of you."

Galeron ran his hands up her sides, whispering her name. She lay on the bed, pulling him on her. He stood, never breaking their gaze. She thought he was intent on leaving, but with his breath ragged, he unclasped his armor. She lifted his tunic and kissed his belly.

"Ruby."

The way he growled her name ignited her and she met his animalistic kisses while he moaned. Heat concentrated intimately within her. "Take me," she said again. Galeron drew in her bottom lip as he cupped her breasts through her bodice. It took several moments to realize someone was insistently rapping at the door.

"Ruby, have you seen Galeron?" Alex called through the door and Sarah's voice rose in attempt to calm his cursing.

"Damnation, where could he have gone?"

They broke their kiss, their breath mingled between them, their chests heaving in time. Neither answered. Galeron's hand still held one of his clasps, the other rested on her breast.

Alex pounded on the door. "Hell's teeth, Galeron. If you are in there, I shall beat you myself."

Galeron cursed and closed the flap of his lower armor.

Ruby covered her laughter in the pillow.

"Ruby, I find nay bit of humor in this!" Galeron hissed.

Still holding the pillow to her mouth, she laughed hysterically.

He chuckled and rolled his eyes. "You are mad."

She hit him with the pillow and stood to straighten her skirts. With a final peck on the lips, she hurried to answer the raps. Galeron turned her and pressed her against the door.

"Not yet."

Ruby ignored the vibrations of the insistent knock against her back while Galeron kissed her with such intensity it turned the voices on the other side of the door into a distant hum. His tongue teased the line from her earlobe to her neckline. She whispered a weak protest and he covered her lips once again with a tenderness that caused her tears to sting against her closed lids. When she met his gaze, she saw moistness glisten and pool in the blue of his eyes.

Galeron turned away and walked to the middle of the room. He yanked on his hauberk and slipped the mail netting over it. "Answer it."

With heat of passion flushing her face, Ruby bolted from her compromising position and fumbled at the latch with her bandaged hands. Finally, she threw it open.

Galeron glanced up at Sarah and Alex while struggling to fasten his armor to the mail netting. "Relax, Alex," he said, breathing heavily.

Sarah grinned at Ruby while Alex helped Galeron finish.

"It seems your farewells have been said." Alex tugged at a clasp. "It seemed an eternity for you to—" Ruby stepped back when he strode to her and reached for the necklace.

"Alex?" Sarah shook her head at his forwardness.

Ruby gasped, bewildered and a bit aggravated. Galeron smiled reassuringly and stood beside Alex.

"The necklace," Alex whispered, rolling it between his fingers. "It fits Father's description exactly."

Ruby held on to the chain while Alex examined it. "I had come to wonder if it even existed." He let it drop.

Ruby pressed the necklace against her chest and took another step back. Her fingers trembled while she wrapped the orb in her hand.

"You have given it to Ruby," Alex said, deep in thought.

"Obviously," Galeron said.

Alex laughed and kissed her brow. "Be at ease, I do not intend to take it from you."

Ruby realized she had nearly imprinted the orb into her palm and quickly let it go.

"Father told us the legend of the necklace many times when we were children."

"Legend?" Ruby moved closer to Galeron.

"Another time," Alex said.

Galeron ignored his comment. "A knight's heart was captured by a beautiful maiden admiring the necklace. He waited until she passed it by and bartered for it. He tried to no avail to find her again, and night was falling with his hopes. Within days, he was at a social gathering and found her again. They danced the night, and he feared losing her again each time she danced in another's arms. However, naught could keep them apart, and soon they fell in love."

Alex nudged Galeron. "Then he would tell us that maiden was our mother and he was the knight." He shook his head. "I thought it was simply a tale he made up to entertain his two young sons."

Galeron smiled. "As did I. Until dawn, when he gave it to me, along with the ring that belonged to Mother. He told me of a promise he made to give it to their firstborn son when his heart found its mate." Galeron gazed at Ruby. "Now 'tis where it rightfully belongs."

"God in heaven, Galeron, I love you," Ruby whispered, completely taken by the story. She pulled him as close as his armor would allow and lost herself in his kiss.

"My brother's heart has finally opened. I always wanted him to be blessed with the love I have found with you." Alex took Sarah into their bit of heaven and shared a farewell kiss.

"What has Ramstone come to?" boomed a voice from the doorway.

The couples flew apart and met Easton's laughter. He strode across the room and tapped his finger on the necklace. "Welcome to the family, Ruby."

Though she failed to find her past, Ruby was more than willing to relinquish the quest in exchange for the future that lay ahead. She was about to tell them her thoughts when Easton said, "My dear sons, the time has come for you to be on your way."

Galeron collected Ruby's cloak from the floor and wrapped it around her. Though she smiled, her eyes could not mask her fear. With a final tug, he secured the hood under her chin.

The group made their way to the inner ward. The fog had failed to lift, swallowing most of their view. Sarah secured a fur cloak over Alex's armor and handed the other to Galeron.

Galeron swung it over his back, embraced his father, then turned to Ruby. He led her a few paces away then ran his hands beneath her cloak and pulled her close. She grabbed at the edges of his chest plate while he kissed her quivering lips. His lips still touched hers while his voice cracked upon his words. "My only wish is to find my way back to you."

She opened her eyes and memorized every nuance of his expression. "I wish to remain in your arms from that day forth." She did not miss the pain in his eyes and leaned closer to ease it with a whisper. "Naked."

Everyone turned at Galeron's roar of laughter.

Chapter Thirty-Three

His Lips, the Last to Depart

Who dares find levity in a time such as this? Sir Jac scanned the inner ward. Gods, it was Galeron! It seemed a hooded maiden was the one transforming Galeron from his usual dark demeanor to outright laughter. Usually, women wept upon seeing their men off. Jac squinted, watching the two through the fog still hugging the ground. He chuckled softly. Though a crowd of men filled the area, Galeron and the woman seemed set apart, as if they stood in a world where only they existed. A pain seared with the memories of the many times he'd laughed with his wife, and for a moment, Jac wished he had never looked their way. Still, he watched the discreet touch, listened to the murmured words, watched the way Galeron bent closer to listen to her. Or mayhap to catch her scent…as only a woman could smell…sweet, touches of whatever they used in their bath. His wife had always smelled of violets. Jac shook his head. Ah, yes, he remembered it well, and naught could ever fill the void of her death.

Now he watched the man who, until recently, had been trothed to his sister. Jac ran his hand along his steed's flank, wishing the woman would turn to face him so he could see who this slight maiden was and how she held such power over Galeron. Was she his mistress? Would Mara, had she wedded this man, have had to compete for Galeron's attention? Why was he even dwelling on this? Mara had made it apparent that she would never marry. Mayhap 'twould have been a blessing had his father been harder on her, but he seemed as powerless as Galeron was with the woman before him now. Women were both a blessing and a curse.

The thought caused a twitch of a smile and Jac shook his head, recalling the wiles his wife used to get her way. Ah, what imagination she had once the doors of the chamber were closed. His heart ached for her worse than his body ever would. He swung into his saddle and tried not to begrudge the happiness Galeron had found. Everything must focus on avenging his family, not on his pain. Not on Galeron's newest mistress. Revenge was the only thing he had left. Again, Galeron laughed. Jac spurred his horse to the gates, unable to watch any longer.

* * * *

Ruby turned at the swift movement of the retreating knight and watched him fade into the fog. Facing the man she loved, she embraced the joy Galeron's laughter brought to the bleak morning. A tremor entered her soul with each kiss he gave upon her fingertips. Ruby traced his face and stood on tiptoe, kissing him again.

Galeron's warmth left as he backed away, his lips the last to depart. She jutted her chin, keeping her tears at bay while he stepped into the curtain of fog with Alex by his side.

Tears blurring her vision, she stumbled toward him. Easton yanked her from the mass of hooves crowding forward. Sarah's fingers interlocked her own and the three of them stoically waited on the outskirts of the army.

A huge thunderclap made her jump. Then, to add to the dreariness, the skies opened and a downpour began. Ruby followed Easton's prod to the overhang.

The inner ward teemed with combined armies. Colorful banners made it seem more like a festival than a gathering for an impending battle. Galeron and Alex sat upon their armored steeds, facing the men.

Galeron guided his horse to where they stood. Ruby forced a smile but his focus was on Easton. "What in hell's fire is Rafe doing among the men? I made it clear he was to stay behind."

"I granted his request."

Ruby's bit her lip to keep from voicing her displeasure. Rafe was but a boy.

"Did you now?" Galeron stood in his stirrups and motioned for Rafe to advance.

Rafe led his horse through the crowd, never breaking eye contact with his brother. Once he arrived, he did not give him a chance to protest. "I leave with you tonight, Galeron. We haven't a moment to disagree."

"Young one—"

Rafe's eyes sparked with anger. "*Sir Rafe.* I am a knight. When are you going to see that?"

Ruby noticed Galeron fist his hand, then slowly released it before he spoke. "I do not deem you ready for this journey. We shall be gone for months."

"Father granted permission. I shall ride alone if I must. Open the blasted gates and I shall take leave now."

Galeron shifted in his saddle. "There are reasons for keeping you here, Rafe."

"Other than the fact you think me a child?" Rafe said. "Daren't say you need me to watch over the women. You need me to fight."

Ruby reflected on how much older he looked in full armor. Mayhap Rafe *should* go, but she kept her thoughts to herself. She saw Galeron's jaw twitch, betraying his fury, but she also saw the indecision in his blue eyes.

"Dare not question me. He is ready. You have trained him well," Easton said.

"'Tis time, brother," Rafe whispered.

Galeron shook the rain from his hair. "Very well, Sir Rafe. You shall ride with us."

Rafe nodded sharply and trotted back into the ranks. Ruby's pride mixed with trepidation. He was of age, but so was every man in the army. It mattered not. They were all risking their lives.

In battle mode, Galeron did not even glance at Ruby before he left to address his men. "Lend thy ears!"

She craned to see Galeron over the crowd. Frustrated, she dragged a bench from the overhang and stood on it. Sarah joined her and gripped her hand, but she remained focused on Galeron. His voice was pure thunder, the cadence a vibrancy of potent control. This side of him she had not seen. A leader of men.

"We shall conquer evil," Galeron shouted. "The dark knights are nay more than immoral demons, possessed with greed and insatiable hunger to kill and destroy. Innocents are slaughtered and left in the streets to die. These demons strike in the night and steal the young. We possess the power and strength to defeat them. We shall end their destruction of peace and bring down their leader, obliterating all he stands for."

The rain chimed onto his armor, mingling with the rumble of thunder. He paused, looking at the somber faces of his men. Not a sound came from the army, albeit the occasional snort and paw of hooves from the steeds. Galeron raised his fist and pumped it in time with his shouts. "We shall slay the enemy! We shall protect the innocent! We shall return victorious!"

A deafening cheer rose from the mass. Galeron's gaze rested on her. Ruby offered a smile then pulled her hood to shelter her face. He would not witness her pain…

At Galeron's signal, the gates opened and Ramstone's army marched through. The armor and weaponry glinted in the light of the torches. The chilled air lent a daunting vision to the steeds' breath as they puffed a whim of fantasy, resembling the snorts of a dragon. With the brothers of Ramstone leading them, the great army galloped into the night.

Once the inner court was deserted, Ruby ran to the gates, watching until she saw naught but darkness. She raised her eyes to the starless sky. Her hood fell back and the rain washed over her. She would not cry. In the midst of a silent prayer, she jumped when Sarah touched her arm. Easton stood beside them. Ruby could not bear to face Sarah, certain the pain reflected in her friend's eyes would split her mask of resolve.

"Close the gates," Easton said to the guards.

She pressed her face against Lord Easton's chest, listening to the heavy gates slam.

"God Almighty, keep them safe," Sarah whispered.

She broke away and fled inside. Sarah and Easton followed, but she continued up the stairs to her chamber. She tossed her soaked cloak aside, threw herself across the bed and released every tear she had hidden from Galeron. The mattress sank beside her and Sarah sobbed just as hard. Somehow, it brought her a bit of comfort. Time and space fled from her until she was spent. She silently bore her dejection while Easton fed the waning fire. The flames shot higher with each log added and she was painfully aware that the warmth it offered could never erase the chill wrapping around her.

Easton sat on the edge of the bed. "All shall be well, my girls."

Neither she nor Sarah responded.

He planted a kiss first on Sarah's brow, then her own. She would've wept at his compassion, but had no more tears to draw from. She touched his hand as he left. Her body felt limp, yet restless, as she stared at him, paused in the doorway.

He shifted his stance several times then quietly called across the room. "I shall send up some warm broth." With a small smile, he left. "Mayhap a carriage ride will distract… We shall go in the morn."

"Aye," Sarah said without conviction. She rose to go.

"Do not leave!" She was shocked at how needy she sounded.

Sarah's breath stuttered with the aftermath of her weeping. "I h-hoped you would ask me to s-stay." She stretched out on her stomach, chin in hands. "We both bear the same heaviness of worry."

Pleased Sarah chose to stay, but relieved when she didn't speak any more, Ruby watched the sparks spit from the fire, dying a quick death in the air. When the broth arrived, Ruby pushed it aside, allowing it to grow as cold as the fear within her.

Chapter Thirty-Four

Quivers

Tiny flakes of snow teased the air and melted on the ground. Suddenly aware of the force of her grip on Easton's and Sarah's arms, Ruby released them. The simple task of getting through the days since the men had left became more tedious with each moment. She thought a ride to the village would distract her thoughts. Now she wondered if her insistence on coming was a mistake.

The few villagers who survived the attack were making an effort to regain a semblance of normalcy in their lives. Did such a thing exist anymore?

Ruby stifled a sigh and returned a greeting from the elderly draper who'd set up on a table in front of the charred remains of his shoppe. She sifted through the small inventory of winter hoods. Holding up one, she waved over Easton and Sarah.

"Jadon needs this now that the weather is changing," she said to Sarah.

Easton dropped a gold coin into the old man's outstretched hand. His eyes widened and he quickly secured it in a pouch.

"You are a kind and generous man," she whispered, a tear brimming. Why such emotion? She must gather her wits.

"Good lord, girl, 'tis simply a hood."

"I speak of the coin." Ruby turned at a nearby shout from a small group of villagers.

"Jacob! Are ye deaf, lad?" The oldest of three lads turned around, nearly tripping over a lad on his heels. It looked as if the man wished to laugh. "Stay nearby and keep your brothers out of mischief."

The lad adjusted the quiver and waved his bow in answer. Ruby watched him scoop up the youngest one and place him on his shoulders, allowing the other to run ahead. A genuine smile alit at the trickle of laughter from the lads and she wished she could join their carefree venture.

She twisted the hood in her hands and watched his boys until they were out of sight. Sarah rescued the hood from Ruby's fist. "'Tis a wise choice that Jadon did not accompany us. The village is worse than I imagined."

"I daren't believe he shall ever wish to leave the walls of Ramstone again." Ruby squinted down the lane. Judging by the litter of remains, she was hesitant to take another step.

"Are you certain you wish to go on?" Sarah asked.

"I must see if anything remains of my home." She owned little, but couldn't pass the chance that her paintings had survived. Especially her latest work, a gift for Jadon. She was comforted a bit when Sarah wrapped her arm around her waist while they rounded the corner. Despite the bite of the cool air, sweat broke her brow the moment she spied her former home.

Tears stung her eyes. "The painting of Jadon's mother. 'Tis ruined." Her gaze roamed the empty space. All that remained was the hearth. "Everything is ruined."

She plopped down on the stone hearth, sending a billow of black soot into the air. Under a pile of rubble, she spotted the cauldron she'd thrown at the knight. A shudder skittered through her. Without a word, Sarah laid out her cloak and settled beside her.

"If only I could wish your loss away," Sarah whispered.

"I fare better than most." There was truth in the statement, but she could not dispel the tightness in her chest, the sting of tears beneath her lids. She drew a line in the ashes and stared at the smear on her fingertip. "After all, I am alive and betrothed to the man I love." Ruby spared a final perusal at the mess. She jutted her chin and wiped a lone tear. "Let us take leave."

"Your face is smudged with ashes." She took the edge of her cloak and wiped Ruby's cheek.

Ruby allowed her ministrations while looking past her at the field nearby. "Not long ago, that field was where I would bring Jadon to play. Now 'tis a final resting place for those who died that night." Her head pounded at the effort to dam her tears. "All for naught," she whispered, staring at the rows of crosses. "Will those deaths ever be avenged?"

"They will." Sarah whispered. "Our men promised."

She squinted, noting movement just beyond the edge of the meadow. "What is that?"

"What?" Sarah followed her gaze. "It seems you were wrong about the field. 'Tis still a place to frolic. Those are the same lads you were watching before."

"Nay, at the trees, Sarah. Something is lurking." Another attack? "Angels in heaven, nay," Ruby said, panic rising in her voice. *Blasted skirts!* She pulled the hem through her legs, jammed it in her sash then ran toward them.

"Wait!" Sarah called, but Ruby never broke her stride.

Once again, she spied movement from the forest edge as she neared. The youngest of the lads had left the group. The lurkers leaped from the trees into the clearing.

"Run, child!" Ruby screamed. "Wolves!"

The other boys looked, first at her, and then where she was headed. They abandoned their bows and ran for their youngest brother as well.

Barely slowing, she snatched a bow and slung the fullest quiver over her shoulder. It took but moments to sprint ahead of the boys. She armed the bow and aimed.

The wolves circled the lad. Too young to realize the danger, the lad's innocent giggle rent the air. His arms reached to welcome the wolf nearest him. His brother's shouts and rock-throwing did little to deter the animals. Wide-eyed confusion, then fear played upon the child's face. Terror froze him to where he stood.

"Hold fast!" The largest of the pack lunged for the lad, capturing him in his jaws. "Nay…" Only one word did she scream, though a thousand prayers shot with the arrow.

The beast yelped but did not relinquish its hold. She rearmed, shouting for Sarah to go for help. The next arrow dropped the wolf on its belly.

It seemed the world slowed but Ruby's mind remained sharp. Several of the pack now circled her. They were close enough for her to see their bared teeth, but she continued to deflect the advance of the rest from the boy.

At Easton's shout, she resisted the urge to pull her focus from the boy. Ruby armed her bow again and again, hoping the quiver was not empty when she reached for the next arrow.

Easton reached her side, armed with a dagger. "Give me the bow and find safety."

She shook her head, striking yet another wolf.

"Silas!" a man's voice shouted from behind her.

Much to her relief, the boy called out. "Papa, Papa!"

Two remaining wolves circled closer to him. His father drew his bow and aimed. One wolf leaped into the air, but the arrow slammed into its flight. The boy cried out when the mangy enemy landed atop him.

The lad's father pursued the lone survivor, driving it into the forest. Everyone else ran to the child, Ruby the first to arrive. The warmth of the demon's fur tangled in her grasp as she tried to remove the animal off the child. It seemed her body was someone else's and it took all she had to stand.

The boy's eyes rolled back.

"Nay!" Ruby slammed to her bottom. She planted her feet and shoved the carcass off him. He cried out when she drew his limp body into her lap. "Shhh…daren't make a sound." Footsteps. The enemy was near. Her heart sped faster, her breath hitched with panic.

The boy's father took him from her arms. Why did she fear him so?

"My life shall be forever indebted to you." His words seemed to echo and a drop of his son's blood hit her cheek, burning away clear thought. Warmth — terrible warmth — trickled and dripped off her chin.

Sarah and Easton's worried faces wavered as if in a dream. She swung her gaze but the child was gone.

"Where are you hurt?" Sarah wiped Ruby's face.

"I am not." Ruby pushed her hand away. *I left him.*

Easton hoisted her to her feet. "Who ever imagined you a skilled archer? Had it not been for you that child would be dead." Still breathing heavily, he wiped his brow. "Leave it to you to meet the possibility."

They strode to the village, Easton still chattering on about her bravery. The thump of the quiver grew louder with each of her steps. His voice muffled.

He is dead. I left him…dead. The thumping became deafening and the weight of the quiver seemed as if it would break her shoulder. A tin taste of bile filled her mouth and she shrugged off the strap, spilling the arrows to the ground. She clenched her eyes, she shook her head, but she still saw the blood dripping from the child.

"Pray tell, what is it?" Sarah's panic was evident in her voice.

Ruby broke into a sweat, clawing at the blood on her arms. A vision knocked into her. She knew she was awake, yet the vision of the child covered in blood — the pain of a dagger carving her face — the terror, continued to jab relentlessly in her mind. She quickened her pace, distancing herself from the field.

Everyone swarmed around, congratulating her when they reached the village. Their faces blurred and she recoiled from the crowd.

"I cannot leave him!" she screamed.

The crowd fell silent.

"He is with his father, Ruby," Easton whispered.

"His father! I must find him." She shoved through the crowd, searching for someone, unattainable anywhere but her muddled memory. She shook her head, plowing forward. "Help him!"

"Ruby!" Easton grabbed her shoulders and spun her around. "Cease this! The lad is hurt, but alive."

Ruby stared at Easton. "He is dead." She wrenched from his grasp. "I cannot release him!" She swayed, sweat trickling from her face. The air thickened and she gasped her plea. "You fail to listen! I cannot leave him like that." Naught made sense anymore, yet she could not cease trying to convey the unexplainable. Her world seemed to shatter as darkness swirled around her.

Someone was running…and she was in his arms. When had he lifted her? Who…who was he? "I shall bring you home."

Home. She knew not where that was anymore. A man laid her across the carriage seat. Easton. 'Twas Easton. Gods, was she going mad?

Sarah scrambled in, shouting at the driver. "Make haste to Ramstone!"

The carriage lurched and the two held her secure. She stared at the inky darkness, the lad's scream still piercing through her. She took a shuddering breath. A whimper, then a full wail.

Easton wrapped his arms around her. She smelled the stench of blood. Ruby mumbled the horrid truth against Easton's chest. "He is dead because of me."

"Ruby, I assure you, the lad is not dead."

"Your bravery saved his life," Sarah whispered.

"My cowardice killed him." Her breath caught. "I remember."

"Killed who?" Sarah asked. "What do you recall?"

Ruby clenched her eyes but could not banish the shocked expression on the lad's face as he died. Nauseated by the vision of blood, gurgling in his throat and escaping his mouth, she lurched for the door. "Stop the carriage!"

Easton pounded on the carriage wall. "Halt!"

Ruby stumbled out, falling to her knees and gasping the cold air. Turning from Sarah's cool hand against her brow, she retched until naught remained but sobs.

"We are just outside the gates, sweet child," Easton whispered while helping her into the carriage. "Daren't try to remember anything more."

"What have I done? What evil creature am I?" No matter how she tried, she could not stop trembling. "S-stay with me," she whispered to Sarah.

"I shall."

Easton ignored her protests and lifted her as soon as they disembarked. "Nay, child. You are too drawn to make it upstairs." He strode through the doorway. "Galeron shall never forgive me if I allow anything to happen to you."

She laid her head against him, relieved to be back inside the walls of Ramstone.

Shortly after her bath, she drank the tea Sarah offered.

"You want your hair pulled back?" Sarah laid her head in her lap and began braiding without waiting for an answer.

"My fear was uncontrollable."

"Shh." Sarah ran her fingers lightly across Ruby's brow.

"My quiver was crushed so...so long ago." The thought she was trying to convey evaporated. "He was...he cut me." Ruby frowned, wiggling her tongue about her mouth. It seemed forever to form words.

"What was in that tea?" Sarah's face became distorted and Ruby's lids closed, nay matter how hard she tried to keep them open.

Ruby woke to find Sarah sleeping beside her. Careful not to wake her, she crept out of the bed and washed her face in the basin. The cold water made her gasp but she welcomed the shock. Jadon's voice echoed nearby and she opened the door enough to slip into the corridor.

He rubbed his eyes and leaned against her leg. "I cannot find Mama," he whined.

She lifted him and nuzzled his neck, making him giggle. "She fell asleep in my chamber. Want to jump on the bed and wake her?"

Jadon's eyes grew round and he scrambled out of her arms, and leaped into the bed. Sarah bolted upright, her hair falling in her face. Jadon squealed, his blond curls bouncing around his face. "Alas! Mama looks like a dragon!"

"You imp!" Laughing, Sarah tried to grab him, but he bounded out of the way.

Ruby laughed, happy for the normalcy.

Jadon glanced up at her laughter, giving Sarah the opportunity to capture him. "Beg for mercy, little knight!"

"Never!" Jadon reached for Ruby, laughing through his plea. "The dragon caught me! Help!"

"I cannot. 'Tis a spell! Your kiss shall set you *both* free." Ruby plopped on the bed. "Make haste and kiss the dragon!"

Jadon kissed Sarah's cheek. "We are free!"

"Ah, my knight, the spell is broken." Sarah hugged him. "Now I am nay longer a dragon and free to live a life as your mother."

Dragon...I played that before. Sarah looked up and Ruby smiled to hide her turmoil.

"I suppose 'twas you who suggested he surprise me." Sarah allowed Jadon to squirm out of her grasp.

Ruby shrugged. "Someone had to wake the dragon." Her stomach tightened.

Jadon gasped and they both looked at him. "I forgot! Grandfather sent me to ask you to break fast with us." Jadon disappeared without waiting for them to answer.

"Did the tea help you sleep?" Sarah asked, closing the doors.

"Aye, deep enough to quell dreams." Ruby opened the door again. "Easton is waiting."

Sarah patted the bed beside her. "You remembered something. Though it was frightening, 'tis a good thing."

"I'm famished." Ruby waited by the door. Could she not see she did not wish to speak of it?

"Alex thinks all your memories shall eventually return."

"I do not wish to know what Alex thinks!" Slamming the door, she grabbed a kirtle and began dressing.

"As you wish." Sarah stood behind her and nudged away Ruby's hands, assisting with the lacings.

Ruby saw the tears in her eyes when she turned to the basin. She waited while she washed her face, repentant for the way she acted. "My words were harsh...I did not mean any of it." She handed Sarah a drying cloth.

"You seldom think before you speak." She tossed the cloth on the table. "Shall we break fast?"

Before they reached the great hall, Ruby pulled her aside. "Forgive me. Alex is a good man. I am blessed to have his friendship. And yours."

"I understand why you lash out, but it does not shield me from hurt." Sarah hugged her. "Forgiven."

Jadon's squeal of delight ended the moment they peered around the doorway to find him perched on the table. With a shake of the head from Sarah, he scrambled into his seat. "There are dried apricots, Ruby!" He offered her a handful in his chubby fist.

A child, trapped in her memory, materialized in her mind. She gripped the table. Stark memories kept catching her by surprise. The child who had died in her arms had the same smile...the same innocence. She accepted the fruit, popping one in her mouth. "Mmm."

Jadon slipped out of his chair, darted from the room, throwing on a cloak at the door.

"Child!" Sarah placed her hands on her hips. "Where are you going?"

"Grandfather said I could play in the snow!" The door slammed.

"Did he even eat?" Sarah asked Easton.

"He had a bit of fruit. Allow him his play." Easton chuckled. "One would think he never saw snow before."

"You are spoiling him." Sarah poured everyone's tea.

Ruby watched Jadon frolic on the frozen landscape. "I believe apricots have always been my favorite. My brother loves blackberries. I think that is what was spilling from the basket." Bewildered, she looked up at Sarah and Easton. "Did I say that or think it?"

Easton and Sarah spoke in unison. "You have a *brother*?"

With her stomach jolting, Ruby jumped to her feet. She headed for the doorway, putting her hand out as Sarah neared. "I have no idea why I said that." Damn these unexpected slips into her past. She grabbed her cloak from the peg and went outside to join Jadon.

She was surprised her face did not shatter in the winter air, for she certainly seemed broken inside. Though she recalled the essence of a brother, she could not conjure a likeness. However, no doubts lingered, she certainly had one. She plopped onto the bench and tucked her hands underneath her cloak. *A brother*. Her gaze drifted from Jadon forming snowballs to the bare branches above him, the boughs bending with the burden of snow. Would she bend…or break under her burdens?

A snowball slapped her arm, shocking her back to her surroundings.

She scooped a handful of snow, her fingers numbing instantly. "You little rogue!" Aiming, she made certain she met her mark. Jadon's squeal of laughter brought true joy and she genuinely smiled.

"My turn!" He ran toward her, emptying his small armory of snowballs.

Ruby ran, her feet sinking deep into the snow. For the first time in a long while, she laughed without something haunting her. After being accosted with snow in the back of the head repeatedly, she changed course and tackled Jadon.

Ice and snow clung to her hair when they stopped rolling on the ground. Out of breath and spent, they lay on their backs, gazing at the morning clouds.

"Ruby?"

She turned to him. "Aye?" She was about to brush the flakes from his lashes when he took her hand.

"I tell naught of that night. Papa Alex asked me once, but I-I cannot."

She wiped a stray tear from his eye. "Poor lad, 'tis a painful thing to speak of. You can talk to me anytime the need arises. You were very brave that night."

"Do you still love me?"

She fought the lump in her throat. "Never doubt that, my knight. I love everything about you." She embraced him, his damp hair soaking into her cloak. "I always shall." She lifted him, holding his head to his shoulder. "Always."

"D-did the bad knight hurt you?"

"Nay, you saved me from him, Sir Jadon."

Jadon raised his head. "I did?"

"Aye, you are my hero."

"I thought Galeron was your hero."

She blinked back tears. "Then I am a blessed maiden, for I have two heroes." Mayhap three…or more.

"Let us tarry through the garden. Galeron once told me holly grows there." Jadon wrapped his arms tighter around her neck and she drew her cloak around them both.

Her cloak knocked the snow from the waxy leaves near the walkway, uncovering the red berries as they entered the garden.

Chapter Thirty-Five

Wanderlust

Galeron stood between his brothers at the fire, scoffing at the snowflakes filtering through the forest canopy. Even though it provided shelter, the wind whistled through the branches.

"I'd hoped the snowfall would hold out. This shall slow us," Galeron said. "We should go."

"What? We barely finished pitching the tents!" Rafe tossed more wood on the fire, singeing the meat. "Can we not reserve a single day for rest?" Rafe turned as Jac approached. "What do you think, Jac?"

Jac shrugged. "The decision is Galeron's."

Alex scratched the growth on his face. "The storm is sure to hamper us either way."

Several more men meandered closer. Galeron stared at the fire, growing higher with each drip of the meal. A smile twitched at the memory of the rabbit he had shared with Ruby the day they had met in the forest.

He raised his voice as he eyed the men. "We shall press on before nightfall."

The only one who smiled was Jac.

Alex carved a hunk of meat from the carcass and nudged Galeron away from the group. "If the men are too weary to battle when we arrive, what use would there be of pressing on?" Without meeting Galeron's eye, he tested the meat. "It is done." He offered half.

He snatched the meat and stuffed it in his mouth, and chewed for several moments. "So be it." He stepped toward the others. "One night of rest." He tore another portion from the spit then strode to his tent, ignoring the cheers from his men. Footsteps crunched on the crust of ice behind him. He quickened his pace, wishing to be left alone.

"Galeron, wait!" Jac said. Galeron opened the tent flap and sighed. Jac caught up, his breath freezing between them. "May I speak freely?"

He motioned for him to enter the tent. Jac ducked in. Galeron sat on his bedroll, threw a blanket toward Jac and popped the last bit of meat in his mouth. "Speak your mind."

"Perhaps a few hours would be a sufficient rest." He sat on the blanket. "Then we could ride through the night."

"Alex is correct. We cannot battle if we are exhausted." His tone softened at Jac's crestfallen expression. "*Our* reason to press on does not completely lie within our duties. You search for vengeance and your family." Galeron pulled off his gloves and blew into his hands. "I, being the one who postponed the journey to Jastar, wish to right my wrong."

"Absolve your guilt. Naught could have altered the outcome. I hold nay ill will."

The burden of guilt would remain until they found Mara and the young lad, Jacson. "Just the same," he muttered.

Jac cleared his throat. "Each day we rest is another day they suffer."

"Which is the reason we have traveled with minimal rest!"

Jac stood and lifted the tent flap. "You lent an ear to my concerns. I respect that."

"Wait, I have something more to discuss."

Jac turned, his brow lined with worry.

"Ease your mind and sit."

Jac dropped the flap and sat cross-legged on the blanket.

"Alex and I noticed how well you fit in with the rest of the men. You have shown loyalty and respect to my leadership." He sat up. "Would you consider joining Ramstone's knights permanently?"

Surprise spread across his face. "I-I am honored. Any time the need arises, I shall aid your army, however, my home is Jastar. I intend to rebuild once I finish this journey. Mara and Jacson shall require the comfort of our home to return to." His smile weighed down with pain. "I pray we find them."

"If they are held behind the gates of Talbot, we shall." He placed his hands upon Jac's shoulders. "I give my word."

Jac swallowed hard. "What if they are not there?"

"Then we continue the search." Galeron looked down, his hands fisting. "Mara would have been on the way to Ramstone when the attack took place."

"You are wrong. She refused the marriage, remember?"

"Indeed." Galeron pulled a flask from his pack. "You mentioned that several times." After taking a long draw, he tossed the flask to Jac.

Jac caught it and squeezed a hefty portion into his mouth. "Do not take it personally, Galeron. She was adamant that love lead her heart."

"Ah, she's in love with another then."

Jac shook his head and passed the ale. "Nay. She had use for nary a soul, much less a man. But she was of age…a bit past, really. 'Tis the reason our father arranged the marriage with you. He wished her to marry well. It wasn't just to join armies as he told her." Jac sighed. "She was furious, to say the least."

Galeron did not interrupt, allowing Jac to reminisce.

"She came to me, begging me to sway his decision. By the time you were to arrive, I believe we had convinced him to turn you away." Jac's smile faded. "Then the attack. All that seemed so important then, dims in comparison." Jac accepted the flask from Galeron. After swallowing another gulp, he winked. "You would have been taken by her beauty, Galeron. She did not realize her fairness."

"A maiden who has beauty *and* strong convictions." Galeron chuckled.

"Strong convictions to avoid *you*."

"I believe you find true pleasure in the constant reminder of the fact. Hand me my ale, cad." Galeron laughed for the first time since they left Ramstone.

With each swig he shared with Jac, the friendship was forged, and before long, the flask was empty. Relaxed, from the conversation and ale, they stumbled from the tent to join the rest of the men.

Long after the men had settled for the night, Galeron lingered outside his tent. He added several more limbs to the fire and ducked out of the wind. After slipping into his bedroll, he began to relax. Ruby's last promise made him laugh aloud. *Naked indeed, my forest nymph.* With familiar longing, his body responded to her. "Damnation, I cannot wait to bed thee." He reached into his pack and found the kerchief he had tucked in the corner. He brought it to his face and inhaled her lavender scent. Comfort eased through him. "When skies darken, I surrender to you. Reside in my sleep, sweet maiden," he whispered, slipping into an ale-induced slumber.

Chapter Thirty-Six

Armored

Toward the next evening, Galeron sent a scout ahead. At the report of a castle a half-day's ride away, a blast of energy surged through him. Nevertheless, he ensured his men were well rested and fed before moving on. The darkness did not hold much cover, due to the full moon, but the deep hours hopefully proved an advantage.

Galeron rifled through the enemy's armor they had scavenged. "If only we could have rescued more armor from the blacksmith's wife." His sigh billowed in the night air. "The wench. Who would figure she was privy to how to melt it down?"

Alex frowned. "She always assisted him. If you took more notice of anything besides tavern wenches in the village, you would have known that."

He had forgotten that. Since Ruby, he had not even thought of visiting the tavern. "Let's focus on what lies outside this forest, not the tavern."

"You are right, though. The lack of Talbot's armor limits who can ride with us past their gates."

Galeron braced against the blast of energy surging through his veins and gave the signal to ready for the advance out of the woods. The moon shone bits of light through the trees, lending an eerie transformation of his army when they donned the horned helmets.

The smoke from the oil burning in the nearby moat wafted to them. Galeron stifled a cough while tying a red sash across his chest plate.

"Excellent suggestion, Alex. It distinguishes us from the enemy." He glanced at the men ordered to wait behind and sensed Alex looking at him. Galeron squinted through the darkness, wishing he could see his expression. "We shall be victorious."

"Aye, I sense the truth of it in my blood," Alex said.

Galeron led his steed to his youngest brother. "Rafe, you shall remain beside Alex. Nay matter what, you must wait for my order to lower the drawbridge."

Rafe nodded, causing his faceplate to clang shut. He pushed it back up. "Then, I shall slay the bastards."

"You stay near me or Alex at all times." He gently closed Rafe's faceplate. "Let's be off."

Galeron jerked the reins, leading the group into the baleful moonlight. Their march was muffled by the snow, but the soft song of armor broke the silence of the night. The moon illuminated the ghostly dance of snowflakes floating into oblivion on the blanketed ground.

Galeron's breath, visible from his helmet, stilled at the shout from the gates.

"Call out!"

Galeron sucked a breath of frigid air.

"Call out or die!" The voice was louder this time.

Sweat trickled down his neck despite the icy night. He shifted in his saddle. Hoping the word the evil knight had divulged would gain him entrance, Galeron's deep voice shouted across the distance.

"Rage!"

A blustery gust whipped at the snow, circling at the hooves of their rides. Galeron twisted the reins around his fist while he stared at the riveted steel lining the drawbridge. The demonic face hammered upon it ran a chill of dread through him. God in heaven, let that be the correct response.

"Lower the bridge!" came a shout from within the castle.

Galeron exhaled. The muffled thump of the drawbridge drew a satisfied grin. The activity inside floated on the air as he led his men across the bridge. The oily smoke lingered, the bitter taste invading his tongue. His cold armor did naught to protect him from the sweltering heat of the surrounding flames and he quickened the pace across the deathly moat.

The scent of hot mead sweetened the air. A group of men gathered by a great cauldron, scooping hefty portions of the brew. High from the effects, they seemed oblivious to the arrival. To the left of the cauldron, a platform had been erected. The torches surrounding it illuminated the deadened expressions of scantily clad maidens. A man, his mead sloshing, grabbed one of the maidens and led her down the stairs. The festival atmosphere collided with the reason for the gathering.

He turned to Alex, knowing he held nay choice but to hold fast. "Not yet."

Alex signaled for the others to stand by. Only moments passed, but it seemed an eternity as the man accosted her against the far wall. He cringed inwardly at the maiden's cries, vowing the cost of the maiden's pain would be avenged.

Galeron's steed pawed the ground when a guard came close. The leatherwork on the back of his cloak was adorned with a banner. Even in the darkness, he could make out the words *Talbot's Rage*.

The drone of the crowd died and guards stomped to attention. The only sound was the weeping of a single maiden as she crawled up the platform and into the arms of her friends. The guard standing in front of him raised his hands. "All hail our Master!"

His focus snapped to the intricately carved doors, spilling light into the yard as they opened. "Spread word. Daren't dismount," he whispered to Alex. He sneered at the hooded shadow in the doorway, sure none other than Lord Talbot would demand such a dramatic entrance.

Lord Talbot dismissed the maiden beside him. She bowed and stepped away. Galeron's attention held to her for a moment. He glanced at Alex to see if his thought was correct. By the surprise on his face, it was.

"Is that Elizabeth?" Rafe stilled at Galeron's glare.

Talbot accepted a mug from one of the drunkards and eyed Galeron and his men. Galeron ignored the stable boys, unwilling to hand them his reins, never breaking his stare as the leader shoved the guard aside.

With one swift motion, Talbot pushed back his hood, wiping what looked like paint from his forehead. Even his hair was coated, but blond streaks shone through. The firelight lent the illusion of an abyss of darkness to his eyes though they were light in color. The strange man barely looked human. Galeron braced himself against the stare, reminding himself the man was a mere mortal.

"Where are your offerings?" The soft voice barely reached Galeron's ears.

With the taste the metal and oil in his mouth, Galeron dismounted. "Our captives weakened and died against the elements, Master."

The immense leader cocked his head, the motion oddly familiar. In spite of his faceplate, Galeron dreaded the man could read his deceit. Talbot flipped one corner of his cloak, his tunic straining against his muscular chest. The earlier gentleness in speech shredded with his scream. "You dare return without a single offering? Indeed, you must crave the singe of fire." He spat on the ground. "Show your face, useless bastard."

Sweat trickled down Galeron's nose as he lifted his faceplate. He noticed Alex's grasp on the hilt of his sword and gave a warning glance. "Master, may your disappointment be appeased. We *do* have an offering, though 'tis not the regular fare. We replaced our horses with a much better quality. In all your wisdom, you must realize Ramstone is famous for their stallions."

Lord Talbot advanced so close his two-toned hair moved in the breath from Galeron's steed. "Ramstone's stock?" Seemingly able to sense his evil, it snorted and pawed the ground while Talbot traced his long fingers along its sleek muzzle. The leader cast several glances at Galeron as he examined Alex's horse as well. Talbot's heavy footsteps left small canyons in the snow when he stepped back, braced his muscular legs apart and scanned Galeron from head to toe.

He met his glare, careful not to disclose uncertainty. "Master" — oh, how he despised uttering that word —

"the stallions are bred for battle. A grand addition to our army."

Lord Talbot's whisper hissed through yellowed teeth. "Ramstone?" Unsettled, shifting, unstable were his moods, and his voice pitched yet again. "Ramstone was to be spared. Why did you disobey that order?"

Galeron swallowed hard. "We found the place in ruins. We were able to capture their horses from a nearby field."

His footsteps crunched beneath his boots as he paced. "In ruins, you say... You mentioned prisoners who died—where did you acquire *them*? In the field, tending the horses?"

Galeron did not hesitate to respond. "Nay, Master. The nearby village, of course."

Talbot weaved between the men, stopping from time to time to peer at the riders. Galeron stiffened when he stopped beside Rafe's horse. "You there. Remove your helmet," Lord Talbot ordered.

Galeron palmed his dagger, hoping the fear that flickered on Rafe's face once the helmet was removed went unnoticed.

Talbot peered up at him. "Now, remove the coif."

Rafe did as he asked, his hair spilling to his shoulders. Galeron did not understand why the man was doing this, and it unsettled him. Why pick him out of many? Why examine with such scrutiny? Galeron slowly began to slip his sword from the sheath on his saddle.

"Your age?" Talbot asked.

Rafe darted a glance from Talbot to Galeron, then answered. "Ten and six."

"Dismount. I want this horse as my own." He grabbed Rafe's boot. "Dismount!"

Rafe smiled, surprising Galeron. "Master, I shall." He leaned over. "However, you may wish to give it to a lowly servant to tote things about, for this horse is nay worthy for a powerful man as you. 'Tis not a Ramstone stud." He made as if to dismount.

Galeron spoke out, following Rafe's lead. "Lord Talbot, the young lad is correct." He led his steed to Talbot and bowed. "Mine is the most spirited stallion. 'Twill serve your mares as the best stud."

He laughed, deep and disturbing. "Breeding of horses 'tis nay concern. The seeds I require come from chosen knights. The breeders are such as those." His finger extended from the cloak, pointing like a reaper to the platform. "Stallions cannot seed a maiden's vessel." A sneer dripped from his lips. "Though that gives me a pleasurable thought."

Galeron's jaw twitched. *Fucking pig.*

Talbot strode to the platform, his cloak flowing in his wake.

Galeron whispered to Rafe, "Don your helmet, stay mounted and remain silent."

Talbot towered over the maidens and laughed when one scooted away on her bottom. He grabbed her and dragged her down the steps. Her struggle earned a backhand, leaving cuts from his ringed fingers. Though she did not cry out, her tears cleared a clean path down her smudged face. She closed her eyes and shivered as Talbot ripped at her rags. Barely perceptible, she began to cry. She bowed her head, her tangled hair hiding her exposed breasts.

Rafe shifted in his saddle and drew his dagger, returning it to his belt at Galeron's glare.

Talbot traced the tips of his long nails across the cringing maiden's breasts. "Steeds cannot serve this little morsel." Her body heaved with a sob. He pulled her hair and savagely muffled her cries with a kiss. Still grasping her hair, he jerked her in front of him. "One of the few virgins left. She shall do well."

Galeron swallowed the vomit rising into his mouth while her sobs turned to wails. How he wished to kill the man, rescue the poor girl, but wait he must, or all the innocent would end up dead.

As if Talbot had just remembered, he swung around. Still holding the maiden's hair, he motioned toward Rafe, pitching her forward. "Did I not order you to dismount?"

Rafe dismounted and stood beside Galeron. Talbot released the woman and strode to them, then nearly tore the helmet from Rafe's head. "Now, son. Tend to your duty."

Confusion filled Rafe's face for a moment, but he quickly recovered. Had Talbot seen as well? Ill prepared for the heinous implication of what was expected, Galeron stepped in front of his youngest brother. "I shall tend to her. He is but a lad we found in the village." He stared down Talbot. "With all due respect, Master, allow him time to learn our ways."

The man's body seemed to take on an energy…trembling by every limb. His eyes, crazed and wide. His voice quiet, yet screaming insanity. "Dare not deny me the seed of Rage. Rage. Rage." Had he repeated it? Or did fear cause it to reverberate through his brain? Galeron knew not at first. But then he realized Talbot led the drunken men to join his chant. With the increasing level of shouts, he realized he must take action. Now.

Galeron scooped the maiden into his arms. He proceeded to the platform, hiding his confusion at the crazed leader's screams.

"I do not wish it, but you shall die if you continue to defy me!" Several of his men drew weapons and approached Galeron. "Do not draw a sword against him!" Talbot shouted. He circled the platform raising his hands to the heavens. "The seed of your future king has arrived!"

Galeron lowered the woman onto the furs and she cowered away. He locked eyes with Rafe, trying to reassure him. Knowing he couldn't take the chance to attack with Rafe on the ground, he signaled his men to wait.

The drone reached a crescendo. "Bless the seed, bless the seed." Talbot stomped a rhythm and swayed with the chant.

Galeron unclasped his cloak and laid it over the maiden. She stared with the protection of detachment in her eyes. Galeron knelt, hoping she could hear him over the chants. "Trust my actions. You shan't be harmed."

Her eyes widened as Talbot pounded the edge of the platform. "Dare not lay with her! Not thee! I must have the seed of the youngest Ramstone!" Talbot dragged Rafe toward the platform.

Still, Galeron did not give the order to attack. Not until Rafe was safe. His hand twitched at the hilt of his sword. "Master, the halls of Ramstone were deserted. No family remained. Naught even a servant."

Talbot's throat rumbled with a chill of laughter while he advanced to the bottom of the steps. "You fucking lie like your father."

Galeron fought to keep the utter shock from his expression, fought to regain some sort of sense, but naught came. How was he to reason with insanity? "Forgive my ignorance, Master, but I do not understand."

"I offer but two choices." Talbot shoved Rafe up the steps. Galeron caught him. "Serve my vengeance with Rage's seed." Talbot motioned toward the maiden. "Or with his blood. His life is in your hands, *Galeron*."

"How does he know your name? Who is Rage?" Rafe froze, his gaze traveling past Galeron. "Fuck."

Galeron swung around. Calen stood beside Talbot, a smirk of satisfaction on his face.

"You shall pay now, Galeron." Calen's jowls shook with his shout, his plump fist jabbing the air.

Curses flowed profusely as Galeron drew his sword. Calen fled into the crowd, elbowing, shoving, anything to retreat.

Talbot seemed unperturbed at the commotion. As were his drunken men. It was as if a nightmare played out before Galeron's eyes. One he could not wake from. The epitome of insanity approached even closer, stopping at the edge of the platform. "And now, you upon the stage, shall play out the end of this journey."

"I shall play naught but revenge for the innocent." Galeron growled, giving a signal for his men to draw their weapons. Even then Talbot did not retract his order not to draw a weapon against them. Was this a trap?

Talbot bellowed with laughter. Again the sick, demented thought of familiarity bled through...for a split hair of a moment. "After Lord Calen decided you were unworthy, he joined my army. Oh, and his daughter? Already she carries my seed. So, she shall bear a child of Ramstone after all." He chuckled at the thought. "Calen told of your plan to destroy me. I waited ever so patiently. Blessed is such patience, for the reward is Rage. I was not aware *he* would enter my gates."

Galeron shielded Rafe with his body. Alex advanced. "Stand fast, Alex!"

"Spill your seed into the virgin, son," Talbot shouted at Rafe. "I have waited many years for this holy night."

Rafe was trembling. "Galeron? Think of something!"

The chants grew louder, seeming to shut out reality. The platform vibrated at the many stomping feet. "Rage, now!" screamed Talbot, his veins pulsating in his throat.

"I am not Rage!"

Talbot took a step, stopping at the point of Galeron's sword. "I named you, son. Your name is Rage." He pushed his throat against Galeron's blade. "Do you dare spill Ramstone blood?" Naught made sense. Galeron's face tingled, as if all the blood drained from it. Talbot sneered and stepped away from the blade. "You are a bigger fool than your father. Now step aside and allow your brother to follow his destiny."

Rafe grabbed Galeron's arm. "What does he mean?"

"He is delusional," Galeron whispered. "I shan't leave your side."

Lord Talbot outstretched his arms, swaying hypnotically in front of the platform. His blond-streaked hair slid like a sheet of oil down his back as he prayed. "Bless be the seed of Rage. Nestled in the womb of purity, may the heavens grant the quest of a king's bloodline!"

"*My* child is to be king!" Elizabeth shoved through the crowd, stopping at Talbot and tugging his cloak. He yanked it from her clutches and turned away.

Her hair whipped from side to side. "Father!" she shouted. "Where are you? You promised I would be queen!" Tears hung on her lashes when Calen did not answer. "F-father?" She stood and clutched Talbot again. "I am your queen!"

"My only queen is dead." He cradled the slight swell of her belly. "This child is destined to *serve* the new king." He shoved her to her knees, pressing her shoulders to keep her down.

Though Galeron pitied her, he also hated the woman for being a part of the betrayal. Blood dripped from Elizabeth's shoulders as Talbot raised his face to the stars. He joined the prayers of his people, his nails digging deeper. Elizabeth's weeping was drowned by the crescendo.

Galeron focused on the white sheen of Talbot's throat, glistening in the moonlight. "Slip beneath the cloak and appear to take her," he whispered to Rafe.

Rafe wept as he knelt by the maiden. "What does he mean—he named me?"

Galeron nudged Rafe with his boot. "Do it!"

He locked eyes with Alex, motioning him to advance. Amazed the others continued to chant, he wondered it wise to believe the order to spare him would hold true. No one stopped Alex's advance as he brought Rafe's horse alongside the platform. Not one person opened their eyes. Evil permeated the air and if a demon would have risen from the cauldron, Galeron would not be surprised. Chills ran the length of his body.

Rafe kicked him and he looked down at his brother and the maiden in his arms. Galeron's heart broke at the terrified eyes asking for guidance. "Hold fast a bit longer," Galeron whispered, hoping Rafe could decipher his command over the chants. The inner ward seemed to sway and vibrate, except for Calen. He led a horse along the far wall.

Talbot tossed his head side-to-side, drugged in his madness. "Bless his seed! Bless his—"

"Bless *this*, you blasphemous bastard!" Galeron plunged his sword into Talbot's throat. He did not care the consequence of his action. He wanted the man dead. Time stilled. The gurgle of blood choked off Talbot's prayer. His blue eyes flew open and he grappled against the blade, blood spilling from his palms and onto Elizabeth's screaming face. She crawled away as his lanky fingers released their hold. Death spurted in rhythm with the chants as his blood melted the snow beneath his boots.

Talbot dangled on the sword, his arms flopping as Galeron shouted at Rafe. "Release the bridge!"

Rafe leaped into his saddle. With his sword unsheathed, he kicked his mount into a gallop.

Galeron twisted the sword, nearly decapitating Talbot. His shoulder welcomed the release of the weight when his victim slumped to the ground. The last of his body heat melting the bloodied snow, Talbot's mouth gaped with his last plea.

The bridge dropped, breaking the hypnotic chant of the crowd. Calen attempted to gallop across it but Rafe's sword met his advance. The horse continued on. Rafe jumped from the saddle, held Calen's head by the hair, and bellowed a battle cry.

"Rafe! Get on your horse!" Galeron shouted, relieved when he did so. However, the distraction cost Galeron. A punishing clash knocked him in the back. Galeron swung both his sword and battle-axe as he fell into the crowd. Prepared more for the garish festival than a battle, many of Talbot's men fell at his feet. Galeron lost sight of Rafe.

"Rafe!" Galeron shoved Elizabeth under the platform. He swung into the saddle, catching a glimpse of his reinforcements galloping over the drawbridge.

Galeron deflected a blow, nearly sending him to the ground. He slammed his battle-axe squarely into the attacker's head. Still searching for Rafe, he rocked the axe out of the skull. His voice raw, he continued to scream for his brother. Blood splashed his face as he slashed the enemy. He froze, mid-motion, his sword nearly dropping from his hand when he spotted Rafe's injured horse buckle, throwing him. He uttered a prayer that the enemy would protect their newly named heir. Yet through the utter chaos, he feared for his youngest brother's life. He motioned to Alex, for he was nearer. Without hesitation, Alex's sword plunged into one, then another as he cleared a path to where Galeron pointed.

"Rafe!" Galeron bounded to the ground. He hacked through the crowd, swinging with abandon. He took a blow to the head, knocking off his helmet. Blood splattered across his eyes and he blinked past it. His shoulders aching, he sent the enemy off in pieces. "Rafe!" A chill of terror tore through him as he searched.

"Over here!" Alex was flinging bodies aside. "He was here."

Cold air raking his lungs, he sprinted to him. Alex uncovered Rafe as he arrived. Time seemed to sway. The clang of weapons, screams from dying, thunder of hooves, all ceased to exist. The air itself stagnated.

Galeron repeatedly shouted Rafe's name, each time denying death did not stare from his brother's eyes…tears already freezing on his bloodied, young face.

Grief screaming from his lungs, he armed himself with fury and killed with abandon. He did not leave Alex's side as they fought, and little time passed before the purity of the fallen snow transformed into a slushy red river.

Victory was Ramstone's as the darkness relinquished its hold to the gray dawning of day. Exhausted, Galeron stumbled over bodies as he made his way to Rafe's body.

Alex intercepted him. "Let me tend your wounds."

Galeron wiped the blood running into his eyes. Struck dumb at the horrid reality, he shoved past, dragging a trail through the battle slush. Galeron dropped to one knee, his tears falling onto his little brother's armor as he lifted him.

Rafe's head lolled to the side, his blond hair, dripping with blood, trailed in Galeron's stride. Galeron's mind closed as he left footprints of his deathly march in the snow. Meeting the gaze at Alex's grasp, he began to shake. Foreheads together, he stood with Alex, Rafe dangling between them. Fellow knights walked by, offering prayers, while he held the sacrifice of the battle in his arms.

With shadowing grief, Galeron handed Rafe to Alex. Standing before his men, he made sure his stance relayed his anger. "Behead the enemy and post them on their own lances. The devil's spawn shall rot outside the gates for all to see!" Throwing back his head, Galeron released a roar, setting the men into motion.

While the men gathered the dead, Galeron carried Rafe inside. He found a bed and lay him upon it. "How are we to tell Father?"

"By the time we send a messenger, we will be there ourselves." Alex's voice shook. He leaned against the bedpost. "What did Talbot mean when he said he named him?"

Galeron brushed the hair from Rafe's eyes. "I draw nay sense of it." He stood and started for the door. "The ravings of a mad man."

"He knew your name and called Rafe his son."

Galeron swung around. "He is *our* brother."

Alex stared at him for several moments. "I am simply trying to understand."

"There is naught to understand." Galeron ground his eyes with the heels of his hands and stormed out of the room. Talbot's words haunted him as well, but he refused to believe any of his rantings. He gave Alex a sidelong glance when he caught up with him.

"A safe haven for the innocent must be attained." He grasped Alex's shoulder. "Then we shall find Jac's loved ones." He looked down the corridor. "Where is he?"

"Outside, helping the men clear the grounds." Alex started down the stairs after Galeron. "Wait." He grimaced, cracking the blood on his face. "Did you witness what happened?"

Galeron raked his hand through his hair. "His horse went down, unseating him. I saw naught how he... I saw naught. I should have ordered him to stay at home."

"Father granted it anyway. And, Galeron, Rafe would have followed, nay matter the decision."

Galeron embraced his brother, swallowing the enormous lump forming in his throat. "He died an honorable death, brother."

"One of the men said Rafe beheaded Calen."

Galeron's eyebrow rose. "That I did witness. He was proudly displaying it when I shouted for him to get on his horse. He killed a traitor, even to his daughter." He held the door to allow the men to carry their wounded inside. "I hate them both." He blinked at the morning glare and released his chest plate as he entered the inner ward. "I am glad to be rid of this vile disguise." The clang of the armor muffled into the snowdrift. He sneered, pointing to the platform. "Make certain all maidens are looked after and then dismantle the reminder of their horror."

Alex set off and Galeron dispatched three men to retrieve Ramstone's armor from the woods. The clump of hooves against the drawbridge drummed finality and he turned away, glad the horror had ended. He locked eyes with a maiden, approaching from across the yard. Still wearing his cloak, he realized she had been the one on the platform. He gave a weary smile.

Hair fell over her breasts as she slipped off the cloak and handed it to him. "Sir Knight, I return what is yours. For my life being saved, I offer the rest of my days as your servant."

"You owe me naught." He wrapped it around her shoulders and clasped it, covering her nakedness. "All men are not demons. My brother never would have harmed you."

"I realized that the moment he took me in his arms. He said a prayer with me."

His resolve nearly gave way. "He died an honorable knight."

"He died?" Tears sprang to her eyes. "Strength be granted to bear the loss, Sir Knight." She sighed. "His eyes held compassion and I felt safe with him in the few moments we shared." She watched the other maidens following Alex into the warmth of the castle. "Until him, the only kindness I received was from the other maidens." Her stance stiffened. "Except that wench."

"Who?"

"Elizabeth." Her voice grew cold. "She ignored the rapes of young maidens and willingly gave her body to the same men who stole innocence. Then she made her way to Talbot's bed, and became even crueler." Her hands fisted. "Your compassion is nobler than mine. I would have killed her myself had I a weapon."

"You are misguided." Galeron's jaw set. "I haven't any compassion for that vile traitor, despicable harlot and evil—"

"I was under the platform when you pushed her beneath it."

He shrugged. "She was in the way." And carrying an innocent babe within her, but he was not going to even try to explain. "Now, hurry inside and get warm. The castle is yours to do with as you please."

The earlier sadness and anger swept away. She grinned and touched her lips. "Ah, I forgot what 'twas to express happiness." Her lips parted in a tiny laugh. Still fingering her smile, she ambled inside.

He called the nearby men together. "I need volunteers to stay until winter has passed." Jac was among those stepping forward. He nodded sharply. "Many are with child and unfit to travel. You are to provide and protect. Come spring, your duty shall be their safe return home." He sneered and kicked Talbot's limp body. "Drag this vermin outside the gates. Nay, better yet…"

He grabbed his battle-axe and finished off the damage his sword had left. "Burn his body and post his head—" At the sound of hooves on the bridge, the thought that his men could not have returned so quickly speared through him. "Arm yourselves!"

He spotted his shield where he had lifted Rafe, deciding against retrieving it as he drew his sword. Three horned knights galloped into the inner ward, dragging the men he had sent for the armor behind them. He dodged them, but tripped over a body. Though he regained footing, the slip allowed his opponent's blade to plunge through his hauberk.

Blood rose in his throat as he fended the next swipe. He dove toward his shield and met the ground hard, sinking into the snow. Grasping the leather strap of his shield, he sprang to his feet. His blood was warm against the frigid air and he fought to keep darkness from overtaking his mind. He shielded the next strike, then thrust so hard his wrist snapped.

Though the knight was unseated, he continued a relentless attack from the ground. As if in a dance, Galeron's body moved with the familiarity from years of training and experience. Despite his weakness, he refused to cease his attack until he stood over his dead opponent.

He stumbled away. Where was Rafe? He tried to call his name, his blood blurring his voice. A faint buzzing in his ears muffled Alex's shouts.

"I downed a bastard as well, Galeron! This one is for Rafe." A knight lay at Alex's feet, the horned helmet still rocking in the snow.

Galeron could hear other men celebrating the victory and he forced himself to take a step. He looked down, realizing he still stood in the same spot. Alex approached, stopping to pick up Galeron's sword. "We were fortunate this time. The bridge should have been secured." He eyed the men. "Get it done."

Numbness tingled through him. When had he dropped his sword?

"Where's your battle-axe? Did you lose that too?" Alex chuckled.

Galeron choked on blood when he tried to answer. Time slowly halted. He pressed his hand against his chest. He stared blankly at his bloodied glove, surprised at the lack of pain.

Alex sprinted to him, screaming his name, but Galeron barely heard over the pulsating swarm in his head. Snow filled his mouth as he sighed, welcoming the chill upon his wound. He tried to protest when Alex turned him to his back. His eyes widened and he took in the beauty of the cloudless sky. Galeron's whisper mingled with a moan, but he found peace in the single word. "Ruby."

Blood pulsated as if in a song. Alex pressed upon his chest, making it hard to breathe. "Goddamn fools, secure the fucking bridge!" Alex's shout faded.

* * * *

Ruby snapped awake and clutched the sheets to her chest. She scrambled from the bed, fell to her knees, and prayed with such fervor, she scared herself. Not understanding what frightened her, terror emitted through each beat of her heart.

"God, I beg thee. I beg thee." Tears flowed, but she did not unclasp her hands to wipe them. "I know not what I pray for, Lord. In Your wisdom, I have faith that *you* do." Ruby pressed her forehead to her hands and clenched her eyes, knowing if she stopped praying, all hope would be lost.

Chapter Thirty-Seven

The Queen

Jac knelt beside Alex. "Let us bring him out of the cold."

Alex rose higher on his knees, lending his full weight of pressure. "By God's eyes, Galeron, hold fast."

Jac slid his arms under Galeron, shouting for someone to grab the other side. With a grunt, they lifted. Alex sidestepped into the castle, never letting pressure off his wound.

The moment Galeron lay on the bed, they were surrounded by maidens. Alex accepted muslin from one, replacing his blood-saturated glove over the wound. Never had he experienced panic while caring for wounded. Until now. "God in heaven, I beseech thee!" He abandoned prayer and cursed at Galeron instead. "You ignorant arse! Why did you unclasp your armor?" His eyes widened at the paleness replacing Galeron's ruddy complexion. A gurgle of air fought to pass and he turned him to the side, pressing deeper into the wound. "His lung." He clenched his eyes, barring his tears. At the sound of ripping leather, his eyes flew open to see Jac, cutting the hauberk from Galeron.

"Swallow your doubt or grieve yet another brother," Jac whispered.

Alex blew several breaths. "I need wine — boiling wine — to cleanse the wound."

Jac strode to the door, telling one of the maidens what needed to be done. "Anything else?"

"My medicinal bag," Alex said. "On the bed, beside Rafe." The mention of his name brought tears to his eyes. "And clear the room." Though the maidens seemed eager to assist him, a chance remained that any one held ill intention. He trusted no stranger within the walls at this point.

"Very well." Jac guided everyone out of the chamber, motioning for one of the older women to stay behind. "I beg thee, assure wine is boiled and brought up." He met Alex's gaze. "I shall make haste and return with your medicinal bag."

Alex welcomed the solitude. "I beg thee, Lord, grant me the knowledge. I have never successfully mended a pierced lung. Daren't take another brother."

After flushing the wound with the wine, stitching, then bandaging it and finally wrapping it tightly, Alex sat back, his body aching. "I am truly grateful for your assistance, Jac." He had not asked him to stay, and he knew well Jac paid a sacrifice by doing so. "Now go search for your family."

He seemed reluctant to leave. But Alex assured him. "Galeron's breath remains labored, but he shall improve." *God willing.*

"Very well," Jac said quietly, rubbing the back of his neck. "I have not seen..." He hesitated. "But I must hold faith." He strode from the room.

Alex resumed his prayers. Moments slipped into hours, but not once did he rise from his knees. His eyes fluttered at the sound of a woman's voice. At first he thought it came from the corridor. But then she spoke again, this time much closer. He opened his eyes, ready to scold anyone who dared enter without his permission. Elizabeth stood at the foot of the bed, her arms crossed.

"Leave before I—"

"A shame," she said in a singsong manner. "He is ruining my bed. Put him in the servant's quarters."

He stood, his knees aching with the effort. "Get out." Hate infused every pore as he stared her down.

"You cannot order me. I am the queen." She smoothed her satin dress over her belly and patted the barely perceivable swell. "And this is the future king."

"Get out!" Alex strode toward her, backing her out of the room.

Jac hurried into the room. "Ah! My queen!" He bowed before Elizabeth. "I was told you are in need of a *new* chamber. It is now readied. It has more room for your babe."

"My babe?" She stared at Jac, tilting her head to the side like an inquisitive child. "Are you his father?"

Alex looked from one to the other, too stunned to speak. What was Jac going on about? And her? She was mad. Fully mad.

Jac led her from the room, all the while carrying on the insane conversation. After a moment, he returned. "Ease your mind. The poor woman is harmless. Quite mad, she is."

"She is not to be trusted. No one is." Alex sank into the chair, more exhausted than ever. "I do not want her near Galeron."

"He is as my own brother, Alex. I assure you I guard him with my life. I shall do as you ask, but she is to be pitied, not shunned."

"I pity her child." Alex muttered. The lines of worry embedded on Jac's face and Alex realized his harshness. "Very well. Assure Elizabeth is watched over…cared for. Just keep her away from Galeron." He checked his brother's bandage. "Have you found your family, Jac?"

"The ones housed here are willing to help the wounded, but they do not trust enough to answer questions."

"Then do not ask. Take some men and search."

"You have been with Galeron all night. Allow one of the men to watch over him so you can get proper rest."

Why was he so hesitant? There was a good chance they were here. "Go. Find your family," Alex repeated. "I shall watch over mine." Without awaiting a response, he knelt and prayed once again.

* * * *

His first full night of sleep was a waste. Alex rose from the side of Galeron's bed and stretched his stiff muscles, but it did no good. Each step to the door was pure torture. He stuck his head in the corridor, surprised to see Jac standing by the doorway.

"What are you doing here? Did you find Mara and Jacson?"

Jac strode to the bed without answering. "How does he fare?"

"Nay better, nay worse."

"Death failed to claim him for three days now. I have faith he will remain in this world to see the morrow."

Alex sank into the chair. "Have you found them, Jac?" he repeated.

"I have not." Before Alex could reply, Jac hurried with his report. "The enemy has been displayed as Galeron ordered."

Alex saw the weariness in his stance. Sensing Jac did not want to discuss his family, he simply nodded.

"Though most of the maidens are wary, we assured them their care is our only aim." Jac watched several children run past the doorway, their laughter filling the corridor. He continued to stare long after they passed.

"That laughter should be proof enough to turn the others' trust." Alex closed the door, never taking his eyes from Jac.

Jac pointed at the untouched tray of food. "You need to eat."

Alex shrugged and checked Galeron's dressing.

"I moved Rafe to the underground room." Jac sighed and sat to face him. "Alex, you must prepare. The ground is frozen, so the bodies must be burned."

"I shall bring him home." Alex swallowed hard. "Store all our dead in the underground room." He looked up at Jac's sigh.

"He died an honorable death," Jac said.

He had found no comfort when Galeron said the same thing. He recalled many a widow's grief when he spoke of their husbands, Alex wondered if they had found the sentiment as hollow. He blinked at Jac, trying to grasp the conversation.

"Inventory the food. There is plenty to sustain everyone throughout the winter. Though we must find another place to store it now that it is to be used for the — Rafe and the others."

"Do what you must." Alex stretched his legs, propping his feet on the edge of the bed. "Tell me of your search. Anything?"

Jac's mood darkened. "It seems they would have found *me* by now. Especially Jacson, but he is not with any of the children."

Alex detected tears in Jac's eyes and turned to the tray of food, grabbing a handful of dried fruit. "The place is enormous. Three days is a short time to complete a thorough search."

"Mayhap." Jac rose and nudged his chin toward Galeron. "Tell me of any change."

Alex popped a dried fruit in his mouth and chewed for a moment. "He is too stubborn not to survive."

"Mara and Jacson have the same temperament as your brother." He flashed a grin, but it did not quell the torture in his eyes. "I have an idea."

"What is it?"

"A last effort." Jac strode to the door. "I pray 'tis fruitful."

Chapter Thirty-Eight

Search

Jac's newfound hope faltered when he spoke to the children from Jastar and the connecting village. Some clung to their siblings, a few to their mothers, but most appeared to be orphans. All insisted they had not seen Jacson or Mara since their arrival at Talbot Gates.

Reeling with the discovery, he failed to face the despairing facts. Frustrated at the lack of cooperation from most of the maidens, he sent word to gather all of them in the main hall.

He waited by the doorway, his heart skipping in anticipation. He offered a smile of reassurance to hide his growing disappointment. He stepped to the front of the room and raised his voice over the mumbling of the crowd. "Are *all* the maidens gathered here?"

Several nodded. One spoke out. "Except for a midwife, and two others giving birth. What do you want of us?" She cleared her throat and added, her eyes filled with worry, "Sir Knight?"

He spread his arms in attempt to ease the tension, Jac said, "I have nay ill intentions. I only wish to find my son and young sister."

"Are they here among us?"

"Mara?" He scanned the crowd. "Are you here? Daren't be afraid. Jacson, son, I beg thee to answer."

"Be off with you," called a voice from the crowd. "If they were, they would have run into your arms by now. How can you assure us that they are even your family?"

He suppressed a sigh and gave a description of Mara, trying to spy a spark of recognition. His hopes faded when he was met with stony silence. It was obvious the cooperation so freely given when helping the wounded did not extend to any questioning by a stranger, a male stranger at that. He sat on the deep window well and drew a breath.

"I should have begun by giving my name," he whispered to no one in particular. He turned to the crowd and rested his arm on his leg. "I am Sir Jac of Jastar. Is anyone familiar with my home?"

Again, the room dripped with silence. Jac scanned the occupants and locked eyes with a maiden.

"I am," she whispered.

Hope shot to each nerve. A path quickly opened for Jac's long strides. The maiden yanked her arm from the insistent tugging of her friend. Her eyes grew bigger with each of his steps. His towering presence dwarfed her and she swallowed hard. "S-Sir Knight," she stuttered, craning her head. "I shan't bow to ye."

Jac cursed under his breath, realizing what a brute he appeared to be in his haste for an answer. He could see the slight shudder of fear travel through her and he took a step back. "I expect naught but cooperation. I fought for thy freedom. I beg you show the same compassion and tell what you know. Anything shall be of help."

She stared at him, and for a moment, he thought she would flee. "I am Andelina." Her head swung at the collective gasp. "Aye, I am finally free to speak me name." She jutted her chin, raising her voice. "Sir Jac is nae one of the evil men." She squinted and cocked her head. "Me kenning tells he be trusted."

Her attitude was so like his sister, Jac fought to keep from smiling his admiration.

The crowd grumbled louder. Andelina shouted above the protests. "Do ye nae see?" She caressed her swollen belly. "Our wee babes shall be delivered into freedom due to this mon's army."

He began to correct her assumption, but when Jac's eyes scanned the faces, he saw them nodding and decided it did not matter who they thought led Ramstone's army.

His gaze returned to Andelina when she tugged at his sleeve. "Sir Jac, I ken of the lass."

He tampered a gasp. "Are you certain?"

"Certain? Nae. However, she spoke of Jastar as her home. Though 'tis certain she nae admitted the name Mara."

Her Scottish tongue spoke riddles and Jac doubted her sanity. "Andelina, is it?" She nodded. "Many were taken from my home. Mayhap 'tis the reason she answered to another name." He smiled. "I believe she may be in hiding...with my son." The happy thought lent to ease his worries.

"Non surrendered their true name, Sir Knight. 'Twas the only bit of ourselves they could not take." Her hand came to her chest. "I do not wish to douse yer hope, however..." She shook her head.

He kept his doubt hidden and motioned for her to continue. "Though Talbot lorded over the castle, 'twas her who led us. She spoke of Jastar often and said she would return and we would return to our homes as well, if we but believe time will grant us freedom."

Jac wiped his palms on his breeches. "Why is she not leading you now?" The blood pounded as his eyes traced the clear path left behind on her smudged cheeks and tried to brace against the reason for her sudden tears.

Andelina wiped her face with the cuff of her ragged sleeve. "S-she fought against the appointed one."

Jac blinked. "Talbot? Fought him? Are you daft?"

Andelina stiffened. "Nae, Sir Knight, I be of sound mind, and a mon as bright as yerself should deem it best to lend an ear to the only one willing to speak oot."

Jac paced in front of her. "Go on."

"She is gone." She glanced around, then rested her gaze on him. "I shan't teel all detail, for 'twas horrid."

He wiped his brow. "Tell me everything."

"Keep your mouth clenched!" Andelina heeded the shout from one of the maidens.

"Let her speak!" He gave a warning glance to the others. "Carry on."

She looked away. "I cannae relive that night. I wish now I had not spoken at all. What matters is Mary…yer fair Mara, is gone."

"You already said that. Gone where?" Jac clenched his jaw. "Tell me."

"I dinnae wish to deliver heartache."

"My heart aches with uncertainty." Patience thinning, it took all he had not to shake the answers from her. "Come out with it."

416

Andelina met his angry gaze. "She is nae longer among us, Sir Jac. Yer son would be in yer arms as well if he was among us. 'Tis best to spare the sour details."

"*I* choose what is best."

Andelina glanced at the woman who'd silenced her, irritating him further.

"Cease speaking in riddles and get on with it!" he shouted.

She took a step back.

He knelt. "I beg you."

Her eyes softened. He rose and waited. After a moment, he tempered his impatience and continued his questioning. "You say my son is not here either." Jac shook his head, refusing to release hope. "Mara would watch over him. Perhaps they escaped."

"No one escapes—alive anyway. The male children were not allowed contact with anyone in their family. I pray forgiveness for dashing hope, Sir Knight."

"I shall find him." Jac fisted his hands. "What of the defiance against Talbot you spoke of?"

Andelina stared at her feet. "Aye, at the festival of maidens."

"Festival? Like the one last night?"

She tucked her hair behind her ear and stepped back. "The night she was offered, the fool mon had a dagger tucked in his belt. The bright lass took advantage of his stupidity and plunged it into him whilst he lay upon her."

Jac's fury bubbled forward, resonating against the walls. "'Twas not Mara!"

"Me kenning nary leads me astray."

His face tingled and he wondered if it held a drop of blood. "It does now."

"Jastar's maiden 'twas the only lass brave enough to defy the evil lord." She bowed her head. "Fer that, she paid with her life."

"Her *life*?" He dragged his hand over his face, recalling something Galeron had said. He hadn't given much thought to the woman the knight spoke about during Galeron's questioning months before, but now it made perfect sense. Heat rose to the back of his eyes while a chill emanated through the rest of him. Fear began to snag sanity. "All were summoned at first light," he softly quoted.

Andelina blinked several times. "Pray tell? Who were summoned?"

Silence filled the room. Jac could not stop Galeron's earlier description from splintering his mind. He focused on the vaulted ceiling and answered. "You witnessed her death. She was thrown into the flaming moat and nay other dared defy Talbot again."

Andelina's mouth gaped.

The air filled with whispers. "How did he know?"

The room spun. "Mara." His whisper hissed past the mumbles of the crowd.

"Sir Jac?" Andelina cautiously approached him.

Torture wreaked havoc through his mind.

"Be proud of her. Stand strong was her last shout to us."

Jac struggled to keep his legs from buckling. "Stand strong?"

"In honor of Mary — your beloved Mara, I *stand strong* to teel of her courage."

Jac clenched his eyes, the air around him closing in. He saw Mara, begging him to speak on her behalf. Be it her unconventional behavior or pending nuptials to

Galeron, she always ended her plea with a command. "Stand strong," he whispered.

A hand touched his face, jarring him from the sad vision. His mind disconnected as she tentatively touched the tears clinging to his lashes. He backed away, hating her. Hating them all.

Jac fled. With his boots slamming up the stairwell, he rushed for respite on the highest turret. The cold stung his lungs as he gulped several breaths. He dug his fingers into the stone wall and unleashed his anguish into the bitter wind.

"Maaa-raa!" Repeatedly, he called her name, until exhaustion and grief overcame him. Jac slid his back along the turret, landing in a heap. He lay his head into his bloodied hands and wept.

* * * *

Alex woke to the eerie howl of the wind. He shuffled across the room to close the far window. He listened closely and realized 'twas not the wind, but repeated shouts of Mara's name. He bowed his head in prayer, then latched the window.

Galeron began to thrash. Torn from the pity of Jac's grief, he hurried to the bed and held him down. "Be still, you fool, or surely you shall reopen your wound."

Steely blue eyes fluttered open.

"Praise be to God." Alex, instantly furious, yelled, "Daren't ever do that again!"

The brothers stared at each other several moments before Galeron spoke. "What have I done?"

Alex slumped next to him, still gripping Galeron's arm. "You nearly died."

"What is this place?" Galeron blinked several times.

"We are within the walls of Talbot." Touching Galeron's flushed cheeks, he said, "You are still fevered."

"We must return home."

"God's eyes, Galeron! You must allow time to heal."

Galeron tried to sit up and moaned, flopping onto the bed.

"Stubborn oaf, lie still!"

Galeron winced as Alex checked his wound. "Prepare the men."

"Enough orders." Alex retied the bandage.

"We must leave before the winter is—'tis still winter, nay?"

"Aye, winter is still upon us. Now rest."

"Ready the men."

"Enough!" Seeing the worry in Galeron's eyes, he softened. "We shall discuss departure come morn."

Galeron nodded. "I owe you my life."

"You owe me naught but rest."

"On the morrow, we depart." Galeron closed his eyes.

To Alex's relief, the command drifted into a whisper. Within moments, Galeron's snore filled the room. After placing a cool cloth on Galeron's brow, Alex sank into the comfort of the mattress beside his brother. For the first time in days, he slept.

Chapter Thirty-Nine

Subsist

Somewhere in the quiet of his dreams, Alex woke to Galeron's shouts. He rolled out of bed, trying to slice through the thick wall of confusion. He grabbed a wet cloth in such haste that the basin of water clattered to the floor.

"Burn them!" Galeron shouted, wildness clouding his eyes.

Several men came at the noise and helped hold Galeron down. Alex staunched the fresh flow of blood and restitched several places. Galeron fell limp as he replaced the dressing. Alex's own strength was depleted as well.

His voice hoarse, Galeron tried to speak between shallow breaths. Alex leaned close to make out his words. "She does not answer me."

Alex blew a breath, certain he spoke of Ruby. "Ease your mind." He looked up and gave a slight smile to the maiden carrying a fresh basin of water.

"Would you care for food or a mug of ale?" she asked, wiping the water from the floor.

Alex shook his head.

Galeron moaned. "Ruby? Is that you?"

Heat emanated from Galeron as Alex pushed hair from his unfocused eyes. "Nay, Galeron, she is not here."

"Send Sarah to fetch her."

Alex motioned everyone to leave. "Close the door on your way out," he whispered to the maiden.

He dipped the cloth and watched the water trickle, the tiny splashes captivating him. Galeron's mumbles brought him to reality. Once again, he bathed his brow. At the rap on the door, he wiped his palms across his face, stomped across the room, and swung it open.

"What!" Seeing the pain etched on Jac's face made him wince. Alex motioned him in.

Jac bent over Galeron. "I heard the shouts and came as soon as I could. How does he fare?"

Alex dipped another cloth, worried how quickly the first one warmed. "He is fevered." He wiped Galeron's face. "How do you fare, Jac?"

"The search is over."

Alex met Jac's tortured eyes. "Are you certain?"

Jac slumped against the bedpost, crossing his arms. "Remember the knight Galeron tortured in the village? How the knight told of the defiance of a single maiden?"

"Aye."

"The defiant maiden was Mara." His voice, though steady, could not hide the vacancy in his heart.

"God in heaven!"

"There is nay God in heaven, Alex." Jac stomped to the hearth and snatched a log from the woodpile.

By the fury on Jac's face, Alex feared the log would end up across the room, so he didn't argue the point of religion. Jac stared into space for several moments. The log dropped at Jac's feet. "My son is nowhere to be found either."

"I hold hope he is alive somewhere." Alex offered yet another silent prayer, this time for Jac's son and Mara's soul.

Jac raked his fingers through his hair. "Get some rest, Alex. I shall watch over your brother."

"I fare well."

"You are cursed with the same stubbornness as your brother."

"Be it a curse or a virtue, 'tis what kept him alive." *That and prayer.* He gazed out of the window and added. "Hold to hope, Jac." Upon hearing the door close, Alex discovered Jac had left.

* * * *

"Hold to hope, indeed," Jac muttered. "How am I to do that?" He stormed down the stairs and through the main hall. By the time he reached the inner ward, his fury had abated. Then pain seeped in once again. Jac wandered the grounds, searching for Mara's ghost until he was numb with cold. Though God failed him, he still knelt in the snow, praying his son fared better. He could not bear to return inside, and he refused to go near the moat. Broken, that was what he was. Shattered. But he must find a way…any way possible to mend his soul, for he must remain whole for his son. His sigh clouded in the air. "I shan't fail you too, Jacson. I shall find you, lad."

Dawn broke and he braced himself to face yet another day. His heavy footsteps echoed as he entered the castle. A young lad, no older than his son, rekindled the fire and stepped aside to allow Jac to near.

Gripping the mantle, Jac could not draw enough warmth to melt the icy strangulation of his heart. Peace on his land caused weakness, inattentiveness. He had failed miserably as a knight. A son. A husband. He could not live with himself if he failed as a father as well. Alex and Galeron had done well today, and he was proud to be a part of the revenge. The brotherhood between them warmed him at times, but sometimes he was an outcast. Especially when they were at Ramstone, sharing family.

"Family," he whispered as he strode up the stairs. How many here had lost theirs? He fought back tears. He could not bear to think of what Mara had gone through. He struck it away as he opened the door to his borrowed chamber. Mayhap he should rest. Mayhap God would give respite with dreams. Fishing with his son, holding his babe, bedding his wife, laughing with his sister...arguing with his father. Even that was a treasured memory now. He rubbed his eyes, trying to recall the last time he had slept. He lay on the bed, stared at the ceiling and wept.

Chapter Forty

The Last Cart

Ruby blinked away the flakes of snow clinging to her lashes. The bitter air stung her face while she tried to fight the swell of panic. The weary army plodded into the inner ward. Her eyes teared at the many vacant saddles. Where was Galeron? She feigned a smile at Jadon propped on Sarah's hip. Though Easton was by the gates, distance did not hide the worry etched on his face. She curled her fingers even tighter into the heavy folds of her cloak.

Sarah shouted over the wind, echoing Ruby's thoughts. "Alex and Galeron should be leading the men through the gates. They are *always* at the forefront." She squinted and stood on tiptoe. "Where is Rafe?"

Ruby marveled how the beat of her heart did not stop altogether. "Quiet, Sarah."

"What is Father discussing with that knight?"

Ruby sucked in a breath. "Perhaps Jadon should get out of this cold." She squeezed Sarah's hand while a shiver of doom quaked through her.

Sarah turned pale, but did as Ruby instructed. "Keep him occupied in the nursery," she said to her maid.

Ruby's effort to remain calm fell to the wayside when she saw the shock on Easton's face. Sarah's hissed her protest, but Ruby ignored her and crept nearer to the gates. The knight's back was to her and she could barely hear what he was saying. The snow filled her boot when she stepped into a snowdrift in an attempt to eavesdrop on their conversation. Sleet cut her eyelids, but she strained to listen and a snippet of the conversation ambushed her.

"The pain you must bear from his death. Alex had nay chance to save him."

Time halted. Her boots shattered the icy layer on a puddle as she ran to the knight's steed. Horrible thoughts screamed in her mind but all she could do was move on.

The scowl on the squire's face did not deter her. She wrenched the reins from him and swung into the saddle. Kidnapping the messenger's steed, Ruby dashed through the open gates, her cloak whipping behind her.

With her face to the wind, she welcomed the icy refuge, and encouraged the horse on.

"Nay…nay…nay." The wind bit each plea from her.

She yanked the reins so hard the horse reared and hoofed the air when she reached the first cart. Ruby struggled to remain in the saddle, Ruby's fear numbed her senses. She met the stunned faces of the knights. Though she had the urge to scream, her voice froze.

One of the knights shouted over the wind. "You shouldn't be out here. Climb aboard and I shall tie your ride to the cart."

She averted her eyes to his load. "What is in your cart?" she choked out.

The knights glanced at one another. "The dead, milady."

She nearly choked. "In which cart does Sir Galeron lay?" *Dare not answer. Know not of what I ask.*

His gloved hand pointed behind him, unaware he was sealing her worst fear. "The last one, milady."

Her eyes remained on his hand, still pointing. "The last one," she repeated.

When he dropped his hand, she continued to stare, still envisioning the pointed finger. "If you do not wish to ride in the cart, you can ride alongside."

"Be off."

"Milady, I daren't leave you alone in this —"

"Leave!" Her shout surprised her as much as it did him, but he shook his head and moved on.

She slumped, motionless in the storm, the wind whisking her tears before they could fall. The creak of the next cart made her cringe. She ignored the call from the driver as it passed. From the corner of her eye, she could see the dented armor in the back, wondering if Galeron's was among the pile. Slowly raising her head, she spied the last cart in the distance. She shoved back her hood and squinted into the swirling snow. She began to pray for the elements to rip her to shreds and deliver her from what she must face.

The steed snorted its impatience and she dug her heels into the warm flanks. When she met the lumbering cart, she found no amount of courage could force her to witness the contents and she closed her eyes.

"Ruby!" Her eyes flew open at the voice.

Alex shoved back his hood, leaped from the cart and reached up to her. "What are you doing here?"

She stared at him, all strength seeping from her.

Alex took her by the waist and lowered her to the ground. He grabbed the edge of her cloak and pulled it tight. "You are freezing! Climb on the cart and I shall tell you everything on the way." He took the reins of her horse and began to tie it to the cart.

She snatched the reins. "Is that Galeron?"

Alex pulled her hood up and tied it. "Aye, Ruby, 'tis he."

"Nay! Galeron!" She unleashed her anguish. She ran her hand over the furs, his body. Unable to bring herself to peer beneath the coverings, she sank to her knees.

"Why have you taken him?" she shouted to the blackened skies. She rammed her fist against the wooden cart, screaming his name.

Alex tried to pull her away, but she shrugged him away. Easton galloped up, leaping from his horse before it had fully stopped. He lifted her out of the snow and buried both Alex and her in his embrace.

He gave Alex a mixed expression of relief and confusion. "What is she going on about?"

"I just figured it out." Alex held her face, forcing her to face him. "Ruby, you little fool, Galeron is alive!"

She dragged herself from the vast hole of grief. She stared at him, trying to absorb his words.

"You poor heart. Look." He pulled back the furs, drawing a soft groan of protest from Galeron.

She scrambled over the edge of the cart, barely believing Alex's reassurances. Galeron's face was hot beneath her caress and she sobbed with relief. She rejoiced with each glorious breath, freezing in the air above him. She bent closer to savor it against her cheek.

"Galeron, I believed fate dealt thee death," she said between kisses.

Galeron opened his eyes. "Ruby. 'Tis nay dream?"

"I am here." She fought another wave of tears and whispered in his ear. "Though not naked as I promised."

His lip cracked with his smile and a rivulet of blood seeped from it. She yearned to take him into her arms, but feared his injuries.

She crept beneath the furs and lay beside him, filling her with bliss.

"Ruby," he whispered again.

No longer able to see his smile when Alex tossed the furs over them, she still could sense his relief. His breathing seemed labored, but thank the angels he breathed. He ran his hand over the contours of her body. She snuggled, tucking her head under his chin. She tried to remain stoic. He needed her strong.

"I love you." Galeron inhaled, then moaned. "Your hair…I missed the smell of it."

"Rest, sweet man." She gingerly held him and soon he fell silent.

She peeked out and strained to listen to Easton and Alex's conversation. Though a sin to eavesdrop, she had to learn what she could of Galeron's injuries.

"Seeing him eases my worries." Easton turned to Alex. "He looks weak, though."

"The journey sapped most of his strength."

Easton secured the kidnapped horse to the back of the cart. "How bad is his injury?"

"He was unarmored. Lung injury." Alex glanced at the cart and she ducked. "At times I feared he would not make it. His wound did not heal well at first, and now the journey aggravated what progress he'd made."

Easton shook his head. "Could you not have waited until he healed to travel?"

Alex sighed. "I tried, Father. He set out on his own, with nay regard to his wound and mad with fever. Galeron doles orders. He is not one to take them, so I followed his wishes. He was nay longer bleeding, the infection was gone, so we stopped only when absolutely necessary to cut the time of the journey."

"Then let us not delay it any longer." Easton mounted his horse and Alex called to him. "Father, forgive me, but I deemed it best to send a messenger ahead to tell of Rafe's death. I did not wish to burden you all at once."

She covered her cry at the news, but Alex must have seen her movement and turned to her. "How is Galeron faring?"

She looked back to check. "Sleeping."

"Let us bring him home." Easton spurred his stallion forward.

Alex climbed into the seat and whipped the horses into motion. The cart jerked and Galeron moaned. She kissed his brow. Heat emanated against her lips. "Galeron?"

"All is well." He placed a broad hand against her head. She sighed, relishing his fingers running through her hair. Her contentment vanished when his hand landed with a thump beside her head.

With a prayer on her lips, she pressed her ear against his chest. Too fearful to move, she listened to the steady beat until she the noise of the inner ward surrounded her. "Galeron." She pushed the fur from their heads. "You are home."

His mouth twitched. "My nymph." He turned, peering at her from one eye. "I was home the moment you called my name." With a deep groan, he closed his eyes again.

She caught sight of Easton and motioned for him to near, but his focus lay with another cart—the death cart. She tucked the furs around Galeron.

"Warm enough?" The alarm, still so fresh, threatened to tear her apart when he did not respond. She brushed the snowflakes settling in his hair. "Galeron?"

Sarah cried out for Alex and she scanned the crowd, ready to call out to him as well. Tears filled her eyes when Sarah flung herself into Alex's arms, nearly knocking him into a man standing nearby. Her heart dropped, knowing all too well how Sarah had feared for her husband, but Galeron needed him now. "Alex!" He did not hear her over the din in the ward. Afraid to leave Galeron's side, she brushed his hair from face and kissed his brow.

"Rafe is dead because of me. If I—" His words were drowned out by a shout nearby, but he said enough for her to understand.

"Oh, Galeron, my heart aches for you, but the blame does not lie with you."

Galeron shook his head, his eyes clenched, his deep voice replaced with such weakness it tore through her. "F-fetch Alex."

Her breath caught when she did not see Alex where he had stood a moment ago. "Alex!" she called.

Easton motioned for her to wait as he scooped Jadon into his arms.

431

A maid ran to him, shouting at Jadon. "Master Jadon, you were to stay inside. There is too much about!"

Easton's back was to her but the wide-eyed expression on a maid's face told of his displeasure.

"Easton," she called, but his focus was on the scolding, not her.

Galeron opened his eyes. The vacant gaze frightened her. Several stable boys passed with horses, blocking her view. "Make haste, you bleeding imbiciles! What is wrong with you?" she screamed.

Both Alex and Sarah came running with Jadon on their heels. "Why isn't he inside? I ordered—" Alex shook his head. "Gods. I should have tended him myself."

"Galeron needs your help." She locked eyes with Alex, struggling to keep the fear from her voice. She forced a smile for Jadon when he grabbed Alex's hand.

"Dear lad, I shall spend time with you and your mother, but first, I must get Galeron inside," Alex said.

"Why? Is he hurt?"

He picked up Jadon, gave a hug and passed him to Sarah. "Go inside."

Jadon stared over Sarah's shoulder as they walked away. Alex took one look at Galeron then bolted to Easton to intercept him from the path to the cart that held Rafe's frozen body.

"Not yet," she overheard Alex say, "I cannot bear any more, Father. Not yet."

She wished he would allow his father to do what he must, be it viewing his dead son, even falling into grief. Selfish as it was, she wanted to scream at them both to make haste to the one who still held on to life. Easton looked from the death cart to the one holding Galeron, then made his choice. She rose on her knees as they advanced. "Galeron, you shall be in a warm bed soon." Dampness permeated her clothing and she feared he'd wet himself. She tucked the furs tighter around him. The wetness was sticky, not liquid. Ruby lifted her hand. A rivulet of blood snaked down her arm. Flashes of a child's face — a bloody face — wavered like a fog.

Alex leaped into the cart. Spatters of blood hit her face. Easton helped lift Galeron. Several men cleared a path while they carried him through the inner ward.

Ruby's legs nearly gave out when she climbed from the cart, but the thought of parting from him spurred her to focus. She quickly caught up and breathed in unison with Galeron's gasps, as if the action would help him to breathe normally. His head lolled with each of the men's footsteps and the sight of him falling weak ripped through her.

She clutched the doorway, trying to focus on anything other than the trail of blood on the stone floor of the main entrance. Someone grabbed her arm and she looked away from the bloody mess.

"I am here," Sarah whispered.

Ruby watched the gap widen between Galeron and her. "He should not be bleeding. I do not understand."

"Sarah! Ruby!" Jumping at Alex's shout, they hurried to him. "Sarah, fetch bandages and bring them to Galeron's chamber."

Sarah ran to do as he asked. Ruby stared at the drips of blood.

"Make haste." Alex said. "The servants are readying his chamber. Make certain there is a fire started. Assure someone boils wine. Plenty of it. Can you do that?"

Ruby nodded.

"I need at least two basins of fresh water as well."

Ruby wasn't sure if he was still speaking to her, but she nodded again. Her eyes remained on Galeron. He looked dead. Death seemed to grip her as well. "Should he have not healed in all the time it took to return?"

"Now!"

Alex's shout startled her into motion. She tripped in her haste and grabbed the stair railing for support. Her heart shook. Her breath stuttered. Even her feet refused to cooperate and she stumbled up the stairs. *Naught* cooperated — including her mind.

In dazed confusion, she stood immobilized in Galeron's doorway. Out of rhythm with the synchronized frenzy, she dodged a servant carrying a fresh load of firewood and nearly toppled another loaded with extra blankets.

Everyone seemed to tend to their tasks. Except for her. Someone nudged past her in the rushing waves of activity. Alex's orders came to mind. She shrugged off her sodden cloak and threw it across the chair.

"Boil water and fetch two basins of fresh wine!"

The flurry stopped. Every servant stared at her. Immediately realizing her blunder, she raised her voice. "I mean — hell's teeth! You know what I mean. Do it!" She gritted her teeth against the vision of Galeron's blood on the pristine floor. Drip. Drip. Drip. It kept time with her heartbeat. Was his fading in the same rhythm? "Sweet merciful God, You brought him home. I beg Thee, dare not take him now."

Sarah dropped bandages on the table and went to her side. Sarah's fingernails gouged Ruby's arm while they rushed to the stairway. Fear tinged Alex's orders, magnifying her own, and she started downstairs to meet him.

She reached the first landing with Sarah close behind. She froze midstep, pressing her back against the railing, allowing room for the men to pass. The pallor of death on Galeron's face took her breath, but she swallowed her fear and started to follow. Her skirt caught and she turned to see Sarah holding it.

"Ruby, 'tis best we wait downstairs."

"As long as I guard his soul, he shall not leave this world." She didn't wait for Sarah's response. She yanked away and hurried to his chamber.

With a nod to Alex, she took Galeron's hand. "You tend to his wound. I shall tend to the prayers." She knelt beside the bed and closed her eyes.

The remainder of the night, Ruby remained on her knees, an unwavering sentry against the reaper.

Chapter Forty-One

Past and Future

Ruby squinted at the sun's reflection on the scant remainder of snow. "I must return. He may wake again."

"Take a moment to breathe something other than the air of Galeron's chamber. The skies are clear and spring has finally arrived." Sarah smiled and pulled the hood over Ruby's head. "Alex assured he survived the worst."

"Nay, the worst is the death of Rafe. How is Alex dealing with that?"

"He speaks of him often, many times with laughter. He prefers to remember him as he lived. Not as he died." Sarah shook her head. "Alex told me Galeron deems himself responsible."

"He said as much." She shielded her eyes and looked up at his window. "I worry about him."

"I fully understand." Sarah grasped Ruby's hand. "I have prayed over my man as you do now."

Ruby turned to her. "You never made mention of it!"

"'Tis painful to speak of, even now. Death had a grip on Alex when Galeron carried him through the gates." She twisted the edge of her cloak. "However, like him, Galeron has been granted another chance at life. You must give him time to gather strength."

She started for the door. "I do not believe I thanked Alex for all he has done."

"You did, countless times." Sarah latched her arm with Ruby's. "You are simply fashioning an excuse to return inside." She pointed toward the gardens. "Alex did well in the preparation for the medicinal garden this year."

She glanced at Galeron's window. "Uh-huh."

Sarah continued to steer Ruby down the garden path. "Our men were taught their mother's skills from a very young age. Alex told me she would spend hours in the garden, educating them on the many combinations of plants for various ailments."

Ruby's attention peaked. "Galeron knows of these things? I always thought Alex was the one skilled in the healing arts."

"Aye, he is. Galeron paid nay heed to lessons." Sarah drew a rare smile from Ruby. "Alex actually listened, but Galeron ran through the garden with a wooden sword, whacking a path instead."

She could not help but laugh at the vision. "I suppose 'twould bring ire to his mother."

"Nay, Alex said she would smile, sit upon the sword, and go on with the lesson." Sarah grinned. "Galeron would sneak off as soon as her head was turned. That is when the chase would begin."

"Chase?"

Sarah stopped and pointed down one of the paths. "More often than not, the lessons would end in a chase. Alex always laughs when he recalls how she would catch and tickle them in the dirt."

She was surprised at the bit of insight. The painting hanging in the great hall did not depict one who played in the dirt with her children. Ruby examined the portrait. The artist had caught a sadness in her eyes. "A shame they lost their mother at such a tender age."

Sarah hesitated as if she wanted to say something, then decided against it. Just when Ruby intended to ask what it was, Sarah spoke. "I do not believe Galeron shall ever recover from her death."

"Easton told me as much."

Sarah took a step back. "Really?"

"Well, he mentioned that Galeron thought he could heal her."

"Hmm." Sarah resumed their walk. "Easton never talks of it."

Ruby blew a breath. "He was forthcoming with me, then sadness seemed pull him away from the subject."

"Well, he never spoke of it with me. But Alex does recall Galeron's fury when he would not let him near his mother after Rafe was born. He concocted a mixture of herbs in a tea, thinking it would heal her."

"What was wrong with her?" Ruby crouched beside a holly bush.

Sarah grimaced. "Whatever are you doing?"

"I was remembering something Galeron said about the holly." Ruby brushed off her hands and stood. "Now, you were saying?" She sighed at Sarah's blank stare. "About what was wrong with his mother."

"Oh. From what I understand, she fell ill after bearing Rafe and then died the same night. Alex said it frightened him to see his big brother scream so." Sarah shook her head. "Daren't repeat this. I do not believe Alex would appreciate me sharing it."

"I shan't." She swallowed the lump forming in her throat. The vision of a mere boy scratching in the garden to find something to keep his mother alive played in her mind's eye.

"Our men's lives are hard, Ruby. What Galeron is going through is a part of it."

Ruby swerved the conversation. "Who did Alex learn from after she died?"

Sarah studied her a moment. "In addition to training as a knight, he experimented with the concoctions his mother created, and then improved them. His determination to heal has become indispensable."

"Which is a reminder, 'tis past time for the horrid-smelling potion he concocted for Galeron." Ruby motioned for Sarah to follow her inside. "I hope he wakes enough to sip it."

Sarah's laughter echoed inside the main entry. "That *horrid potion* gives the strength Galeron needs." She nudged her. "I fancy 'twill fill him with enough energy to tarry to thy chamber?"

Ruby dismissed her jest with a roll of her eyes and started up the stairs.

"'Tis not unusual for a man to have a taste of his betrothed before marriage."

"Sarah, you are shameful!" She nicked Sarah with her hem. Both erupted into a fit of giggles.

Relentless suggestions followed Ruby as they ascended. "Aye, you desire his rippled body under your canopy." Encouraged by Ruby's laughter, she continued to whisper. "The coverlet shoved to the floor. He slides you across the bed with his thrust."

Ruby laughed so hard she had to grip the banister to keep from falling.

"The laughter of my beloved fills my ears."

She slowly raised her gaze. "Galeron." His name tasted sweet again.

He slipped his hand from the crook of Easton's arm and reached for her, but she saw how Alex had to support him. She did not feel the steps under her feet, but her breath came in gasps at the top of the stairs. Struck dumb, she wrapped her arms around Galeron's waist, her cheek against his chest.

His warmth seeped into her soul. The tension harbored for so long released with a sigh. Galeron nudged her hood with his chin and buried his face in her hair. Silence embraced them.

"I wanted to surprise you," he whispered.

Ruby's voice muffled in his chest. "You succeeded." She looked up, hardly able to grasp the fact he stood before her. Galeron cradled her face in his hands and kissed her, lightly then with growing urgency. She wrapped her arms around his neck and relished the delicious taste of him.

Alex cleared his throat. Easton chuckled. Sarah simply mentioned something about telling her so.

She pulled back. "Dare not frighten me like that again. I feared for your life."

"My sweet forest nymph, how could my soul leave this world when 'tis imprisoned by thee?" He winked. "You have stolen it, little thief."

His weight bore down. Easton grabbed him about the waist.

"You found me. Now, off to bed." She blushed at the suggestive raise of his eyebrows. "I did not mean it like that."

Sarah snickered.

"I ache from lying so long. I am going downstairs," Galeron said.

"Against Alex's advice," Easton interjected. "Mayhap you can convince him otherwise."

"Galeron, you need to regain your strength," she said.

"I have a whim you shall be the recipient when I gain it," he whispered.

Heat filled her cheeks. "Let the brute do as he wishes." She stepped aside, not missing the grins, certain her face turned a deeper shade of crimson.

Galeron continued teasing, though he directed his next comment toward Alex. "Brew more of that concoction of yours. I shall require it to tame the fire in my betrothed."

She glared at Sarah when she joined the men's laughter. "Galeron, enough. They do not need... Enough." Though she meant to sound stern, her words ended in a giggle.

Galeron winked, his eyes crinkling with his smile.

"'Tis not a hint of privacy within these walls," she said to Sarah. No longer smiling, Sarah responded with a stare. "What?" Ruby asked. Sarah sighed and looked away. Ruby pulled her aside as soon as they reached the bottom of the stairs and called ahead. "We shall join you in a moment. I wish to hang my cloak."

"Here, take mine too." Sarah shrugged out of hers.

Ruby hung them on the hall pegs. "What ails you?"

"I believed you would have told me."

Ruby blinked. "Told you what?"

Sarah looked about and cupped her hand over Ruby's ear. "That Galeron shared your bed before leaving for battle." She stood back and crossed her arms.

"*What*?" Her voice pitched into a squeak. "Sarah, we — well, he — " Ruby grinned. "We did not."

"So I am mistaken?"

"Aye, though I wanted him to." Ruby blushed, remembering the waves of pleasure he created. "Best be said, *he* kept control over passion."

"Galeron? Controlled? That is a surprise."

"Why?"

Sarah dismissed her with a wave. "Do not dwell on it. Past is past."

Ruby glanced to the room the men went into. "He had many?"

"I could instruct you on ways to make him lose that control of his."

Ruby clasped her hand over her chest. "Sarah, we shall be wed soon enough."

"'Tis the best thing for an ailing man," Sarah whispered loudly. "There are many ways without undressing."

"I realize that!" She swung around. No one was about, but she felt exposed.

Sarah's eyes widened. "Ah, so his control came about late."

Her whole body seemed to undulated in constant blushes. "A bit."

"Naked?"

"Not completely." Ruby huffed and headed for the room.

Sarah was in full-fledged giggles by the time they reached the doorway. Ruby pinched her arm. "How naked?" Sarah whispered.

"This conversation is over," she said, hardly moving her lips.

"What took so long, fair one?" Galeron whispered, nuzzling her neck with a light kiss.

Ruby's body heated with familiar tremors. "Sarah thought we—that you and I…" She glanced at Sarah. "Honestly, Galeron, 'twas embarrassing!"

His eyebrow rose. "Women talk of such things?"

She shrugged.

He brushed his lips against hers. "I promise to deliver a taste of my attentions later."

"Will they be delivered naked?" She smirked at his expression.

His hand slid beneath her bottom. When he squeezed, she jumped, trying to figure out how he had gained the upper hand. "You do not realize what you are toying with, sweet nymph," he whispered, kissing below her ear. "I have been away far too long."

Tremors fluttered like wings. She failed to notice Alex holding two mugs in front of them.

"God's eyes," Alex said. "All my work shall go to waste if you continue to maul your betrothed."

Galeron laughed against her neck, totally filling her heart. She grabbed the mugs before he made a show of removing his hand. Alex raised his brow and chuckled. She turned away, happy Jadon picked that moment to run into the room. Galeron took his mug. With both hands.

Jadon skidded to a stop in front of them and shook the curls from his eyes. "You are healed!"

"That I am." Galeron ruffled his hair, sending it back into his eyes. "It seems you are healed as well."

He nodded. "Did you slay the bad knight?"

"I did."

"He slayed you back." Jadon squinted. "Your blood was everywhere. I saw it."

"Have a seat." Ruby patted her lap.

Jadon climbed up and planted a kiss on her cheek before returning his attention to Galeron. "Did it hurt?"

"Nay need to fret, I am well."

"I am happy you did not—that you are better."

Ruby hugged Jadon. "Ah, so am I."

He eyed Galeron. "You made her sad."

Galeron glanced at Ruby. "Well, she is smiling now, little one."

"Do you know what Papa Alex said?"

Galeron chuckled at the change of subject. "Perhaps you should tell me."

"He said you are stubborn."

Galeron's eyebrow rose. "Did he?"

"Aye, and brave." He placed his hand on Galeron's shoulder. It seemed tiny in contrast. "I am going to be a brave knight like you and Papa Alex."

"Indeed? I thought you already *were* a knight."

"I am Ruby's knight. I want to be a Ramstone one as well." Jadon puffed out his chest.

"Then you shall, young one." Galeron winced.

Ruby ached for Galeron. She fear 'twas not the pain that made him wince, but the reminder of calling Rafe 'young one'. By the expression clouding Alex's face, she assumed the same thought entered his mind.

Jadon hopped down and squeezed between his new parents. He leaned forward, continuing the conversation. "I need a sword."

Galeron coughed and held his chest. "Perhaps a wooden one for now. Papa Alex and I shall train you."

Jadon clapped, bringing a smile to everyone. "And Ruby shall train me to be a great archer!"

Ruby's smile dissipated.

Galeron smiled. "Nay, young one, 'twould also be left to us."

Jadon shook his head at Ruby. "I want *you* to teach me."

"Jadon, you are mistaken," Sarah whispered.

Jadon giggled. "You jest, Mama. You told Papa her aim was amazing when she killed those wolves!"

Galeron swung his glare at his father before resting it on her. "What does the child speak of?"

"Wild imaginings." She pulled her hand from his and wiped it on her skirt.

"Go play in the nursery. I shall be up shortly." Sarah prodded Jadon with a loving pat on his bottom. Unaware of the damage he'd done, he waved and skipped out of the room.

"I pray forgiveness. I did not realize he overheard me telling Alex about your extraordinary skill with the bow." She silenced at Ruby's glare.

Ruby turned to Galeron. "Pay her nay mind. The woman exaggerates."

Galeron accented each word. "You. Killed. Wolves?" The fury in his eyes rendered her speechless. And a bit afraid. "Damnation, do not flinch at me like that, woman!"

He glared at his father. "You assured me you would keep her safe."

Easton frowned. "I did."

A prickle of sweat danced upon her brow. She rose, trying to think of a way to close the subject altogether. "'Tis of nay consequence now."

Galeron nearly touched his nose to her face as he rose. "Such a foolish risk! What were you thinking?"

Her ire fired. "I did not have the luxury of thought! A lad was attacked. I had nay choice but to protect him."

A spasm of fear crept in with the memory. "I w-was not aware I could arm a bow until then."

"She is amazing," Easton added. He took a gulp of mead when Ruby glowered at him. "However, the memory gained proved painful."

Ruby rolled her eyes.

"You remembered something?" he whispered, drawing her closer.

Dread pulsed through her. "Let it rest. You are healing. Jadon is safe and everyone is home. Is that not enough?"

Sarah spoke before he could answer. "It will continue to haunt you. Your response to that night frightened us all, and he should be told about—"

She pushed Galeron's arms from her waist. "Sarah, you have naught a bit of say in this!"

Sarah sighed. "Then you tell him."

"Enough!" she ordered. Turning to Galeron, she could see the pain on his face as he sat. "See? Now you are hurting. Go rest."

"Do not steer this my way. This is about you." He tugged her, guiding her to sit beside him. She resisted, wanting only to run from the room. "Ruby, do not pull away from me. I shall let it rest. For now. Alex, pour a round of mead."

She sighed and settled beside him.

Alex strode to the table and poured a single mug of mead. He sauntered to Ruby and stopped in front of her, drawing a long swig.

"Alex, leave her be," Galeron said.

Alex swished the ale and continued to study her. He glanced at Galeron before swallowing. "Ruby, from what Sarah told me, 'tis apparent the recovery of your memory is underway."

"Alex." Galeron's voice lowered, his warning clear.

Alex sat beside her. "I can assist in remembering fully."

Galeron stood, yanking Alex by his tunic. "I said leave her be!"

"Galeron!" She tried to stand between them. Easton jerked her out of the way.

"You see what she is doing!" Alex shouted. "I cannot stand by and watch it happen."

Galeron's jaw twitched and he let go of Alex. He swayed and took a step back. Ruby ran to him. Her eyes widened when he nudged her aside.

"Watch *what* happen?" Galeron asked.

"Are you blind? I believe you fear her memories more than she does!"

Galeron swung. Alex blocked his fist. Ruby darted in front of Galeron, nearly struck by his next blow.

"I shan't watch you fight with the only brother you have left!" Standing between them, she bore the heat emanating from their bodies. Galeron and Alex's eyes held fury, but she stood her ground. "Make peace." She locked eyes with Galeron.

"Not until he swears to leave you be."

"I refuse to utter an empty oath." Alex straightened his rumpled tunic. Sarah gasped.

"Enough!" Easton shouted. "Alex, stand back. Ruby, take leave with your man. Sarah, serve mead or…something."

She could not decided whether to laugh or be fearful. "You should rest. This needless fighting has taken what strength you have."

To her surprise, he relented. "You are right. I am tired." He took Ruby's arm and led her from the room. Once at the stairs they realized he would need assistance and she started back to the room. Before she entered, Alex's angry voice made her pause by the doorway. Alex paced the room. "Stubborn oaf! He does nay justice by protecting Ruby from herself." He slammed his mug on the table. "She cannot deny her past forever." He ignored Sarah's insistence to calm down. "Those memories shall consume her."

Sarah laid her hand on Alex's arm. "She shall face them in her own time."

"I pray she is not alone when it happens, for Galeron stands the chance to lose her forever."

"That would never happen. She would never leave him."

"Nay, Sarah, you fail to understand."

"Alex, let us take a walk, my legs are stiff." Easton started for the door and Ruby ducked back.

"Unseasoned knights have been known to bury the gore and death of battle deep into their minds without dealing with it. I am able to help most, but there were those who—" Alex blew a breath when Easton placed his hand on his shoulder and lowered his voice. "They end up losing their minds."

Sarah slowly turned to Easton. "Is that true?"

Easton nodded.

"We must do something." She plopped into a chair.

"We cannot push either one of them right now," Easton said. "Galeron is gaining his strength and Ruby apparently is not strong enough to deal with her memories."

"We cannot simply stand by." Sarah's eyes welled with tears. "I cannot bear to think her denial can drive her to madness."

"Madness?" Ruby's gasp caused them all to turn toward the doorway.

Sarah snapped to her feet. "I — we — "

"Galeron needs help up the stairs." She choked out her request and backed from the doorway, a vile mixture of anger and fear shaking her. Animosity faded when they gathered at the stairs. The men stood on each side of Galeron at the bottom of the stairs.

"Lean on us," Alex said.

Easton went to his other side and they started up.

She shrugged from Sarah's attempted hug and ran ahead. She opened the door to his chamber. She stepped inside, admiring his mahogany desk. She pushed a parchment out of the way. Fully aware she should not meddle with his things, she did it anyway. She recognized bits written in his hand. "Pray tell, how many times did you rewrite the letter to me?" She smiled, touched he had worked so hard on it.

With the window hangings in her hands, she looked down on the snow-spattered garden imprinted with footprints from the morning walk she shared with Sarah. Remorseful for the way she had treated her moments before, she hoped Sarah would forgive her.

She spied the knights' quarters. Even from here, he oversaw his men. Groups of knights were stringing bows, others were setting up stuffed targets. A shiver traveled down her back and she yanked the hangings closed. She drew back the covers and pounded the pillows into shape. Still fisted, she turned when Sarah spoke from the doorway.

"'Twas slow going up the stairs," Sarah said, not quite meeting her eyes.

"Is he well?" She hurried to the door.

"The argument took much out of him."

She frowned, still watching him, his head down. "Sarah…"

She smiled at Galeron when he looked up. He straightened his stance and smiled back.

Sarah fluffed the pillows.

"I already did that."

Sarah let the pillow drop. "Very well." She went to the hangings.

"Leave those pulled."

"I was making sure the window was closed." Sarah crossed her arms.

"I should never have shouted at you," she blurted.

Sarah rushed to her. "I only wished to help. You should not bear your memories alone."

"I am not certain I want to bear them it at all, Sarah. Any I recall either have been horrid or make nay sense. Either way, I am always left with the sense I am at fault for something unforgivable." She dropped her confession to a whisper as the men neared. "I did something horrible. I fear if Galeron knows, I shall lose him."

"Ruby, none of us, especially Galeron—"

"Step aside, ladies." Alex helped Galeron into the room.

Ruby followed them to the bed. Galeron lay back, his feet still on the floor. She glimpsed the pain etched across his face before he placed his forearm across his eyes.

"I shall take my leave," Ruby whispered.

"'Twould be best," Easton said.

Galeron patted the bed with his free hand. "Come, share my bed." He peered from beneath his arm and grinned.

Easton chuckled.

Ruby sighed. "Daren't encourage him."

Alex took off Galeron's boots and swung his legs onto the bed. "Now, get some rest." He leaned closer and whispered. "I mean it, Galeron, *rest*."

"I shall rest well, with Ruby beside me."

Alex threw his hands in the air. "I highly doubt that."

"Ruby, dare you make me come and get you?"

She sighed at Galeron then assured Alex. "I have nay intention of lying on the bed."

"Why not? I am not yet strong enough to take advantage of you." He grinned.

A blush slapped her cheeks. Easton and Alex's laughter echoed in the corridor as soon as they stepped out of the room.

"Mead turns men into fools," she whispered to Sarah. "I am taking leave now, Galeron."

"Very well, leave," Galeron said.

She rolled her eyes, kissed his brow, and walked to the door. Sarah guided her back into the room.

"What are you—" Her eyes widened with each word Sarah whispered into her ear. She glanced at Galeron, glad he had finally closed his eyes, for she feared he would see her growing interest on her face. Sarah crept out and closed the door. She changed her mind about leaving, dwelling on Sarah's secret.

She tiptoed to the bed.

Without opening his eyes, Galeron spoke, making her jump. "You cannot creep up on a knight." He opened one eye. "It has been much too long since we have been alone. I need you close."

She toed off her boots and curled up next to him. "I can meet that need." She slipped her hand into his breeches.

"God in heaven, woman!" He grabbed her wrist. "What are you *doing*?"

"I'm not sure, but Sarah said— Oh, I can tell you like what I am doing. Sarah assured all it would take is a touch." She moved her hand as her friend had instructed.

"Damnation. Dare not mention her name with your hand in my breeches!" Galeron chuckled. "However…you are right. I do so enjoy your ministrations." His eyes fluttered closed as he let go of her hand.

He grew harder and she pushed his breeches down a bit to allow her to move more freely. Watching his profile, she figured Sarah was correct about easing his pain as she moved her hand in a rhythmic pace. Her breath quickened with his and she longed for his touch, but stayed to task.

Time passed without a word and she closed her eyes, swaying with his uneven breathing. His eyes flew open and he clutched her hand.

She looked up at him just as his groan rallied through the room. She regretted ever listening to Sarah. Terrified at his moans, she let go, sure she had hurt him. When he lurched and grabbed the cloth by the bedside, she was sure of it.

"Forgive me, forgive me!" She sat up. "I was trying to speed your healing! What did I do wrong?"

He pulled her to him and kissed her, his body still trembling. "Nay, my love. Shh." He smiled and wiped her tears. "That was…damnation, woman!"

"You are not hurt?"

He kissed her again, his breathing still ragged as he reached beneath her skirts. "Were you hurt the last time I did this?" he whispered, caressing her through her undergarment.

"N-nay," she whispered, her blood rushing to where his fingers roamed.

He pulled his hand away. "Then you understand."

"Show me once more, just to be certain I understand."

He closed his eyes. "You understand full well."

She laughed and kissed him. "Explain to me how it grows so big. I could barely wrap my —"

"Hell's teeth, woman," he whispered. "I never can predict what you may say next."

She watched his chest rise and fall for several moments before resting her hand upon it. He placed his hand over hers and she studied how hers looked tiny in comparison. His gaze met hers. "Whatever possessed you —" He cleared his throat. "To place your hand in my breeches?"

"Sarah said there is nay shame in it. She told me what to do and that it would speed your healing. She does it with Alex and he —"

"Enough."

She grinned. "Are you complaining?"

"Nay. Though 'tis not why I asked you to stay." He drew her closer. "Too much is left unsaid. What have you remembered?"

"Let us rest for a while first." She snuggled, closing her eyes without waiting for him to agree. She listened for his breathing to slow. Thinking he had fallen asleep, she gasped when he spoke.

"I did not miss what you said to Sarah."

"'Twas simple prattle." She kissed his neck. "Sleep."

"Nay matter what you remember, you shan't lose me. Do not ever speak of such a thing again." He propped himself on one elbow, running his fingers along her side.

She swallowed hard. "Galeron, your love for me dims reality. I am certain you shall regret ever sharing a bed once—"

"I shall never regret sharing *anything* with you." He winked. "Especially a bed."

She traced the dimple in his chin. "You do not know what kind of maiden I was. I fear it was not a desirable one."

"Nay, sweet one, you are definitely desirable."

Ruby sat up and hugged her knees. Her hands shook so violently she had to clutch them tighter against her legs. "Galeron, I cannot give myself fully to you."

He rubbed her back. "Sweet jewel, I did not intend on taking you now anyway."

"I do not mean I cannot give my body to you. I mean my *self*. As long as I am void of memory, I live a fantasy. I cannot continue to do that."

"This is nay fantasy."

"I must face my past. If I could but figure out how."

He guided her to lie with her back against his chest. "We both shall heal in time. All shall be well, of that I am certain."

"The only thing I am certain of in my distorted life is my love for you."

"Your life is not distorted, simply injured."

She rolled to face him. "You deserve me whole. I am in pieces."

He cradled her face. "Give it time, sweet one."

She pressed her cheek against his hand. "Galeron, if I tell you something, can you promise you will not be angry?"

He tilted her face up. "Tell me."

She furrowed her brow. "I went to fetch Alex and your father and overheard Alex speaking of the danger of madness like mine."

He stopped rubbing his hand along her waist. "*What*? Alex is overreacting."

"It seems he not the only one concerned. They all fear I shall be lost in madness if I do not face my past, but I do not know how to do that!"

"Sweet Ruby." He traced several kisses across her brow. "Give it time."

"*Time*? Time for what? To go mad? Time only haunts me with night terrors." Everything seemed to pour out of her. "I dream the oddest things. Innocent things, like berries falling from a basket or honey drizzled on fresh bread, and at the worst, a bloodied child." She quickly changed the path of her recollections. "However, sometimes my dreams bring comfort. Lately, I dream of arming a bow. I find joy in that." She grinned and pretended to release an arrow.

"You are doing it again."

"What?"

"Ah, once again you switch course of the conversation. This time, I am glad you did." Galeron tapped her chin. "You must tell me about what happened with the wolves."

Dread suffocated her. Intent on keeping it at bay, she grinned at him. "I am skilled."

He rolled his eyes. "Aye, my father seemed quite impressed."

"That stands to reason. I am quite impressive."

He raised his eyebrow in the way she adored.

"You doubt it? Do you not believe I can excel as an archer?"

"You, my little gem, have a way of avoiding certain points of conversation with your wit as well."

She ran her hand across the waist of his breeches. "I do not wish to discuss it now, Galeron. Would you like me to help you heal again?"

He grinned. "You also ploy avoidance by using your wiles." He snuggled beside her. "'Tis quite a weapon."

"Cease your talk and enjoy this instead then." She ran her tongue across his lips.

"You are tearing at my resolve, my lithe vixen."

She sighed when he kissed the hollow of her throat, arching into his touch while he swept his fingers along the scoop of her neckline.

"I shall never tire of your reaction to me." He kissed her eyes closed. "I love you, Ruby," he whispered, the emotion catching in his throat.

She slowly opened her eyes at the force of his words. "I wish I could explain the depth of what I feel for you."

"Try."

She swallowed hard. "My heart aches when I am not with you, yet my body aches when I am."

He slowly unbraided her hair, the familiar smell of lavender wafting from it. "Sweet Ruby, the love and the passion you created are blessings I have never experienced before."

"Your love is new, but your passion is not."

Her hair fell from his hand. "You doubt me?"

"Even Sarah says — well, she didn't quite say it." She tried again. "The night I first came here someone mentioned you always end up with a fair maiden."

He chuckled. "You remember that? That was simply jest."

"While I lived in the village, rumors abounded of your popularity among the tavern maids."

"They were meaningless."

"Yet you bedded them," she said, her jealousy tainting the moment.

He looked at the ceiling. "That was the past. Over. Done."

She took a breath and blew it out slowly to keep her doubt from stealing her trust. Would he visit the tavern in the future? He tilted her chin, making it impossible to hide her tears.

"My heart never knew love before you, Ruby. 'Tis the reason I keep our sexual play from taking us fully. I wish to experience bedding you as your husband. We deserve the newness of our wedding night. Though it shall be your first time, it shall be a new beginning for me as well."

"You speak of my first time. I have nay guarantee of my purity."

"You are innocent."

She furrowed her brow. "You cannot be sure of that that until you..." She blushed.

"That constant blush tells of your innocence." He cut off her reply with a kiss and ran his hands the length of her body. "You are delightful," he whispered.

He guided her to her back. The coolness of the room made her shiver when her skirts rode up. He pressed against her. "You are going to hurt yourself."

"Mmm."

"Galeron. Sleep." She wanted naught more than to enjoy the torturous pleasure of his hand against her undergarment. She readjusted her skirt and gently pulled his hand away.

"Sweet Ruby." He pushed her hair from her face. "I am trying to give you the same pleasure you bestowed on me."

She tried to focus. "Alex will hear my cries and throw me out." She giggled. "So cease mauling me or I shall…" She gasped as he lowered his face to her cleavage. "Or I shall…uh. I am not sure what I shall do."

He laughed against her breasts. "Mauling?" He peeked up at her. "Very well, I shall refrain from mauling you." He winced as he fell back on the pillows.

The poor man was hurting. She kissed his forehead. "For now."

He sighed. "I *greatly* anticipate our wedding night." He closed his eyes, a smile still on his lips.

"We should spend it away from Ramstone."

"Pray tell, why leave on such a special night?" he said without opening his eyes.

"If your touch makes me cry out, your body moving within mine is certain to cause such passion, even the villagers shall have to cover their ears."

He laughed so hard she feared Alex would come and drag her away so Galeron could rest. "I'm serious!" she said. "I have nay control when you touch me there!"

"God's eyes, I adore your wit." He ran his finger along her cheek. "Before you, I did not experience true laughter."

"I wish I remembered life before you. I am sure of one thing. When I regain my memory, my heart shall remain yours."

"What if you belong to another?"

She stared at him. "Another?"

He caressed her jaw, avoiding her gaze. "You mentioned that in the past."

She nodded. "I put you through pain that night in the village. For that I am sorry." She blinked back tears. "I never told you how sorry I was."

"We haven't spoken of it since then." His hair brushed her face when he looked away. "Yet, it doesn't make it any less of a possibility."

Ruby struggled to explain. "My heart knows nay other." Her voice fell to a whisper. "My heart melted and poured every bit of my love into yours by our first kiss."

"You felt that strong?"

"Strong enough to comprehend how a heart shatters when the one she loves leaves her behind to claim another woman."

Galeron closed his eyes. "I loved you, even then. I did not realize you felt the same."

She did not miss the shakiness in his voice. "My unrequited love was...like dying inside. It killed me that I held nay right to you."

He wrapped his body around hers. "Fate gave you the right."

Within moments, his steady breath signaled slumber. She crept out and closed the hangings around the bed. She sat at his mahogany desk and bowed her head.

"Lord, I am ready. You are aware of all, though I am at a loss. The child dwelling in my memory met his death. If I am at fault, then punish me. Have mercy, Lord. Spare your wrath if it means turning Galeron against me." Ruby tucked her feet underneath her skirt. "However, if you deem my punishment should be losing the man I love, then I pray you strike me dead."

"Ruby." Galeron pulled back the hangings around the bed. "My heart surrenders to thee. My allegiance is to thee," he whispered.

She clasped her hand over her mouth.

He sat up, still reciting his letter. "Your past remains a mystery. Your future remains to unfold. Allow it to unfold in my arms." He spread his arms. She ran to the bed then snuggled in his embrace.

Though he had held her many times, something special ran through her as he combed her hair with his fingers. "I meant every word of the letter. If you are able to recall your past, then so be it. I shall remain in your future, of that be certain."

She pulled his face to hers and kissed him, a shaky breath ending her tears. "My prayer is answered," she whispered.

"I need you as much as you need me." He led her to the pillows and kissed her eyes closed. "Rest, we are both weary."

She smiled. Still uncertain of what would come next, she was finally secure knowing they would face it together.

Chapter Forty-Two
Determined

Ruby grinned at the sight of Galeron pulling off his sweat-soaked tunic. She reined her mare and swung out of the saddle. With the forest as her shelter, she sat with her sketching supplies in her lap.

She followed every detail of his bare chest with her eyes. His muscles twitched with each movement. Her charcoal remained poised as she thoroughly enjoyed the devilish tremble invading her body. Watching a moment longer, she scratched the charcoal furiously on the parchment. Intent on capturing the essence of his rhythm, she paused to study his steady movements.

Even from the distance, she saw the many battle scars. She hesitated, remembering how the latest wound had nearly taken his life. Her fingers scrambled to sketch him when he halted, his sword glinting in the sun. She blurred the charcoal with her thumb to shadow the dip between his shoulder blades.

"Sweet angels in heaven, deliver me."

The sketch forgotten in her lap, she followed the single trail of perspiration as it dipped and rolled over his rippled abdomen. The spring breeze ruffled the leaves, but did naught to cool the heat he created in her.

How could craving him be sated? Marriage was a joining, sex was a need. Why could they not be separate?

She bowed her head. "Forgive me for my wanton thoughts, Lord." Though she repeated the prayer each day, her body still reacted to the mere sight of him.

Finished with her sketch, she blew the hair out her face and wiped her hands after packing up her parchment and charcoal. She hefted herself onto the mare Galeron had given her. "Be off, Abby," she said with a gentle kick.

Galeron spun around with his sword raised, his expression still engaged in concentration.

"'Tis I, daren't slay me!" she shouted while galloping to him.

A grin replaced his frown. He sheathed the sword and shielded his eyes against the sun as he waited.

She ambled to him, allowing Abby to graze beside his stallion. He hooked his thumbs in his belt. "What are you wearing?"

She shrugged, eyeing his glistening chest. "More than you."

His eyes skimmed her body. "I thought you were in the village with Sarah and Alex."

"I decided not to go."

"You cannot avoid the village forever."

Ruby nudged her head toward the quiver and arrows latched to her saddle. "I decided to hunt instead."

He pulled her by the waist of her breeches, causing her to lurch closer. "Wherever did you get these clothes?"

"I made them," she answered, glad he was easily swayed from talking about the village. "I like it."

"You should not be out without an escort."

"I am with you, am I not?" She planted a kiss on his lips. "Accompany me on my hunt."

Galeron grimaced. "Fair one, maidens do not hunt."

"Pray tell, why?"

"They simply do not." He wiped the smear of charcoal from her cheek. "Nor do they dress in breeches."

She flipped her braid from her shoulder. "I *like* to wear breeches." She kissed the hollow of his neck. "Why does it matter?"

He stepped back. "Because it's sinful."

"Sinful?" She toyed with the lacings. "Should I act sinful as well and remove them?"

"Breeches are for men, and nay, you should not remove them." He chuckled. "I was about to head home. Want to race?"

She was tempted, for she had almost won the last challenge. "I'm not headed that way. I told you, I am off to hunt."

"If fresh meat is what you desire, I shall hunt for you."

Ah, this man did not take well to her doing things her way. Best he learn. And quickly. "Lend me your ears, arrogant knight."

"Arrogant?"

She ignored his interruption. "My strongest memory came when I shot an arrow. This time I am ready for what lurks in my past. My hunt has naught to do with treading on your masculine self-importance."

"My masculine self-importance?" He slid his hands around her waist.

Thoroughly captivated with their banter, she prodded him on. "Do you have words of your own, or must you continuously repeat mine?"

"You possess a wild tongue, best you tame it."

Thoroughly enjoying the faint taste of his salty skin, she flicked her tongue on his nipple. "Are you certain you wish to tame this tongue of mine?"

Galeron's growl blended with her laughter. Her hand deftly outlined the crease of his muscles on his stomach.

"Ah, I surrender, speak all you want." He ran his hand along her body, cutting her giggle short. "Mmm, your curves are unhampered. Perhaps breeches are fitting attire after all." He kissed her neck.

A small moan escaped as her body responded. "I can step out of them this very moment if you so wish."

He tucked her head under his chin. "Your wiles shall do me in."

"The power of your manly scent shall do *me* in." She sprinted to the water hole. "'Twould do nay harm to wash off your stench." Hard on her heels, he threw her over his shoulder without breaking stride. She screamed when they hit the water.

He trod the surface, holding her. "Do not fear. I shan't let you drown."

She shook her hair out of her eyes, dunked him, and wiggled out of his grasp. She swam a distance and broke the surface, grabbing a breath.

"Hold fast!" Galeron swam to her, his body gliding through the water.

She dove back under, raced to the bank and climbed out. "I beat you."

Galeron, wide-eyed, shouted to her. "Hell's teeth, woman, you can swim!"

She teetered between fear and surprise. "I-I suppose I can!"

His voice carried across the water. "I feared you drowned!"

She balanced on one foot, pulling off her boot. "Cease your shouting." She grinned when she nearly fell.

"Why would you trick me like that?"

Galeron's tone shook her. She tore her gaze from the water trickling from her boot. Barely resisting the urge to throw it at him, she sat and pulled off the other one. "I was not tricking you."

"I know not of a maiden who can swim."

She sprang to her feet. "Ah, lest I hear it from your lips, I shall say it." Furrowing her brow, she tucked her chin and mocked him. "Maidens do not hunt, fair one. They do not wear breeches, and they certainly do not swim."

"Well, they do not," he said without pause.

She squeezed the water from the hem of her breeches. "Pure ignorance," she whispered. "Pray tell, can a maiden do *anything*?"

He stared for a moment. "Well, they can wear skirts, cook the meat their men bring home and warm the bed with their body." He chuckled when she delivered an exaggerated smile. "There is another thing a maiden does not do."

With hands on hips, she glared at him. "You are treading more than water, Galeron."

"They also do not stand in direct sun in wet attire." He dove under and resurfaced, resting his arms on the bank. "I can see every curve and peak of your body."

Oh, she had not planned that, but this could very well be a good thing. "Does that distress you, Sir Knight?"

He grinned. "Nay, I am blessed by the chill of the water."

She frowned, wondering what he meant. "Well, I am blessed by the sun." She lay on her back. "It shall dry me."

He hefted himself out and stood over her. She found it difficult to ignore the water trickling down his body. She slapped his calf. "Step away. You are dripping on me."

"You are soaked already, my gem." Galeron lay down, tucked his hands behind his head and grinned at her. "Some of the buds have sprouted and the trees shall be full soon."

"So." She undid her braid.

"What ails you?"

"You do not accept my breeches, or ability with the bow, or even that I can swim." She was pouting like a child, but didn't care. "You do not accept anything."

"I accept everything. I was simply taken by surprise." He stroked her arm. "Do not hold anger toward me, Ruby."

Ruby sighed. "You shall come to understand my ways." She absently rolled her necklace between her fingers. "I suppose we shall do that together."

Galeron stole at glance at her soaked bodice and linked his fingers tighter behind his head. "Where did you acquire the bow?"

"I borrowed them." She glanced at her mare, Abby, grazing nearby. "What does it matter?"

"It matters." He stepped over her and went directly to her horse. He hung the quiver on his shoulder and held out the bow. "Who would dare lend these to a maiden?"

She scrambled to him, cursing when a stone pierced her foot. "They hung idle, so I took them." She lunged toward the bow, but he snapped it out of her reach.

"Ah, so a maiden can be a thief as well?"

Still hopping to snatch them, and quite frustrated, she resembled a frantic rabbit, she said, "Jest noted, though 'tis a poor one."

"I have the mind to punish you." A raised eyebrow and grin accompanied his comment.

She placed her hands on her hips. "How might you do that?" She squinted at him, holding back a smile, certain he would not dare do such a thing.

"Like this." He grabbed her bottom and pressed against her.

"*That* is not a punishment." She laughed and wiggled her hips, pressing harder against him. *Oh my, what a glorious warmth creeping where our bodies meet.*

He dropped the bow and lowered her to the ground. "This clothing does naught to hide your succulent body. You are hardly wearing anything at all." His blue eyes clouded with passion, his breath mirroring her own. He nibbled her bottom lip and she opened her mouth to his probing tongue. The kiss ended much too soon and she nearly said as much when he brushed the hair from her face. "I have never been kissed by a half-clothed thief." He slipped the quiver from his shoulder.

"Nay?" She cocked her head, deflecting the next kiss. "Has a half-clothed thief ever done *this*?" She rolled, pushed him to his back, and straddled him. His muscles tensed against her thighs as she stretched, pinning his wrists above his head. Her pulse quickened when he didn't fight her. "Do you not defend thyself from this thief, Sir Knight?"

"I have nay defense. You have already stolen my heart."

Ruby kissed his eyes closed. "Hell's teeth, knight, you think you are clever with your sweet words?" She continued to kiss his face, her hand creeping along the edge of his breeches.

"Nay," he whispered.

Her teeth caught tiny bits of his chest. "Are you sure?" She tugged on the lacing.

"Woman, must you always torture me?" His eyes shot open when she squirmed on top of his bare belly.

"Must you insist on keeping your betrothed pure?"

His brow rose. "You are serious!" He laughed. "What a show that would be. As much as I wish to take you, it shan't be here."

Still holding his wrists, she drew his nipple between her teeth. Galeron hissed. "S-stop."

"Very well, my love." He tried to grab her ankle as she whisked the weapons from the ground and ran.

"You slinky vixen!"

She knew it would not take long before he caught up and was nearly to Abby when he did. "I have yet something else a maiden can do." She burst out laughing at his frown.

"Ruby, enough." He snatched at the quiver, but it was *her* turn to dart out of his grasp.

She laughed harder, waving him off with the bow. "*This* maiden can outwit her man."

Galeron stopped trying to take her weapon, a serious expression on his face. "Just this moment, the sunlight captured your essence." He stepped closer, gently pushing the tendrils from her eyes. "You…are beautiful."

Her laughter faded into a shiver as he stroked her cheek. She moved to keep him from touching her scar.

"Do not do that, Ruby." He tilted her face to him. "The vision of your face in this moment is one I shall always treasure."

"Kind words, my love, yet I have seen my reflection. Time has not been favorable to my hideous scar."

"There is *naught* hideous about you. Are you blind to the men's eyes following you?" He sighed. "Anywhere you go, they stare."

"Aye, at the scar." She shrugged. "It does not bother me."

He kissed where the slash had been, his breath hot against her cheek. "Your beauty fades the scar, not the other way around."

"Then you see through the eyes of a blind man." She kissed his chest. "Galeron, if I loved you any more, my heart would be in danger of shattering."

"Aye, my jewel, I feel the same."

She stepped back and cocked her head.

"Every time you tilt your head like that, trouble is brewing."

She waved the bow in front of him.

"As I said, trouble."

"Take me hunting." As soon as she spoke the words, she had the eerie sensation she'd made the same request many times in the past.

He grabbed the quiver from her and slipped it over her head. "Very well, we shall hunt." He adjusted the strap to fit her slight frame.

Ruby watched his eyes focus on the strap nestled between her breasts. She cleared her throat, but he took no notice. She poked him in the ribs with the bow. He winced, but did not avert his gaze. She strode off, calling over her shoulder. "Brute." Used to the way his one stride matched her two, she was not surprised when he caught up. "Cease your stare."

"Then wear clothing that does not display these." He brushed his finger across one of her breasts, causing her nipple to pebble. His lips curved with delight. "The night of our wedding you shall not hamper my touch."

"'Tis not hampered now." She slapped his hand. "You are the one who chooses to wait…so wait." She elbowed him when he tried to cup her breast and strode to her mare. Her hands trembled as she grabbed the saddle horn. "You tease me incessantly."

He boosted her before her foot met the stirrup. "I tease myself as well. Imagine when our longing is unleashed."

She swung her leg over the horse, wishing it were him. "I cannot imagine. Now, shall we hunt?"

He shook his head, crossed his arms and looked up at her. "You honestly believe you can hunt?"

"Probably better than you."

"I believe I finally met my equal." He grabbed his tunic from a nearby branch and pulled it on. "On nay account did I envision 'twould be a maiden."

"Of course not," she muttered. "How will you face the men when you cannot match my aim?"

"That rings of a challenge." He settled into his saddle.

She laughed. "Be off, Abby. You can probably outrun his stallion."

"Wait, I must tell you something before we go," Galeron said. "More of a confession, I suppose."

She smoothed Abby's mane. "Are you going to confess you have poor aim?"

"I know what happened the night you killed the wolves." He guided his mount beside hers. "Father told me everything."

The lighthearted mood dissolved. She twisted the reins. "He had nay right. I asked him to let it rest."

"*I* refused to let it rest. He feared…" His eyes spoke his doubt.

"What?" She wondered if he would drain her patience completely.

"He feared you fell into madness that night." He said the words so quickly they ran together. "The night you overhead them talking? You never told me the details. I am glad he went against your wishes and told me about the wolf attack."

She shifted in her saddle. "Well, I do not wish to dwell on it. There is naught to worry of now. It happened some time ago."

"Are you *certain* you wish to go hunting?"

Ruby's stomach tightened. "I am not certain of anything, Galeron, but I cannot continue this way." She gripped the bow. "I need to discover who I am before we are wed."

"You know your essence. Anything which happened in your past does not change that."

Unable to explain any more than she already had, she stared at the forest and what may lie beyond.

"You do not recall your past for a reason. Give it time."

She grinded her eyes with the heels of her hands. "I must do this, Galeron. If it brings a memory, I want you there." She shivered, despite the warmth of the spring day. "I am afraid." How she hated the admission. "I shall go alone if I must." She met his eyes. "However, I feel safer with you."

He put his hand over her fisted reins. "Ease your mind. I shall do as you wish."

The weight of her future bore down as she raised her bow. A longing call began in her throat and pitched into a shout of determination. "Memories, unleash your demons. I shall slay them all!" She kicked Abby into a full gallop, wishing she were as brave as her words.

Chapter Forty-Three

The Hunt

"Stand aside. I am quite sure I do not need your assistance," Ruby whispered. The rabbit darted into the brush and she glared at him.

"What?" Galeron said. "You are the one who spoke."

"I would have kept silent had you not insisted on showing me how to aim."

"When have you ever kept silent?"

She scowled and propped the bow on the toe of her boot. "I shall now. I am not speaking to you." She grinned at Galeron's playful nudge. Stepping aside, she tried to spy what he was aiming at. Did he see game she did not?

He released the arrow into a tree several paces away. "Galeron. You need to practice. For that is a tree, not food."

"I thought you were not speaking to me."

"That was a wasted shot."

"Nay." He grinned. "See how close you can get to mine."

"Your arrow?" She blinked. "'Tis foolish. I came here to hunt, not play silly games."

"I do not see a rabbit at the end of your arrow. Mayhap your aim is faulty and *you* are in need of practice."

She met the toes of his boots with her own. "I haven't even the chance to draw my bow!"

With a wink, he kissed her forehead. "Prove your aim first."

"You are a brute," she said, accenting each word. She stood on tiptoe, pecked a kiss and rearmed her bow. "Step aside, arrogant knight."

"Aye, I suppose you need all the space possible."

"Do you taunt everyone this way?" She rested the arrow across the bow.

"Nay, just the one I can get a rise out of."

She ignored his comment, finding it hard to enjoy their usual good-natured sparring. She hooked her finger over the shaft of the arrow. Everything about this was familiar, even the teasing. She lowered the bow, trying to absorb the memory.

"Oh, fair one, your aim is off already."

"You—" She turned, her response forgotten. Though Galeron stood before her, she had the uncanny sense that she should be seeing someone else's face. Someone she loved. Unnerved, she blankly stared.

"Ruby, what is it?" He tucked her hair behind her ear. "I will cease my teasing."

"For a moment I recalled someone—at least I think I did." She did.

"Who?"

"I am not sure, 'twas more emotion than anything." *Love.* Ruby shook her head, trying to dispel the thought. Her elbow locked as she raised her bow. "Stand aside."

Galeron stepped back, eyeing her. "I am beginning to regret agreeing to this hunt."

She pulled the bow, inhaling the new growth of the forest. *Now, hold your breath.* Peace enfolded her and she heeded the instruction of the phantom memory. *Be certain of your aim before you let it fly, young one.* She released her breath, the bow raking her fingers. The muffled thump of the arrow echoed within her. Peace fled and the cold drip of fear stole her breath.

"Nay."

"You are mistaken." Galeron pointed to the tree. "Look, you hit it!" He sprinted to their target. "Father was right, you are—" He fingered the arrow, splitting his down the middle. "Amazing," he whispered.

The forest swept away and Ruby slid with it. "Let them be!"

He whipped around. "The arrows?" A bead of sweat trickled down her temple. She methodically drew another arrow from the quiver and armed the bow. He would not get away with such treachery. "Wait."

"Release the boy!"

He slammed to the ground just as the arrow whizzed overhead. Damn him. Ruby grappled for the next arrow. "Bastard! Leave him be!"

Galeron scrambled to his feet and charged her, landing with her on the ground. The loud crack of the quiver blended with her scream. She lost grip on her bow and it landed with a thud beside them.

He pulled the shattered quiver from beneath her. "Are you hurt?" He swept the tangled mass of hair from her face. "Ruby? Ruby!"

Air escaped her lungs when the quiver shattered against her back. She tried to answer his shouts, but Galeron's voice faded.

A knight slammed her against the stone wall. Her ears buzzed and spots blotted her vision. "Spunky lad, you shall make a fine knight." *His breath nearly made her vomit when he grabbed her face, making her face at him.* "Though, I am beginning to wonder if you are worth all the trouble."

"Unhand me, swine!" *My dagger! Ruby struggled to breathe.*

"'Tis I. Galeron. Dare not fall away from my voice." Galeron's voice wavered. Where was he?

She wrapped her fingers around the hilt of her dagger and slipped it from her boot.

"Aye, a spirited lad ye are. Yet, young enough to learn our ways." *The knight laughed when she tried to squirm away.* "For the death of my brother, you shall pay." *His putrid breath brushed her cheek.* "For the rest of your days – " *His mouth gaped in a scream.*

The splash from his eye hit her face. She gagged and relinquished the hold on the dagger when he slammed the back of her head into the wall. Her eyes wide, she clawed at his armor as he ground his arm into her neck.

"I. Beg. Thee." *Her vision tunneled.*

He yanked the dagger out of his eye and pressed the blade against her face. "Beg, coward. Save your putrid soul."

Unable to draw a breath, her tears slipped into the slice as he carved her cheek.

"This battle shall be your last."

She drew up her feet and pushed against his chest plate. His raspy laugh intermingled with the surrounding battle while he drilled his fist into her stomach.

Her legs hung limp. His cold armor slipped from her fingers. The scant bit of air remaining now knocked from her. Death, deliver me!

His fury spewed. "My remaining eye shall witness your last breath." *He pressed harder.*

Her eyes closed, her stomach twitching with the effort to breathe.

"*You shall never see the sun rise again!*"

"*Nay beast, you are mistaken.*" Recognizing the blessed voice of her brother, she slid down the wall as something crashed against her attacker's armor.

Chapter Forty-Four

Injured Souls

Galeron knelt on the forest floor, cradling Ruby's pale, trembling form. She coughed, uttering random bits of nonsense. "My jewel, I beg you, listen." The vacancy in her eyes dimmed his hope. "There is nay threat. All is well!"

Ruby clutched his tunic. "You must come. I cannot do it alone."

He nearly wept with relief. "I am here, Ruby." He assured her, pressing her head against his chest. "You are not alone."

"Help me release him."

The chill of realization shot through him. He took her by the shoulders, shaking her. "Ruby!"

"He is h-hanging! *Listen* to me!"

"Ruby, 'tis not reality."

"'Twas my fault. You should have let me die." She tried to crawl away.

"Ramstone. Remember Ramstone!" Galeron's mind raced. "The necklace. Sarah. Your paints. The garden. Ruby, we are to be married in the garden." His voice pitched. "You are safe!"

"I could not pry it." Ruby clawed at his arms. "Do not push me away. You fail to understand."

He raised his hand. Unable to strike her, he smashed his fist into the ground. "Lord in heaven, she does not deserve this persecution. Deliver her from the depths of her hell." Frantic, he kissed her. The lack of response forced his heart to skitter like a pebble across a pond only to sink. "Come back to me." Tears filled his eyes. "Ruby, *please*."

"Follow me." Her voice jilted in a monotone. "I cannot leave him like that."

"Leave him. He is but a memory—a terrible dream."

"'Twas meant for me." Her body shuddered then fell limp.

Helpless, and utterly useless, Galeron watched her succumb to madness. "Daren't leave me." Her body dangled in his arms as he sprinted to the horses. "Be off!" he shouted, slapping Abby's rump. "Find your way home!"

He gulped several breaths before he hoisted her across his saddle. He jammed his boot into the stirrups and pulled her into his lap. "Ruby, hold fast. We are going home. You shall be safe there." He prayed his words held true as he kicked his stallion into a gallop. Nearly passing the water hole they'd frolicked in earlier, Galeron was struck with an idea. He brought her to the water's edge and splashed her face. She never flinched at the icy water.

"Dammit to hell, do not do this!" The drops of water sprayed from her face when he slapped her cheek.

"Forgive me." He landed a slap to the other side. "You are more stubborn than this." Hoping the icy depths would shock her, he jumped in with her in his arms. He whisked her to the surface and trod water. "I beg you, speak to me."

She sputtered, but said naught. He swam to the edge and pulled her out of the water as he spewed curses. The sun dropped in the sky, no longer providing warmth. They both shivered uncontrollably as he carried her to his stallion. The limpness of her body shot fear into him, but he reassured himself by constantly placing his hand in front of her face, her breath warming his hand and holding his hope.

They cut into the path of the carriage as it entered the gates. Easton jumped from the carriage before it came to a full stop. He clutched Ruby and slid from the saddle. He stumbled, nearly knocking down his father in his haste to get inside.

Easton jerked Galeron's sleeve and pushed the hair back from Ruby's face. "What happened?"

"Out of the way." He fled up the stairs, Alex and Sarah's shouts following him from the entryway. He turned at the landing, witnessing his father staring at the puddle of water. "I believe she drowned," someone said behind him. Sarah's scream tore through the corridors, but Galeron did not waste a moment and continued to the upper level.

"Move!" Galeron shouted at a servant unfortunate enough to be in Ruby's chamber. "Boil water for a bath, you fool!"

"Is she is alive?" Easton asked, now running full force into the room with Alex and Sarah on his heels.

"Aye!" Galeron said over his shoulder as he laid Ruby on the bed.

"What happened?" Easton stepped aside, allowing a servant to drag the tub into the room.

Sarah squeezed past and went to Ruby. "Poor dear." She rubbed Ruby's hands. "Angels in heaven, you are freezing." She tucked a blanket around her, her gaze pinned on Alex. "She is awake, yet doesn't speak. What is wrong with her?"

Alex grasped Ruby's jaw. "Can you hear me?"

"She does not respond to anything," Galeron said, through chattering teeth.

"Damnation, Galeron, I demand an answer!" Easton shouted. "What happened?"

Sarah frowned at Easton and draped a blanket on Galeron's shoulders. "Did she fall into the water?"

Galeron shook his head. "Nay, I dunked her in it."

"You *what*?" Easton stomped to him and pecked his back. "Are you daft?"

Galeron swung around, his body as numb as his mind.

Easton sighed. "Warm the poor child beside the fire until the tub is filled."

Galeron brought Ruby on the hearth, cradling her head in his lap. "Ruby, you are home." A wisp of a sob escaped before she closed her eyes. He shouted for his brother. "Make her open her eyes, Alex!"

The fear in Galeron's voice seemed to paralyze everyone for a moment. Alex sat beside him. "Relax and tell me what led to this."

"Relax?" he shouted. "Look at her!"

Alex waited.

"She remembered," Galeron whispered. "I am uncertain what, but 'twas something horrible."

"What is wrong with her, Alex?" Sarah repeated, sinking onto the edge of the bed.

"She is lost. That is what is *wrong* with her." Galeron scowled. "She trusted me and now she is lost in her madness."

"M-madness?" Sarah's hand stifled her sob.

Alex threw several more logs on the fire and gripped the mantle. "Do not give up on her, Galeron." He blew a long breath. "She has a strong soul."

He clutched Ruby tighter, hoping she could draw comfort from his embrace. "You did not witness what she went through." He buried his face in her hair. "Her soul shattered before my eyes."

"We have seen much worse with good recovery, brother."

He looked up. "She was sucked into the breath of her demons."

"Galeron —"

"Leave me be, Alex." He closed his eyes, focusing on the sound of the water pouring into the tub, focusing on anything besides the fear pulsing in each thought. Sarah placed her hand on his shoulder and he realized she had been speaking to him.

"Can wait in the corridor until I am done."

He stared at her. Though he was unsure of what she had said, he didn't like waiting anywhere. "I shall stay."

Easton sat beside him. "You cannot, son. Sarah needs to bathe Ruby."

"I. Shall. Stay," Galeron said, between gritted teeth.

"You may lower her into the bath as she is." Sarah unclasped Ruby's necklace. "I shall undress her after you leave."

Galeron gazed at the necklace, wondering if the promise of marriage was hopeless.

"Get on with it!" She pursed her lips and motioned toward Ruby. He lowered Ruby into the tub and then planted himself in a chair by the fire, his back to her. Sarah raised an eyebrow at Alex, sighing when all he did was shrug defeat.

"I shall be nearby. Call out when you are done." Easton walked to the door.

Sarah pointed at Galeron's back.

Easton glanced at him as he left. "He shall stay."

Alex followed Easton, pausing at the door. "I should be finished by the time you have her ready."

"Finished with what?" Galeron and Sarah asked at the same time.

"I need to brew a medicinal tea." Alex strode to Galeron's self-appointed post. "You should use this time to change out of those wet clothes."

"The fire is doing a fine job of drying me." The door closed. Something wet slapped to the floor. Most likely Ruby's clothing. "Pray tell, she dared leave the gates dressed like this?" Sarah asked, obviously trying to draw him into conversation. All he could think of was the way he had teased her in the meadow about her attire.

"Aye, Sarah. She was off to hunt."

"Hunt? Well, let us not dwell on that." Sarah scrubbed so furiously, he winced. "Her color is returning."

"Were you aware she had arrows and a bow?" Surely she had been, for the two were quite full of secrets by the way they always whispered to each other.

"She had *what*?" Sarah was either nervous, or sloppy, for water splashed on the floor. A moment later, Sarah's slippers landed by the bed.

"Where did she get them?"

"Do you believe I am privy to where she would acquire such a thing? I am not even certain how she acquires the breeches she so loves." She giggled, but even with his back to her, he sensed the lie.

"She tells you everything."

"I believe she fashioned the breeches herself." She paused several moments. "How did she get so many twigs in her hair?"

"Who gave them to her, Sarah?"

"The breeches? I told you, she—"

Galeron turned and Sarah shielded Ruby. "Do not be coy. I need you to tell me about the blasted arrows!"

Sarah filled the pitcher, and with her back to him, began to rinse Ruby's hair. "Does it really matter?"

"It matters."

"Why?"

"I need to know who to slam the next arrow into."

Sarah's head jerked up. The pitcher slipped, shattering at her feet. She tried to step out of the way, but ended up slipping in a puddle. "Oh!" She looked down and paled as she locked eyes with Galeron. "Look what you made me do!"

Chapter Forty-Five

Culpability

"Do not move." Shards crunched under his boots and he glanced down. "Not a step, Sarah."

Sarah spread her arms, shielding the tub. "I beg you, do not approach. She would be *horrified*."

Galeron took the blanket from his shoulders. "I shall drape this over the tub." He eyed the blood snaking through the puddle. He sidled past Sarah and covered the tub. "Now, wrap your arms about my neck."

"Nay, first lift Ruby out. The water grows cold."

"Very well." He was relieved at the warmth of her silky skin beneath the blanket. Sarah begin to cry as he laid Ruby on the bed. "Sarah, I beg you, do not weep." He raised his voice. "Alex, come quickly!" He lifted her from the puddle of blood and lowered her onto a chair. "Forgive me, forgive me," he chanted, pulling shards from her feet. He looked up to see her push her fist against her mouth. "Not to fret, the cuts are not deep."

He examined them closer. "Quite a bleeder, you are." He pressed a drying cloth against it.

Her breath shuddered as she wiped her tears. "I pray your forgiveness."

He wound the cloth around her feet. "I should send someone to fetch your husband." He strode to the door and called for a maid. "Get Alex."

"I gave them to her," Sarah whispered from across the room.

He feigned he did not hear as he opened a trunk. "Get her clothed." When Sarah made no move, and began rummaging. "Breeches?" He frowned and dangled several from the contents. "How many does she *own*?"

Sarah limped over and snatched them out of his hand. "Lend your ears. I—"

"Damnation, Sarah. Get off your feet!" Her mouth gaped and regret flashed through him. He turned, snatched a night-rail from the trunk and slung it over his shoulder. He scooped a stunned Sarah off her feet and unceremoniously plopped her onto the bed beside Ruby.

"I gave her several of Alex's arrows, an old quiver and bow," she blurted, tears filling her eyes. "I was responsible. I am the one you wish to kill."

He winced at her words, not the confession, but the fact that she believed he wished to kill her. "I would never harm you, Sarah. And I gathered you gave them to her when you dropped the pitcher. Now, dress her before she chills." He tossed the night-rail on her lap.

Sarah vigorously rubbed Ruby through the blanket. "Grant forgiveness, I feared she would go to the knights' quarters herself had I not—"

He took her hand and kissed it. "There is naught to forgive." The blame was his alone.

"All is well with us?"

He kicked the trunk closed, glanced back and tenderly whispered, "It never strayed any other way."

Sarah smiled through her tears. "You have changed."

"Get on with it." He cleared his throat. "I shall wait by the fire while you dress her."

"You shall wait outside the door. Go." Sarah nudged him. "You have done enough."

He had indeed. The damage may never be undone. Galeron raked his hand through his hair and stood over Ruby, relieved to witness the glow on Ruby's face. "Very well." He sighed, following an order instead of giving one, how novel. He offered his thanks to Sarah before backing out the doors and closing them, nearly slamming into Alex.

"You sent for me?" Alex tried to nudge past him. "Is it Ruby?"

"Sarah is hurt—wait!" He blocked Alex as he reached for the door. "She is dressing Ruby." He paced in front of his brother. "Sarah dropped a pitcher and cut her feet on broken shards. Worry not, I cleansed the wounds. They are not deep." He glanced at Alex. "Forgive me brother, for I am at fault for her injury."

"Did *you* cut her feet?"

Galeron stopped midstep. "Of course not." He eyed his father coming toward them. Had the maid fetched him too?

"Then you are not at fault," Alex said as Easton arrived.

"At fault for what?" Easton peered from one to the other.

All the reasons he was at fault seemed too immense to count...or explain. "Everything. I am at the fault for so much."

Alex put his finger up to silence him. "Fate plays a part here, brother."

Easton stepped in. "You take blame for what you cannot control. You did it as a lad and you continue to do so."

"Do not bring boyhood days to mind now, Father." Galeron eyed the door, willing Sarah's call to come through it.

"I refuse to dwell on this nonsense. I must fetch the tea and salve." Alex sprinted down the hall. "I shan't be long."

Easton pressed on. "Your obsession with guilt began with your mother's death." Apparently his father had no issue with dwelling on this. Why had he even mentioned it? He did not expect him to understand.

Out of respect, he quelled the urge to roll his eyes. "I am too weary to discuss this."

Easton held up his hand, ticking off on his fingers. "The cuts are nay fault of your own. Or Ruby's demise, the loss of Mara, or..." Easton swallowed hard. "Or Rafe."

"Enough!" Galeron rapped on the door. "Sarah, are you nearly done?"

"Enough? What are you shouting about?" Something clattered and he was surprised to hear a curse. "Patience," Sarah shouted. "And cease pounding on the door."

"You wield nay control over pain or death," Easton pressed on.

He closed his eyes, weariness flaring to anger. Respect thrown outside, he mocked his father. He thrust his hand, pointing to one finger. "Pain? Had I not allowed Ruby's foolish whim to hunt, she would not be in pain." Pointing to the following fingers, he counted off with each name. "Mara, Jacson and the tiny babe's lives could have been spared." He fisted his hand and dropped it, too pained to add Rafe's name to the list. "The fault lies with me."

"You said nearly the exact thing about your mother."

What? Galeron pressed his temples. Why did he insist on doing this? Very seldom did he bring up that night, for it caused his father pain. Yet tonight, his father chose to bring that up? "Mother hasn't a thing to do with this."

"Everything stems from it!"

He stared at his father. The man he loved, hated and obeyed was unraveling before him, his eyes wide and crazed. Ruby lay lost on the other side of the door and his father could focus on naught but the past. "You never speak of her, yet you choose now to bring this to light."

Easton took Galeron's face between his calloused hands. "The only one who could deliver your mother did so. Now she resides with Him in the heavens." He kissed Galeron's furrowed brow. "You must focus on healing your burden and releasing your guilt or there is nay hope for Ruby."

Galeron took a step back. "What does *Ruby* have to do with this prattle?"

"Ruby harbors guilt as you do. I see it in her eyes whenever she holds Jadon in her arms. I am certain 'tis linked with guilt from her past. I believe it has to do with a child."

Mayhap he misjudged his father. He made sense. Ruby was torn with guilt. He had witnessed it. Galeron inhaled deeply, remembering something she'd said. "She shouted something about releasing a lad."

"Ruby has strength beyond her years, but she is ill equipped to handle her past alone. Her trust lies with you. Only you can help her to finally free herself from her guilt."

"How?" Galeron thrust his hands toward her doors. "You saw her." His voice cracked and it took a moment to regain his composure. "God in heaven, hope is slipping with each moment."

Easton motioned him to follow into the next room. After a tap on the door, he assured Sarah he would return.

Easton stood, hands clasped behind his back, his expression foreboding. "Sit down, son."

Instead of taking a seat, Galeron stood, flexing his hands in an attempt to ease tension. He recognized his father's stance well. When told of Mother's death. The demise of his beloved uncle. What, pray tell, lay in wait now? "Why must we come here to speak?"

The man looked deep in thought, a soft expression on his face. "The corridor is not the ideal place to carry on a conversation. Now, sit."

Sit. *Hmph.* It did naught to ease his worry over Ruby. "Never has fear gripped me before now." Ah, he would not have confessed *that* outside Ruby's door. His father was right. He heaved a sigh and sat. "Naught I did helped her. Ruby is more lost than the day I found her."

Easton leaned forward and brushed the hair back from Galeron's forehead, like his mother used to do. It made him uncomfortable…wary. "And naught you can do will help until you heal yourself. Only then can you lead Ruby back from her battles."

Heal himself? Galeron studied his palms. "I believe it shall prove to be the hardest to fight. I haven't a weapon."

"You have two. Love and perseverance shall slay the guilt."

With a rush of emotion, Galeron embraced him, clutching at the bit of hope offered. "Guilt is a horrid beast, Father."

His father stiffened. "A horrid beast," Easton repeated, stepping back. "A beast I buried with your mother's death."

Barely a day passed that Galeron did not pay her memory tribute, but he seldom spoke of her. Especially to his father. Even as a lad, the grief in his father's eyes had silenced him. Yet now, it seemed all Easton could dwell on. Galeron slowly sat back down. "Seriously, Father, I am beginning to think you are the one going mad. Are you reliving her death?"

"The birth. The death," Easton whispered.

The only brightness to those days had been his infant brother. Galeron stayed silent, waiting, dreading, and painfully watching his father.

"She did not die giving birth to Rafe," Easton blurted.

Galeron's mouth gaped and he quickly recovered. "Have some of Alex's tea and get some rest." He led his father to the door. "I shall walk you to your chamber."

Easton shrugged away. "Do not treat me like a child. I was there!"

"And Mother died within hours of Rafe's birth, Father. Though I was but ten years, I remember well." His father added to his worry, but he smiled. "You are merely overwrought."

"Aye, 'twas *indeed* the night of his birth." Easton's eyes filled with tears. "I should have told you long ago."

Galeron's brow furrowed, a chill permeating his body. He could not recall ever witnessing his father cry. "What is there to tell?"

Easton strode to the table and lit a candle. Galeron noticed how it illuminated his age. "You and Alex were so young...so very young." His eyes glistened in the firelight. "By the time you were old enough to understand, I couldn't bear to mar her memory."

It seemed all blood pooled to his feet, leaving his face numb. "I do not wish to hear any more." Galeron barely forced the words out. "Enough."

"Your guilt is a product of my sins." Easton displayed his hands, as if to explain. "Because of my silence, my horrid sins, you..." He shook his head.

"You make little sense. Cease this." His heart racing, Galeron strode to the door, intent on fetching Alex for help. Was he to lose everyone to madness? Was there a curse floating through the air they breathed?

"She took her own life, Galeron."

Unable to take another step, to think, to absorb anything more than a spider crawling into a crack by his boot, Galeron stared at the spot where it had disappeared.

"Fault lies with me. I banished her from Ramstone as I snatched Rage from her arms."

Galeron swung around, the air in the room bearing down on him. "R-Rage?"

Silent tears streamed down his face, tripping on each wrinkle. "Aye, I changed the spiteful name after your mother died."

His mind twisted and froze as the words pierced him. Nay response, nay denial, nay speck of logic. Naught.

"I planned on telling him who his father was upon your return from battle. However, fate decided he leave this world without knowing."

Galeron made his way to the chair and plopped into the seat, the whole time blathering torn pieces of what his father said. "Telling him? Name? His *father*?"

Easton sat, seemingly crumpling into the chair. "Aye, Rafe's father. I left him for dead. 'Tis apparent he is — was still alive. I did not realize until…" His expression faded with his unfinished thought.

"What?" Galeron's head throbbed. "Who lives?" He heard Alex call and strode to the doorway.

Easton met him at the door, his eyes wild. "Wait."

Galeron had no pity left for the man. "He must hear this." He nudged Easton aside. "What more have you to add to this horrible night? You chose *now* to do this?"

"I did not intend — lies have a way of being bared." He shook his head. "I meant to speak of guilt, to ease your own…to help *Ruby*. All the rest" — Easton reached out, as if trying to grasp words from the air — "all the rest was happenstance."

"Damn happenstance." He swung the door open and spied Alex by Ruby's chamber holding the salve and mug of steaming tea. "Leave that. Get in here. Now."

Alex hurried to the room, his hands still full. Galeron closed the door behind him, took the things and put them aside.

Alex's face paled. "Angels in heaven, tell me Ruby is not worse."

"Nay." The door was cool against his back, realizing how flushed he was. "This has naught to do with Ruby."

Alex looked from one to the other. "Then what is it?"

"Our dear father was telling of Mother's death. Oh, and lest I forget, he has an interesting tale about our little brother, Rage."

"Rafe!" Alex corrected. "Are you *mad*?" He winced. "That was callous. How can you call him by that name is…it is vile."

"However, 'tis apparent his name is Rage." Galeron took a step toward his father. "Is that not so, *Father*? Or should I wonder if I should address you as such? Am I your son? Is Alex?"

"Galeron. Enough! You are my son! Both of you. All of you," Easton sputtered. "Let me explain."

"Then do so. What of Mother's death and what does *Rafe* have to do with it?" Alex glared at Galeron. "*Rafe*," he repeated.

Easton shook his head. "Where do I begin?"

"Start at the beginning, you lying bastard," Galeron said.

Chapter Forty-Six

Unveiled

"Your weariness does not excuse such disrespect! How dare you speak to Father like that?" Alex faced him.

Easton motioned toward the chairs, but no one took the suggestion. He sighed and walked to them.

It took all Galeron had not to crush his fist into his father's face. "The beginning, Father. Spare naught."

"Your mother did not seem to mind when our marriage was arranged."

"That is a bit more of the beginning than we need," Galeron said.

"'Tis where all the lies began."

"Lies?" Alex glanced from one to the other. "What lies?"

"Everything is a lie," Galeron said, watching a lone drip of wax glide down the candle. "It seems our brother, Rafe, did not have the same father as us."

Alex blanched "He *what*?"

"I beg thee," Easton said. "Allow me to explain."

Alex sank into the nearest chair. Galeron placed a hand on his shoulder, too tense to take a seat.

"Your mother gave me two sons—the two of you. Years later, she blessed you with a younger brother."

"Rafe," Galeron muttered and crossed his arms.

"Aye." Easton paced for a moment then stopped in front of them. "My brother, Zane, was Rafe's father."

Alex shook his head. "Uncle Zane?"

"He died in battle when we were young!" Galeron shoved past Easton and leaned on the mantel. "Apparently, yet another lie?"

Easton shook his head. "Do not interrupt me."

"I shan't remain silent. You *lied* to us! Now you smear the names of our mother *and* Rafe!"

Easton marched to Galeron. "You shall hold your tongue!"

He spoke softly but Galeron saw his fury. He clenched his jaw and slammed into the chair beside Alex.

Easton retreated to the hearth. Even from the distance, Galeron could see his knuckles whiten against his grip on the mantel. He was glad his father did not turn their way. Angry as he was, he still did not wish his father to see the hate harbored in his heart.

"Galeron speaks the truth. Zane did not die in battle, however, I believed he died by my hands." Easton turned from the fire. "I-I stabbed him and left him for dead."

Alex gripped the arms of his chair, rising out of it. "You did this to *your brother*?"

"Alex could never make me angry enough to do such a thing!" Galeron began to wonder if he ever knew his father.

"Even if he bedded Ruby? Gave her a child?"

Chilled by the shock, Galeron reeled at the realization of his father's words. His mother, her smile, her loving eyes was all he could see. "Nay, Father, you are mistaken."

Easton shook his head, tears dripping from his jaw. "They *told* me. The timing of the birth proved it. They were so bold as to tell me they loved each other. I trusted him. Most of all, I trusted her."

Galeron's face softened at the grief in his father's voice. He glanced at Alex. Neither said a word.

"I saw the looks between them." Easton shook his head. "I chose to lie to myself."

"As well as everyone else."

Galeron heaved a sigh. "Ruby is fighting for sanity and you bring more pain." Galeron stood. "Why not continue your deceit?"

"I do not think I wish to know," Alex said.

Galeron squinted. "I do. Has Zane returned to uncover your lies?"

"He did not return to Ramstone. Then or now. I did not mean to deceive you." Easton swallowed hard.

"I could have lived with the lie." Galeron walked to him and spat into the fire, the sizzle matching his anger. He looked at Alex as he rose, his stance defeated.

His voice carried uncertainty. "I assume there is more to this, though I am not sure I wish to hear it."

"I lost my wife and my brother that night. You both lost your mother. And an uncle you loved. All because of my rage." Easton's eyes widened. "Anger—I meant anger." He shook his head. "Guilt has ruled my days. I helped naught by lying about it. Now, Rafe is dead because of it."

He clenched his fists. "Did you ever love him?"

"As my own. That came easily." He sank into the chair, his movements of a man twice his age. "I returned to your mother, Zane's blood still on me, to tell her he was dead."

"Tell her?" Alex gasped. "May the Lord grant forgiveness."

Forgiveness. Father deserved nay more than Uncle Zane. Why such deceit? Such hatred? What had twisted Zane's smiles to sneers? Where were laughing memories, jousting with make-believe lances and wooden swords? All these questions speared through Galeron, clattering with wasted energy. His father's confession skewered his thoughts.

"She was sleeping, Rafe cradled in her arms." Easton's eyes took on the distant memory. "She was so beautiful." His resolve faltered. "I handed Rafe to a nursemaid to tend to him." His voice pitched, cracking at the end. "She woke calling his name."

Alex whispered, "Rafe?"

"Nay, she woke calling for Zane."

Galeron winced. Pity—unwelcomed—crept on ghostly feet. His father suffered double deceit.

"She begged for forgiveness, but I turned from her, telling her the babe died. I shouted over her sobs, I banished her to the village and swore never should she lay eyes on either of you again. She fell silent when I told her Zane was dead." He put his face in his hands. "I loved your mother, even then. I never meant a word of it. I returned later that night to tell her all was forgiven." He was met with silence. "She was dead."

"The childbirth…too hard on her?" Galeron wished he hadn't asked when his father began to weep.

"Nay, *I* was. She lost her s-sons, her home and her lov—Zane. I left her with naught to live for."

Beads of sweat dripped into Galeron's eyes. "Enough, Father," he whispered.

"Rafe may not have been of my loins, but he was my son. He knew nay different. It seems Talbot did."

"Talbot?" Alex nearly wrenched his neck.

Galeron shook with the surge of adrenaline. "Hell's fury—you mean—nay. Talbot? Tell me I am wrong." Galeron strode to Easton. "Tell me!"

"When you told me the word Rage would gain passage through Talbot's gates, I was shaken, but never thought—I thought Zane was dead!"

Alex pushed between them. "You make nay sense!"

"Rage," Galeron whispered, grabbing Alex. "Talbot called Rafe—"

"Rage." Alex finished his sentence. "I thought 'twas the ranting of a madman. He called him son." His eyes widened. "Talbot was *Zane*?"

"Talbot…messenger of destruction." Easton wrung his hands. "When you told about the battle, I had nay doubt who he was. He saw past your masquerade. He knew all along."

"He was privy to our plans because of that bastard Calen," Galeron said.

"Nay, I fear Calen only convinced him he was right. Talbot was hoping that you would claim vengeance upon him when you found Jastar in ruins."

"You are delusional, old man. He had nay knowledge of that."

"You think not? He followed Rafe's life. Dare you doubt he would not find out about your upcoming marriage to Mara…and of her home?"

Galeron opened his mouth to argue, then clamped his lips, uttering not a word, it made sense. Insanity made sense.

"You rode into his trap because I kept my suspicions to myself. Mad though he was, my brother ached for Ramstone from the beginning. He tried to acquire all I had. Wife, family, future. And he almost succeeded." He shook his head. "And I took it all back, and more. I left him with naught. Killing him. In his madness, Rafe was the way to reclaim everything…I suppose. I cannot claim to read his mind, or what was left of it." He snapped his gaze at both of them. "Aye, sons, his reach clawed into our lives after all these years."

Numbness crept over him. "Nay, it could not be. Father, you told him Rafe died that night." Blood pounded Galeron's ears as his mind revisited the night Rafe died in battle.

Vehemently shaking his head, Easton said, "I lied to your mother. Yet, I taunted Zane with the truth. As his blood dripped from my dagger, I told him his son would be given to a villager to raise."

Galeron strode to him. "How did Mother die that night? Did you kill her?"

His shoulders sagged. "Her knowledge of medicine saved lives, but ended hers. She drank a potion. There was nay blood, just a note clasped in her fist."

Galeron's throat went dry. "What was penned upon it?"

Easton sighed. "My sons, forever I shall love thee."

"Nay more?" Alex asked.

Easton bowed his head. "She died thinking her babe gone. Zane dead, and the two of you taken from her." He heaved a sigh, shattered with a sob. "I *told* her I hated her. I never had the chance to take those words back."

"You may as well have killed Rafe at birth. You killed him just the same." Galeron yanked his father's tunic and pushed him against the wall.

"Galeron!" Alex shouted.

"With your lies and silence, you killed our brother!" Galeron's voice dropped, each word dripping with hate. "Your fury killed our mother." Galeron slammed his fist into the wall and strode to the door. "Are you coming, brother?"

"My sons, can you not grant forgiveness?"

"For what, Father? Your lies, Rafe's demise or Mother's death?" Alex did not wait for an answer. He and Galeron slammed from the room.

Alex cursed as they reached Ruby's door. "I left the salve and tea in there."

"Fetch it later. The tea is cold anyway." Galeron knocked. "As cold as his fucking heart." Sarah told them to wait. Why so long? Was Ruby worse? Galeron stifled the urge to storm into the room.

Alex leaned against the wall. "Galeron, what do you make of what Father told us?"

"I will not discuss that now. My only concern is Ruby."

Alex spoke quickly, as if the words were coals, scorching his tongue. "Father begged forgiveness. I do not think I can grant it. What am I to do?"

Galeron did not bother to answer. What was he to say? He did not know how to guide anything other than a fist, much less his younger brother. "You may enter now." Sarah looked from one to the other. "Do not be so distressed. Ruby is resting quietly." She hobbled to the bed on her heels.

"You bandaged your feet?" Alex asked.

"I have indeed." She smiled at Alex's raised eyebrow. "I also applied the salve we used for Ruby when she injured her hands."

Galeron nudged past as Alex kissed her. "Just the same, I shall examine them."

"Later," she whispered. They met Galeron at the bed. Sarah tucked the blanket under Ruby's chin. "I spoke to her and she seemed to respond to my voice." Galeron did not respond but sensed her gaze. "She is not resting well, but refuses to wake, or mayhap she cannot."

"I expected as much," Alex muttered. "I should fetch the —" His gaze darted over Galeron's shoulder.

Galeron turned to see Easton at the door, the mug and salve in his hands. He strode over, snatched the mug and salve and kicked the door closed.

"What —? Why —?" Sarah looked to Alex for answers but all he did was shake his head.

"Let it be, Sarah." Alex accepted the mug from Galeron. "Prop her up." Sarah stacked several pillows behind Ruby and Alex tipped the mug to her lips, the contents dribbling down her chin.

Galeron grabbed Alex's arm, sloshing the contents. "What are you doing? She cannot drink. I thought you were to apply it." He realized how foolish that was. "Or something."

"This is to make her fall into a dreamless sleep. Deep and restful." Alex steadied the mug. "Trust me."

"Trust?" Galeron scowled. He snatched the tea, slammed it on the bedside table. "She is already distressed. She does not need —"

"What ails the two of you?" Sarah sighed when they ignored her question. "I wish I had left you both outside the door."

As if she hadn't spoken, Alex argued with Galeron. "Ruby has been drinking this for months. It staves off her night terrors."

Why was he not aware of this? Because of his questioning, that was why. Galeron ran his finger along Ruby's jawline. He should have never relented, never allowed Ruby's evasions when he asked about the dreams. He had failed to help her face them. And now they devoured her.

"Trust me," Alex said, "She shan't rest well without it. Especially after all she has been through today." Alex placed the drink in Galeron's hand. "Just give her a little. A few drops will do."

"Very well, Alex." Galeron whispered Ruby's name and pressed the mug to her mouth. When she did not swallow, he filled his mouth. With his lips against hers, Galeron trickled a bit of the concoction down her throat. He sat back, swallowed and wiped a drop from the corner of her mouth.

"Aye, I suppose 'tis one way to do it." Alex smiled. "I noticed you swallowed the remainder of it."

Galeron nodded, his mind clouding. He turned at footsteps to see his father hesitating in the doorway. "I believe she kished me. Kished." He frowned and tried again. "Kissed me." *Was the room moving?* Time seemed to slow. His eyelids even seemed to move in a wavering blink.

Alex chuckled. "You should have spat it out. Best be off with those wet clothes before it takes effect." Galeron fought to stay awake, but his body seemed weighted…and soaring at the same time. The last thing he saw was the canopy above the bed.

* * * *

Easton rushed to the bedside. Sarah grabbed Alex's sleeve. "Is he ill?"

"Do not fret. I doubled the brew to help Ruby sleep heavily." Alex glanced back at his brother and chuckled despite the tension. "Galeron swallowed quite a bit."

"There is nay humor in this, Alex. He cannot lie there. Get him up. He is damp and muddy," Sarah said, hands on hips. "And in Ruby's bed."

"I cannot move him." Alex pulled off Galeron's boot. "I suppose we must strip the heathen here." He chuckled when Sarah huffed, her face crimson.

"You shall do that without me." She limped out of the room.

"Why do you tease your woman?" Easton asked, making to grab the other boot.

"I have this." Alex frowned. "Be gone." As disillusioned as he was, it was wrong to show such disrespect. "When you return, assure you have a nightshirt for him."

Easton did not acknowledge the tension. "From the time he was a lad he chose to sleep in the skin God gave him. Does the man even own a nightshirt?"

Alex shrugged. A deep silence permeated the room. Could Easton not give him time to digest everything?

"I beg you, Alex, forgive—"

"My doubts are high that he owns a nightshirt," Alex said. "Fetch one of mine." He realized a servant could be summoned for the task, but he wanted him gone. Easton left the door ajar as he left. Still holding Galeron's boot, Alex dropped it and sank on the edge of the bed.

"All seems lost. Even you, Ruby." His bravado dissolving, he carefully lifted the necklace around her neck. The orb spun and sparkled in the candlelight. "My mother lives on with this promise of love, Ruby." He wondered if his words reached her. "And when Galeron gifted it to you, it lives on in you. He needs you more than a man ever needed anyone."

Alex wiped his sleeve across his eyes. "Remember the legend of the necklace. I beg you, hold to that promise." Alex's whisper brushed her cheek. "Pull away from the loss, Ruby. Fulfill your future." He drew a deep breath and exhaled. "And the future of my brother. He has lost so much, he cannot lose you too."

Easton and Sarah's voices drifted down the corridor. Alex darted to the other side of the bed and yanked at Galeron's other boot. His smile was genuine when he caught a glimpse of Easton gallop by with Jadon on his back, Sarah stopping at the door. "Sarah, you must get off of your feet, dear one." Alex took the nightshirt from her arms.

"Papa!" Jadon squealed, using Easton's hair as reins and leading him to the doorway.

Alex feigned surprise. "You are gaining stealth, my little knight!" He lifted Jadon off Easton's back. "Where did you come from?"

Jadon peered over his shoulder but Alex turned, shielding him from the doorway. "Where is Ruby?" His laughter filled the corridor when Alex propped him on his shoulders and whinnied, then galloped down the corridor.

"Alex, he shall not be able to sleep," Sarah said, trying to catch up.

"Whoa!" Jadon yanked Alex's ears. "You must wait for Mama."

Alex winced. "Very well, Sir Knight." He kissed Jadon's feet, still warm from his bath. Jadon fell into a fit of giggles. "Aye, so that tickles, does it?" Alex kissed him several more times.

"Alex, you are nay help." Sarah pulled Jadon from Alex's shoulders and handed him to Easton. "Tell me—" She glanced at Jadon. "How things progress."

"I shall." He watched until they turned the corner, returned to Ruby's chamber and tossed the nightshirt on the chair. After assuring Ruby's breathing was steady he focused on Galeron, his body hanging halfway off the bed.

His mood lightened and he chuckled at the sight. He yanked at the leg of Galeron's breeches. Thankful the task was difficult, he had an excuse not to speak when Easton hurried in and assisted him.

"'Twould be easier to slice these off with his dagger." Easton removed the sheath from Galeron's belt and tossed it aside.

"Is Jadon in bed?"

"He is used to Ruby putting him down, so Sarah is staying until he falls asleep." Easton hit the wall when the breeches finally gave. Alex did not bother helping him up. Easton chucked the breeches on the floor. "Alex—"

"Enough."

Easton sighed. A quiet calm came over the room while he stood over Ruby. "She always wears that, nay?"

Alex looked where Easton pointed. "The necklace? Aye, she treasures it." Alex was shocked at the tears in his father's eyes. "Father, the worst is over." He hefted Galeron to a sitting position. "Help me remove his tunic."

"The necklace was a wedding gift." Easton yanked the tunic over Galeron's head. "'Twas from my brother, not I."

Alex let Galeron plop on the bed. "*What?*"

Easton busied himself drying Galeron's chest. "It was from Zane."

Praise be God, Galeron was drugged and unable to hear yet another confession. Alex wished he was as blessed. "The legend of the necklace," Alex said. "Yet another lie?"

Easton tossed the drying cloth on the floor. "Not at all. The story rings true, though I changed it a bit to heal my heart. Your mother cherished the necklace, always speaking of how it held the promise of love." He shook his head. "I believed she meant our love. She must have loved him from the beginning." He seemed to drift to happier times. "He was here often. Do you recall?"

Though he was too young to recall him fully, Alex remembered the laughter during his stays. The memory was now tainted in sharp contrast to who he had become.

Easton would not leave it be, torturing himself and Alex as well. "I was blind to it. Zane chose to live far from Ramstone after the wedding. 'Twas I who convinced him to live here when the two of you were young. I deemed he was the best man to protect my family while I was gone." His brow creased as he gazed past Alex, as if he were no longer in the room. "Ironic, isn't it? 'Twas my fault tragedy befell us all."

"I see now where Galeron gets his penchant for guilt." Alex was not sure whether to strike or show mercy.

"Alex…I beg thee." The sorrow etched on Easton's brow.

Mercy trickled in. Alex realized how deep the secrets haunted his father. "I want to forgive you. I suppose I will in time. Galeron shall too." He gave him a weak smile. "'Twould be best to let the fantasy of the necklace abide."

"'Tis nay fantasy, Alex." Easton slipped the nightshirt over Galeron's head. "The love promised abided in your mother's heart. It simply was directed elsewhere."

After a struggle, they finally accomplished dressing him.

Alex grinned when they wiped their brows at the same time. "I suppose we should clean this mess." He motioned to the tub.

"Already been ordered." Easton gestured toward Galeron. "We cannot leave him in her bed, son."

"Do *you* dare attempt moving the beast?" Without waiting for an answer, Alex pulled the coverlet over the both of them. He gathered the tunic and breeches and laid them on the hearth. He was about to place Galeron's boots by the fire when his father whispered his name. "Aye?" Alex dropped the boots on the hearth, peering at him.

With a shaky sigh, Easton pointed at the bed. Galeron had shifted to his side with Ruby instinctively molded into the curve of his body. "A part of her remains with him," Easton whispered.

Alex put his arm across his father's shoulders and led him out. They each grabbed a handle of the double doors and pulled them closed.

Chapter Forty-Seven

The Awakening

Ruby sensed the sun upon her face before she peered out of her dream. The breeze carried jasmine and lavender from the garden where they were to be married. A steady breath brushed the back of her neck. Dread tore at her as she opened her eyes, certain it was Galeron.

Moving as little as possible, she turned to him and saw he still slept. The sunlight filtered through the hangings, illuminating his face. Her eyes glided over his profile and she tucked each detail into her memory to savor when they were no longer together.

"Sweet angels, give me strength to carry this through." She crept from the bed. Chills shot through her while she dressed, despite the spring air. Boots in hand, she ached to hold him. "Forgive me."

She placed a wood panel upon the easel. Her hand shook while she dipped her brush, for once, nay heed to what color. The paint precariously clung to the bristles. With a final glance to assure he still slept, Ruby painted her farewell.

Her words severed her ties, breaking her heart in the process. She read over the message, searing it forever into her mind. Her head bobbed with the effort to muffle her sobs while she placed her necklace on the pillow beside Galeron. Tears blinded her while she pulled on her boots. The familiar sweep of memories scattered her resolve. The window hangings billowed in the breeze and she stood, lifting her face to the warmth.

The vision of a knight grabbing a boy struck so hard she stumbled from the shock of it. The tin taste of bile made her gag and she slumped onto the window seat, holding her head. Nay more, she had remembered enough. She stared at the stone floor, unable to hamper the memory. The horrible thump of a babe hitting the floor echoed in her mind.

"Ruby?"

Wordless, she was trapped as Galeron approached. Able to glimpse her past, she grasped just how capable she was of terrible actions and clenched her eyes, ready to shove him away and run from the room.

"Do not avoid me," Galeron whispered, kissing her brow. A tear escaped from the corners, but she kept them closed. He kissed her lids.

"You should remain in bed." He carried her over and assured the covers were about her. "I beg you, love, speak to me."

She swallowed hard and looked at him, despising her cowardice. "I cannot."

"Aye, of course, you must rest." He grabbed his breeches and gave her a crooked grin while slipping them on.

She turned away, unable to watch the beautiful movement of his muscles while he pulled off his nightshirt, but detected a smile in his voice while he spoke.

"My jewel, you gave us all a scare. I feared I lost you to madness. Alex tried to assure me—" Galeron fell silent. The easel. She faced him. Her heart fractured at his expression. Unable to find a word to erase his confusion, she focused on the throb at his temple.

The man seemed to grow with each step toward her. She didn't even try to pull away when he jerked her to her feet and led her to the easel. It may as well have been the gallows. "Explain this." His voice held no tenderness.

She looked down. "There is nay more to explain, Galeron."

"Damn you." His tone tore through her, ripping tiny pieces out and scattering it at her feet. "Woman, there is *everything* to explain."

Her tongue was as heavy as her heart, unable to convey more than she already had on the wood panel. She met his gaze, fighting back tears.

He raked his fingers through his hair. "*This* was to be your farewell?"

Her head pounded, yet she welcomed the pain. "It is my farewell."

"Ruby, you are confused. You simply need time to gather your wits. You cannot mean this."

"I do mean it, Galeron." She jutted her chin. "I must go home."

"This *is* your home." Galeron pulled her close. "What memory would cause you to even think you must leave it?"

She buried his face in his chest. "All of them."

"What is it you remember?" His lips brushed her temple. "Naught can turn me away. Naught can change how I feel about you…love you."

"I remember enough to realize I cannot remain here." She stepped back. "I do not expect you to understand."

"Yet, you expect me to stand here and watch you go?" Anger filled his eyes. "Perhaps you *have* gone mad."

Though his words wounded, she couldn't blame him. She watched the tensing of his jaw and fisted her hand to keep from stroking it. "I recall my home. I must find it."

"Why would you not simply ask me to take you?"

"Simply ask? There is naught simple about this." So much was packed in her mind, she could not explain any of it away. "I wrote you to explain…" She took another step back.

His fingers pressed against the wood panel and he began to read. His voice held no compassion as it echoed into her soul. "My dearest Galeron. You shall always own my heart. I have given it freely. I treasure our betrothal, but I shall not bind you to a murderess. Reality snuffed dreams, leaving a nightmare of truth."

He stared at her until she looked away and continued to read aloud. "The maiden you love nay longer exists. I am but a wisp of the woman you believe me to be. I beg forgiveness for leaving without a spoken farewell. I could not bear to gaze into your loving eyes and then turn away. Forever I shall cherish you. The only truth of our days together is the love we shared. The rest are unintentional lies. I love you, Galeron, for this reason, we must part. Forever, your Ruby." He looked up at her. "*My* Ruby, eh? Forever?" He kicked the supports, sending the easel crashing to the ground. "Damn you!"

She jumped back, the red paint spattering on her boots reminding her of the blood she'd spilled.

"Look at me," Galeron shouted. Slowly scanning the length of his body, she reached his face. His gaze remained on her neck and she placed her palm where the necklace used to be. "What have you done with it?" he whispered, anger disappearing from his face.

"I cannot accept it any longer." She motioned to where it rested on the pillow. "Your life shall be tarnished with me in it." She started for the door.

Galeron's voice faltered with his plea. "Sweet jewel, daren't do this."

Her heart slowed to a ragged beat. "'Tis best I leave. All this has been a lie." His gaze followed her to the door. She turned away and opened it.

Galeron slammed it, wrenching it from her grasp. She bit back a cry when he grabbed her, digging his fingers into her tender flesh. "Our love is not a lie!"

"Galeron, let go. You are hurting me."

Galeron eased his grasp. "You are hurting *me*."

"Angels in heaven, 'tis why I wanted to leave while you slept!" She began to cry. "A-allow m-me to go."

"Never." His words, soft...so soft it slammed through her like a lance. Like the one that had killed the child.

"You do not know me!" she screamed.

He whispered in her ear, taking her gently into his arms. "Nay, fair one. I do, with every part of my being."

His breath upon her cheek tortured her. "Release me."

Galeron crushed her against him, his urgency bruising her lips with a kiss. Every sense heightened, the stubble on his chin like tiny daggers piercing her resolve. She did not resist when her lifted her, cradling her as he walked to the bed.

The warmth of his body drew her instinctually closer. His voice was raspy when he finally released her from his embrace. "I love you, Ruby, and I am certain of your love for me. Nay memory shall spoil any of what we have."

All she had was spoils of her past. "Galeron—"

"Not a word, fair one." He kissed her neck, sending familiar tremors through her. "Not until I have my say." He cupped her chin and made it impossible to turn away. His eyes never strayed from hers as he brushed her lips with his own. His kiss was gentle, probing...forgiving.

She fisted her hands to keep from running them under his clothing. "You are n-not saying anything, Galeron."

He pulled back, taking a deep breath. She wondered if he could read her thoughts by the way he studied her. "Your past cannot possibly change my devotion to you. It shan't tear my heart from yours. Now, tell me why you chose to leave me."

"I chose? I haven't a choice." She bowed her head. "I could not face you."

"I never realized you were a coward."

Her eyes darted up. "I am not a coward!"

His brow rose. "Nay? Yet you intended on spiriting away while I slept?"

Damn him. "I was sparing you the truth of my transgressions, Galeron. I am a sinful, horrid maiden. I have remembered everything."

"Your name?" He raised his damn brow again. "Do you know your name?"

Ruby blew a breath. "Nay."

"Your home?" He crossed his arms and waited for an answer. "What of your home?"

She remembered what it looks like engulfed in flames. "A bit."

"You have not remembered everything then."

She sat up. "You are infuriating! I remember enough." The clammy sweat of panic began to dampen her tunic. "I did many things — too many to forgive."

Galeron pulled her back onto the coverlet, his tender touch brushing tendrils from her eyes...torturing her. "Do you not realize how your damn painted farewell would *shatter* me?"

"Shatter?" She swallowed past what seemed a piece of coal in her throat. "If I stay, you are doomed to a *shattered* life. I am only a whimsy...a fantasy." She searched his eyes for a bit of understanding. "Now you know."

"What is it you presume I know?"

"I am not the Ruby you created."

"Allow me be the one to decide on that."

She scrambled from the bed. "Hell's teeth, Galeron. Why do you choose to make this more difficult than it already is?"

"You are the one making it difficult." He rose, towering over her. "Tell me what is so horrible that you find it imperative to leave." His eyes widened. "Do you belong to another?"

"I do not." She blew a breath at the revelation. "I do not," she repeated.

"'Tis the only thing that matters then."

Fury engulfed her. "Simplistic oaf." She shoved him, hating him as much as she hated herself. "What matters? I killed a child and left him hanging from a lance. I still am tortured by a babe crying in my dreams! I *left* them!" Ruby's screams raked her throat, but she could not stop the flow of her confession. "I left my f-

515

family with only death to d-deliver them. I am a terrible wench. I fled." She ignored the pounding on the door. She didn't have the strength to push Galeron away when he pressed her head against her chest. "I am not worthy. I b-beg you, r-release me." *Hold me. Hold me.*

Alex kicked open the door and he and Sarah nearly fell over each other trying to reach them. They both began to talk at once. "Ruby, are you well? What happened? Have you remembered?"

Galeron put out his hand. "Enough!" Everyone fell silent. His grip tightened and she wished he would crush her altogether. "Now, get out," Galeron said.

Alex and Sarah began to protest just as Easton came rushing into the room shouting. "I heard the screaming—"

"Damn you all to hell, get out!"

The door slammed. Galeron's muscles twitched against her cheek, his heart racing. She pulled away, her breath stuttering from her sobs, but she could not help but smile as she looked about the empty room. "You scared them."

He shook his head, his face still red with anger. "Unbelievable! You find humor in this?"

"You really are a brute, Galeron."

"I was *trying* to protect you."

"From what? Myself?" Swallowing, she wiped her tears, a calmness seeping into her. "My confession freed me from my burden. You have naught to protect me from. Naught has changed, but my courage to face telling them what I must do. You should have let them stay."

Sarah cracked open the door. "Oh. We can stay?"

He stepped toward the door and Sarah slammed it.

She nudged past him and opened it. "Enter." She rolled her eyes when Sarah was the only one who stepped inside. "All of you."

He crossed his arms. "I see your stubbornness remained with the *new you*."

She glared at him until he sat on the edge of the bed. She faced the others and motioned to the chairs. "I have something to say to each of you." Her judgment imminent, she braced herself. Ruby looked at each concerned face, hardly believing it was her voice speaking so calmly. "I have remembered disturbing events."

"Ruby, wait," Galeron said from behind her. "This is not necessary. You have not thought this out."

She raised her voice. "I need you to understand why I must go."

"Go? Where?" asked Sarah.

"She is not going anywhere," Galeron said.

Ruby's sash whipped the air as she turned to him. "Silence, Galeron!"

"I shall not remain silent." Galeron strode to her and grabbed her shoulders. "You are staying."

"As you wish to think." She stared into his eyes. "Now, cease being an ogre and sit!" Easton cleared his throat, but she never veered her gaze.

Galeron took a seat between his father and Alex. "That is the first order I have seen you take in a long time." Alex nudged him.

"Shut your damn mouth."

He stared at Galeron then turned to Ruby, realization spreading across his face. "You intend to *leave Ramstone*?"

Her shoulders ached with tension. "I do."

"Nay!" Easton stood.

"Sit. I have much to confess before I leave."

"It seems the air is filled with damn confessions." Galeron eyed his father.

Ruby tilted her head in question. "I did not intentionally mislead you. I assume you all believe me to be a good maiden." She winced when they all nodded. "I am not."

Easton leaned forward. "I refuse to believe—"

"I have killed."

"I am certain you had reason," Sarah said.

"A child. I killed a child." Ruby watched Sarah's face blanch. Her silence said everything. "Then, I left him hanging from a lance." She shuddered at the memory of his limp body swaying with her hands clinging to the weapon. She retold the story she'd just told Galeron. "I also left a newborn babe crying in a nursemaid's arms. I believe he was mine."

Galeron jumped to his feet. "You told me you do not belong to another!"

"I do not sense another in my heart. I suppose I must have been a..." She stiffened, speaking her fears. "A whore who left her babe behind."

"You are mistaken." Galeron rose and went to her.

Ruby stepped away. "I killed a path of men as well." Unable to hold back, she put her hands in her face and wept. "After murdering, I *fled*."

"Ruby, certainly, you had reason." Galeron took her into his arms, but she turned out of them.

"How did it happen?" Alex was close by, but she continued to hide her face. "Perhaps we can sort it out."

She accepted a kerchief from Galeron and wiped her nose. "What does it matter anymore? There is naught to sort. 'Tis all horrid. I must leave. Today."

"Nay," Galeron said. "I will not have it."

"I care naught for what you shall have!" She glared at him, thinking it easier to leave if he was angry.

"Coward."

She swung toward Sarah. "What. Did. You. Say?"

Sarah rose, her fists at her sides. Her voice shook with each word. "You are a damn coward. You fled from your past. You now flee from a beautiful future. How much longer must you flee?"

Her accusations stung. "Sarah, I beg you to understand."

"All I understand is you have chosen the coward's path once again."

"Listen—"

"I have heard enough. How *dare* you? Do you doubt the depth of our love and acceptance?"

She stared at Sarah, her calm, sweet Sarah, shouting at her. Her words stabbed with truth. "I never doubted your love, Sarah."

"What of mine? Do you doubt it?" Alex asked, standing beside Sarah.

Ruby's throat closed. "You could never doubt my love, Ruby." Galeron wrapped his arms around her waist and kissed the top of her head. His heartbeat drummed against her back. It was racing as fast as her own was.

Easton rose, shaking his head. "Ah, Ruby." He cradled her face and kissed her brow. "I love you as my own. Your departure would create naught but empty souls and a broken heart. Ramstone would lose its treasure." Easton looked up at Galeron and back to her. "Aye, the treasure which sparkles with laughter and shines with denial of conformity." He took a shaky breath. "Ruby, our jewel of Ramstone. This place, void of our treasure, would never be the same." Easton pressed his lips to her brow, lingering for a moment, before he sat.

She shook from the intensity of his words. "I am a murderess."

"It does not matter." Galeron walked to Easton and rested his hand on his shoulder. "It does not matter to any of us. Love still abides, nay matter what crimes were committed." Easton clasped his hand. Galeron gave him a nod and then led her to the window seat.

She sank into the cushions, trying to grasp the unconditional love surrounding her.

"Tell us everything," Sarah said.

She took a deep breath. "Hold me," she whispered to Galeron. She closed her eyes. "I decided to leave one morning, without my brother's watchful eye. We competed in a way and I was hurrying home to tell him of the pheasant and rabbits I hunted on my own. I expected his ire, for I left without an escort, so I picked a whole basket of berries to appease him." She opened her eyes and smiled at Sarah. "Blackberries, remember? I told you they were his favorite."

Sarah smiled. "Go on."

"As I crested the hill behind my home—" The vision seemed to tremble in her head. "My home was in flames." Her stomach lurched with the reminder. "We were under siege. I found the way in, through the lower level." She jumped to her feet, and began to pace. "The *dream*! I dreamed of tearing away the ivy blocking the door!"

She did not realize she had left Galeron's side until he led her back to the window seat. "All is well, go on."

She slowly shook her head. "This part is not clear. I came upon a child. A knight held him—I killed him."

"The child?" Easton asked.

"Nay, the knight. A maiden was fighting with him for—" She frowned. "*Her* children?" She closed her eyes, trying to recall. "The child fell. Yet I grabbed a child and ran." She paused. "It makes little sense."

"Enough Ruby, 'tis too difficult," Galeron said.

"I was running to the lower level with a lad...I believe the newborn was the one that—aye, I left him with the nursemaid." Her nails pierced her palm. She dreamed this so many times! Wide-eyed, she turned to Galeron. "You were right, 'twas not a dream."

Galeron blinked hard. "The one where the knight killed you with his lance?"

"Aye."

He looked at her as if she was feeble minded. "'*Twas* a dream. You are obviously alive."

Ruby paced, the memory now searing her mind. "The lance did not pierce my chest as my night terrors deemed." Her sides heaved, the air becoming heavy. "The lad was on my hip—c-crying." She turned to Galeron as he came to her. He would never forgive her. She shoved back the memory as she pushed Galeron away and wrapped her arms about her waist, digging her fingers into her sides. "He was begging to stay with me." She still could remember his little body as she tried to push him to freedom through the door to the back field. "I promised I would find him in the woods after I helped the others, but he...he..."

Ruby did not realize she quit talking until Sarah tugged, urging her to sit. Ruby's hair hid her face as she bowed. "I covered his little mouth when he begged me to come with him. Poor lad was sore afraid."

Galeron swept Ruby into his arms. "Cease this. You are pale."

The flush of memory spat at her. She buried her face in his chest. "I covered his mouth to stifle his cries, but it was too late. We were discovered. I pulled him away from the doorway and hid — the casks. The row of casks, we hid between them."

The clammy fingers of doom clutched her and she wished Galeron's arms could fight them off. For the first time, she could not find refuge in his embrace.

"Had I not placed him on my hip—" She tried to banish the thought. "I-turned away from the lance. Oh God, I—the *thump!* H-he was r-ripped from my embrace."

The utter disillusionment of who she was, and what she had done, no matter how innocently, was now in the open. She could not bring herself to face Galeron or anyone one else in the room, so she continued to cry into Galeron's chest.

"I am an animal. I ran from the knight. I ran from — he was *hanging* there!"

She looked up, trying to make Galeron see she was not pure evil, pure cowardice. "I went back. I tried to release him from the lance, Galeron. I *tried*."

She looked down at her hands, surprised her arms were not covered in blood. When she looked up, she saw the boy's face, blood dripping from his mouth, tears slipping from his lifeless eyes. She blinked hard, her breath coming in ragged sobs. Galeron's face was once again before her. Was she truly mad?

No one spoke. The rustle of the hangings on the window sounded loud against their silence and she turned to face the punishing stares. She glanced at Galeron, thankful it was his face and not the murdered child.

"You did not kill him," he said.

"I couldn't—the lance was too…"

"Was too deep." Galeron sighed. "Now it makes sense."

"What makes sense?" Alex interjected.

"She said something about this in the forest."

"I left him." Ruby's wooden words splintered their conversation. "I left him and the babe." In all this horror, there was a sliver of light. "That much is true. There is a babe. Alive." Her breath labored as the memory took its toll. She watched Sarah pace from the window to Alex, then glanced at Easton. The one she couldn't face was Galeron while she continued to relive the past.

"I left the lad next to the dead knight. Nay, first I straddled the knight and stabbed — or did I?" She began to blubber. "He pushed her and the babe fell. Someone was with me, when I handed her the babe, she fled." The racking sobs raked her throat. "I was left with the lad. I had nay time t-to find the b-babe!"

"Ruby, cease this," Galeron commanded.

"I c-called for my brother. I fought another k-knight. H-he…" She tried to breathe through her sobs. "It hurt s-so bad."

"Ruby, please."

She vaguely sensed Galeron's embrace. "He pinned me against the wall—choking me. I pulled a dagger from my boot"—Ruby tasted the blood from long ago—"and jammed it in his eye."

"Damnation, I said stop!" Galeron's voice seemed to come from another room.

"Let her be," someone shouted…shouted…so far away.

"He did not flinch. He pulled it from his eye, his hatred was full." She ran her finger along her cheek. "He did this."

"How ever did you escape?" Sarah's touch sucked her back to the present.

"My brother saved me." The brightness of the morning tunneled into darkness. She was small and insignificant in Galeron's arms. The legs beneath her seemed foreign. Sweat chilled and heated her at the same time. "I killed your son. Forgive me, Jac." She wished she could slip into darkness, yet it remained out of reach.

"Ruby!"

She was coherent enough to realize he carried her, but she gave into the dark void. She wanted to slip away.

"Let her be, you say!" Galeron shouted at Alex. "How much more can she take?"

"Did she say *Jac*?" Alex said.

"What are you talking about?"

She tried to tell them to stop shouting, but words twisted in her head, naught making sense.

"She said, 'Forgive me, Jac'."

Galeron brushed Ruby's hair from her pale face. She opened her eyes. His relief showed on his face when she focused on him. "Ruby?"

She wished to sleep, escape...find Jac and make up for her wrongs.

"'Tis a common name." Sarah looked at Alex. "Isn't it?"

"Aye, but Jastar was attacked." Alex nudged past Easton and leaned over her. "Do you remember Jastar?"

His face blurry, she struggled to focus on what Alex was saying.

Galeron shoved him back. "She knows naught of Jastar."

The name tugged then yanked her painfully back. "Jastar." Her trepidation remained, yet it mixed with strange excitement. "Aye, I know of Jastar." She closed her eyes. "I can nearly smell the bread baking in the kitchen." The corners of her mouth twitched at the vivid memory of honey drizzling over it.

"Did you work there? A scullery maid perhaps?" Galeron asked.

Ruby held her head in her hands. "Nay."

"What does it mean to you?" Galeron whispered.

"'Tis my home."

Easton gasped. "Oh, sweet angels in heaven. When is Jac expected back?"

Strength surged through her at the mention of his name. "Jac?" Ruby grabbed Easton. "Is he alive? What of my father? The babe?" The heavy silence weighted the room. She turned to Galeron. "Do *you* know where they are? Were you at Jastar? *Someone say something!*"

Galeron laughed.

"You, my dear, are the missing Mara." He kissed her.

She tried to speak past his lips. "I most certainly am not! Dare not assume I am Mara." She kissed him lightly then pulled back. "I *hate* her. I grew to despise the one who took you from me." She frowned, realizing how horrid that sounded. "Uh…I am not her. Now, about Jac. Where is he?"

"There is a possibility she isn't Mara," Alex said. "However, Jac shall have the answer when he returns."

Ruby asked about Jac again, but no one paid mind.

"Nay, she called Jac her brother." Sarah ignored Ruby tugging her sleeve.

"Did he mention any other sisters?" Alex looked from Galeron to Easton.

Easton sat on the edge of the bed. "I never asked about other siblings. I suppose we cannot assume anything."

"But the babe…" Galeron argued with Easton. "She mentioned a babe and another child."

"Galeron." Alex glared at him then glanced at Ruby. "We only found a —"

"He is dead!" Ruby shouted.

Everyone turned to her. "Who?" they asked in unison.

"The other child Galeron speaks of." Her tears stung. "Jacson…the child slain by the lance." Relentless information flooded her mind.

"Enough for now. She must rest. Out," Galeron ordered.

Sarah bent to kiss Ruby's brow. "I shall send up a tray. You have gone without nourishment much too long."

Ruby feared she'd lose anything she swallowed. "I cannot eat now." She stifled a gag at the thought. "Tell me about Jastar."

"Have a tray brought up just the same," Galeron said. "Now, leave us be."

Easton opened the door and motioned them out.

Ruby waited until the door closed. She looked to Galeron for answers. "Why isn't anyone saying more about Jac?"

"Because he is not here to tell us anything, Ruby. He will not be here until late spring. He knows naught about you being here."

"I have nay closure." She sighed, ashamed she ever thought of leaving. "I still am unsure of my identity."

His silence made her nervous. She was uncomfortable under his scrutiny and wondered what he was thinking about. His hands were warm against her, gentle as he laid her back.

Galeron slipped off her boots and rubbed her feet. "Let your burden rest."

She closed her eyes, relaxing with his tender caress.

"Nay more searching. Allow me to just hold you." He climbed in beside her.

She pulled her kirtle over her head and threw it at the end of the bed, then snuggled beside him in a chemise and breeches she had stitched for herself.

Galeron chuckled. "I intended the only thing removed to be your boots."

She grinned at him.

"Get in here, you breeched forest nymph." He lifted the covers. She snuggled against him, thankful for the lighthearted moment, but it ended when he spoke.

"It pains me that you would have left me."

He swallowed hard. "I couldn't bear you hating me when you discovered the truth."

"Ruby, understand this." He pulled back and glared at her. "You had naught to do with what happened to the lad."

"I put him in harm's way."

"It was a *murder*. A vile man killed him, not you. You did everything you could to save him." He was actually growling. "Release the damn guilt!"

"I cannot help how I feel."

"That, I well understand," he whispered. "Your guilt is what held these memories at bay for so long. A part of you must realize 'twas nay fault of your own."

She tucked her head under his chin. "Had I not—"

"Enough, never again are you to take blame of what happened."

She nodded, knowing full well she would never forgive herself. "Galeron?" She shifted closer. "Do you believe me to be Mara? Or do you wish it to ease your mind?"

"I haven't an answer to that."

"Jac does." What would come of her once he realized who killed his child? She tried to gain comfort from Galeron's embrace, to no avail. Weary as she was, she fought off sleep, for she feared the ensuing nightmare of the child she had murdered.

Chapter Forty-Eight

Flowers and Forgiveness

"Pray tell, do my eyes deceive me?" Alex called, strolling into the garden with his hands in his pockets.

Galeron grinned and plopped a handful of lavender stalks into a basket. "Good morn, Alex."

"Do you need a bonnet?"

Galeron dropped the basket and lunged for him. Their deep laughter filled the morning air while he pinned Alex's head under his arm.

"Enough," Alex said. "You are sure to hurt thyself."

Galeron chuckled, released him, and picked up the basket of flowers. "Ruby's favorite. I thought she should wake to something she loves." He picked up the flowers he dumped on the ground. "I mean, other than I."

"Lord in heaven, you have turned soft." Alex put up his hands and backed away with merriment in his eyes. "Easy, brother. I could not resist."

Galeron draped his arm over Alex's shoulders and they started inside. "I was thinking…"

Alex glanced up at him. "What?"

"I do not believe she is Mara."

"Who? Ruby?"

"Nay, Sarah, you oaf."

Alex came to a halt. "You must face the possibility. It makes perfect sense."

"Jac told me of Mara. She had no desire to marry. Ruby, as you well know, wants naught more." Galeron ignored the shaking of Alex's head. "Any word from Talbot?"

"Aye, a rider arrived earlier. He was exhausted. Jac and the others are readying for the journey and should be here within a month or so." He sighed. "We shall uncover more when he arrives."

"If she is Mara, she would realize that by now." Galeron gripped the basket tighter.

"Well, I believe she *does*. Her guilt keeps her from facing it." He sighed. "Give her time."

"Mara did not wish to marry," he repeated, picking up a flower and twirling it between his fingers.

"Ah, you fear she will not marry you if she faces the fact." Alex eyed the crushed flower in Galeron's fist. "I mean the possibility."

Galeron wiped his hand on his breeches and walked ahead, knocking several petals off the rose bushes on his way out.

"Sarah is already planning the wedding. Will you be arranging the flowers for the bride?"

Galeron swung around, grinning. "Mayhap."

Alex strode to him, matching his steps when he caught up. "In all seriousness, are you certain a wedding will take place?"

Galeron's boots skidded in the gravel at the end of the path. "Of course!"

He looked at her window. "She was leaving you, Galeron."

"She shall marry me."

"Very well, brother."

He detected Alex's doubt, intensifying his own. "I still cannot fathom how she made the unwise decision to leave, nay matter what happened in the past."

"Guilt," Alex said. "Guilt twists one's thoughts."

"In a skewed way, she showed me what Father must have been dealing with all these years. It was he who was injured the most."

"You have forgiven him?"

Jadon ran by the window and Galeron's first thought was how his children would play in his home as well. "I have forgiven him. He is our father and soon to be the grandfather of my children. Now, I must forgive myself for Mother's death, as well as Mara's demise. Which brings me right back to Ruby." He sighed, knowing he would never forgive himself for Rafe's death.

Alex picked up a stone and tossed it. "'Tis a vicious wheel of events that we must stop from turning."

Galeron sighed. "Only Ruby can do that." He motioned to the basket of flowers. "Do you think Sarah will help me arrange these for Ruby?"

Alex chuckled and took a few steps ahead. "Why? Doesn't the sweet, flower-picking, knight know how?" He broke into a run with Galeron on his heels.

Chapter Forty-Nine

Converging Time

"Sir Jac has arrived!" Sarah gasped, looking out of Ruby's window.

Ruby turned, nearly tripping on the hem of her wedding attire. The final fitting had gone well, filled with laughter and hope for the future. And now the past haunted her once again. She yanked the dried wreath of flowers Sarah had plopped on her head in jest a mere moment ago. She had hoped for a bit more time. "Are you certain? It could be yet more guests for the celebratory dinner."

"'Tis Jac and he appears as if he has traveled hard." She craned out of the window. "He is dismounting... Galeron is greeting him."

She took a step to join her, but stopped. "Come away from the window and help me undress."

"Is this not exciting? May I stay while ye speak to him?" Sarah turned from the window and hurried to her. "Why do you look so fearful? This is a good thing."

Ruby nodded.

"I think you should leave your hair down for the celebratory meal tonight. Now let us get you changed so you can meet with Jac."

Ruby flung the wreath onto the bed. "This could change everything." The wedding attire was suddenly uncomfortable and the crisp rustle of silk grated on her. Her stomach twisted and she smoothed her hands over the lace with a shuddering breath. "I am not ready."

"What? You have known he was coming for over a month now." Sarah hugged her. "He made it in time for your wedding. Is that not what you wished for?"

"I wished to discover if he—if I—what if I am not Mara? What if I *am*?"

She paled at the rap on the door. "They dare not send him up?" she whispered.

Sarah peeked out the door and spoke in hushed whispers. A huge smile graced her face as she closed the door. "He could not wait to see you."

Hell's teeth, why did he pick now, the day before she was to be wed? She suddenly did not wish to hear the news he would bear—or the confession she must give him. If she were Mara. Mayhap she was someone he had never met. So many thoughts jumbled in her head. She grabbed Sarah when she turned to open it again. "I cannot do this. Not now."

Sarah took her by the shoulders. "You *must* do this." She stroked the side of her face. "I would stay, but he requested to see you alone."

"What of my wishes? I am not ready to see—"

"You must do this," she repeated. Sarah kissed her cheek and opened the door.

"Blast you." She cast her gaze to the floor, memorizing every bead on her skirt's hem. His boots were the first thing she saw. She studied each scuff, waiting for him to speak.

"Prithee, dear maiden," Jac whispered. "Raise your face."

Her heart threatened to cease with confusing fear and excitement. She scanned the length of him as she looked up, hoping to recognize a scar, a freckle, a piece of jewelry, but naught struck her as familiar. Then she met his blue eyes and gasped in recognition. Their shared childhood shot faster than an arrow, taking her breath. His mouth gaped and tears flowed freely down his cheeks. Still, he said not a word.

"I never thought 'twould be the day I would witness you weeping like a babe in a cradle," she said, laughing and weeping simultaneously.

Jac grabbed her, swung her full circle and placed her on her feet. "Mara." He kissed every part of her face and picked her up again. "Ah, my little Mara."

When he lowered her, she wondered how her legs held up. She fingered the scar on his chin. "I did that." She smiled, remembering how she had accidentally racked him with the bow when he was teaching her to shoot. "It did not even raise your ire." She felt disconnected, yet certain he would be angry when the truth was told.

"Mara, I feared you were dead." He ran his hand against her hair. "I was so close, yet never knew."

She nodded, entranced. The events of the hunt with Galeron swarmed through her head. "*You* taught me to hunt!"

"Aye, 'twas I, my young one."

She smiled. "You always called me that."

Jac grinned. "Young one?"

She clenched her eyes and opened them again, bits of memory pieced together.

Run, young one. Go, Mara!

Jacson is —

Enough! I shall find them all. Now go!

"Mara, what is it?" Jac turned her face to him, worry creasing his brow.

The flood of memories no longer denied her access. The air cooled the beads of sweat prickling her face. She stumbled to the window seat and slumped into the cushions. "The attack."

Jac sat, taking her hands into his. "Galeron warned me this would be hard on you. Slowly…tell me slowly. All is well."

"You *forced* me to leave." Her mouth was parched. "I tried to tell you."

"Tell me what?"

She tugged at her high collar. "Did you throw me upon a horse?"

Jac blinked at the change of subject. "I did. You were arguing with me the whole time. I could not fathom why you fought to stay during a battle."

The acrid smell of blood filled her nostrils. "I killed Jacson." She winced at the painful crush of Jac's grasp. Though he sat beside her, she barely made out his hiss of a whisper.

"You killed my son?" Jac released his grasp and placed his hands on each side of her face. "Nay, you would never harm my boy. What is it you speak of, Mara?"

The more he said her name, the more she remembered. "I lifted him to my hip and turned to avoid the lance."

"What lance?"

She shook her head. "I took Jacson to the lower level."

"You were wise to take that passage. How did you ever remember it was there?"

"You and I played there as children." Her memory turned a page, like a book scribed by the devil. "I searched for the outer door on the day of the attack. When I couldn't find it, I thought I'd imagined it."

Her face was hot when he removed his hands. She rubbed her fingertips, recalling how the splinters from the door ripped at them through the vines when she had returned from her hunt. "I couldn't open it and used my mare to free the door."

Jac did not say a word. She continued, sure she was sealing the fate of her brother's hatred and shunning. "Our home was already in flames, but I found the boys and Ann." She glanced up at his sigh.

"Ann and Seth did not survive," he whispered. "Now you say Jacson is gone as well?"

Petals fell from her hair when she shook her head. "You are mistaken. Seth is alive! He was in Ann's arms when she fought with the knight." Flashes of detail made her nauseated but she spared Jac the details of his wife's death. "I tried to aid her, but she died. However Seth was in her arms, alive."

Jac swallowed. "Nay, Mara. He died."

She refused to be deterred. "I gave Seth to the nursemaid when the knight grabbed Jacson!" She smiled, knowing he would be pleased. "Seth is *alive*…somewhere." She looked up with hope radiating through the painful memory, but Jac continued to shake his head.

"Galeron told me he buried the babe with Ann."

She watched the horrible truth reflect in his eyes. "Nay, not Seth too."

"Tell me, what of Jacson?"

Ruby swallowed back a sob. "I took him with me once I—" She remembered thrusting the arrow into the knight, narrowly missing Jacson. How many had she killed?

Jac pulled her to her feet. "What happened to him?"

She fisted her hand. Hating to tell him the horrors, she realized Jac needed to hear the truth. "He began to cry when I tried to push him through the doorway."

"Push him through what doorway?"

"In the lower level. 'Twas partially blocked by the casks." She tried to look away, but he pressed his forehead against hers. "I covered his mouth, fearing the knight would find us." She closed her eyes. "I propped Jacson on my hip to comfort him, but 'twas too late. He heard us."

She could not tell him. His hands pressed hard into her face. "Tell me, Mara. Tell me what happened to my son."

When she did not respond, he tilted her face up. "Damnation, look at me." She opened her eyes. Though his voice was harsh, his eyes filled with defeat.

"I had him in my arms when the knight found us," she whispered.

"That, you said."

"I-I turned away, avoiding the knight's lance—"

"You brave soul!"

She began to sob. "N-nay, you fail to see. When I turned…oh God, Jac. The l-lance pierced his little body! He stared at me, the look of surprise and pain faded quickly. Then…"

She couldn't see anything but a blur as he wiped her tears. "I ran. I shamefully ran. The knight grabbed for me as I squeezed out the door."

Hearing her brother weep shattered her, but she had to tell him everything. "I backtracked and tried to free Jacson from the lance." She took a breath. "I came to find you, but the enemy found me first." She looked down, waiting for his wrath. "You killed the knight that killed your son. I pray you can gather some peace in that."

Jac clenched his eyes. She lied. She actually lied to him. Aye, Jac had slain the man who thrust the lance, but 'twas her that had put the child in danger. She wanted to tear off her wedding attire, slip into breeches and ride as far as her mare would carry her. "I lied. I am the one who killed your son. Had I not turned—"

"Dare not!" His deep voice broke through her pain. "The fault does not lie with you!" His sobs racked his body as he bowed his head. "Where is he now?"

"At home, still in the lower level," she whispered.

Jac released her and crushed his palms against his tears. His labored breathing pierced her heart while he tried to regain composure.

Now that she had discovered her identity, she no longer wished to be the maiden called Mara. She cursed the fact her memory regained power, seeping into her new life like a disease. "I have caused naught but pain."

"You have caused naught but *joy*."

Shocked that his red-rimmed eyes still shone of love, she took a step back. "J-joy? I think not."

"I found you." He hugged her. "I found the one who insisted on wearing my boyhood breeches. The one who would sneak out in the wee hours of the morn to hunt. The stubborn sister constantly thrusting me into dire straits with father for *ever* teaching you the way of the bow. Aye, Mara, my little love, you are the one always bringing me joy with your unconventional ways." His sadness turned into a tremble of a smile. "And the only one left in my family."

She tried to believe him, but her guilt ripped her hope away. "Forgive me."

"There is naught to forgive, Mara. 'Twas a battle. Jacson's death was nay fault of your own. You did all you could to save him."

Ruby turned from him, and caught a glimpse of the garden where the wedding was to take place. Did she even deserve what lay ahead? Concentrating to make her feet cooperate, she walked closer and unclasped the window.

The breeze carried the smell of the gardens, the sweet melody of the musicians practicing, the merriment of those readying for festivities of tonight's meal, all wafted up. Now she was not deserving of the glorious celebration or the wedding the next day.

She realized how tense her body was when Jac stepped behind her and gently massaged her shoulders. She faced him, pain searing her. "Jac, I should return with you. I cannot go on as if naught happened. Had I been braver, I would have returned sooner."

"You were as brave as any knight. You fought with all I taught you." He sighed. "I have relived seeing the knight wounding you every night since." He traced her scar with his fingertip. "You are not to return to Jastar. You are to live the life of a knight's lady. The life Father chose for you." Jac's chuckle rang out of place with the sadness they bore. "Ironic, isn't it? I shall bring you to stand beside the man you swore you would never marry."

"The final time I spent with Father was filled with curses and refusal to follow his wishes." She bowed her head. "I never thanked him for trying to do well by me."

"He never held ill will. He adored you even though you chose to hunt and scratch in the dirt to gather roots for your paints. So many times he voiced that he raised another son." He tipped her chin. "Father intended on releasing you from the agreement, Mara. He was willing to give up the joining of armies with Ramstone to make you happy. You fled on your hunt before he could tell you."

"He intended to free me from the agreement?" she repeated.

Jac gasped. "Damn, I did not even ask how you feel about it now." He eyed the door before turning to her. "I shall free you from the agreement if you wish."

Ruby fingered the necklace Galeron gave her. "I nay longer wish to be free of it. I love Galeron. He has awakened my heart." She tried to accept Jac's forgiveness. "And you have awakened my hope, dear brother."

"Then all is well." He gave her a hug and strode to the door. He opened the door to find Sarah cupping her ear. "I shall take leave and share the wonderful tidings. If they have not been shared already."

"They haven't, for I was too busy eavesdropping." Sarah entered the room. "However, everyone is sorely impatient to meet with you. Tell the others we shall join them as soon as Ruby is ready."

Jac gave a sharp nod, winked at Ruby and closed the door behind him.

Ruby fled into Sarah's waiting arms. "He forgives me."

"I heard every word." Sarah wiped a stray tear. "It shall take some time to get accustomed to calling you Mara."

Ruby shook her head. "It shall take time to *be* Mara," She tilted her head. "I do not think I even wish that anymore."

Sarah laid out her clothing. "Get dressed. Drink mead until you dance with abandon. Enjoy your brother and the celebration." She started unlacing Ruby's dress. "Decide about that mystical maiden Mara on the morrow." She laughed. "Mara. Morrow. That is clever."

"But ever so true." Ruby sighed. "I must decide."

"Ah, that you must, for Galeron needs to know who he is to marry."

Ruby giggled. "You can lighten even the darkest mood."

Chapter Fifty

The Wedding

"Ouch!" Ruby's sleeves rustled as she rubbed her head. "Must you poke those pins so deep?" The room was too hot. Her wedding attire was too heavy, her boots too tight. Everything was too…too much. Why did she agree to such a grand affair? Why did they not simply marry on the church steps?

Sarah rearranged the wreath of flowers in Ruby's hair for the third time. "Hold still. Partaking of an overabundance of mead last eve 'tis the reason your head aches so. And I am not poking." Sarah handed her a steaming mug. "Drink, it is cool now."

As soon as the smell of the concoction reached her nose, she smiled. "Mint…and something dreadfully familiar." Ruby took a sip. "Ale. Is this a cure or curse?"

Sarah shrugged, a huge smile on her face. "Alex, Galeron and Jac show nay residual effects of the casks they emptied into their gullets after they partook of the same cure." She motioned toward the open door. "Ah, he is awaiting to speak with you." She spun Ruby around to face her. "You are beautiful."

Ruby took three large swallows, banged the mug on the table and blew a long breath. "Let the merriment commence!" she shouted, mocking Galeron's cheer from the night before. "Dare I believe this day has finally come?" she said over Sarah's laughter. Only to be tinged with guilt. As usual, Sarah noticed her hesitance.

"Ruby—Mara." Thankfully she forgot to dwell on her change of mood and said, "'Twill take eternity to remember to call you by that name."

"I have thought of that at length." Ruby was about to tell her what she decided, when Jac knocked on the partially open door.

"Mara? The time draws near, and I must… Ah, my breech-clad sister looks more like a beautiful bride now." He smiled at Sarah. "Grant a moment?"

Sarah scurried out of the room, closing the door quietly behind her.

"Ah, the breeches I wore at the meal still shock you?" She scratched at the itchy wreath and then pulled it from her hair. "They were trimmed in lace."

"I learned years ago naught shocks me about you, but some of the guests were taken aback at your choice of attire." Jac chuckled. "Galeron, however, could not take his eyes away from you all night." He kissed her brow. "I can see his adoration and acceptance. He shall make a fitting husband."

"Jac?" Ruby toyed with the beading at the cuff of her sleeve. Now she must tell him. What if he did not agree? "There is one thing…"

"What." He grinned. "You wish to wear breeches to the wedding?"

She walked to the table and lifted the chain girdle. The rubies hanging from it caught and held the light. "These rubies were given to me by Easton as a wedding gift." She looked up at him.

"A mighty fine gift indeed."

"The rubies…" This was more difficult than she thought it would be. "They symbolize so much. The name Ruby was given to me by Galeron." She coiled the girdle on the table, staring at Jac before she whispered, "Our parents dubbed me Mara."

He nodded slowly, but she saw pure confusion in his expression.

"Yet I have changed my life…changed everything in the year that has passed. Would it be a misstep to live by the name Galeron gave me? It is how I am known by everyone, both here at Ramstone and the village." She inhaled slowly. "And in my heart."

Jac's footsteps echoed on the stone floor as he paced. Twice he glanced at her, but said not a word. Was he angry with her?

"I shall be Mara." Anything to appease him. She had already caused so much pain. A slow smile, a shake of his head and a low sigh punctuated his stilled pacing.

"Nay." He approached her and ran a finger along her jaw. "Ruby. A new name to begin a new day…a new life." His eyes, though still filled with grief, sparked with bits of happiness. "Follow thy bliss and release the horror of the past."

She wrapped her arms about Jac's waist. "A new day with the two men I love by my side." She turned at Sarah's shout through the door.

"Ru—Mara, they await! Is all well?" She did not wait for an answer and rushed into the room, her blue silk skirts rustling in protest. "You are not even ready!" She grabbed the wreath of flowers and pinned it to Ruby's hair again. She began to repair the face makeup. "Why have you been crying, Mara?"

"It matters not." She smiled. "And call me Ruby."

"But your name is—"

Jac shrugged. "Be it Mara or Ruby, this woman does as she wishes." Jac laughed at Ruby's disdainful grin.

Sarah took the girdle and clasped it at Ruby's waist. "Oh, I well realize. However, this one does not seem to know exactly how to go about getting what she wishes for."

She swung around. "Cease speaking as if I am not here before you. I was always certain where my heart belonged from the first time Galeron kissed me. Even more so when he dubbed me Ruby of the Forest." *And every moment since.*

"So, Father was correct in his choice for you?" Jac crossed his arms and leaned against the bedpost.

"Naught could have forced me—you witnessed my refusal when father told of the agreement." She sighed at his knowing grin. "Very well, Jac, he was correct after all."

"I never believed you would grant *anyone* the right to be correct."

"You win." She winked. "This time."

"Poor Galeron." Jac laughed at her expression. "Does he know you hunt? In breeches, nay less?"

"Of course."

"He accepts that?"

"He accepts everything about me." She smiled, realizing she was responsible for that.

Sarah arranged Ruby's red hair about her shoulders. "Well, nay breeches today." She tugged at Ruby's skirts and stood back to admire at her. "The blue of the dress matches Galeron's eyes."

Sarah hurried ahead to join the wedding guests.

"You are beautiful." Jac offered his arm. "Ruby, allow me to lead you into your new life."

Ruby detected a tear in the corner of Jac's eye when they paused in the garden.

The lyre ceased playing. One of the jugglers looked away from the task of keeping his objects in the air. The ball dropped and rolled to her feet. She picked it up and tossed it to Galeron. "Next you shall have me in those hands, my love, do you think you can handle it?"

The crowd broke out in laughter as Jac led her to him. Galeron's teeth flashed in a grin.

The priest began the vows. "Mara, do you take your betrothed, Galeron, as your husband?"

"Nay," she whispered.

Galeron spun toward her, his eyes wide and mouth hanging open. The crowd began to whisper.

She raised her voice. "Nay," she repeated. The breeze blew her stray tendrils into her eyes. "My name is Ruby."

Galeron exhaled. "Ruby of the Forest."

"Ruby of the Forest," the priest repeated, the edges of his mouth twitching. "Do you—"

"Aye, I take this man as my husband forever."

Galeron slid his mother's ring on her finger. "I accept this forest nymph as my lady. For always."

The priest frowned at all the interruptions, but Ruby could see by the glint in his eyes that he wanted to laugh. "Do you have *more* to say?"

She giggled in answer, though her face warmed with embarrassment, or excitement, she was not quite sure.

The priest scanned the crowd, silencing them. "With these vows so eloquently spoken, may this joining be blessed and sealed." He shook his head and whispered to Galeron. "I am certain it will prove to be an interesting marriage. God be with you."

She slipped from her past and into her destiny as she drank in Galeron's kisses. Flower petals caught in his hair as they passed through the guests and into the center of the ward.

Her feet skimmed the grass when they began to dance. He pressed his face close, so she could hear him over the music. "I just realized we never danced together before." He spun her, knocking her hair from its pins.

"I would rather we danced in bed, my husband," she whispered, nibbling his ear.

Galeron's laughter blended into the music.

Sweet mead flowed freely and she partook, dancing with abandon. She swayed from one partner to another. Laughing, each time Jac took her in his arms and lifted her from her feet in a hug. She caught sight of Jadon, dancing with a young girl. The look in his eyes was one of adoration. A young woman she vaguely recognized from her days in the village kept staring at her each time she danced with Jac. She searched for her husband, grateful when he cut in and led her into the garden.

She looked behind to see Jac taking the stranger into his arms and dancing with her. She tilted her head up and kissed him. And her brother did not pull away.

Galeron tugged her deeper into the garden. "Cease your staring. He deserves a bit of levity in his life. It has been over a year since he lost his wife."

"True." She grinned as he spun her around. The wafting smell of the gardens mixed with the sunset as they glided in a dance of their own. His hands roamed her body. She moved in rhythm with the music, pressing hips into him.

The music slowed and she rested her head against his chest. Her head swam from the mead and the festivities showed no sign of ending. "Galeron, shall we ever find a moment alone?"

"We are alone now."

She looked up, sighing at his kisses upon her neck. "Steal your lady away, sweet knight."

Galeron swept her into his arms. A cheer rose when they broke into the crowd. Well wishes followed them as he carried her inside.

"Galeron, wait!" She looked over his shoulder when he stopped. "We should bid everyone farewell."

"Nay, my love, we have waited long enough."

She looked into Galeron's eyes, wondering if their babe would have the blue of his, or green of hers. "Perchance we shall create a son."

Galeron strode faster. "We shall create more than that." He bounded up the stairs, then hurried down the corridor and kicked open the doors to their wedding chamber. "We shall create new heights of lovemaking." He lowered her to her feet, his tongue tangling with hers.

Her urgency met his. Without breaking their kiss, her fingers pulled at his clothing while he fumbled with the clasp of her jeweled girdle. The clink against the stone floor told that he had accomplished the task just as she pulled the lacings from his breeches. His fingers ran along each curve of her body, sending jolts where his fingers journeyed.

He unlaced her then set about the task of undoing the long cuffs. After a few moments, and whispered curses, the buttons pinged about the room, sending her into a fit of giggles. Galeron chuckled. "Dammit all, I believe I like your breeches better."

She stepped out of her skirts and grinned, watching his eyes scan the nearly see-through breeches she had made days before. "I have been blessed with an angel," Galeron whispered.

She twirled the red satin ribbon holding up her breeches. "Nay, my love, I shan't be an angel tonight."

Galeron raised an eyebrow, picked her up and tossed her onto the bed. His throat rumbled a low growl as he touched the hollow of her neck with a kiss. He caressed her face. "My angel...my devil...my wife."

She locked eyes with him, her pulse quickening while he unlaced her chemise, baring her breasts. Her nipples tingled, aching for his touch. Closing her eyes when he lowered his warm lips upon her, she whispered, "Then again, I believe I must be an angel, for your touch brings me to h-heaven."

He raised his face and grinned. "'Tis just a taste, sweet jewel. 'Twill be a night of passion you shan't forget."

"I shan't forget anything ever again." She smiled, knowing how true her words were.

About the Author

J.M. Powers grew up with a book tucked under her arm. On rare occasions when she wasn't reading, she invented stories for her younger siblings. She never outgrew her love of books, and now creates witty, feisty and unconventional characters of her own. New worlds swirl from J.M.'s mind with such intensity, she ends up following her characters around, jotting down whatever they may do or say.

This author eagerly plunges into the world of writing, and more often than not, J.M. Powers answers with a glassy stare when family asks if dinner is ready. Her alter-ego, Jeannie, wakes up, and embraces life with her family on a tiny island in Upstate New York. Despite the craziness between reality and the world of writing, life falls together...despite the fact J.M. keeps popping in with medieval story plots while Jeannie is trying to cook dinner.

J.M. loves to hear from readers. You can find her contact information, website details and author profile page at http://www.totallybound.com.

TOTALLY
BOUND

Home of Erotic Romance

www.ingramcontent.com/pod-product-compliance
Lightning Source LLC
Chambersburg PA
CBHW032255020726
47495CB00001B/120